secret shape-shifters live, love, and scheme. Laurell K. Hamilton readers will enjoy this edgy world."

"It's only taken two books for the dynamic duo of Adams and Clamp to cement their position as premier authors of paranormal fiction. Gritty and unique, with amazingly Byzantine character development, this inside look at the unconventional world of shape-shifters is a page-turner in the truest sense."

"It's rare when a second book surpasses the first, but *Moon's Web* explodes onto the scene, earning a Perfect 10. If you're a fan of Laurell K. Hamilton or Kelley Armstrong, *Moon's Web* is definitely a book for you!"

"C. T. Adams and Cathy Clamp have outdone the wonderful job they did with *Hunter's Moon*! The action begins on the very first page and doesn't let up throughout the story."

Cold Moon Rising

C. T. ADAMS
and CATHY CLAMP

TOR®

paranormal romance

A TOM DOHERTY ASSOCIATES BOOK
NEW YORK

This is a work of fiction. All of the characters, organizations, and events portrayed in this novel are either products of the authors' imagination or are used fictitiously.

COLD MOON RISING

Copyright © 2009 by C. T. Adams and Cathy Clamp

All rights reserved.

A Tor Book
Published by Tom Doherty Associates, LLC
175 Fifth Avenue
New York, NY 10010

www.tor-forge.com

Tor® is a registered trademark of Tom Doherty Associates, LLC.

ISBN 978-0-7653-5964-3

First Edition: August 2009

Printed in the United States of America

0 9 8 7 6 5 4 3 2 1

DEDICATION and ACKNOWLEDGMENTS

As always, we would first like to dedicate this book to Don Clamp and James Adams for all their help and support in our writing careers. We'd also like to thank our agent, Merrilee Heifetz, and her wonderful assistants for their continued faith in us and the worlds we write. Of course, every book is only as good as the editing inside, so kudos to Anna Genoese, Heather Osborn, Jozelle Dyer, and Melissa Frain for everything you've done in getting this book from the computer to the shelves. You guys are the best! Finally, we lost the brilliance of several authors this year, and we'd like to say a final, heartfelt thank you and good-bye to those authors who inspired us and let us live in their worlds for a time. Rest in peace Michael Crichton, Tony Hillerman, Arthur C. Clarke, Barrington J. Bayley, Aleksandr Solzhenitsyn, William F. Buckley, Jr., Janet Kagan, Thomas M. Disch, and so many others who made life more enjoyable. Also a fond farewell to Tor editor Brian M. Thomsen and publishing legend Robert Giroux. May you have all possible rewards in the hereafter for your efforts to enrich our lives. If you've never picked up one of their books, please do. You'll understand why we're thanking them.

AUTHORS' NOTE

Welcome back to the dangerous, supernatural world of Tony and Sue Giodone. For those of you who hoped to be brought up-to-date about everything that has happened in their life since *Hunter's Moon* and *Moon's Web* . . . well, we tried. But in Tony's world it's only been a year (though quite an eventful one!) since he and Sue met, and some of the things you've wondered about haven't actually happened yet. So we did the best we could to catch you up without too much "name dropping."

We do hope you enjoy meeting Liz Sutton-Kendall. Liz is about to start her own adventures in a new series, and we expect life will be every bit as . . . *interesting* . . . for her as it has been for Tony.

As for Tony, as you'll see here, life as a Sazi is never, *ever* dull. Still, he's adjusting to his new job as a Wolven agent—which in his opinion really isn't that different from his old job freelancing. But the past has a way of catching up with people when you least want or expect it.

In answer to the most frequently asked questions we've received by e-mail and in blogs:

Asri still hasn't had her babies. Sazi dragons have long gestation periods. And they are no fun to be around during the process. So Bobby has wisely been giving his new bride a wide berth and putting in some extra time with Wolven. While we don't know yet whether the babies will be dragons or pythons, it *will* be a multiple birth, and they will both be very glad when it's over.

The Chicago pack is doing well. Nikoli is representing the wolves on the council quite well, and the Duchess is becoming a force to be reckoned with. Yurgi and his "Pemela" have found the house of their dreams and will be having a barbeque soon to celebrate the birth of their first child. Yes, those of you who guessed that the werespider took her for that reason were right!

We hope that you enjoy this latest adventure, and we look forward to bringing you more tales of all sorts in the future.

To sign up for our newsletter/fan information, contact us at catadamsfans@gmail.com.

Cold Moon Rising

Chapter One

SWEAT ROLLED DOWN my forehead, trailing ribbons of salty wetness through the layers of caked-on grime. I swatted at another black fly intent on sucking my blood.

There were a lot of bugs hovering just outside my reach, but only the extremely hungry ones dived in for a meal. They just don't seem to like the taste of magical blood.

The muscles in my right arm were starting to get tired from all the swinging. Although sharp and efficient, the machete did little to clear a path through the dense canopy of green surrounding me. I heard Will Kerchee having to cut his own path, even though he followed close behind. Shadows still enveloped us, but a reddish-gold glow on the horizon told me two things: it was going to be hot, and it was going to rain. Both of which meant it was going to be muggy as hell for the rest of the job.

"We apparently have different concepts of *access,* Kerchee. When you said we could get here easily, I presumed there'd be a road." The jungle seemed to swallow my words so they were barely a murmur above the raucous noise overhead. I suppose I couldn't blame the various prey animals for screaming about our presence here. The alpha magic that enveloped me, tethered me to Will, did keep away the press of the moon that struggled to pull wolf fur from beneath my skin. But it also pressed against the animals, warned them of our journey through their home. The sheer weight of it was like being stuffed inside a dry suit in the heat—or a sausage casing. It was enough to make *me* want to scream too. As it was, I had to fight an urge to climb the trees and rip out their screeching, furry little throats.

Everything was too intense, a by-product of the supernatural power that made me a creature bound to the moon's whim. Every scent was like a knife through my brain for the three days surrounding the full moon. If people wonder whether animals feel joy or worry or frustration . . . yep, they do. I could smell their emotions drifting on the air. But the mere reality of emotions doesn't mean I'm not going to eat my next burger with all the enthusiasm of the wolf inside. I'm more of a carnivore now than I ever was. Raw meat smells like heaven now and blended with the hot-and-sour-soup scent of terror around me, around *us,* the glands at the back of my jaw were drooling in time to the growl from my stomach.

"Geez, Giambrocco. Whine, whine, whine," Will replied with at least as much of a wheeze as I'd hoped to hear. "I said *I* could get here easily. Why in the hell Lucas stuck me with a partner for this job who can't *fly* is beyond me."

It was beyond me, as well. Lucas Santiago is our boss and is usually pretty bright. But this time I was wondering. It was bad enough to deal with the reality of being a shape-shifter, when such things aren't supposed to exist. But Will could shift into a *bird*? No, that was still a bit too much for this former mobster brain to handle this early in the morning. Yeah, I've seen him shift and fly off as the massive bald eagle he is, but it's no less hard to deal with for the experience.

Another fly bit me, and I slapped my neck. My normally sensitive ears, made a dozen times worse by the sting of the moon, registered the clap of flesh on flesh and the slight squishing sound at the level of a jet takeoff. I'd probably be deaf already if not for the healing powers us imaginary monsters have. I took my hand away from my neck to look at the smear of blood-covered insect legs on my palm. Got it! The scent was enticing enough to cause me to bring my hand up to mouth and lick the blood off. Yuck. I hate it when I do that. I spat onto the ground to clear out the taste.

A clearing appeared in front of me, and I took the opportunity to lift my canteen to my mouth and take a long swig. What I wouldn't give for a cold beer right now.

Will was still chopping away at the thick undergrowth several yards back, so I took the opportunity to take a long sniff of the slight breeze that finally stirred the leaves.

It wasn't far now. Oil, diesel, and unwashed humans with supernatural blood fought for dominance in my nose from the distance, yet we were still too far away for even my sensitive hearing. But there were no telltale outlines in the darkness. I can see colored auras around other Sazi, giving me warning when they're nearby. Will stood out like a beacon in the sunlight. But I'm told that nobody else but me and one or two others can see the lights—they call it *second sight*.

We could hope I wasn't missing anything.

A swishing sound next to my ear made my instincts take over. I moved sideways, fast, and reached out to stop the arm holding the long, curved machete in midstroke. The black leather glove I've started to wear on jobs squeaked from the sudden effort and slid against my sweaty palm. Then I pulled the body attached to the arm into the clearing beside me.

"Think you might be a little more careful with that thing?" I asked in a harsh whisper, because now I was starting to catch whispers of machinery in the distance.

Will took off his pith hat and mopped at his brow. I thought the pith hat was a little overkill. A green cotton headband served me just fine.

When he set the hat back on he replied, "Wuss. You'd heal. Besides, I missed, didn't I?"

I shook my head and adjusted my backpack and rifle sling. "Not for lack of trying. And keep your voice down. We're close now."

Will began to remove his backpack. The khaki cotton shirt hung like a limp dishrag from his bronze skin, sopping wet with sweat. The smell was almost enough to make me retch. I glared at him with disgust. None of the other Native Americans I've met dripped sweat like this guy.

"What?" he asked with irritation, as he dropped into a squat on a moss-covered rock.

"Have you ever heard of deodorant, Will?" I asked in the same whisper.

"Birds sweat in human form, Tony. We just do. I have antiperspirant and deodorant on," he replied in a normal voice with a withering look. "But I only put it under my arms, like everyone else in the world. I didn't coat my body with the shit. Wish we would have had enough time to get some of the Wolven cologne that would kill our scents. This job is going to be tough enough without the bad guys smelling us coming a mile away." He paused and shook his head in frustration. "Damn wolves and your touchy noses. Hope the snakes aren't as sensitive." He pulled a slightly less damp cloth from his pants pocket, then took off his helmet and set it on the ground beside him. I was a little surprised that he kept his hair high and tight, regardless of regulations. Once again, many I met around Nevada tended to fight for their tribal right. But he did strike me as the strict law-and-order type. He wiped his face again. "It's hot, and we're not exactly going to a fashion show. Besides, you've been keeping a pace that would kill a draft horse. My calves are killing me. Don't you *ever* get tired?"

He opened his pack and removed a roll of beef jerky. I've always been fond of beef jerky. But after three days tramping through the jungle eating nothing but, I was starting to change my opinion.

I let the backpack slide from my shoulders and leaned my Kalashnikov against the nearest tree. My own shirt was wet enough to wring out, so I figured I might as well. "Hell, I didn't get tired back when I was a vanilla human. Plus, we're on a tight schedule," I replied quietly, stripping the faded green ex-army jacket from my body. "I don't know about you, but I had other plans this week than wandering through the jungle hoping to find where a captured Wolven agent is being held. It's just good luck that I stumbled on that guard last week in the restaurant bar and could use my hindsight to fix Rayna's location. Who knew that three-day snakes got drunk on tequila so easy?" I twisted the shirt diagonally and watched as wetness poured onto the green grass. A pretty easy way to mark my territory, I had to admit.

"I'm pretty sure my foresight might have had something to do with us *being* in that bar, so back off, wolf." I think he was annoyed that one of my Sazi magic abilities is hindsight—the ability to see and experience someone else's memories when I touch them, while his is foresight—the gift of seeing the future. The hindsight is the reason for the gloves. It's a skin-on-skin thing, and fortunately, although annoying and uncomfortable, gloves do help slow down accidental images. Hindsight is very matter-of-fact, and pretty damned useful. You're seeing what already happened, which lets me see details of an event that Kerchee's *ever-changing future* visions can't provide. It's not a gift that a three-day wolf should have, since we're the lowest of the low in the supernatural world. I can't even control my own change, which was why Will was with me.

In all honesty, though, the hindsight part doesn't annoy him nearly as much as the fact that I even work for Wolven, the shape-shifter law enforcement agency. Will Kerchee is a state cop in Texas, and despite the fact that I'm slightly reformed, I'm still an accused gangster from the Midwest who would be pretty easily convicted if put in court. The new identity as J. Anthony Giambrocco doesn't negate the fact that Tony Giodone— while presumed dead—still has an arrest warrant on the books in two states, and is guilty of a lot of things that would make a jury pale. So it bugs him that we're partnered. He'd much rather be slapping cuffs on me. I don't have to do much more than watch his fingers twitch to where his sidearm would be in uniform to know that. At first, I couldn't resist making sudden movements at the edge of his peripheral vision just to watch him react . . . and a bird's peripheral goes back nearly to his spine. But then came the moon, when we were all supposed to be out of here a week ago, and now he's expending energy to keep me from turning. I'm being nice, but it's not really in my nature. That's more Sue's nature—my wife. We're bonded with more of that Sazi magic. She's in my head right now, tethered to me just like I am to Will. But she doesn't really like watching when I go on jobs, so I keep the door between us locked off. I'm getting better at that. At first, I couldn't control her involvement at all and killing people really trips her trigger. Like Kerchee, she'd much rather save a person than off 'em.

Flies began to buzz around Will's head. His face lit up with a pleased expression when he discovered a fat, nondescript black beetle that had managed to crawl into the jerky roll. I shook my head as he popped it in his mouth and crunched down cheerfully. Birds and bugs. Ick.

I looked around the clearing as I put the now wrinkled, but drier, shirt back on. I looked like hell, and probably smelled as bad as Will, but he was right—we weren't in a fashion show.

Life rose up around us in the growing sunshine like a wave. I saw flies and gnats hover around both of our sweaty heads, and heard larger insects and animals farther out in the jungle. I could see them, smell them, taste them. A python in the grass had considered us prey, but stopped as it sensed that invisible magic that screamed

Sazi . . . shape-shifter . . . *predator*. It slunk back, retreated, and now was giving us a wide berth. The monkeys and colorful birds in the trees continued to screech and call and scold, their numbers growing as daylight made them bolder. And somewhere, deeper in the green sea of vegetation, a panther watched us. Sensed me sensing it. I turned my eyes toward the shadows and stared. I could feel a growl try to escape from deep inside of me. I didn't let it surface, but I sent a trickle of magical energy out toward the hidden eyes and felt it react. This was my territory now. For as long as I was here. It disappeared into the artificial darkness.

This seemed an odd place for a clearing. But no trees had been cut down for a homestead or anything. The canopy of trees and tall ferns just seemed to . . . *stop*. The undergrowth had no such problem, and the vines and grasses were almost knee high. Damn, it was already getting hot! But luckily, the humidity's only 100 percent.

"So," said Will through a mouthful of salted meat, "what now? Which way do we go, *bwana*?"

"Who put me in charge?" I asked irritably. "You're supposed to be leading *me* to the spot, remember?"

He shrugged gracefully, nearly a flapping of feathery wings. "That ended in the bar. You're the one with the hindsight. Lots more accurate than my vision. I could tell you where we were if I was flying above. But on the ground, I'm not much better than human. I'm pretty sure we're going the right way, and you seem to be doing just fine."

Pretty sure? Great, just what I needed—to be lost in a jungle in Central America. Actually, though, as soon as he said it I realized he was right. I *was* sure where we were. We should reach the spot in less than an hour, if the breeze wasn't playing games with my nose. I didn't understand how I knew, only that I did. Living out someone's memories is always strange, like déjà vu. Part of me doesn't like this weird Sazi shit. But the other part, the hunter part, finds it perfectly natural. Like it's the logical next step.

Maybe it is.

I took another drink out of the big canteen in my pack and carefully filled the smaller water bottle on my belt. Most of what was in our packs was water. But the load was getting lighter faster than I'd planned. I hadn't counted on three days of blistering heat during the rainy season.

My elbow did the pointing toward the next thicket of green. "That way, another hour, give or take . . . if the bugs don't chew us down to bone by then." Another fly, another slap. I winced at the sound before the background settled into a monotonous droning of a thousand different insects that I never used to notice.

Monotonous . . . regular.

My brow furrowed. That one whine, high-pitched and steady, was a little *too* regular. No rise as it ventured closer, no fall as it darted away. Had it been there a minute ago? I couldn't remember. But whatever the expression on my face was made Will cock his head and lower his brows.

"What?"

I shook my head again. "Don't know. Something's not right." I stepped a few feet in one direction and then the other—in a pattern of ever-expanding circles with Will as the center. Still the whine persisted, as though coming from everywhere. "Can you hear that hum? It's really high-pitched."

He crossed his arms over his chest and turned around slowly, face intense. But then he shook his head, and lowered his voice to a near whisper. "Nothing, and my hearing's pretty sharp. Tinnitus maybe?"

Could a Sazi get ringing in the ears without magic healing the nerve damage before it could register a sound? Well, I *am* as close to human as a werewolf can get, and don't heal for shit, so who knows? "Lower your shield on me for a second. Let's see if it gets better or worse."

I felt the release before I even registered the dip of his chin—sudden enough to nearly drop me to my knees from the sheer weight of the moon that crashed down on me. Pinpricks slashed at my arms and legs, as the sharp tips of fur struggled to emerge from my skin. I stayed standing, but just barely, and had to clench my fists and jaw to keep from letting out a raging howl from the abrupt pain. He watched me, not so much in concern for my welfare, but to see if I could manage the strain.

I've had worse, so I could.

Once I could focus my head a little, I concentrated on the sounds around me, trying to filter out everything except that one whine. The thing was, I recognized the sound, but couldn't remember from where. Whatever it was seemed out of context—familiar, but in the wrong place.

"Ignore it," Will said while shouldering his rifle again. "It'll go away soon enough."

"Nope. Can't do it. I've learned to trust my instincts . . . even the wolf ones. We'll have to stay here until I figure it out." I tried to think of other high-pitched sounds, but none of them matched in my brain. *Electri-*

cal lines . . . no. Bats . . . huh-uh. Fluorescent light, compressor, computer . . . nope. But the word *mechanical* kept swimming up to the top of my brain over and over. This wasn't a natural noise.

Will let out a frustrated little chirp, like a strangled screech—which it probably was. "We're already running late. We can't *afford* for you to figure it out." But I ignored him and kept trying to find a name for the sound, until finally he lowered his rifle and pack to the ground and started to strip off his shirt. "You keep watch on my stuff. I'll fly ahead and find their camp and then come back here to let you know how far it is."

I couldn't help but snort even though I didn't bother to watch him strip. "Uh, right. And you don't think a bunch of other shape-shifters will notice a *bald eagle* floating a few thousand miles out of range over the jungle? Feeling a little suicidal today, are we?"

He let out his own rude noise that was accompanied by a weird combination of scents—oranges and burnt coffee. He was apparently both amused and annoyed at my comment. Oranges is humor and laughing. Caramelized coffee tells me the person is pissed. "Give me a little credit, newbie. I've been doing this since before your granddaddy was a glimmer in his pappy's eye. My eyesight is exceptional. I probably won't have to do much more than get above the treetops to spot the camp and even if I have to take a few flaps, I'll never be close enough for them to spot me through the canopy."

The moon picked that precise moment to drop me to my knees with a strangled scream, and I had to bite my lip to keep more sound from coming out. The door between me and Sue flung wide open and I was abruptly in two places at once. She was grocery shopping, of all things, and the phantom image of shelves and produce overlaid on the ferns and vines. The squeak of the cart wheel was lower pitched than the sound in my head, but I suddenly realized I was hearing the same sound in *two* places.

What the hell?

Tony? I could hear Sue's voice drift over the whine and the animals in the trees, and could sense a feeling of panic take her over. **What's happening? Are you okay? I see a jungle and hear lots of screaming.**

I thought I shook my head, but I really couldn't tell if it was moving or if I was only imagining it. Something was wrong . . . very wrong. Hearing the sound in Sue's world only confirmed that and made my heart race faster. **Animals, and they're just ticked off, not hurt. But I can't talk now. Bad things are about to happen.**

Two things hit at once. First, Will shifted forms in a blur of motion that my eyes really couldn't follow, and spread his massive wings while bunching his legs to spring upward. Then, Sue moved her cart to near the automatic doors by the soda machines, out the way of other shoppers in case she couldn't pull herself out of the crisis. The whine got louder in that part of my mind and the realization of what the noise was suddenly crashed home. I spent a dozen years of my life as a security consultant—installing and repairing alarm systems and the like. It was the shoplifting sensor near the door I was hearing, a beam of light between two contacts that lets out a nearly imperceptible whine . . . until it gets interrupted by an activated item.

I turned and shouted at Will, no longer caring whether anyone heard. "No! Don't fly up!"

But it was too late. He'd already let out a flap that took him soaring a dozen feet high. Another click told me I was right and all I could do was race for cover as gunfire from a dozen points in the trees shattered the morning air. I stood a better chance surviving as a smaller target and could run faster in wolf form, so I stopped fighting the pressure of the moon on me. I felt Sue partially collapse against the shopping cart as fur began to flow and every bone in my body broke and re-formed at lightning speed. The pain that filled my mind wasn't from bullets . . . or at least, I *hoped* it wasn't from bullets. It was a little hard to tell.

When the automatic rifles had expended their clips a few seconds later, and acrid smoke and silence filled the air, I finally poked my head out from beneath the heavy log that had taken the brunt of the damage. No surprise that the animals had booked it for the border. I would too in their place.

It was hard not to be impressed by such a subtle trap. Now that I knew what I was looking for, I could see the bits of metal scattered among the tall trees around the open space. We must have somehow tripped a switch when we entered the clearing that activated the sensors. Then, with no cover, any intruder trying to *leave* the clearing would be eliminated. No fuss, no muss—and plenty of warning to the bad guys to close up shop in case they missed anyone.

Will was on the ground, still in bird form. One wing was covered in blood, but he smelled more angry and embarrassed than in pain. As I stepped closer, struggling to ignore the scent of bird blood while my stomach growled, he opened that yellow beak and ticked his tongue across the edge, making a sharp sound that was probably a curse word in bird language. "Note to self . . . listen to the villain standing next to you so the villain in the brush doesn't kill you."

One of my ears flicked forward, the wolf equivalent of a shrug. "Can't say I didn't tell you to stay put. Anything other than the wing . . . winged?"

He shook his feathery head. "No, but my forearm's busted clean in half. They were apparently expecting Sazi, because the bullets were silver. That's why I haven't turned back. I don't want it to heal wrong during the change. Mind setting the pieces back together so I can shift back? Now that the camp's been warned by the gunfire, we don't have much time."

I looked at him and down at my wolf form and raised a paw. "Any clues how to accomplish that? I'm not an alpha, remember? I can't change back by choice, and as you can see . . . no opposable thumbs."

Those too-bright eyes stared at me before he blinked once, down to up, like my python-shifter buddy, Bobby, does. "Well, hell. Doesn't that just suck moss-covered swamp rocks? Yeah, I can change you and hold you, but I'm going to wind up healing damned slow."

"You going to be able to handle a rifle? We're going to need them to get out of here, I'm betting." I was starting to hear shouts in the distance. Either they were coming for us, or pulling up stakes where they were. I looked toward the sound and so did Will. It occurred to me that I wasn't seeing grocery items anymore, and couldn't seem to sense Sue in my mind. It wasn't uncommon that she would shut the door on her own when the crisis was done and there was blood on the ground. It turns her stomach and the fact that someone else's pain excites me now isn't something she likes to think about much. But I had to admit that the desire to pounce on my partner just to hear him yelp, and then savor sweet, metallic blood, was strong.

Kerchee interrupted my thoughts. "Don't see why not. Just switch rifles with me. The auto has a shorter sling and my trigger finger is fine. It's a room broom anyway, so aiming isn't much of an issue." He winced just then and his wing twitched. So did I, and that bothered me.

A lot.

"Actually, we're going to have to speed up the process. The bone's already trying to knit, and with it snapped like this, it's going to try to fill in the gaps with new bone."

"And that would be bad?" I've had more than one time since turning wolf that I considered it a really good thing that my body filled in missing gaps. Nothing like barely surviving a dragon feasting on you to appreciate healing abilities.

"Oh, that would be *very* bad. My arm would be crippled and I doubt my fingers would work right. And even if a healer re-broke it, it would try to remember the *new* form. It would take months and months to get it back to normal and it would be impossible to explain to humans, so I'd have to be off work until it was right again. Magic's sort of like quirky software. If you stay in the parameters, it's awesome. But press just one wrong key—"

Ah. Got it. Yeah, I'd noticed that myself. "So, you want to change me back and I'll hold it steady?"

His wing twitched again and the feathers started to move. I didn't think he was doing it because he stumbled a little and wound up having to catch himself with his other wing. "No time. Just grab it with your teeth.

It's a clean break, so all you have to do is hold it steady while the magic does its thing."

I looked at him as askance as a wolf can. "You want *me* . . . the three-day wolf with barely enough magic to have human thoughts, to grab onto your bloody wing with my mouth? On the first day of the moon? You're either very brave or very stupid, because I haven't eaten since dinner last night and it's everything I can do right now not to have you for breakfast."

His lower jaw moved in what might be considered a laugh. "You forget I'm an alpha. I'm going to hold you motionless once you've clamped on. You won't be able to move your jaw enough to chew."

It was true that I've seen him do the magical freezing thing. He and Bobby, the third member of our crew, had a duel of sorts after we'd had a few rounds at the bar. Most Sazi can't get drunk, since our brain cells heal too quickly to be impaired. But just the ceremony of drinking relaxed the two tough-guy alphas enough to try stupid things. I was supposed to be the judge to determine who had the strongest magic, but I had to call it a draw since neither of them wound up *completely* unable to move and the overload of magic was making fights break out all over the bar. Still, I was betting he could hold me just fine.

There are some things that are against my better judgment that I wind up doing anyway. This was going to be one of them, just so we could finish this and get out of here. I stepped forward, trying not to think too much about the plan. It seemed simple enough, but I've learned that not everything is simple in the supernatural world.

"Let's go over to that tree," he said, and I struggled

to listen. But the closer I got to him, the stronger the smell of blood was. It filled my nose, started my saliva dripping, and tried to turn my brain to putty and put a red haze over my vision. "I can prop my wing tip on that broken branch so you can keep the bone straight." I could see the bone now, the two sharp ends poking up through the feathers—bright white against the dark brown background. He turned and hopped toward a tree and I followed, transfixed by the spots of red that marked his path. My nose dropped to the ground without my willing it to and more of my brain shut down as the sweet scent filled me.

"You still with me, Giambrocco? Is the moon getting to you too much?"

"No, I'm fine." Even as I said the words, I knew the wolf was taking over, lying to the bird so he could replace the fire in his belly with red, warm meat.

Cautious, slow. I moved toward the wounded bird carefully. I didn't want to startle it enough to fly. The part of my mind that was still human was rebelling. There was something about feeding on another human that it objected to. My heart started beating faster as I ran my nose slowly over the wounded wing. My mouth opened and I felt the sharp end of bone press against the roof of my mouth and feathery softness glide over my tongue. Clamping shut my jaw suddenly made the bird gasp and writhe and made my jaw convulse, tighten, until I could feel my teeth sink beneath the feathers into firm flesh. More warm, salty wetness slid down my throat and I swallowed it, but it only made me hungrier.

No more of this toying with the prey.

A growl escaped me and I started to twist and rip at the wing. Human words that I recognized as cursing filled my ears, and a second wing began to beat at my head. I laid my ears down, closed my eyes, and continued to feed. Pressure then against me, forcing me to stop. I tried to open my jaw, but it was fixed tight. That wasn't acceptable. The prey doesn't control the hunter. I reached out to fight against whatever bound me, kept me from the food, and felt my mate in the background. She was eating meat too, and the taste of it drove me wild. I fought harder and touched a thin line in my mind that was my pack. I hadn't felt the other wolves for so long, but now they were with me. They could taste the prey too and wanted to share in the feast. I felt fur replace flesh and other teeth struggle to reach what I was tasting.

With renewed vigor, I snapped and ripped at feathers and flesh until it began to shrink in my mouth, change until it was an arm, not a wing. Then hands opened my mouth, threw me to the ground, forcing me to raise up again and pounce.

But the bird was gone, replaced by a man, who quickly climbed a tree and sat on the limb staring down at me with both anger and amazement. But it was the jaw-tightening scent of fear that made me jump against the tree, tearing bark off in my effort to get back to eating.

Then the moon eased against me, pushed away by an unseen force, until I was in a bubble of magic again, turning, changing until I was back in the accursed human shell once more.

"Whoa." I blinked and stared down at the blood staining my hands and bare chest. "Man, I hate it when that happens." I didn't even want to think about the revulsion I felt. I'd killed a man before during another blind wolf moment, and I still have nightmares about it. Strange that a trained assassin would flinch at death, but there's something that's just ... *wrong* with ripping out a throat with my teeth.

"Jesus f-ing Christ, Tony!" Will was staring at his arm, now whole again, but with more than a few teeth gouges that were slowly filling in as I watched. "How in the hell did you defeat my magic like that? I should be able to hold you like you were an insect."

I took a deep, shuddering breath and held it until I could think my own thoughts again. "Power of the pack. You weren't just holding me, you were trying to hold a dozen hungry wolves. I didn't think I was attached to the Chicago group anymore, but apparently I was wrong. I'll bet Nikoli is having an interesting day just about now, turning wolves back human." I was betting I was still in central time zone, meaning it was also morning in Illinois.

Kerchee climbed down out of the tree slowly, keeping a close eye on me. I should probably find it weird that we were two guys naked in the jungle, but *Brokeback Mountain* this wasn't. It was more locker room of the weird than any sort of turn-on. Will turned and started to put on his clothes and left me to find my spares from the pack that was now mostly ruined near the log where I first turned.

We quickly and silently picked up our weapons and returned to the task of tracking down the camp, which wasn't too hard anymore, as much noise as they were making. The hard part was keeping to the undergrowth and staying quiet so the roving bands of troops didn't spot us. I could smell them as snake a mile away, and they could likely smell us too, but the scent of Will's blood was too strong, and it led them to where we'd been ... not where we were going.

By the time we passed through a small stream where we washed off the blood and got to the edge of a rock out-cropping near the camp, I'd returned fully to my mind. I'm glad that Kerchee didn't feel the need to "talk" about what happened. I'm not good at apologies, and saying *I told you so* didn't really seem appropriate either.

We couldn't ask for better timing, because a helicopter arrived just as we did, scattering our scent in every direction. It must have made us seem a much bigger force than two, because everybody started sticking out their tongues and getting panicked looks. Snake-shifters stick out their tongues a lot to scent the air when there aren't humans around. Even Bobby used to lick his lips so much he had to keep a tube of lip balm handy so they didn't crack.

"Keep an eye out for where they might be holding Rayna."

I glanced around at the canvas tents and corrugated metal shacks that wouldn't do much more than provide limited protection from the weather and shook my head. "She's a tiger, right? Well, unless she's underground, or they've got a steel cage in one of the buildings, she's not here. Nothing I'm seeing would hold *me,* much less an alpha cat."

But then what before my wondering eyes did appear but a Sazi woman, surrounded by a bevy of creosote-scented men of all nationalities, pushing her toward the copter. I have no idea why snakes smell like creosote, but they do. The woman, on the other hand, had a definite "cat" smell. Yeah, just like the small ones when you walk into someone's house, only bigger.

The bevy of men weren't admirers, although the woman deserved a second look. I counted twenty, then thirty, armed soldiers. There's a vast difference between a "guard" and a *soldier.* A lot of it is how they carry themselves, and their weapons. These guys looked both ready for action, and eager for it, from the way they were searching the jungle . . . but keeping to their posts. One thing I've learned about snakes, though—only a very few of the species are what they call *day hunters.* Those of the night-hunting variety have really shitty eyesight and hardly any nose. If the soldiers were sticking to the formula I've encountered before, they would be tasting the air for our location and feeling for a heat source. Good thing we were still wet from the river and in a shady spot.

I was expecting one woman prisoner, but the second one who was dragged out of the nearby tent took me by surprise—not only because she was there at all, but because of *who* she was.

"Um, wow. That's not who I expected to see."

"What in the hell is *she* doing here?" Will's quiet voice held the same surprise as mine. But when Angelique Calibria, the über-tough, bitchy-as-hell representative of the raptors on the Sazi council, was abruptly slapped to the ground by another woman who got off the helicopter . . . and stayed there looking scared, Kerchee's voice turned much more worried.

"I think we're in some serious shit here."

Chapter Two

A HINT OF movement caught the corner of my eye before it disappeared with lightning speed. But once I saw the flash of black-red fire, I knew what . . . and *who* was there. An ally, or I would already have fired a shot his way.

"So," I whispered in a breath so low that only those standing closest to me would hear. "Do you know her?"

Will shook his head and answered in a similar low pitch. "Never seen her before. I wish the helicopter wasn't blowing all the scents around so I could smell better."

My brows raised, because I was a little surprised Will hadn't noticed the new arrival. "I wasn't talking to you. I was talking to Ahmad."

It did my heart good to see how fast his head whipped around. Even the snake king himself raised a brow from where he now crouched behind us. "Perhaps your reputation is . . . *partially* deserved, agent."

Ahmad al-Narmer—and no, I have no idea how he came about that name—is like his namesake, the king cobra. He's slender, muscled, and very, very deadly.

Even the bleed-over from his power was like crawling through stinging nettles. It both itched and hurt and you knew, just *knew* that if you touched your skin, you'd be screaming for a week.

I shrugged slightly, while focusing my eyes back on the scene in front of me. Trying to ignore the sensation of biting ants on my body was like asking a ten-year-old to ignore chicken pox. It could be done, but it took effort. "Second sight is handy that way. You have a really unique signature color. Not particularly *pretty*, but unique." His aura was the color of old dried blood, with a touch of oozing tar. Up until last Christmas, it had been a healthy red-gold, but something happened to him to change it, and apparently I'm not high enough in this new family to know the details.

He ignored the statement and returned to my earlier question. "She looks like a thousand other snakes from the back. I need her to turn around. Until she does, tell me the details I'm not seeing . . . both of you."

This was something that Wolven really did well. Lucas has started to require our reports to include specialization. For example, I see auras, so he wants to know what color and where the weak points are in the person's power. Will can see a mite on the back of a flea, so from him, Lucas would want to know the tiniest details, from a chipped fingernail to whether the person has dandruff. It's actually creating a better profile on the known criminals that we haven't caught up with yet. People not only have tells in their personality that resurface time after time, but also have tiny things they don't bother to cover up, from moles to ordinary scars and even the position of teeth.

"Aura's really bright. Bigger than Will's . . . so at

least yours and Lucas's level and the color of—" I
paused and glanced around without moving my head.
When I twitched my chin, it was toward the helicopter
door. "The call letters on the chopper's tail, but a shade
darker, toward orange. Scent is all snake, heavy on the
creosote. Probably venomous."

"Small tattoo of a coiled snake inside a triangle on
her wrist. The watch nearly covers it, but I noticed when
she slapped Angelique." Which she proceeded to do
again. The problem was that the chopper, and now the
trucks, were loud enough that I couldn't seem to focus
in on the words. Pity I suck at reading lips. I should really look into classes.

The wind was whipping around her long hair and I
noticed a second tattoo at the base of her neck . . . the
same second as Will spoke again.

"Another tattoo, this one of what looks like a pad-
lock on her L-five neck joint. Is that what it looks like
to you, Tony?"

I frankly didn't see it long enough, but, "Yeah, sort
of. I'd have to see it again to be sure. Weak spots in her
power at her left ankle." The woman turned just then,
so I got to see her face. From her golden-brown skin, I
was expecting her features to be from one of the Latin
countries. But no, she was definitely Middle Eastern.
Damned if I could figure out where she hailed from,
though. I kept reporting, figuring I didn't have much
time before we were going to have to move in, or move
out. All those flicking tongues were starting to zone in
on our location. "Another weak spot at the hollow of
her neck."

"Yeah," Will whispered with a nod. "I can see the
barest remnant of a scar, just above her collarbone.

Looks like it was made with a curved blade—probably silver if it interrupted her aura enough to leave a weak point."

"Poisoned silver." Ahmad's voice was dull and flat. "She barely survived." It didn't sound like he was trying to hide his reaction as much as he was too surprised to remember how to inflect. The turmoil of emotions that started to roll off of him was startling. Council members have access to a sweet little invention of Bobby's. It's a cologne that disguises a Sazi's scent. Turns the person into a blank slate, smell-wise. It was confusing as hell to me when I first encountered it and I could have sworn that Ahmad was wearing it when he arrived. So, either he didn't have any particular emotions when he arrived, or he was *really* surprised now.

"Sounds like you know her."

He gave me a look that would have signed his death warrant if he were anyone else. But he answered. "Her name is, or *was,* Tuli al-Ur . . . and she should be long dead. That she's standing there says that either I am wrong about her identity, or wrong about the power I'd ascribed to her. Either way, I suggest that it is past time to remove those we came to rescue, and capture her for further investigation."

I flicked my eyes around to the thick foliage, but nope . . . I wasn't seeing any neon lights except for us and those with the guns ahead of us. "Did you bring along a cavalry that you haven't mentioned?" There's outnumbered, and *outnumbered.* This is the latter category that even movie heroes are smart enough to avoid. "In fact, why are you here at all? Is there something going on that we should know about?"

Instead of answering he flicked his chin toward the

hills to the north and muttered so low that I had to struggle to hear, even with his lips almost close enough to touch my ear. "At the base of those cliffs, there is a cave where we can take the women to rest for a time before getting them back to headquarters. You, wolf, will provide ground cover with the rifles. The bird will change forms, fly in, and carry the women away with his talons. I will kill any opponents you miss."

Will's jaw dropped and his scent was filled with a burst of soured milk, which tends to come from disbelief. "Speaking as *the bird,* the only way I'd be able to pick up the women with my talons long enough to fly would be to sink them into their shoulders and even if I could manage the weight of both, I couldn't keep the load steady enough to gain any altitude."

If he'd expected that logic to sway Ahmad, he was wrong. "Locking your claws *is* the most expedient way to maintain your grip. Angelique would expect no less of a rescuer. Surely you've trained for rescues of this sort. Why else would you be selected for this mission?" He let out a sigh that sounded angry and put upon, but his scent was closer to the nauseating, cloying scent of dark humor. "Must I question the other skills Lucas boasted you inherited and simply dismiss you as a risk to this assignment?"

That's Ahmad for you. He can simultaneously insult both your abilities and family tree, while looking at you like you're shit to be scraped from his boot. Unlike the rest of the council, there's little Ahmad likes better than to watch people fail. Gives him some sort of kick. I hate guys like him because their arrogance is usually what causes things to go bad. Still, I'm not stupid enough to say anything to his face. People don't survive a smart mouth in this world.

Will's obviously been around long enough not to rise to the bait. You could almost hear his teeth grinding, but he stayed polite while at the same time throwing all the potential blame on Ahmad. "Our instructions were to remove the prisoners without damage. But if you're confident the guidelines have changed, naturally we'll follow your direction. You'll both have to keep those with guns busy so they don't shoot the hostages. I doubt they'll consider a single gun much of a threat. You'll also have to either turn off that chopper prop or get them to move the ladies out from underneath. I'm a good flyer, but I'm not a magician."

Ahmad stayed still and unblinking for a long moment and then narrowed his pupils. Yeah, he didn't squint his eyes in anger. He narrowed the pupils until they were slits and let out a foul scent that was like poisoned coffee. That's just creepy. Still, that was the only outward sign of his annoyance which was a good thing.

Whatever questions Tuli was asking Angelique weren't getting satisfactory answers, because she slammed my least favorite bird in the face with a rifle butt and then with gestures made it clear that they were to be loaded on the helicopter. We didn't have much time. "Very well. Wolf, you will lay down ground fire while I move around the flank to eliminate the perimeter guards. I expect two-shot kills, if a three-day can manage that."

Once again . . . skills and heritage. I stuck out my right hand and pasted on my best smile. "Hi, my name's Tony. I'll be your *trained* assassin today." Yeah, yeah, I know. Short walk to a long grave, but I couldn't help myself.

Will let out a noise that could only be interpreted as a strangled laugh. If it weren't for the fact that he sounded curiously like a howler monkey and there was too much noise from the chopper, we'd probably be diving from bullets.

I decided that it would be prudent to separate myself from the snake man when his jaw opened enough to let out a low hiss. I picked up both my weapon and Will's and slipped into the undergrowth to get a better location for shooting.

Things happened pretty quickly after that. It didn't take any great amount of skill to aim and fire on the first guy who caught my eye at the far ring of guards. Like Ahmad instructed, a two-shot kill. That's the rule for taking out Sazi . . . once in the head and once in the heart. Pop, pop, too fast for the body to heal. I've been practicing to lower my time and increase my accuracy, because you really do only get two chances with these guys—especially the powerful ones. But, as expected, once one guard went down the others got all riled up.

Sprays of bullets started firing every direction. Stupid, in my opinion, and I changed my mind about these guys being pros. Movies make it look like there's unlimited ammo in the world. But in reality, a fifty-round clip takes about five seconds to dump with a full auto, and close to a quarter minute for even a Sazi to reload it. Sure, you can slap in another clip and keep going, but your average-joe-villain on a payroll isn't considered worth the money to give a dozen clips to. They had the standard taped double-stack clip and probably a load more in an ammo dump somewhere. But *somewhere's* a long way away when you're taking fire.

Ahmad actually didn't have a bad idea. Everybody was concentrating on my fire as I raced back and forth between multiple points and switched weapons so they'd think there were more of us, while he was sneaking around the edges and just . . . touching people. It was sort of hard to concentrate on my own predicament because he was just strolling up in human form and putting a finger on their neck. A guard would freeze in place with an expression of abject fear and intense pain and then they'd just drop to the ground with a glassy stare seconds later. It was like they weren't even seeing him walk up, bold as brass. I know alphas can cast illusions to make themselves appear to be almost anything, but it just seemed really odd that they wouldn't notice him at all.

I well and truly need to learn to keep my mouth shut around him.

Out of the corner of my eye as I was taking out another guard, I saw the woman named Tuli starting to push the other women toward the open helicopter door. Angelique wasn't even resisting. She just looked confused, but the other woman was fighting like a . . . well, a *tiger* to stay on the ground and she was apparently important enough to them that they weren't willing to kill her. But the chopper needed to be eliminated from the picture anyway, so I turned my fire and first took out the pilot through the windshield and then started to systematically fire at the base of the prop . . . between bouts of keeping my ass alive.

There was finally a satisfying spray of fluid as I cut a pressurized line and then wisps of smoke began to appear in the sky. Shortly thereafter, people started darting away from the machine as the whirring thup from the prop turned into an angry screech of tortured metal.

Unlike the movies once again, it didn't explode. While there's something really satisfying about watching a kick-ass explosion, helicopter manufacturers would have a hundred lawsuits a week if the unit exploded just because a coolant line went down. No, it just started smoking and then ground to a halt, all parts intact. No harm, no foul.

Well, unless you wanted to *go* somewhere.

Will was there in a flash, diving down in a blur of speed. He did some fancy flicking of a few feathers at the back of his wings, and suddenly he was coming out of the dive, a shoulder and arm gripped in each powerful talon as he fought to gain altitude with two-hundred-plus pounds of weight dangling under him. I've noticed that some of those tiger women are *really* dense, muscle-wise. But the birds are light as . . . well, a bag of feathers, so I'll just bet he was having loads of fun trying to stay level.

Blood poured and the women's screams of anger and pain were nearly equal to the panicked shouts of the soldiers as their tickets to employment were fast rising above the tree line. The few that weren't smart enough to watch their *own* backs were soon on their backs with a quick succession of dual shots.

But it was getting harder and harder to concentrate on shooting as the scent of blood, fear, and anger drifted up on the rising warm air currents. Will's cocoon was still tight around me, but I could feel it lessening as he pulled back power to carry his load.

The farther away with the women Will got, the more the moon started pressing down on me—messing with my head and making every bone in my body scream in pain. But been there, done that, so I guess it was time to put on my big-boy undies and fight off the moon myself. Fortunately, there's a good reason for Sazi to have mates. There's extra life energy available to draw on when it's crisis time. And y'know, when there's suddenly a dozen guards looking pissed and staring right at your location while flipping ammo clips, it's a good bet a crisis is heading your way.

A pair of shots rang out from behind me. It was only my paranoid nature and slightly hyperactive survival instinct that made me dive and roll the moment I heard the first shot, so the chunk of hot lead only grazed my neck and shoulder instead of splattering my brain across the landscape. I fired multiple shots toward the blur of light through the leaves and was satisfied to smell the scent of new pennies join the anger and pain on the wind. It didn't make my arm feel any better, but at least I had company in my misery.

Of course, now everybody knew where I was, so I didn't really have time to tend to my boo-boo. It was all I could do to grab my two weapons, race toward the fallen scout to grab his extra ammo . . . kicking him sharply in the head first, so he didn't get any bright ideas about following me, and dive face-first into the wall of green in the approximate location of the cliffs. Ahmad was going to have to be on his own, but he's been around for a very long time, so I was betting he was fully capable of handling his end.

Thankfully, most of the trees in the area were tall enough that even the lower branches were over my head, so I could see the cliffs looming ahead of me without having to constantly readjust my path. It made escaping a lot easier, since the guys after me probably knew the terrain better. It also helped that they considered their guns to be an asset. They'd actually be quicker in their snake form, and could probably overtake me and take me down by sheer force. But having no arms really limits ranged weapon opportunities in case there was more than just me out here, or I was a tougher opponent than they expected.

The trouble was that I was getting out of breath quicker than I should and the rifles felt like they were getting heavier and heavier. A glance down told me that the slick on the metal wasn't sweat. It was blood, and there was a lot more of it than there should be. I slung the Mac-10 over my neck and reached up with my left hand to feel distinct spurts of wetness that matched the beating of my heart.

Crap. The bullet had nicked the carotid artery. I was bleeding out.

Chapter Three

No WONDER THE snakes weren't bothering to speed up. In a few minutes, they could stop running altogether and leave my corpse for the animals.

One of the worst things about being a three-day dog is that even though I heal better than when I was human, it would still be hours before I'd recover. Still too slow of a process to make up for the loss of blood.

I had limited options. If I kept running from the snakes and kept my heart pumping hard, I'd die just that much quicker. If I slowed down, instead of a relatively painless descent into oblivion from loss of blood, I'd die in agony from a snakebite or torture. These Sazi snakes are really into torture, and that's not a road I cared to go down.

So, running it was.

I pressed the palm of my hand against my neck to slow down the escape of the blood and raced for the relative safety of the cliffs after throwing a few sprays of bullets behind me to keep heads down for a moment. I didn't think that Will or Ahmad would be overly appreciative of me painting a scent trail right to the prisoner's hidey-hole, since it sort of defeats the whole purpose of the rescue. But a cave is more easily defended than open air, and I was pretty sure that the blood from the shoulder wounds Will had inflicted were being tracked as well.

The sounds of rifle fire and the occasional shotgun blast as I neared the cliffs told me I was right. It was a pleasant surprise that the majority of weapon fire was coming out of the cave. Either Will had picked up some artillery during the flight, or Ahmad had already stocked the cave in preparation of a firefight. Magic against magic is fine when it's one on one or even one on six, but the best alpha will wind up toast against a dozen or more other magic users. Ranged weapons are a good thing, which is why my skills have become valuable to the Sazi command.

I hoped that his eyesight was as good as he claimed, and he'd been to the range recently, because I was starting to get gray flowers erupting in my vision and my left leg was starting to drag every time I lifted it. "Kerchee! Incoming!"

The clearing right before the cave was going to be a problem, but at least if I was shot, it would be quick. I pulled on the cord of energy inside my mind until I could feel Sue's heart speeding up to match the adrenaline-laced one in my chest.

The cave mouth was looming as I raced forward and I hoped that the tiny bursts of light from the darkness were aiming at targets other than me. With a primal yell, I threw my last bit of energy to lifting the AK-47, the only gun that still had ammo, and pointing it upside down over my head before pulling the trigger. I probably didn't hit much more than dirt, but I thought I heard at least one scream before I flung myself face-first into the cave with an appalling lack of finesse and disturbing flash of pain.

Will spoke without even looking back toward me. "About time you got here, wolf. Grab something from the arsenal and give me a hand picking these guys off."

I flipped over with effort and then scooted on my butt until I was sitting against the wall. The left arm was completely useless now and it was hard to keep my head upright. My voice came out way threadier than I liked and I also didn't care for the pants for air it took to even get the few words out. "No . . . can do, flyboy. I got . . . tagged. Just felt like . . . dying from something . . . other than a snake . . . bite."

He turned his head then and took me in with an up-down flick of his eyes. "Well, shit. Rayna, you got anything left to stop that bleeding? Lucas will be pissed to no end if I let him die."

I saw something move out of the corner of my eye and forced my head to flop so I could see. A pale blond woman who smelled of cat knelt down beside me. She moved my head to the other side so she could see my neck and let out a low, concerned rowr. "The bullet went right through it and part of the vein is missing. It'll take more skill, or at least more power, than mine to fix it. But you're a shaman, right, Will? Can't you heal it up? I can man the entrance until Ahmad gets here."

The bright light behind Will began to fade to gray as Rayna stood and hurried forward, and the retort from the muzzle seemed to grow fainter as my heart slowed down. Really, if I had to go, this wasn't so bad. I just wished I could find Sue in my mind. I could feel her body, but it was like her voice was muffled behind a brick wall. I could only hear the tiniest sound, but her voice too was fading fast.

I'd like to say I dreamed, but that wouldn't be quite right. It was more that things were happening around me, but I wasn't a participant. There were female voices now, and the sounds of quiet chanting in a language I didn't recognize. Fire appeared in the form of a torch and the cave was suddenly brightly lit. I was looking back toward the cave entrance and it was farther away, like I was deeper in the cave, and standing.

The standing part was nice. It gave me hope, however false.

Shadows appeared at the cave entrance, but instead of panicking like I should, it felt *good* . . . right that they'd finally arrived. Like they should be here. Both men and women walked carefully into the cave, their bodies painted and covered with feathers and fur. They smelled of more than just skins, though. They were shifters, like me. Some were wolves, some cats, and a few raptors and snakes. They walked with quiet deliberation deeper into the cave and I moved with them, like I was floating overhead. Or sometimes beside. There was a path worn smooth in the stone from a thousand other treks like this one. But this visit was more important. There was a sense of something nearly sacred about these people. Maybe they were priests or shamans or even seers.

They could fix the corruption that was to come, could mend the damage already caused. The chanting started again and one man stepped from the middle of the procession and raised a book high over his head, turning as he spoke. The book was fuzzy and had the sickly pattern and color of the science experiment you'd find in a cup of sugared coffee forgotten for a week. The faces of the others turned from placid to angry and the few people willing to glance at the book wore an expression of loathing.

Now a question. I only knew because of the lilt of the words at the end of the sentence. The others met his eyes as he turned and they all nodded assent. The man turned again and now I could see the blackened hole that had been dug into the cave wall. The book was lowered onto a flimsy patterned skin, like a python shed from a man-sized snake. Over and over it was rolled until it was encased, sealed from the humidity of the cave. There was a sense of relief that permeated the small room. As firelight flickered across the wall paintings of squat men with fierce faces offering food to their gods, the man with the book put the book in the hole. Not with a sense of ceremony, but with the same disgust reserved for roaches found under the fridge.

Darkness, and then the scene changed. Hands were reaching for the book in the hole and I couldn't stop it. But I knew it was a bad, bad thing. The scent of the shifter who was in the cave was a creosote so strong that it burned my nose. Stronger than Bobby, stronger than Ahmad. This was a force to make the world bow. And somehow I knew the book couldn't leave the cave in his possession. Bad things would happen and everyone would suffer. Yet I couldn't move. Couldn't breathe. I could only watch as the man smiled at a second, shorter man, his thin face familiar, but not enough to put a name to. They left in silence, not a word spoken. Yet the stench and fear they left in the cave would last for years.

More sounds now, mechanical and soft. Pain ripped at my neck and arm and I was amazed I hadn't noticed it before. Then the pain faded and I was looking again at the helicopter, but from a different angle. Most of the men with the rifles lay dead and those who weren't dead were dying. Only two figures remained in the scene . . . me and the woman Ahmad had called Tuli.

She smiled and her voice was the sultry sound of a Bond girl, all smooth and sexy with evil undertones. "I'm surprised to see you here, Rimush. I'd heard that you turned against your father's goals." I'd never heard the name before, and couldn't really figure who I was supposed to be.

But then I figured it out, only because of the voice. A moment of panic flashed through me before I recovered enough to say with disdain laced through the words, "Not as surprised as I am to see *you*, Tuli. Especially since I was told there was no one left here with any sort of leadership ability to continue his plan."

The frown was sudden and burned metal joined the taste of bitter shame on the air. "We have progressed . . . even though our lord has not seen fit to visit of late."

Should I feel, or at least *show,* sorrow? No. Better to let her see the truth. I let the satisfied smile part my lips. "He has not visited because I killed him in combat. Did Nasil not consider you important enough to tell that my old debt is finally repaid with his blood?"

Tuli reached out to grasp the edge of the helicopter. She tried to make it look like a casual gesture, but her scent betrayed her as both surprised and frightened. She stared warily and flicked out the pink tip of her tongue before she spat the words, "You lie! You haven't the strength to have killed Sargon."

One brow raised like rehearsed so many times and I settled my stance into casual indifference. "Haven't I?

Are you so unable to taste truth after living among my father's minions for this many years that you cannot trust your tongue?"

A pause then. It was necessary to let her think, consider the implications. Would she be more concerned about Sargon's plan, or her own welfare? Or, it might be amusing if her first thought was something else entirely.

"If you speak true, then that would mean—"

Yes, let her see the small smirk . . . and try to interpret what it might mean. If she was close to the plan, she could be useful. More flicks of that so-pink tongue to try to read me. I'd forgotten that tongue, and that dark hair, longer now than I remembered. But I've spent far too many years becoming unreadable to give her anything to ease her discomfort.

Now her pupils narrowed and an intoxicating mix of worry, anger, and fear flowed through my flared nostrils to paint the back of my throat. But hidden among the other scents was something I hadn't tasted in centuries— and had certainly never expected to taste again from *her.*

"So. You are here to claim right of succession."

No movement. No expression. Her only answer was direct eye contact and a wave of power toward her . . . enough to throw her off balance but not sting. Both were critical while I struggled to find meaning in a term I hadn't heard since childhood. I was the youngest, so it was never expected I would gain the throne of Akede unless by assassination or happenstance. In fact, since my father had gained the throne by conquest, it would be only Tuli's clan—the Hurrians—who might have created meaning in the term.

"Well? Do I hold so little of your interest that I am not to even be told if you plan to own my key?"

Ah. I remembered now. Why was I not surprised my father held fast to the reins of such an outdated notion like slavery until his dying breath? How many wounds did Tuli bear since last I saw her? How many healed bites, how many burns and lash marks to keep her from rebelling? No, I had little use for slaves. They were unreliable at best, and a danger, at worst. Yet, if I hoped to unravel the plan he'd begun down here, this might be my easiest road. "How many keys was he in possession of?"

The question came out too matter of fact from the flinch and stiff, barely polite answer. "There are only a dozen left, plus those who are paid to serve. Is that sufficient for you to *bother* with us, or are we to be cast to the winds?"

The pain in her eyes took me far into the past—when we were barely more than children, and my mother threatened to have Tuli returned to the Hurrian king as an inadequate treaty gift for serving a meal that was nearly burnt. There was no worse insult to the gifting royals, who would immediately kill her and her family for the shame they had brought.

But so many years had passed now. There was no family to return to if I threw off her chains. No country, no king.

I stepped closer to her, until we were only inches apart. The taste of her power was still as intoxicating as it was a dozen centuries ago. "Would I have risked my mother's anger by teaching you to cook properly if I planned to cast you off now?" There was no escaping the logic, and the blush that came to her face said she also remembered the other, more *pleasurable,* things I taught her in those sultry nights in the kitchen.

"We swore we would never speak of those few stolen moments."

The smile came to my face unbidden as I glanced around at the still ground. "We swore we would never speak of it to another living soul . . . and I see none."

She tried hard not to smirk. No doubt she knew, and possibly liked, some of the soldiers. I wondered if any were her lovers. "You inherited your father's talent for death."

My *father.* Would he dog my every step until my final day? The sudden clenching of my fists and hiss that was pulled out of my throat at the memory of Sargon's last few moments was enough to make her step back a pace. "I *ripped* the talent from his worthless hide. He made one too many mistakes, and he paid as dearly, and as painfully, as I could make him."

The vengeance finally swam up into her eyes like a fish breaking the water's surface. The nod of her head was tight and the smile as filled with darkness as the blackest depth of my anger. "Whatever you gave, he deserved more."

He did, so there was no reason to reply. But it wouldn't be long before the searching guards returned, so we needed to leave. I didn't hold much hope that the bird and the wolf could remove an army. And, it might be that the raptors would have to find another leader to sit at the council table. But none of that mattered now. For now, all that was important was to find out what my father was planning. As much as I hated him, there was no denying his intelligence and strength of will. That even the greatest Sazi minds and seers couldn't unearth his project spoke of something so diabolical that few in the entire world would survive it.

And since my father's right hand, Nasil, still lived, the plan was likely proceeding. It was quite possible Nasil was Sargon's primary planner—helping find the flaws before others discovered them. He must either die, or be made to believe that I'm in concert with him until I can sabotage the scheme.

"You seem lost in thought, my lord."

Hearing that term brought me back to my senses. I didn't like it then, and find I still don't care to be anyone's *lord*. Yet, without that distance, I might not be able to bring the charade to fruition. No, as much as I hated it, Prince Rimush must return for a time.

Without any warning, I grabbed that long hair and yanked her tight against me. She gasped in fear, but her scent was filled with more than that. It tasted both sweet and hot on my lips. I leaned down briefly and hissed in her ear. "Never interrupt me when I'm thinking, Tuli. You'll find me much more civil if you hold your tongue until spoken to."

Apparently, Sargon had let loose the reins on her much more than I'd expected, because the way her head whipped back and the anger that came into her eyes said she wasn't accustomed to being spoken to in such a manner anymore.

I found I liked the look on her. Proud, confident.

Her own stinging magic fought against mine, and even though I'd been forced to share the power I'd gained from my father with Antoine Monier, the leader of the cats, the magic at my command was formidable enough to cow her. The longer I held her gaze and let the dark power rise into the hand that held her to sting her skin, the less confident she got. After a few long moments, she flicked her gaze down to my collar and unclenched her fists, with effort. "As you wish, my lord."

I released her hair and smoothed it gently, then ran a slow finger down her jawline until she shivered. I always enjoyed watching her shiver from my touch. There were few women in the world who could make me feel true desire—rather than simple lust, but Tuli was one of them. She met my eyes again with confusion as she caught the scent, which is exactly where I wanted to keep her for a time. "I'm not my father, Tuli, even though I *can* be if required. But neither am I the Rimush you remember. I am Ahmad al-Narmer, and I rule *all* the snakes in the world, including the ones who formerly answered to my father. Those who accept my rule will be treated fairly. Those who challenge me—" I looked around again at the bodies of snakes that covered the ground. "Will meet the fate of those you see."

The anger was back again, and I let it pass this time. "But you helped the prisoners escape and allowed the bird and wolf to kill those you are supposed to protect. Why should we follow a traitor to the cause?"

"The *cause,* my dear Tuli, wasn't to bring down the wrath of the Sazi council on our heads before the final event. The plan was to remain unnoticed until it was too late." That part was easy to fake knowledge of. It was *always* my father's plan to remain unnoticed for as long as possible. I forced my own anger to rise, because if I really had favored my father's plan for conquest of the earth, I would be furious at the ineptitude shown here. "Of *course* I helped them. I'm not an idiot like whoever planned this kidnapping. Did you even realize you held the raptor councilwoman as prisoner? Do you know they are organizing for war against you at this very moment? Why do you think I've been under cover as a councilman for this long, except to keep them lulled into complacency? This debacle has ruined *decades* of my efforts!"

Plans within plans. Another thing my father was known for, and it certainly wouldn't be out of character for him to have thrust me into a seat as a spy for centuries and pretend that I was an enemy until needed. Time had little meaning to him. I find it more precious, but Tuli didn't need to know that.

Now the confusion was in her voice, blended with the horror that I hoped to hear. "A *council member*? War? But why would Nasil—?"

Ah. Now we were getting somewhere. Taking Angelique was *Nasil's* plan. For what purpose, though? He didn't take actions lightly. I let disgust rise into my voice and walked away, stepping over a dead body with the same distaste my father would exhibit. I was expecting she would follow, and she did. "Tell me more of *Nasil's* plan. Since he witnessed my father's death in Germany, his goals are his own and may or may not include the result my father and I expected."

I flicked my gaze toward her to see suspicion of my father's trusted aide rising into her face. Good. Exactly as planned.

Searing pain erupted in my neck and shoulder. Reality lost meaning and there were suddenly both jungle and cave in my view. Dark and light blended and blurred. Too many faces and too many legs peering through a fog at me now, and I couldn't seem to move. Fear wasn't something I'd experienced much, but I felt it now.

Suddenly I was looking down on me again, as though from outside. Will was swearing and slamming palms down on my chest, which was bouncing enough to spray rocks out from under my back. My ribs hurt now, and they hurt a *lot,* so more than one must be broken. How long had he been doing CPR on me? At least my neck didn't hurt as much so whatever Ahmad had done did the trick. I wasn't surprised he wouldn't deign to touch me to start my heart again, though.

Will bent down to push air into my lungs, but he's not my type. I threw up a hand to fend off his face. "No . . . thanks." I coughed up something that tasted a lot like blood. "My wife . . . wouldn't approve."

He collapsed backward onto his butt with a relieved sound. I noticed that the two women were watching the scene from the wall. The tiger, Rayna, was looking exhausted. Angelique was looking . . . confused. But I didn't see Ahmad. Still, I didn't hear any gunfire either, so he must be outside finishing off the rest of the soldiers.

I was starting to feel a lot better now and could almost move enough to sit up. It hurt to breathe deep, but it was nothing a little athletic tape and a couple of days' rest wouldn't cure. "Tell Ahmad to wear gloves next time he feeds me magic. I'm getting to where I really hate flashbacks . . . especially from snakes. The tongue flicky-tasty thing is just creepy."

Will furrowed his brows and shook his head. "What are you talking about? Ahmad hasn't gotten here yet. Rayna's the one who fed me magic while I healed you, so you should thank the nice tiger that you're alive. In fact, we should *all* thank the nice tiger we're alive, since she's also an awesome shot with a sniper rifle."

Rayna? I stared at her closely and she didn't resemble Tuli in the slightest. It was too detailed for imagination and didn't feel like a dream. No, it was definitely Ahmad's head I was in, which meant—

"Someone needs to get back to the helicopter then. Ahmad got attacked and I was there for the ride. Don't know how exactly, but I've learned not to ignore the seer thing." I nodded toward Rayna. "Oh . . . and thanks. If it helps any, I feel worse than you look."

It pulled a chuckle from her. "It does help a little bit, actually. My ego, at least."

Will was obviously puzzled. "You get hindsight, so without touching him, you shouldn't have a clue what might have happened to him. How do you know?"

The Jeep honking outside the cave interrupted any answer I might have given . . . if I had any idea how to respond.

The only thing I knew for certain was that Ahmad was toast if we didn't get to him in time.

Chapter Four

"So, STILL NO sign of him, huh?"

Will was flat on a couch in the Sazi clinic waiting room in Boulder, Colorado, trying to get his breathing back to normal. Bobby was checking his vital signs, looking more like an M.D. than the chemist he was. His nearly blue-black skin was an interesting contrast to Will's nutty red. The regular rooms were already full of doctors treating the women . . . Sue included. Asking questions was the only thing keeping me out of the exam room. I'd already had my ass kicked out twice by the healers.

Bobby answered because Will was still out of breath. After searching the jungle for Ahmad for the past day, he'd flown straight here.

Without a plane.

"Nope. You were right that there was a struggle, and some of the blood Will collected definitely tasted like Ahmad's. Normally, I wouldn't worry about him, but he's never gone missing without checking in either."

I opened my mouth to reply, but Lucas's voice from the doorway made us both turn our heads. He's not a big man, but he's solidly built, so he filled most of the opening, not even counting the pulsing blue-white aura that surrounds him. His salt-and-pepper hair had gone to mostly silver since I'd met him, but I knew more than one person who aged rapidly in a high-stress job. Right now, there was no higher-stress job in the world—human or supernatural—than being the head of Wolven. Things are going to hell in a handbasket all over the world, and he's responsible for fixing anything that involves shape-shifters. That's most of the problems in the news right now, even though the humans don't realize it. "He's not missing anymore. I just got off the phone with Ahmad and he's on his way to Boulder. Should be here tomorrow. He wants a briefing about what he missed." He rolled his eyes and shook his head before glancing at me and Will. "As you might guess, he was annoyed he had to travel this far just to talk to you two."

I shrugged. "You couldn't have just handed us both the phone?"

Another shake, but this one with a level of agreement. "Doesn't work that way in a debriefing. It has to be in person. You know that. And you had to come here to heal up. It was the closest location with full lab facilities. Rayna's coming along, but we're still trying to figure out what happened to Angelique. She's definitely not herself . . . she's actually *cooperating* with us without argument." Like the rest of us, he was flummoxed at her attitude. Yep, she knew who she was. Yes, she remembered her imprisonment and was willing to talk about her captors. But gone were the demands and the haughty attitude that she'd carried for, apparently, her whole term on the council . . . which was more than a century. The change of personality was worrying enough to the physician in charge, Amber Wingate, that she'd called in her husband, Charles, to visit. He's the chief justice of the council, a polar bear–shifter that pretty much everybody has intimated is the de facto ruler of the Sazi. "Amber's got her under sedation magic until she can arrange for one of the traveling MRI rigs to come up here to see if she had a serious head injury that didn't heal right." He looked right at me, flinched visibly, and then added, "She'll probably want to have Sue checked too, if you have no objection. Apparently, it's . . . *necessary* at this point."

That wasn't something I liked hearing, and it spurred me to stand up and push my way past Lucas into the hallway. Yeah, he could probably hold me with magic and make me freeze in place for hours. He's got the oomph to do that. But this time he didn't. He's mated too, so maybe he understands just what not feeling Sue in my head is doing to me. It wasn't just the normal kind of twitchy that every husband feels when his wife is sick. This is deeper, like the phantom pain of a missing limb. Yet with a magical tie, you can't see for certain whether the limb is still there. It was making me crazy.

The machines were beeping softly as I walked into the room. A wave of smooth, warm power tickled my skin, rising up from the bed. Healing magic isn't like anything else. It's a warm bath, a fluffy towel, and hot cocoa in front of the fire, all rolled into a cozy sensation that makes you feel like an hour after a big turkey dinner. Lazy, content, and sleepy.

But it didn't make me feel lazy or content. It just washed over me and then past. My every nerve was on edge as I watched all the machines flicker and beep. "So, what's wrong with her?" There was a gruffness on the edge of the words that spoke more of my fear than I liked anyone to know. But no doubt the healer's heard it all. She's been doing this for centuries.

Dr. Wingate—Amber to those in Wolven—pulled the stethoscope plugs from her ears and let out a sigh. "I wish I knew. I'll be straight with you, Tony, because I think you can handle it. Her body just seems to be breaking down. The tissue and joints are degrading at a rate I can't keep up with." She reached forward and lifted the edge of the sheet. I had to suck in my breath in a hiss at the nasty bruise that covered half of one thigh. "Any idea how long that's been there?"

I shook my head. "I haven't been home for a few days, but it wasn't there last week. She said she'd been working out at the Wolven obstacle course with your sister-in-law, Tahira. A couple of the women there have been working at beefing up her self-defense skills. She prefers to be out of my head when I'm on jobs, and I figured it was a good way to keep her busy." A thought occurred to me and it made me growl. "Did someone there hurt her?"

Amber shook her head and then sat down in the chair next to the bed. "Not according to Tahira. I just got off the phone with her. But the trouble is, when I try to heal it, the bruise just grows. It's like it's reacting negatively to my magic, which doesn't make sense. I heal humans all the time . . . without them realizing it, of course. But I've never seen anything like this."

"What about plain old human diseases?" My background as a human is too wide and deep to ignore, and I've noticed that an awful lot of shape-shifters forget about the obvious. "Have you done blood tests and checked her organs and such?"

Amber didn't take offense at the question. That's one of the things I like about her. "It's the first thing I thought of, since she's full human . . . not even a Sazi family member that we can find in her family tree. Kidneys, liver, and heart are all fine. Platelet count well within normal, so it's not that her blood is too thin and her red and white cell counts are right in range. She even has a decent cholesterol count and absolutely average blood pressure. No autoimmune problems, cancer, meningitis, Lyme disease or chemical poisoning. But, she's got necrosis in her nasal linings, spots in her lungs, bruising, and a rash on her back." Another shrug, accompanied by a frustrated sigh. "I've got her on antiviral and antibiotic drips, plus an antiinflammatory. I'm starting into the rare diseases, but I don't know . . . this just *feels* wrong. It feels magical, but backward. Like she's allergic to the cure."

"Well, people *can* be allergic to drugs. Why couldn't a human be allergic to magic? Lucas told me that most attack victims don't survive their first change. Could that be part of the reason?"

She tapped her fingers on the clean white sheet and got a thoughtful look on her face as she stared at Sue. "I wouldn't even know how to begin to test for that, and it would be a *really* bad thing if she were."

I couldn't really see why. "If it's healing magic that's making her sicker, then just let her heal in a human hospital."

She turned her face fully toward me and raised both brows. "And then what, Tony? If it's magic she's allergic to, then she's allergic to *you*. You're her tie to our world. So if it really is affecting her, every minute you spend with her, every moment you're mated, is putting her closer to the grave."

That logic leap was so obvious it shouldn't have clubbed me upside the head as hard as it did. As it was, though, I sagged against the doorway and found my knees wouldn't hold me very well. The queasy feeling in my stomach wasn't helping my mood any, either.

"So how do we fix it? There has to be something that can be done. Can you shield her from me like you did when she was in Boulder? Are you shielding her now?"

She stood just as I spotted Lucas and Bobby coming down the hallway. "Yes. No. Maybe. I'm not shielding her now, so if you can't feel her, then it's worse than I thought. Frankly, I don't know if that even is the problem. And, if it is, shielding might make her deteriorate faster. I'm going to have to consult with some other healers and maybe a few seers. My sister Aspen *might* be able to tell me what will happen. She likes you because you both have hindsight, so maybe. But don't count on the seers being too horribly helpful in this. They look at the bigger picture, and that often leaves us little people out in the cold. For now, though, I'd say that it would be best if you weren't here. I noticed the process speeding up when you walked in the hospital. It might be coincidence, but we can't be sure and I'd like every advantage I can get."

So. That was it then. It would make me laugh if I didn't scream first. Sue wanted to hire me to kill her, one year ago this month. I said no, but amended that maybe I could in a year or so, if the heat on her from being a local celebrity where we lived, died down. Well, it did and a year has now passed.

Prophetic? Who knows? All I know is that it sucks. But I wasn't going to let it sit until there was no other choice.

I was a kid when my mom got sick and died, and I couldn't do anything but watch. This time, I wasn't so willing to be a bystander. I stepped farther into the room as Lucas and Bobby reached the doorway and found myself staring down at her pale, perfect features. I didn't want to leave her. Not for a second. But could I kill her by staying?

"Will's ready to head back to Texas, Tony. You need to tell him anything?"

I shrugged and shook my head, not taking my eyes from Sue. Her auburn hair was shorter now, in a wedge cut. She told me on the phone last week she liked the way it bounced when she walked. Yeah, we can talk mind to mind, but sometimes a voice on the phone is just comforting when you're alone. And too, maybe she realized what was happening before anyone else, because we've been talking on the phone a lot lately. I never really thought about *why* she might call me, unless—

I turned my face to Amber with concern probably etched across it. "Is she in pain? Are these bruises and degeneration hurting her?" I had another sick feeling in the pit of my stomach, like I already knew the answer. It was what had been beating on me from behind that wall. "Shit. She *is* in pain. I can feel it."

Apparently, that was another of those obvious things that made Amber's eyes open wide her mouth form an O. "I can't believe I didn't think of that. If the small blood vessels are breaking and causing the bruising, then there could easily be pain. I should probably start her on something in her IV. Maybe that's why she's retreated into a coma-like state. Actually, there's a weird condition with blood vessels breaking I remember reading about—" She grabbed the chart hanging on the end of the bed and a pen from the pocket of her smock, and walked out briskly, flipping pages and mumbling to the nurse next to her. "Let's get someone up here to do a spinal tap and I'll also need another blood sample. Then . . ."

I wanted to touch Sue, but feared doing so, even with the gloves on. All I could do was look on helplessly until I felt Lucas step close and let out a slow, deep breath. He was pulling in all his magic so that he felt like a normal human next to me. He's one of the few alphas I knew who could do that and I appreciated the gesture if magic really was hurting her. I noticed Bobby stayed at the door. "You need something to take your mind off this before you start to pine."

Yeah, that would be a bad thing. Had *pining* happen once, before they figured out that separating Sue from me with a shield could cause it. It's like the mating magic is a drug and without it, I wound up going through a really vicious, cold-turkey withdrawal. Until Lucas figured it out, I was well on the way to putting a gun in my mouth and squeezing the trigger.

Lucas shuddered lightly, a physical manifestation of what I was thinking. "Actually, we *both* need a distraction. I'm going to leave Bobby here with Amber to do the lab work, so let's get some meat and then I'll drop you at a motel. I need to talk to the temporary Alpha here in Boulder about some business, but then tomorrow morning I'll need you to drive with me to Kansas. We should be back before Ahmad gets here and I want to hear more about your experience in that cave before he starts to grill you for details. Bring your guns. I've already loaded up a duffel with silver ammo."

I nodded and turned away from Sue as I felt her encouragement that I go with Lucas. I couldn't deny that a little mindless action would keep me sane right now. And I've found that wherever Lucas went, action seemed to follow.

Chapter Five

THE HORIZON WAS barely edging to blue from black as we headed down into Kansas under a starless sky. "Remind me again why we're here at such an ungodly hour? When you said *tomorrow,* I'd assumed you meant in broad daylight. And I was pretty sure you mentioned us driving."

Lucas shrugged. I only knew because I heard the fabric of his shirt rustle against the seat. His scent gave away nothing. He was a blank slate, which told me he'd prepared for this trip by putting on that blasted cologne. It was handy when I was wearing it, but annoying when others did. I've noticed that I've started to consider the ability to scent emotions as nearly necessary, which is probably a mistake. Any crutch you rely on too much can be dangerous.

It was still full dark at, according to the altimeter, eight thousand feet and dropping. The lights from the instrument panel bathed us both in an eerie glow, but it wasn't enough to see much more than broad movements. "Plans change. Peter, the local Alpha, had to cancel on me because work went nuts and he couldn't get off early.

Then Amber confiscated my old office for a meeting with the local seers. I tried to get some sleep and wound up having nightmares."

Time to change the subject, because frankly, I don't really like people sharing dreams. They're often odd and have little meaning outside of the person's own psyche and experiences. Plus, having graduated college with a psych minor usually made me listen and comment, which wound up a bad idea on nearly every occasion. "So what's the scoop with the reconstruction? We going to have actual offices soon so I don't have to keep wading through stacks of paperwork in my office in Chicago?" Wolven was going through a rough time right now. They either had a mole in the group, or someone managed to get access to the building in Paris, because the whole place was bugged to the nines. Computers had signs of having been cloned, files had fingerprints that didn't match employees, and some folders were flat missing. Nonessential, nonclassified files had been moved to the headquarters of the wolf councilman—my boss, Nikoli. That's another reason why it sucks to be Lucas right now. He's having to simultaneously interview agents and side employees like cleaning crew, while constantly having to deal with "scope creep" from council members with their own agendas. Naturally, I'd been the prime suspect. Duh. The thing is, though, I'm strongly in favor of Wolven's existence, so I really don't want to see it fail and have anarchy take over. I'd like to think that your average human could truly handle the concept of shape-shifters, but I know better. It'd just be a newer, shinier version of racism and, speaking as one who would likely be discriminated against, I'm against the idea.

Apparently, I have several supporters on the council, although I can't imagine why. But the heat on me died down nearly as quickly as it started.

The frustrated sigh told me the answer without him continuing, but I let him anyway. "Going slower than I'd like. It's as much the *where* as the when. We'd planned to move operations to America, but it's meeting opposition. Paris was a very cosmopolitan city, so agents of different nationalities and accents could come and go freely. The Alpha Female down in Texas reminded me how rare it is for a group of powerful people who make people nervous to descend on an area without notice. I'm afraid that this delay is part of the plan of whoever is doing this. If the council puts Wolven in a smaller and smaller box to keep everyone happy, we'll wind up existing, but ineffective. I'm not willing to let that happen, so we're back to square one. Hang on for a sec."

Lucas turned the dial on the radio to a new setting and started to call the Goodland Airport to check in. I'd been to Kansas City plenty of times, but we were going to be landing the old prop job that Lucas had rented on a private airfield in the middle of nowhere. I'd heard of Goodland since it was on a main east-west interstate and shows up from time to time on the Weather Channel updates, but had no idea where we were headed. Frankly, I'd rather be in the corporate jet we used to get to Denver from Central America. Pipers don't have enough legroom for my taste. It occurred to me that Lucas had started talking again and I couldn't remember what he'd said. "Um, my bad. Tell me again what you said. I was sort of lost in thought. Sorry."

He sighed, not like he was angry, but like he was starting to figure out I wasn't going to be much help on the trip. "You'll have to try to pay attention. I know it'll be hard, considering the circumstances, but this is an important mission and I need your head with me. I was trying to give you some more background on why we're here. Last week I got a call from one of the women in the Boulder pack. A man named Paul Kendall got her number from the regional emergency hotline we have set up for relatives and he told her he needed to get ahold of someone from Wolven right away. He has reason to believe his daughter, Liz Sutton-Kendall, had her first change last month and wrecked part of the town. But there are no other shifters in his family and he's afraid for both her and the locals if she goes feral."

I furrowed my brow and tried to think it through, but failed. "You'd think there wouldn't be a question about that. Either she changed or didn't. Why doesn't he know? Doesn't she live at home anymore? Did she disappear and come back bloody?"

Lucas started to look out the window. "Watch for a pair of grain towers next to a red barn. That's the farm we're looking for. It should be coming up in the next few miles. No, he doesn't know because there was a tornado in Hansen . . . that's the name of the town, the night of the last full moon. The local press is attributing the damage to the storm, but he doesn't think so. She was found unconscious under the wreckage of the tower the next morning—stark naked, but without a scratch on her. If he's to be believed, the girl is a badger-shifter, and he seems certain she dug a burrow under the foundation of the water tower to escape the storm, which collapsed onto a good part of the downtown."

My laugh was unavoidable, despite Lucas's warning growl. "Oh, c'mon, how can that *not* be funny? It just screams tabloid cover story: 'Local Badgergirl Makes Big Splash in Town!' " I framed the headline in the air with my fingers. Lucas wasn't quite as amused as I, but I saw the corner of his mouth twitch a fraction.

"It's fine to laugh in the plane, but keep your jokes to yourself when we land. This is actually quite a serious situation. There's only one badger-shifter in the entire world right now, and if something happens to him, there's nobody to train her. The nightmare I had earlier was about the last time Nigel went berserk in a crowded opera hall in London." He turned his head enough that I could see his lightly glowing eyes. "It wasn't pretty. A lot of people died that day for no good reason and it was hell to keep the press and officials from digging too deep. If the girl really is a badger, and she's feral . . . well, let's just say the tornado will have been the least of this town's worries."

"But badgers aren't carnivores, are they? Don't they eat bugs and stuff? She wouldn't chew up the residents even if she turned."

His light snort made me wonder just what we'd be up against. "Oh, they're carnivores all right. But lesser ones—rats, gophers, snakes . . . that sort of thing. She probably wouldn't *eat* them. But chew them up? Uh, think of a Freddy movie, but with *two* knife hands, equally sharp teeth, and a worse disposition."

That raised my brows, and made me feel for my Taurus in the holster on my hip. Maybe I should have made the loads a little hotter. They're already above average, but I could go up a few grains and stay within extreme barrel limits.

I nodded and pointed out the window as buildings began to appear in the distance. "Looks like a town coming up ahead. Yeah, I think I remember you mentioning a badger back in Chicago. Some English guy who vowed never to set foot on U.S. soil because all Americans are traitors to the crown?"

It was Lucas's turn to nod. "Nigel Sutton, tenth earl of Suttcliffe in his present incarnation. Kendall says the girl's mother was his multi-great granddaughter. Except Nigel doesn't know he *has* a granddaughter, and he was one of the ones who helped eliminate others of his kind when they went berserk. Said his people were too dangerous to live among humans . . . sort of like the were-spiders. But for the girl, it's a black sheep issue, I think, so even if he doesn't kill her outright, it's not going to be easy to convince him to teach a 'colonist' the ropes."

A red barn passed under us, but without grain silos. Then a pair of silos, but no barn. Then three silos and a white barn. And all appeared to have plenty of room to land a plane. "You sure about the directions? Lots of barns, lots of silos, but no matches so far and we're just about out of town." I could see now where the water tower had been, owing to the massive crane parked next to the remains of the supports. Okay, maybe it *was* a big deal that she killed the tower. There wasn't a stream or lake to be seen for miles, and close to a dozen buildings were rubble. "You can force this earl to train her, though, right?"

The old white wolf chuckled and tilted the wings a bit to head toward a spot of red on the horizon. "I'd have about as much luck forcing your pack leader to tap dance in a tutu. It could be *done,* but it wouldn't be pretty."

Yeah, Nikoli might not be as powerful as some, but

boy is he stubborn! "Ah, got it. And thar she blows." I pointed out the window just as Lucas spotted the same thing—two silos and a red barn. Right next to the barn was an old bi-wing crop duster that had seen better days. But it was parked on a tidy, smooth runway that looked easier to land on than a country road. I've done that, and it's not much fun. "There's our target. We got some way to get from point A to point B, or is this the Kendall farm?"

He shook his head and lowered the flaps to slow down. "This is the Sampson farm. Fringe relatives to one of the Boulder pack members. The Kendalls live in town and Ralph Sampson is going to let us borrow a car for a few days . . . if it takes that long. I want to have a look at the site before I visit the family."

Lucas landed the plane with nary a bounce of the wheels. I suppose if I'd had a hundred or so years to practice, I'd be pretty good too. "So what's my purpose here? I can't imagine *you* need an enforcer for one badger. Or am I the bad cop to your good cop?"

The whine of the prop spinning down was replaced by the sound of a tractor far out in the field. It was a good thing Lucas was damping the moon's effects, because right now I'd be screaming if not for it. Ever filled up a water balloon until it was so heavy it could break with each new drop from the faucet? Now imagine you're *inside* the balloon, waiting for it to break. That's what it felt like under the shield Lucas had over me. It was a lot different than Will's cocoon—not quite as stifling, but more ominous.

"I need your second sight, mostly, to tell me if she's exhibiting any feral qualities."

"And I do that, *how*? What does *feral* look like in

the aura stream?" I've seen lots of different auras on shifters, and they all had a sort of personality. It's like a woman going to find hair dye that's "brown." Which brown? Chestnut, or honey or auburn or a hundred shades in between?

"According to my former second in command, it's really easy to tell—like spotting meat that's spoiled even through cellophane where you can't smell it. You'll know it when you see it and it'll be unmistakable." He paused before opening the plane door. "But the cop thing isn't a bad idea. The Kendall girl has, as her father phrased it, *anger management issues.* Most badgers do, and Nigel still can make even your old enforcer in Chicago seem like a fluffy bunny."

Ah. Considering said enforcer had once shredded my back until you could see ribs and organs, I decided to steer clear of old Nigel.

Lucas slid off his headset and gave a small wave to the lanky man in grimy coveralls who was walking our way. The old white frame house behind him had probably been a stage stop a century before. The light that shone out through the windows was fading as the sun rose. A cat jumped lightly onto the railing of the wraparound porch. Reminded me of Sue's old house, back when I met her.

Thinking of her threw open the door in my mind without even intending to. There was a gasp inside my mind and then a stab of pain that felt like an ice pick drilling through my temple. I've never felt like I had to be particularly gentle or careful with Sue, so now I felt really strange, wanting to apologize for a simple mind brush.

You don't need to apologize. It was amazing how good it felt to hear her voice, however tired.

I won't stay, but Amber said my contact with you is hurting you. Is that true? Has it been happening for long? I felt a twinge in my shoulder, like a shrug. Sue can do that sometimes . . . make my muscles move when she moves.

A month or so, I guess. I don't remember the exact day it started. But you've been so busy, I didn't want to worry you. I . . . thought I could handle it.

I growled then in frustration and worry, and Lucas noticed from outside the plane. He turned and his eyes started to glow slightly. The bubble increased in strength and Sue became a whisper I had to struggle to hear. I realized I hadn't even gotten out of my seat yet and I doubted Lucas would be pleased at what I was doing. Can you tell Amber what you're feeling? She's trying to help.

I know, and I want to help her. But I can't talk. My brain's not connecting to my body right now. But I was doing research last week, and I think there's a ritual that might help. Tell Amber to look at page seventy-four in the old book her sister brought her. They're not numbered so I started counting from the first page, even though it's blank.

A ritual? What kind of ritual? I'm not sure I like this idea.

It's . . . complicated.   There's . . . there's . . . a . . . way to make—

Her voice was fading fast and sounding tight with pain. I didn't want to wear her out or make her any worse. Never mind. Rest now. I'll call Amber.

I felt her smile in my mind like a ray of sunshine through clouds, even though her voice was fading to the barest whisper. I like it that you worry. That's . . .

selfish of me, huh? But I do like it. And no . . . no matter what, I love you.

She meant it too, and that amazes me to this day. Wolf, hit man and all, and she really does love me. Weird. Love you too. Get some sleep.

I pushed shut the door between our minds with some effort and a lot of trepidation. I really didn't like how her voice sounded at the end—way too slow and slurry.

Work. I definitely needed to get back to work and get my mind off this. There was well and truly nothing I could do from here. But first I pulled out my cell phone. Of course, no signal here in the boonies. I'd have to borrow one or find a landline to get Amber started at that end.

GETTING INVITED IN for coffee had been a good thing, both because I really *needed* coffee, and I needed a bathroom. Plus, they were happy to let me make a call to the clinic to talk to Amber. Well, they weren't *happy*. They smelled scared as hell. Sampson's wife kept hovering near the staircase, and her eyes and scent told me she would fight to her own death if we even thought of heading upstairs to where, I presume, her children slept. But the scent of fear made my stomach clench, so it was good that I found a quiet spot in the living room, away from people, to make the call.

Amber wasn't pleased that Sue and I had been in contact, but she promised to check on the page in the book Sue mentioned. Once the call was done, I just sat back and enjoyed coffee with real cream from the cows in the barn, and stared out the window at the rising sun. It was coming up with that rich gold color that said it was going to be clear and hot. The sun forced back the pull of the moon until it was just background noise, instead of a steady pulse against my skin . . . and my stomach.

As we were getting in the old pickup that would make us blend in nicely, I realized my stomach was growling again, but this time not because of the scent of fear. This was the plain ole "haven't eaten since dinner yesterday" variety. "Let's see about finding a café in town. I could use a steak and eggs about now."

Lucas nodded. "Not a bad idea. I'd like us to pose as contractors looking to put in a bid on the water tower rebuild. That should open up some mouths and a local restaurant is a great place to find out the gossip to see if there's anything Kendall didn't mention. You know anything about water towers?"

I pursed my lips and tipped my head with a twitch of my shoulder. "Enough to get by. I've found it's better to be personable but vague to lull suspicions. I notice you brought along a clipboard and measuring tape. Pick one and I'll man the other. It's probably good it's Saturday. Then we can't get the answer of, 'Go talk to someone at city hall' when we start asking stupid questions."

"That was my plan."

I rolled down the window to let in the cool morning breeze. I'd gotten used to cracks from Sue about being her favorite puppy with his nose out the window, but I couldn't deny that the scents and motion from passing air were invigorating. I also noticed Lucas wasn't complaining.

We were still several miles from Hansen on a narrow county road. The barrow ditches were so tall with weeds and volunteer wheat that we had to poke the bumper nearly into the oncoming lane to see at each intersection. It told me that either the county didn't have enough of a tax base for a road maintenance budget, or nobody cared enough to complain. It's amazing how much you can learn about a town and the residents by just driving around a little. Carrying that air of blindness to your surroundings is critical to blending in. Too many tourists fail at it because they carry along with them what's "normal" from where they left, instead of adapting to where they are. If nobody else notices a particularly nasty scent, then a smart tourist doesn't either. If locals flock to a hole-in-the-wall restaurant that looks like a dive over a fancy, shiny eatery, it's wise to follow if you want to stay healthy.

So when we hit the edge of town, I started scoping out who was hanging out where. The little building with a sixties pole sign reading, CUPPAJOE'S was our best bet. Probably half the town's vehicles were in the lot with more arriving every minute. "Let's make a swing through the site while everyone's busy."

Lucas didn't reply. He just drove past the restaurant casually, keeping the speedometer a shade under the posted limit and hanging his arm out the window like he belonged. The people exiting the restaurant didn't even look up, meaning he's apparently done this before.

We had to go slow around the wreckage of the water tower and swerved once or twice to avoid some particularly large potholes that were dug into the pavement from where the unyielding steel met the ground. Lucas was taking everything in as he drove, his eyes flicking back and forth while appearing not to. I started making notes in my head to put on my "expert" persona and tried to spot where there might have been a big

burrow dug into the sand. It was mostly sand in town—
the fine, nearly powdery kind that would compact really well, but would probably require shoring during
the excavation. I added that piece of information to my
mental list as we passed by an old adobe motel that had
seen better days, on our way around the block to head
back to the café.

"And he swears it was Tony the Nose?"

My head and upper body snapped around so fast that
the seat belt thought it was an accident and jerked me
back. But it was too late. I couldn't see who the speaker
had been. "Turn around!" I ordered, fast and low. "Go
back past that motel. But don't make it obvious."

He twisted his head as he flipped on the blinker at
the corner. "What's up?"

The doubts started to set in as Lucas increased his
speed slightly on his way to the next corner. Maybe I
heard wrong. After all, what would someone who knows
the stupid name they gave me in the mob be doing in a
small Kansas town? I shrugged and tapped my fingers
on my knee. "Could be nothing. I could have sworn I
heard a guy with a Jersey accent say 'Tony the Nose.'
That was the idiotic nickname my friend John Corbin
gave me when we were kids, and it stuck through the
whole time I was in the family."

Lucas suddenly started to take it seriously and
stomped on the gas after we rounded the next corner,
sending a spray of dust into the air. The Sazi, for some
unknown reason I couldn't fathom, had expended a lot
of time and energy to make me "dead" to my old life
and welcome me onto the Wolven force. I'd asked repeatedly, but nobody would tell me why. Occasionally,
it was against my will, but I was settling in to the role.

It was good money and used my talents well. Now, I'd changed my appearance and had taken pains during this past year to stay out of areas I knew could be a problem, but I was starting to worry that I'd missed something—gotten so involved in an assignment that I hadn't noticed someone noticing me. His voice interrupted my walking through each of my last few assignments, searching my memory for something I'd missed. "Do you think Leone would spill the beans?"

The guffaw that erupted from me nearly made me choke. "It would take even more torture than the Sazi snakes are capable of to make Carmine Leone *spill the beans*. A couple of the guys saw me during the spider attack in Chicago, but they were all made guys. I'd be very surprised if they'd squeal if Carmine told them not to—and he would. And even if they told someone in my old hometown, no way in hell would they tell anyone in Jersey about Carmine's ace in the hole."

That raised Lucas's eyebrows. I started to kick myself, because it didn't come out like I'd planned. "*Are* you Carmine's ace in the hole? You been moonlighting on me?"

I knew what he was really asking. Was I continuing to assassinate humans, risking arrest and revealing the secret of the Sazi? That's an automatic, instantaneous death sentence, because humans have no idea we exist. I shook my head wearily. "No, I'm not still working for Carmine. Hell, I haven't even been in contact with him or Linda since Christmas. And the last time I saw Babs, she was spun up in a spider cocoon. But Joey, Sal, and Louis all saw me that one time visiting with Bobby." I still remember the look on Joey the Snake's face when he came walking up to me in the basement hideout Carmine had dug underneath his estate. The grin he'd worn as he approached me turned into something more serious. The simple words of, 'Thought you were dead, man' had been echoed by the faces of those around him, and was about as emotional as guys like them get. I'd been flattered, at least until I learned Joey'd been undermining my replacement. Sadly, that left two seats open at the poker table each month, because Carmine wasn't pleased to the point that Joey wound up at the bottom of a deep lake.

"Would they talk?"

I shrugged. They never had before, but who knew what had changed in the last year? "I'd be shocked, but I've been shocked before. Joey's dead, and Louis and Sal have always been Carmine's top two lieutenants. But anything's possible, I guess. A better bet, in my mind, is that I did something stupid and got noticed by someone who was in a place I didn't expect. The 'out of context, out of mind' thing."

"We need to check into this motel." He flipped on his right blinker to turn into the motel parking lot, causing my heart to do a drum solo.

I started scanning the lot, looking for pairs of eyes staring. "Are you *nuts*? You trying to make certain they spot me?"

Now he smiled in the corner of my vision, and it was filled with the same amusement he always wore when I'd forgotten about his abilities. "Then we need to make sure you don't look like *you*." When I turned to look at him, gone was the stocky Latino with the silvering hair. In his place was a taller Caucasian with wavy dark hair and a hometown, outdoorsy tan who would fit in perfectly in this town.

I recognized the man. I'd seen him once before in an airport in Indiana on another near-full moon. I'd only figured out it was an illusion because he'd gotten angry and his aura changed colors. It was back to what it had been that night, a thin gold band instead of blue-white, and he now smelled of lemon-lime-soaked cardboard instead of the sweet smell of ripe cactus fruit.

"Ah. It's Greg Hamilton—football hero, today, is it?"

He offered an open, friendly smile that I knew was all mask. "Not quite. Greg is dead and is known in some law-enforcement circles. They do look similar, but I'm modeled after a young man named Josh Sampson. He's the nephew of the man we're visiting. I dropped by their house in Boulder last night. The plane's rented in his name with his pilot's license. Josh is going underground for a few days—an all-expenses-paid trip to a remote island with no electrical service, where the staff waits on you hand and foot. He can use it. He's a pilot and is on leave for burnout. I was a little surprised how subtle the difference is, but the slope of the nose is different and the hair is a touch darker. No reason not to use the scent, though. And don't forget to check the mirror . . . Joe."

I flipped down the visor on the passenger side, but it wasn't a deluxe model that had a vanity mirror. So I rolled down the window farther and stuck my head fully out to see myself in the rearview. My brows shot up because it was so *totally* not me staring at me. I blinked and so did the reflection. I bared my teeth in a kind of smile and so did my double.

My dark hair was now golden and tight against my head. The eyes, once the cold blue-gray of gunmetal were closer to sapphire. The face was more narrow, with high cheekbones, a slightly roman nose, and a weak chin. It was an odd mix of nationalities—Native America meets Scandinavia, via England. "Where in the world did you come up with this face? Do I actually look like a real person you know?"

"Knew. Guy named John Spence. He was a good guy, just doing his job protecting a makeshift fort, during the *War of Northern Aggression*. He was killed by a stray bullet not even aimed his way, and left a young wife he'd only married a few weeks before. Pity. He was tolerant. That was rare in the day."

My lips pursed. I knew that Lucas was as old as dirt, but it's weird when someone talks about events from nearly a hundred fifty years ago as though they happened last week. Bobby does that too, and it's always strange.

"So, I look like a Civil War victim. You have personas picked out for us?" I knew he did. He's always a step or two ahead. It was mere courtesy to ask what it was.

"Like I said, I'm Josh Sampson, Ralph's brother's youngest son from Colorado. You're Joe . . . Davis. How does that sound?"

"Sounds white-bread, middle class, and completely forgettable. Should be perfect. And we're here to put in a bid on the water tower?"

"You are. I'm just delivering you and visiting family. Fewer people ask questions when you're family . . . even shoestring relatives. I know enough about the Sampsons that I can pull it off."

We opened our doors at the same moment one of the room doors opened. I twitched almost visibly as two men came outside. I recognized them both and it was a struggle to ignore them as though I didn't.

I knew the older of the two as Stuart Prezza. He was

the spitting image of his daddy, Vito. Square and short, with dark hair in a buzz cut and hazel eyes. They both hailed from the New Jersey mob. I'd killed Stuart's younger brother, Jeffrey, at Carmine's order—but it was before I even knew the Sazi existed, so I'd already been excused from that job by the council. But I hadn't come close enough since turning wolf to notice his scent, which my head immediately attached to an image of the algae that grows on carpeting left too long in the rain. The younger man I knew by reputation and photographs. He had a metallic scent covered with dirt . . . sort of like a big mound of buried coins. Ricky Mario was slender and tall, his thin sandy hair just brushing his shoulders. From the way he had it parted, I was betting he was going to be a candidate for early pattern baldness in a year or two. He was an up-and-comer hitter when I started freelancing and we occasionally bid on the same jobs. I was a little surprised that Vito had sent him out this far, unless they expected to take me by surprise.

Of course, that led me back to the same questions—what were they doing here in a pissant little town in Kansas, and why would they be expecting *me*?

The longer I thought, the longer I apparently stared at them, because Stuart noticed me noticing. That's never good. He flipped me off with a slap of his palm to his forearm. Normally, that's enough in the big city to get the curious to find other things to look at. It gave me an out without confrontation, so I did as expected and shifted my gaze, trying to look cowed. That particular set of facial motions isn't all that easy for me, since I'm either too good or too stupid to admit I *should* be cowed.

What do you mean, he isn't here? He was expecting me to arrive and knew I had little time.

The inside of the clinic in Boulder was suddenly superimposed over the Kansas parking lot and Stuart's ugly mug. But I wasn't in Sue's head. I could tell that because whoever I was in was taller than Amber, so she had to look up to lock eyes.

"Oh, please, Ahmad. Why are you so surprised? They had a Wolven emergency in Kansas and had to leave. It happens. You weren't supposed to arrive until this evening, so don't give me the *little time* crap. I expect they'll be here by then, so you might as well just sit down and wait. Charles is on his way too, so you'll have to make time even if you don't have it."

I could feel the snake king's brows furrow as he considered what she said. I still couldn't figure out for the life of me why I was attaching to his head right now—and if anyone said anything about having *mating ties* with that guy, they'd get decked.

"Why is Charles coming? He was scheduled to be in Germany for another week."

Amber sighed and stripped off the blue nitrile gloves she was wearing. I only know what they are because I prefer them over latex or vinyl. "It's Angelique. Something happened to her down there. I'm not sure she's ever going to be the same. Decisions need to be made."

A sensation like being punched in the stomach made me let out a whoosh of air. Turned out it *was* something punching me in the stomach . . . my duffel bag. "You still with me there, Joe?"

Stuart and Ricky were long gone, the car a black dot down the highway. Lucas was inches away from my face, his eyes glowing bright as he struggled to shield me against whatever was happening to me. But it wasn't that easy. He was holding a key with a tag in his hand, saying that he'd already checked in while I was stuck out of body. This wasn't a moon thing, because I wasn't in Ahmad's head long enough for all that to have happened. Or, at least I didn't *think* I'd been. "Yeah. Sort of. Got another flash of snake king. He's in Boulder and pissed we aren't."

It was obvious that floored him. He reared back and was actually surprised, not just pretending. I could even smell a shock of something in the air. Surprise isn't quite an emotion, so it's really hard to match it to a particular scent. It's just a poof of scent that's sort of like the gust that hits you as you enter a superstore. "Just now? With me shielding you, you got sucked inside a hindsight?"

I shook my head hard and fast, trying to clear the cotton candy that was fuzzing up my thoughts. "Not hindsight. It's the present, like right this second. I'm still partly there." I held out my hand like I could touch the wall that should be there, but met only air. "I can see the waiting room. He and Amber are talking about Angelique, but I can't hear what they're saying. That part seems to come and go. In the jungle, I was getting his thoughts too, stuff that wasn't spoken. Memories of his father and of the woman who was hitting Angelique. He knew her. They'd been lovers as teenagers." I readjusted the duffel so it didn't fall out from under my arm, and threw the strap over my shoulder.

Lucas mulled for a moment and then sighed. "Well, we don't have time to deal with that now. I'll do what I can to keep it from happening, but you'll have to tell me when it *is* happening. You're still coming into your seer powers, so who knows?"

I didn't respond, not because there wasn't anything to say, but because I didn't want to even acknowledge that possibility to air. Weird things happen when magic's involved, and I don't care if it's just the moon reaching out to touch someone, or a wand turning someone into a frog. The rule is: keep your mouth shut if you don't want to experience what you speak.

THE TRIP BACK to the restaurant was silent, with each of us thinking our own thoughts. Actually, I wasn't thinking so much as listening, because I just couldn't seem to shake the conversation between Ahmad and Amber out of my head and since it involved me and Sue, it seemed prudent to eavesdrop.

"I can't remember seeing anything like this before." Ahmad wasn't fibbing. He was trying to compare Sue's condition to everything he'd experienced in his life, and that was a lot of stuff. Seeing her through his eyes wasn't something I enjoyed, because his next words were, "Waste no more time. Let her die." She was *human,* and should be beneath the notice of their kind. Worse, she was mated to a three-day who should have been put down the moment he turned.

Knowing what I do now, I had a difficult time disagreeing with the *concept.* But I'm somewhat rabid about the object, so I came close to muttering *fuck you* right in the cab of the truck. I wondered if he would hear me. Fortunately, Amber's tone conveyed the same message, so I didn't have to try. "Saving a life isn't *wasting time,* Ahmad. I'd be very careful voicing that opinion when my husband gets here. He nearly dispatched Sargon for that same belief." There was a rather enjoyable moment as Lucas turned the truck into the café parking lot. Ahmad felt taken aback at the same moment the grill of a semi drove right through where his face would be. Made me smile, and the bright rainbow of color that filled my vision for a second said that Sue was inheriting my dark sense of humor.

"Can you hang with me long enough to do this, or should I go in alone?" Lucas was looking relatively concerned and had a worried scent that rode over the emotional blackout of the cologne—a tangy, sharp smell not dissimilar to hot vinegar. He was watching me with the same attention he should be using to investigate the scene, so I understood the question.

And it was a good question, because I was going to be useless for anything if I didn't get a handle on this. "Let me try something first and I'll let you know."

I closed my eyes and reached into my mind, imagining the kitchen door that Aspen had helped me develop. It was a mental trick we'd worked on to let Sue and me disconnect from each other during trouble. The trouble came from my side of the joining 99 percent of the time, so I had to find a way to keep her from experiencing stuff she didn't want to know about. Aspen had talked about building a wall of bricks, but the kitchen door motif worked better for me. It was an old-fashioned one with a dutch half, so I could close it completely or open one half or the other.

Now I started to morph the door I could see. It grew wider and taller. The wood turned to polished steel with a big wheel on the front. But when I pulled on it, the door still moved like a house door—too easily, so I added weight . . . layer upon layer of solid metal until it felt like a vault door *should*. Now when I pulled, the tug sang through my muscles from the effort, but it moved smoothly on oiled hinges.

A breeze hit my face as I swung the door and the image in the clinic became clearer, the small sounds of machines and the light squeak of rubber on polished linoleum as Amber and what I presumed were her nurses scurried with quiet efficiency. With some effort, I braced my hands on the door and pushed hard. It resisted at first and tension caught the muscles in my lower back, making me grunt. But then it gave way and caused a satisfying clunk as it settled into the frame.

The clinic disappeared.

Cool.

There was a weight in my head now, similar to sinus pressure, but I was pretty sure I could manage it. Nothing hurt, but I had to blink more than once and I realized I was pressing my hands flat against the front of the dash. The plastic was dented from the effort I'd used. Oops.

Lucas had a road map open over the steering wheel, effectively blocking us from the view of anyone who exited the restaurant.

"Okay, we'll see if that'll hold. I've never tried to block two sources of energy before. Never had to worry about it until now. With the full moon, it'll be . . . interesting." I had to talk over the crinkling of paper as he refolded the road map with apparent ease. I always get the folds wrong and wind up with a lopsided square that doesn't fit the glove box, instead of a neat rectangle. Naturally, Lucas made a neat rectangle. I snorted as he handed it back to me to put away. "Show off."

He didn't reply, but his eyes twinkled just a bit before he turned his head and opened the door.

As we walked toward the entrance, I tried to come up with a good way to bring up the subject of the water tower, but it turned out I didn't have to. A group of men were seated at a round table in the corner. From the litter of plates, cups, and empty sugar packs, it was obvious they'd been there for hours. "I'm not kidding! That Kendall girl is dangerous."

Lucas flicked his eyes my way as he slid into the booth and I nodded to show I heard. It was hard *not* to hear since the short stocky guy under the John Deere cap had a voice like a television announcer—all midtones and loud.

A tall, thin guy with sleeve tans so dark I was pretty sure he was a farmer or rancher shook his head and leaned back in his chair until it was tipped on two legs. "Oh, come on, Earl. Just because she read that good-for-nothing brother of hers the riot act for the way he's been running the store? You think Paul wouldn't have already tanned his hide if he wasn't still abed? You've seen the place, just like I have. Rats in the grain, bugs in the hay, and half the implements allowed to go to rust."

Earl just snorted, but another of the crew weighed in. "Mike's right. I had to turn away two deliveries of round bales for the herd just last week, and I've cancelled my standing orders until Paul's back in charge. The whole thing was moldy . . . every bale. Now, I don't mind a turn or two of waste. That's normal. But there's no way his daddy would have even *thought* about delivering bales that bad. I don't want to think about rodents in the grain I accepted, so don't give me the details. Rats give me the willies."

A younger guy who might be Earl's son from the resemblance was shaking his head—tiny little movements that said something had really spooked him. "Yeah, but you guys didn't see her. She wasn't like that before she went off to college. Sure, she was always a hothead, but this . . . she didn't throw bottles or nothin' or even scream. But she looked just like those ladies you see on *America's Most Wanted* before they go off and do something horrible. She had a *look* in her eye."

The final man at the table, a tall thin codger who didn't have enough teeth to keep his lips from curling under let out a little chuckle. "Spunk. That's what little Lizzie's got. Why, if I was twenty years younger—"

The waitress arrived at the table just then with a pot of coffee in one hand. She bopped the old guy on the head with her order pad. "*Twenty* years? Try fifty, ya old lech. Liz is just a baby, and in my opinion she had every right to go off on Frank. He's a lazy lout who doesn't deserve to inherit that store. Paul really ought to give it to Liz. She'd run it right."

Mike shook his head. "Nah. She's got her fancy new diploma, so she won't be staying around this dump. Already has a job offer back East from what I hear . . . designing landfills and such. Good money in landfills."

Earl gave a grudging grunt even though he didn't uncross his arms from where they were tight across his chest. "Girl has a good eye for dirt. I'll give her that. I never would have thought to check the west section for that special sand they use for telescope glass if she hadn't walked me out there. Now I've got a lease on it from a German group. The royalties will put Becky through college."

I'd been staring at the menu blindly while listening to the conversation and was so involved that I didn't even notice the waitress until she popped her gum and said, "What'cha have, hon?"

My stomach knew what it wanted without even searching. "Steak and eggs. Rare and over easy. White toast and coffee."

Her pen paused over the pad and her eyebrows rose, making the careful makeup she'd used to cover the crow's feet at the edge of watery green eyes crack just a bit. "Which kind?"

Of coffee? "Um . . . regular? Caffeinated."

She rolled her eyes and tapped the pen on the single-sheet, plastic-coated menu in my hand. Her natural scent of fresh kindergarten paste blended with just the lightest touch of burnt metal from frustration. "Which kind of *steak*?"

I finally looked at the menu. It was the first I'd ever seen that gave a variety of steak for the steak and eggs. Wow. None of those wimpy paper-thin slices of breakfast steak here! There was T-bone, sirloin, strip, and even filet to choose from, plus two sizes of each. Ah, *cow country* . . . best friend to the carnivore, and a town after my heart. The gland in the back of my jaw started secreting enough drool that I had to swallow or risk dripping on the table. "T-bone. Sixteen ounce. And rare."

She nodded. "Got the rare part. How about you?" She pointed the pen tip at Lucas. "Say, you look familiar. You from around here?"

If the question bothered Lucas, he didn't show it. He just smiled. "Nope. I'm from near Denver. We're staying out east of town with my uncle for a few days."

Her shoulders dropped, and she opened her mouth in that universal acknowledgment of surprise. The sour milk scent of disbelief rose into the air, so it wasn't faked. "Well, for heavens sake! I thought I recognized you. You're Dave and Caroline's boy?" She called out to the table of men before Lucas could even reply. "Look here, ya old coots! This is David Sampson's youngest, Josh. He's visiting Ralph. You here for some pheasants? Season starts tomorrow, you know."

Hunting season starts this week? Well, wasn't *that* just handy knowledge? We could walk around freely with shotguns while two Mafia members were looking for me, and hey . . . accidents do happen. My favorite time of year.

The men all gave a little uncomfortable wave, which we returned, but thankfully they didn't head toward our table. They had moved on from talking about Liz Sutton-Kendall to the price of grain, so we were free to ignore each other. Lucas put his menu on the edge of the table. "I'll have the same as him. But say, hearing them talk about that girl reminded me of something Uncle Ralph said. Wasn't someone named Sutton caught in that tornado last month?"

The waitress, who had a name badge reading Jonyye—which I had no idea how to pronounce, raised her brows and put one hand on her apron-clad hip, ready to spill her guts. She had just opened her mouth to reply when a bright ding sounded from behind the counter. "Johnny! Order up!" Okay, good. I knew how to pronounce her name now.

She looked at the pad where she'd scribbled our order and raised one finger. "Let me put in your order and take this plate. I'll be right back."

She disappeared and while I would like to talk about all the revelations, I was probably going to have to wait until we were outside. But then a sharp pain formed in my forehead—a red-hot spike that made me wince. **What do you think?** The words appeared in my mind, almost as though painted across the surface. The voice was Lucas's. I'd forgotten that, as a pack leader, he could communicate mentally like Sue and I do. That would make things easy, if I could stop myself from screaming in pain.

I squeezed my eyes shut and rubbed my forehead to ease the pressure. I knew it'd be better in a minute, since he'd done this to me before. But that didn't remove the knife from my brain right now. I hate it when you do this. Hurts like hell, in case you don't remember my mentioning it the last five times. And I think we're going to find out everything we need to know before I've half finished my steak.

I was right.

She didn't return until she had our order and as she set them down, she set *herself* down, knocking hips with Lucas/Josh repeatedly until he moved over to make room in the booth. I couldn't help but chuckle, despite the glare I got from him and the little stabby pain between my eyes.

I was surprised that Jonyye didn't have a genealogy map tucked in one of her broad pockets. Not that she needed anything in print. She had the entire county's family tree mapped out under her curly mop of bottle-platinum-blond that didn't really cover the gray hairs. It just blended them in a little better. Not only did we hear, in *vivid* detail, about the night of the tornado, but about the entire Sutton/Kendall family tree. Liz's mother was a Sutton, all right, and the *rumor* was she came from European money, which is why she insisted the girl have a hyphenated name. I'd figured she was adopted or was a stepkid, but no. She was Kendall's own daughter, just with a different last name. I've heard of that before, but usually the kid winds up with a weird middle name to keep a nearly dead surname alive. Hyphens must be the new thing.

"So she's really lucky to be alive, huh?" I swept up some yolk with my toast and waited for her to reply with another diatribe.

Another broad expression of her slender, muscled arms made Lucas duck his head before taking a bite of seasoned potatoes. The steak I started cutting was perfectly prepared—fork tender and well seasoned—and so far I wasn't having to go through the obstacle course of Jonyye's hands to eat.

Life was good.

"It was *amazing*! Buried under that rubble all night long, and not a scratch on her! She must have a guardian angel—" She paused and looked sad for a moment. "But of course, she *does*. Her sweet mother is probably still watching out for her, just like she always did before she passed on. Poor Paul really struggled with the three of them before he married his second wife, Tammy. Liz was probably twelve when that happened. Tammy's been a saint, with the kids as wild as they were. All three really took to her, and she's been every bit as good a mom as their real one. She's been a real blessing to Paul, too, since his heart attack."

Ah. That could be useful, a lever to get the girl to do the things that are going to be required of her. None of us really *like* doing all the stuff the council makes us do to protect the public and keep the secret of the Sazi. But we do them anyway, because people that matter to us could die without them.

After Lucas had finished his last bite of steak, he nodded and dabbed at his mouth with a surprisingly wide paper napkin. "We should stop by and pay our respects if he's not well. Mom would be annoyed if I didn't. I think she went to school with Paul, didn't she?"

Jonyye thought about that for a second but then shrugged, just like she was intended to. "They *might* have been in the same graduating class. Or was that Ralph? I can't remember. But they were definitely in school at the same time. And I'm sure Paul would like that. I don't think he gets too many visitors anymore. Lots of folks stopped by right after he got out of the hospital, but you know how it is. People get busy." She stood up and dusted imaginary crumbs from her apron. "I should get back to work anyway. Paul and Tammy live at the other end of town. You can't miss their place. Just go to Twelfth and turn right. It's the pale pink house. Not my favorite color, but Tammy loves it." She reached out to grab Lucas's shoulder with a smile. He tried to get out of the way, but there wasn't anywhere to go. See, the problem with illusion is it's just that. Lucas was broader across than Josh in real life, so if Jonyye did more than just touch him, what she felt wouldn't match what her eyes told her. It could bother her for days.

Fortunately, she only put a light finger on the sleeve of his shirt. "You tell your mama that Jonyye says hi. She'll remember me. I've been working here my whole life."

She picked up our plates and balanced them in her hands as she walked off. Lucas and I were just starting to rise and scoot out of the booth when he sat down abruptly and motioned for me to do the same with a sharp downward movement of his finger. When he picked up his cup and started to sip while watching the door over the rim, I tried to find a way to see what was behind me while not turning in my seat and looking obvious. The convex mirror on the far wall was the best I could do, even though the images were skewed and distances weren't easy to determine. I could tell from the careful placement of it midwall that it let Jonyye know when someone was coming out of the hallway to the bathrooms. I was betting there'd been more than one collision with her while holding full plates as she came out from behind the counter.

The bell over the door jingled. I wasn't surprised to spot Ricky and Stuart walking into the place, along with a third man whose olive skin said he was from the Middle East. The copper-colored glow around him said he was Sazi. His scent roiled over the room and even those without supernatural noses noticed something odd about the man. They just didn't know *what* was wrong. He smelled enough like Ahmad, except weaker, that I was betting he was a cobra. Now, what in the world were two Jersey guys doing with a Sazi snake? I glanced up and Lucas's eyes were asking the same question. But the only way we were going to find out the answer was to stay and listen in.

I held up my cup and caught Jonyye's eye. She nodded and headed our way with a half-full pot. She noticed the new arrivals just as she reached our table. Her sudden frown and the sharp sour scent said she'd encountered them before. "Oh, *them*." She lowered her voice and bent forward as though sweeping up crumbs from the back of the table, then whispered words, her mouth barely moving. "You boys stay away from those men. They're bad news. The sheriff has been watching them since they rolled into town two days ago. Don't know what they're up to, but it isn't good. You mark my words."

Lucas/Josh gave the only appropriate reply. "Yes, ma'am." I nodded in agreement. I couldn't think of anything I'd like more than staying away from those men. The trick was, that wasn't going to be so easy. Having a snake with them meant that illusion wasn't going to help much. He'd taste us coming.

The scent of cherries makes Mustaf quite ill. I blinked. Now where did that thought come from? I glanced at Lucas, but he was busy watching the men over Jonyye's shoulder. He didn't give me any sort of look that said it had been him talking, and it hadn't been his voice I'd heard. It was my own voice—well, as much as you *have* a voice in your own mind. It was weird, but most of my life is pretty weird right now. If I was going to be living in an *X-Files* world, I might as well run with it.

"You got any cherry pie, Jonyye?" She turned her head and looked at me with an odd expression, so I shrugged. "Got a sudden craving. You know how it is." And apparently she did, because she smiled.

"Best in the county. Make it myself. You wait right here."

I raised my hand and gave her a pair of fingers. "Bring two. I know Josh. He won't say no."

Lucas waited until she was back behind the front counter, taking a tall glass dome off a plate of pastries before he spoke under his breath. "Actually, I *will* say no. I don't like cherry pie. In fact, I hate it. And we just ate enough for four people. What's up?"

I repeated the words that had appeared in my brain. "The scent of cherries makes Mustaf quite ill." That caused a raised brow. "Hey, don't know where the thought came from, but I'm game."

My hands clenched suddenly from the sharp pain as he drove his thoughts into my skull. *You know the snake?*

It's tough to have a conversation without appearing to, so I spent some time dusting nonexistent crumbs from the picnic table–patterned red-and-white cloth. *Never seen him before. But maybe I'm still picking up from Ahmad. He probably has a dossier on every snake in the world. Either way, it's worth a try. He hasn't spotted us yet as far as I can tell, but look how fast his tongue is licking his lips. It won't be long before he zeroes in on us. We'll find out soon enough if there's anything to it.*

Jonyye appeared just then with two plates that had light steam rising from them. The scent of sugared warm cherries filled the air and suddenly I really *was* hungry again. She set down the plates and forks with a look of pride. "Warmed it up for you. Pie's no good when it's cold. Just tell me if that isn't the best pie you've ever had in your life."

Lucas managed to fight down his revulsion at the scent pretty well, considering. He smiled, but it was shaky. "Afraid I'll have to make some room if I'm going to have that. It sure looks good, but mine needs to cool a little anyway." It did look hotter, nearly bubbling, so when he scooted out of his seat, Jonyye didn't stop him. "Excuse me. I'll be right back." In my mind he continued. *I'll be listening in from the restroom. We can't just sit and make no noise without being noticed. Now you can just sit and nobody will expect you to talk. Feel free to steal my pie. I promise I won't mind.*

He looked at the pie again as he turned and shuddered a little as I cut my first forkful and stuffed it in my mouth with actual enthusiasm. One bite was enough not to have to fake it to say, "Suit yourself. But don't be surprised if yours is gone by the time you get back. Jonyye makes a mean pie."

She beamed and I was suddenly her golden boy. Never a bad thing for future needs. I made a very deliberate point of holding up my fork and blowing on the next bite. I angled my mouth so it pushed the scent of hot cherries right into the faces of the three men sitting at the table nearby. The snake's tongue went from thoughtfully licking to that same expression a kid makes when they take a spoonful of cough syrup.

Pleased to meet you, Mustaf.

Another slow, deliberate breath followed by a burst of air toward them and it was all she wrote. *Quite ill* was a bit of an understatement, because Mustaf the snake suddenly held a hand to his mouth. His cheeks puffed out and he clawed his way out of the booth, looked around frantically, and then raced out the door. More than one of Earl's crew got a delighted expression and raced to the window to watch the foreigner heaving his guts out next to the Shasta daisies. Mike elbowed Earl's son in the ribs.

"Heck, and he hasn't even *eaten* the food yet. Some sort of record for ptomaine. The rest of us won't get it for an hour or so."

The old codger with the missing teeth let out a whoop of laughter. "Told you that coffeepot ought to be cleaned out at least once a year, Jonyye."

"Oh, stop." She was smiling when she said it. "You shouldn't make fun of a man in distress. I'll see if I've got some Kao in the back for him." But I noticed she didn't move very fast.

I stayed right in my seat because although I'd love to watch him heaving, I found it interesting that Ricky and Stuart *didn't* find it interesting. They didn't seem to mind at all that he was gone. Sort of *relieved*, in fact. I kept casually cutting off tiny bits of the pie, savoring each bite as Lucas shuddered in my head.

"Wonder what set him off," Stuart finally whispered after a couple of sips of coffee, while the other men continued to hoot and holler. "Tastes fine to me."

Ricky waved it off and muttered. "Fugettaboutit. Who knows? Who cares? The guy drives me nuts anyway. What I wanna know is how long we're gonna be stuck in this bumfuck town? It's been two days, and nuttin. I think someone's yanking the Don's chain. Giodone's dead. Otherwise, he would have showed up at the hospital by now or at least sent word. But not even flowers. We're chasin' air here."

Hospital? You know anything about someone in a hospital? I was asking Lucas, and he knew it. The little stabby pain made me wince as I bit down. The men at the table noticed me wince so I fished around in my mouth like I'd found a pit in my cherries, then peered at my fingers and wiped them on the plate. It was enough to make them ignore me again.

Just the clinic. We don't have any agents or pack members in any hospital these guys would have access to.

Stuart shrugged. "Maybe. But Pop says stay here until the weekend, so we stay until the weekend. There was still that plane that landed at the farm this morning, and I still say that farmer was lying about someone flying in."

Ricky raised his hand, trying to attract Jonyye's attention to order. But she seemed to be really, really busy right then and didn't acknowledge the wave. "I just don't see any reason why they'd protect a guy like Giodone, and if roughing up his kid didn't make him talk, nothing will."

Lucas reacted violently and I could hear a low growl come out from the hallway across the room. I agreed. That just put these guys on my shit list. You don't get to hit kids. It was a hard and fast rule of Carmine's and one I always enforced . . . permanently.

Stuart slapped his hand out sideways and thumped Ricky's bicep. "Keep your voice down, stupid!" he hissed. "We're not on home turf here. That dumbass sheriff is already too damn nosy without giving him ideas of where to go look."

My ears were really sensitive today or I wouldn't have even noticed that Lucas had pulled out his cell phone in the bathroom. No doubt he was calling the Sampsons to check up on them.

"Think we ought to call our snitch again to find out when they're leaving? I'd rather spend the weekend at the beach than in this heat."

I'd very much like to listen in on that call to find out who this "snitch" was. I was just starting to think about how to track their car when Lucas came out from the bathroom hallway fast and hard, barely missing Jonyye carrying a tray of food for the family near the door. He didn't even apologize, which wasn't like him. As he reached the table, he pulled out his wallet and threw a pair of fifties on the table, which was waaay more than the bill would be, even with the pie. "C'mon, Joe. We have places to be. *Right now.*"

I wasn't quite done with my pie, but I don't argue

when he uses that tone. He's a lot more like Carmine than he'd like to think. I wouldn't put it past him to just pull out a piece and start firing at anything that stepped in his way when he's on a mission . . . including me.

Jonyye didn't even have time to acknowledge our leaving before I was up and following him out the door.

Mustaf was still on the ground, coughing and trying to catch his breath. We were halfway to the truck when Lucas changed his mind about leaving and made a U-turn toward the snake. A golden light, tinged with blue, shot out from the aura surrounding him and caught the Sazi snake in a vise. I'd seen him do this before, but it's always entertaining to watch . . . from the outside. Mustaf fell to his side as though paralyzed. Which he was. Then the magic tightened around him until he was curled into a fetal position with only his head free to move. Lucas, in his Josh persona, moved toward him quickly. His face wore a concerned expression that would convince everyone still staring out the window of the restaurant. But most of the diners had returned to their meals, so there wouldn't be many people to witness whatever he was about to do to the shapeshifter. I stayed out of it. It wouldn't look right for both of us to race over. Still, I stayed nearby in case he needed help.

Right.

Fortunately, my ears were still in overkill mode, so I would hear every word like it was being screamed next to my ear. Of course, the trouble with that is that ears aren't terribly selective when it comes to loud noise. It's like those "personal amplifiers" you see on television that claim you can eavesdrop on conversations a block away. Sure you can . . . right up until the moment the neighbor kid's car with the bad muffler, or the high-end speakers, drives by. Then you won't be hearing anything at all for a day or so.

But Lucas's whispered conversation? No problem at all.

"Were you with the men who harmed the child on the farm, Mustaf? If you were, it's a death sentence offense."

The man's facial features stilled and instead of trying to fight against Lucas's power—always a futile effort, he froze. "You know my name. Nobody in this country knows my true name."

Josh had one of those smiles that was filled with even white teeth that spoke of years of expensive orthodontic treatments. But Lucas's eyes didn't match the smile. The eyes were filled with anger and deadly intent. He crouched down next to the snake and let his eyes glow bright. "Wolven knows everything, and we're every*where*. Remember that. The men you're with are wanted by the human authorities. If you stay with them, and are put behind bars for crimes they committed, I don't believe Ahmad will see fit to send a lawyer. He will visit you himself and you will never see a fair trial. Now, I will ask again. Were you with them?"

Mustaf let out a slow breath and then shook his head once, firmly. "No. They went to the house alone." I believed him, because there was no scent of black peppers, which I've learned means a person is lying. "I remained behind to watch for the three-day wolf they said was to come. That's my only purpose here. I was

paid to help find the man they seek to bring him back
for crimes he committed. They don't even know *how* I
find other Sazi. I have broken no council laws to become a bounty hunter. But if I cannot get the taste of
that wretched fruit from my tongue, I will do no good
for them, so I might as well leave."

Lucas released his magical hold on Mustaf and
once he'd relaxed onto the dirt, got out of his crouch
and offered him a hand to his feet. His words were firm,
even though the smile was still on his face. "Wolven is
not so depleted that we require vigilante assistance.
Tell those you work with, and for, that to capture another Sazi for delivery to anyone other than the council
will have punishment meted. The Sazi these men seek
is a Wolven agent now. Any crimes have been com-
muted by the chief justice. We will allow him to defend
himself as any other Wolven agent can. Is that understood?"

The ultimatum didn't go over well. He let out a low
hiss and his fists clenched. "You have no right to make
this rule, Wolven! I do no harm. I do not plan injuries
to others. I do not kill or participate in torture or risk
creating a new snake. I merely point out criminals others seek. This is my livelihood, to feed my many children. Only the council can make such a law, and they
must be aware that it will injure myself and others. I
demand to have my say before them, to defend my business."

It was pretty obvious Lucas didn't like it from the low
growl he let out and the scent of burning coffee that
filled the parking lot. But he dipped his head once. "You
will have your say at the next council meeting, two
months hence. Ahmad will notify you of the location.

But until then, *my* word is law. The charter of Wolven, enacted by the council, gives me that right. You will leave this place, and turn away any jobs until then. Am I understood?"

Mustaf leaned back his shoulders fluidly until there was a definite bowing of his spine. I've learned the snake-shifters do that when they're about to strike. I stepped forward carefully and started to plan how to reach the derringer in the holster at my ankle in case I needed to dive for cover and shoot. Since he was a cobra, he might only spit. But even that's deadly. Lucas didn't budge. He stared him down, not even bothering to freeze him with magic, until the snake's shoulders relaxed, fraction by fraction. But the cobra's words were still poisoned darts and I'd bet if he could have found a way to make them cut flesh, he would have. "You . . . are . . . *understood.*"

Lucas turned and walked away, not even bothering to come my way, or look back at the pissed-off snake. All I could do was shake my head as I got in the truck, which was already running by the time I got there. "Gee. That went well." I tried to keep the sarcasm out of my voice, because actually it did sort of go well.

"The problem is that he's right. Wolven *is* depleted to the point where we need extra help. But we can't let the average Sazi know that, because they'll take advantage. All I can do is puff up my chest and pretend at this point and hope the council is going to agree with my position."

The way he was gripping the steering wheel as he backed out made me wonder whether he was going to snap it in two by the time the ride was over.

"Need me to take over driving? You seem a little . . .

stressed. I'd like to make it wherever we're going in one piece."

His own growl, low pitched and vicious, caught him unaware and he had to slam his mouth shut and blink a couple of times. I fingered the door latch in case I needed to dive out. No way was I a match for him if he was pissed and we both knew it.

He sighed and tried to get his emotions under control. I only knew that because there was so much scent overload in the car that I started a sneezing fit. And there wasn't a single tissue in the truck. "Lots of things going on right now. I'm overextended and it's starting to show. Wolven's a mess, Boulder's a mess, the new turn is about to leave town with an unwitting human right at the full moon, and we have a councilwoman down from unknown causes. There's still something big happening out there and the harder I try to figure it out, the faster it slips through my fingers."

There wasn't a thing I could do about any of it, other than the matter at hand, so I focused on that. "I presume it's the new turn about to leave town that's our crisis of the moment? Or are we heading to the Sanderson farm to check out whether there are going to be any new snakes in the region?"

He shook his head. "No, I believe Mustaf. Good job on outing him, by the way. I've actually heard of him, but had never seen him before. Wherever you got the information is fine with me. But if you're connecting to Ahmad's head without him knowing, we're going to have to find some way to stop it. He's privy to secrets that you don't get to have access to."

I couldn't help a small smile. "Afraid I'll sell you out?"

Lucas kept a straight face, and I was pretty sure he wasn't kidding. "It's not beneath you. I don't have any illusions about you, Tony. I'd love to think I could trust you, but there's a divide between our worlds that I doubt if you'll ever cross." I was pretty sure I knew what he was talking about, but I let him continue anyway. "You have morals, of a sort, which is why I'm giving you a chance with Wolven. But your morals are your own, which is pretty typical of a sociopath. Sometimes they coincide with what the rest of society considers normal, sometimes they're even stricter. But more often they're looser, and that's where we have a problem."

"And it's why you keep partnering me with agents stronger than me, magically." The huff of air I let out wasn't really humor. Just irony. I looked out the window at the neat houses with green lawns. I'd had a nice house with a lawn once, on a quiet cul-de-sac where I had friends and people who respected me. But then came the Sazi and everything changed. Now I was in a dumpy apartment in a strange town where I was part of a pack I didn't really belong to. I was the lowest of the low of my kind, living with a woman that I was married to on paper, but had never actually agreed to share my life with before a man of the cloth. And I might lose her any day and could lose my life on any given assignment at the whim of my *partner.* I spent each day trying not to think about a whole bunch of things that it was best not to dwell on. "No doubt with orders of *shoot to kill* if I become too much of a pain." I raised my brows as he glanced at me without responding. "It's not like I hadn't already figured it out."

"I don't doubt it, but it's not like it was a secret. You have plenty of detractors among Wolven and the council, and only a few supporters. That you're still alive says your benefits outweigh your . . . issues. I keep hoping that'll continue."

"Hope springs eternal." This time I did smile and he couldn't help but let out a chuckle.

Chapter Six

"You were right to call us in, Paul." Lucas and I were sitting on a comfortable couch across from a man who shouldn't be out of bed. He was pale, gaunt, and it was obvious moving was a chore. "She's one of us, all right."

Liz Sutton-Kendall had just left the room to check up on her guest, who was missing in action in the bathroom. We hadn't really talked to her about the Sazi yet, but we would. The size of the pearlescent pink aura around the petite brunette told me she would probably wind up an alpha, and she smelled distinctly of warm fur, rich soil, and something sweet and candy-like that I couldn't completely place. "She's not going to be able to travel by the end of the day. Tonight's the first night of the moon. Anything could happen and from what Lucas has said, her kind isn't to be taken lightly."

Kendall sighed, and I would have thought it was from sorrow, but there was also the lighter fragrance of relief that drifted my way on the cool air from floor vents. The small smile that eased his face took a few years, or a few levels of pain, away from him. "She's always been different . . . like her mother, and it's sort of nice there's a reason. I used to worry about her, getting in fights with the neighbor kids over nothing, spending all her time alone, digging holes in the yard. Why, the girl didn't *own* an outfit that wasn't caked with ground-in mud and red clay." Now he chuckled and his scent filled with the warm cookie overtones of parental love. "She was my fishing buddy until she got too grown-up. I'd send her out to find worms for me. She always knew where they were. That's something Margaret talked about having too—how she could find bugs and worms. She could hear them moving underground. It got worse on the moon and she used to have to put on headphones and listen to music to stop hearing them bumping around under the house. But she never did turn."

Lucas nodded and leaned forward until his elbows were on his knees. "That happens sometimes with family members. They get some of the symptoms, but never turn. It used to be that people like them got locked up in asylums. Now we watch the hospitals for near-turns, help them cope. Sometimes we can even heal the damage to their systems so they can live normal lives."

Paul tapped his fingers on the arm of the chair and it was like watching bones wiggle in a Halloween display. "I'm concerned about sending her to her grandpa for training, though. Margaret made it really clear that he wouldn't welcome anyone from this branch of the family. Isn't there anyone else who can teach Elizabeth the ways . . . any other option except to send her away?"

"Send me away where? What are you guys talking about out here so seriously? You heard me turn down the job with these guys, Dad. I'm going to accept the one back East I was offered last week. Heather and I are leaving tomorrow morning, just like we planned."

It seemed a quick and easy way to get the girl to come with us—offer a job to a fresh college grad. We'd hoped that by offering more money than her other offer, she'd leap on it. No such luck. Lucas shook his head. "I'm afraid we can't let you do that."

I finally got a look at Elizabeth's friend Heather, who was now hovering in the doorway trying to stay as far out of the room as possible. She was taller and thinner than the Kendall girl, and while she didn't have an aura, there was a way she held her body—very cat-like and ready to spring away, that made me wonder. I twitched a finger until she came fully into the room. "You're a family member, aren't you, Heather? What species? Cougar? Jaguar? You're too tall and lithe for a bobcat."

She went even paler than she already was, until the dark freckles on her nose stood out in sharp relief. "Not for generations. *Please* tell me I'm not going to turn! God, I wouldn't know what to do." Heather turned to her friend with tears in her eyes. "I know it's not your fault. Truly. But I'm scared for you, Liz. You don't know what these people are like. I didn't want to tell you when I heard your dad talking to Wolven yesterday. I just wanted to run away and hide. But I couldn't leave you. Not like this."

Liz's face was a study in amazement—probably very similar to my own when Bobby first talked to me about stuff I couldn't grasp. "What are you talking about, Heather? What is *Wolven*? And who in the world brought in Chinese food just now? I didn't even know we had a takeout restaurant in town."

Chinese? I took a sniff and suddenly understood. She related to emotions the same way as me . . . by comparing them to things I could understand. To me, fear smells like hot-and-sour soup. I wished there was an easier way to break this to her. She seemed like a nice kid. "You're starting to be able to smell emotions, Liz. That particular one is fear. It smells good, doesn't it? Hard to keep from trying to find the source. Makes your stomach growl."

She turned to stare at me and her eyes got wide as her stomach did, indeed, growl at that moment. Lucas figured out what I was doing and joined in. "You're swallowing a lot now, aren't you? And your nose is trying to follow, which is why your head keeps trying to turn. Like walking past a bakery with fresh bread filling the air. Your kind doesn't normally find such large game compelling, but you're not precisely . . . *normal* anymore. And frankly, I don't know exactly what you *will* need to eat." He paused meaningfully. "Tonight. When the moon is full, and you shape-shift into a very large and possibly feral badger. The same as you did last month—during the tornado. That's why we're here, Liz. It wasn't the storm that destroyed the water tower. It was *you*. What did you eat last month at this time? Can you even remember?"

She was backing away from us now, shaking her head, panic and confusion plain on her face. But there was nowhere to go. Lucas was easing off on the shield he had over me and himself, letting magic fill the air. It wasn't helping the fear level of the others any. Paul didn't move quickly, possibly understanding how that would be seen. But he was so ill right now that his scent wasn't particularly appealing.

Heather, however . . . she started to twitch and make abrupt small movements that said she was about to bolt. Liz couldn't seem to take her eyes from her friend, her muscles spasming with each twitch. "You're all insane." The moment her mouth opened, though, the drool that slipped down her chin gave her away. Heather saw it and shrieked. When she did that, the scent of fear doubled and a low, hungry growl came from my throat, even though I was stuffed full of steak. A flick of her eyes my way didn't help calm Heather. She dove from the room.

I didn't want to follow. I swear. I don't hunt *humans*. But that sudden movement, combined with the fear, was just too much without Lucas's shield. Blood filled my vision and a snarl erupted from deep in my chest. What I found weird was that Lucas didn't try to stop me. What was his plan?

Then it didn't matter anymore because I was across the room, pushing Liz out of the way to get through the doorway where the cat had gone. The new turn didn't push so easily, though. A flare of light, the color of a rainsoaked sunrise, flashed out and then she was on me, pushing me to the ground. We shattered the coffee table in the process and magazines scattered into the air. A shard of glass six inches or more across slashed into my back. I was pretty impressed with Paul, because all he did was lift his legs out of the way, as though we were two unruly toddlers tussling underfoot. The girl's brute force was amazing. It was like having a brick wall fall on me, and the sound that erupted from her was vicious and keening, a counterpoint to my deep snarls.

Seconds later, our hands were raised with simultaneous intent to harm the other when time froze . . . and so did we. I'd had it happen more times than I'd care to count, so I just relaxed and waited. Liz, on the other hand, *freaked . . . out*. All she could move were her eyes and they were twitching and straining against whatever invisible force held her. Her aura roiled and spiked, seeking escape from the bubble. Then, to prove his point, I guess, Lucas released his hold on me. Just me. I was able to crawl painfully out from underneath her, my breath coming out in small gasps. I hoped the glass hadn't hit a lung. I'd had worse before, but breathing is something I've learned to enjoy.

Soon she was perched in midair, one leg fully off the floor, along with the opposite hand. It was still curled into a claw with powder-pink nails pointed right at where my face had been. Her face was twisted into a snarl, teeth bared, and her neck and shoulders were bent forward like either a vulture on a fence, or a gargoyle on a building ledge. I let Lucas slowly pull out the shard and managed to keep the wincing to a minimum. But *man* that stings! Then I moved over to stand on the tiled entry, where I wouldn't add any more blood to the carpet. She continued to battle against something she'd never defeat all the while.

The Wolven chief wiped my blood off his hands then leaned over and sopped up the excess dripping down my shirt with some tissues he grabbed from a box on the end table. He eased back into the couch cushions and continued to hold the lasso of blue-white magic tightly around her while he watched her struggle. When she'd finally settled down, a minute or more later, he spoke, his voice calm, almost soothing. "Do you understand now, Ms. Kendall? You are Sazi . . . as much animal as human now. Magically born and tied forever to the phases of the moon. Can you see why it's vital that you be trained to handle these new abilities and emotions?" Liz's eyeballs rolled up and to the side until mostly white was showing, to be able to see him. She blinked once, with effort. He acknowledged that small movement with a tiny smile. "Now, I'm *hoping* that attacking my associate was because you felt protective of your friend. Defending a human while under stress would go a long way toward the council's approval of you having some limited independence after your training. Just don't lie about your motives. You won't be looked at harshly for your *motives* at this stage. But lying changes your body chemistry. Other Sazi can smell it, and you could be punished. So before you're asked later, think carefully and be honest with yourself. Sort out your exact thoughts while you were charging him. Was he an enemy, attempting to harm your friend? Or . . . and this is something you're going to have to consider long and hard . . . was he a potential *meal*?"

Paul sighed and turned in his chair to face his daughter. "I know all this seems impossible, Lizzie, but you needed to understand why I called these men to meet you. You're nothing if not like me—hard-headed. You have to see something to believe it. You probably don't remember, but even though your mama never turned, she . . . *felt* all the same things you are right now, each and every full moon. And your grandfather in London *does* turn. Now, I truly believe you don't have a dangerous thought in your head, sweetheart. But you see just how fast that all happened? It was *seconds*. There was no time for thought. It was pure instinct, just like during the storm last month. Can't you see the blood where Mr. Davis was lying? You would have *killed* a regular human if there'd been nobody to stop you like Alpha Santiago just did.

She stilled completely then, taking her father's words to heart. Her eyes dropped to the carpet. The blood was starting to dry at the edges, adding a rust color to the vivid red on the pale tan pattern. Heather peeked out from the doorway, apparently noticing it had gotten quieter. She flinched a little at her friend's position and the blood on the floor, but she handled it pretty well, considering.

Heather bent down sideways from the waist until she caught Liz's eyes. She smiled brightly, her scent filled with oranges and cookie spice. "Wow, Liz! You are *amazing.* Thank you so much for trying to stop him. That goes way above and beyond the call for a roomie. You're the best." Then she stood back in the corner again, probably staying as far away from *me* as possible.

Rather than just dropping her abruptly like he's done to me more than once, Lucas released Liz slowly. She was able to get her arm and leg under her before she did a face-plant onto the floor. But even after she was free to move, she wasn't precisely . . . *free* to move. He kept a thin tether on her, the lightest touch, just so she'd know he was there. She did, and it made her rub her arms like they were cold every time she glanced at him.

She turned to me after staring at the bloodstain for a few long moments, and was close to tears. "I'm really, *really* sorry, Mr. Davis. That wasn't like me. I swear. But when you—" She paused and flicked her eyes toward Heather before returning to me. "I've always had a temper, but this was—" She just shook her head, unable to continue. Her eyes closed and she wrapped her arms around herself, withdrawing inward to let it sink in until she could deal with it. Her remorse was obvious from the thick, misty scent of fog in the air and lasted until her father put a comforting hand on her leg. It apparently helped a little, because she was able to stop shaking and look up again. "And here you are, standing bleeding like a stuck pig when we should be getting you to the hospital for stitches."

I held up one hand. "It's okay. No stitches required, and no apologies necessary. My fault entirely and don't worry, I'll heal. That's one really good thing about this whole magical, shape-shifter crap. We heal really fast. By nightfall, you'll never know I was hurt. For the record, I don't *think* I would have hurt your friend and I *know* Lucas wouldn't have let me. I normally have pretty good control over myself, so I'm a little surprised I went into chase mode. I don't eat people." I locked eyes with her and then raised my brows. "I don't think you do either."

She went a little green, with eyes moving toward the stain of red and then back to me. "The thought of meat right now makes me nauseous, frankly. At least the blood blends in with your dark hair enough that it's not noticeable, but you need different clothes before you leave here. People will definitely talk in this town if you walk out with blood on you."

All four of us looked at her oddly, but for entirely different reasons. Heather was the first to voice it. "Um, he has blond hair, Liz. And the red shows up really well."

Liz blinked once, looked at me again, and then looked to her father for confirmation. He nodded. "Pale as your brother's when he was little . . . a regular tow-head."

Heather started to speak again when Lucas held up a hand. "Describe the two of us, Liz. Tell me what you see. Nobody coach her."

She seemed uncertain now, her fingernails tapping a staccato on her jeans. "Well . . . Mr. Davis must have an Italian mother, because he's medium height, with dark hair and a sort of broad nose. Early thirties, I think. Oh, and sort of blue-grayish eyes. It's hard to tell from here. And lots of muscles. You must work out a lot." I nodded as Heather stared at me again before rubbing her eyes in disbelief. In fact, the soured milk smell of disbelief was pretty thick in the room about then. I was thinking that everybody in the room was bleeding it out their pores.

Then she turned to Lucas, and even I was surprised at what she said. "You're Native American, but I can't really tell from which tribe. Probably in your late twenties. Dark hair, dark eyes, bronze skin—the whole package. Might even be a little Mayan in your heritage. There was one guy in school my junior year who was Mayan, from way up in the Andes, and you sort of have his nose."

The seconds ticked by and Lucas remained silent. He didn't confirm or dispute the claim, which sort of answered it as far as I was concerned. The girl could see through illusions. I'd heard of that from Bobby, but it was one of those really, *really* rare gifts . . . like my hindsight. In fact, I didn't think anyone alive had it right now. That made her extremely dangerous, because illusion magic is the stock and trade of the Sazi. Especially Wolven and the council. Unless they drafted her straight into Wolven . . . but a lot of that depended on temperament. She might not be suited. I know more than one Alpha who isn't law-enforcement material. It only works with me because I came out of being an enforcer for Carmine, and the rules of the Sazi aren't all that different from the mob. They hate it when I say that, but it's true.

At last the big guy spoke, his voice flat and firm. I wasn't surprised at what he said, but it obviously wasn't what *Liz* wanted to hear. "You'll be flying back to Boulder with us today. We'll get you on your way to England to train as soon as the full moon is over. I'd suggest starting to pack if you want to take your own things."

Her hands went to her hips and the hazel eyes were flashing pink-gold fire. It was sort of cute for the few seconds the fit of temper was going to last before Lucas choked it off. "Uh, hello? I don't think so. I'm leaving tomorrow for the coast. I have interviews for an apartment. Fine, I won't travel at night. I'll find some cave or something to hide in for a few days a month. But I'm not going to Boulder, or to freakin' *England*! I don't do flying, and I don't even own a passport."

It made me smile, because it sounded a lot like me when I'd first found out about the shifting stuff. But eventually I was going to have to watch that bright spark of enthusiasm and . . . *spunk* get crushed into cracker crumbs.

Well, heck! What better time than now? I held up a pair of digits. "Two problems with that scenario, kiddo." I lowered my middle finger when she turned to face me. "First, you can *say* you'll lock yourself up and not go out at night, but it won't work that way. Let me regale you with the tale of shredded doors, broken windows, and hunting ducks at the petting zoo someday . . . with a bonus interview of what duck bones and feathers feel like coming out the other side. I can't imagine that typical badger food of mice or prairie dogs will feel any better."

She and Heather both made a face. "Eww—"

I lowered my index finger until I had a nice tight fist before I dropped it on top of the other arm crossed over my chest. "Second, you remember that nifty trick Santiago did, holding you motionless? Guess what? He can make you *walk* even better. Been there, done that. He's just offering you the *courtesy* of going under your own power. But trust me, if he says you're going, you are. And there's not a person in this town who won't believe that you got in our truck completely willingly—with a smile on your face."

She paused to consider that and looked again at Lucas like she couldn't quite believe it. I saw the rope of magic increase just a bit and then her hand rose to the top of her head of its own accord, while she stared at it in panic. She even grabbed the arm with her other hand to tug it down, but it stayed firmly in place.

I shrugged. "Any more questions?"

Heather leaned closer and whispered in her ear. "Like I said . . . these guys are scary. My cousin has told me stories that would curl your hair about one of the female big cats. She's French and gets a kick out of pain."

I heard a sigh and turned my head. So did the girls. Paul had been watching Lucas the whole time, apparently. Probably trying not to watch his daughter get her lessons. That can't be fun for a dad. "Wolven specializes in tracking down shape-shifters who break the law, Lizzie. Sometimes they have to get rough. Just like our own police."

"But we don't get *a kick out of pain*." Lucas stood up and walked over to the girls, releasing Liz's arm as he did. He put a fatherly hand on Heather's shoulder and looked at her with real concern. "I'm sorry that the only stories you've heard of us are bad ones, Heather. While it is a difficult life to lead and the secret of our existence is a heavy burden, our only real goal is to live in harmony with the rest of the world. People don't know we exist because we *can* live in harmony that way. It's the reason for everything—the Sazi council, where we set down laws so we *don't* impact humanity, to Wolven and even individual groups that are ruled by leaders we select. It's the promise we've made to our people and we've stood by it since the dawn of civilization."

Liz had her head cocked and was listening closely. I could also see her nostrils flare as her animal took the measure of him. Whether or not she realized it. "You're not kidding. That really *is* what you want." Then she shook her head. "But you're only one man. Who's to say that's what *all* your people want?"

Spunky . . . and sharp. Good combination. He ought to snap her up before someone else does. "Lucas here is the head of Wolven, the law-enforcement branch. But until he took over the post, he was the councilman for the wolves—the top dog, so to speak. He may not be able to tell you what every person in every species wants, but he's fully capable of making them keep the promise. The kind of power he's got is legendary. He says *jump,* we ask how high—snakes, cats, bears, birds. And wolves, of course. All of us." Well, *most* of us do, and even I know it's not a very bright idea to flat refuse him something. She looked at me curiously, not quite sure what to make of what I said. "Think of your having even *met* him in your lifetime as being sort of like meeting J. Edgar Hoover while investigating a local crime scene back in the fifties. It could happen, but it's damned rare."

He shrugged it off modestly, even though I knew why he came. Still, his scent didn't betray anything other than the baking-bread scent of concern. "I was in the neighborhood. Joe's right, though. What I say, goes, so long as it's within the rules the council has set down. And one of the rules is that we keep new turns, and those around them, safe. The storm kept you occupied last month on your first turn, Liz. But what about this month? Are you willing to risk your family, or your friend here, if something went wrong? It's high stakes. You're gambling with their lives until you're better equipped to handle the change."

I didn't get a chance to hear her answer because all of a sudden the vault door in my mind slammed open, throwing me to my knees with either a grunt or a scream. Hard to say which, but with my luck, I was probably screaming like a little girl. I can't remember if I grabbed my head and pressed or if it was the magic that made it feel like it was locked in an ever-tightening vise. I must be locked in Sue's head, rather than Ahmad's, because everything was dark and there was an incessant beeping in the background, along with whispered conversation I couldn't make out. My throat hurt, but I couldn't seem to move my mouth to swallow, so I was betting they had in a breathing tube now. It's not a good thing when they have to do that. Means the body is shutting down, unable to breathe by itself.

To hell with Kansas and the new turn. I focused inward, trying to find Sue's mind while I still could. You'd think that was an oxymoron. After all, I was *in* her mind, so how could I not find it? But not so. I was in her *body*. Brains are big places when you're looking blindly for where a person in a coma might have hidden themselves to escape the situation. Was she lost in her memories, or trapped in her own pain center, too hurt to focus? It was sort of like searching for a black cat in a dark room. You're looking for small and furry, and near the floor is the *likely* spot. But not the only one. I tried the likely spots first, near the vault door I was visualizing and near where I could hear voices.

I found a tiny, bright thread huddled near the door—like she'd used everything she had to get it open to find me. Sue?

Knew . . . you'd come. Not too . . . much time now. They're arguing . . . not . . . sure it'll happen in time.

I'll give you whatever time you need, Sue. I'm tough. I'll keep you going as long as you need.

A tiny bit of golden sunrise filled my head and it made me smile. You're . . . sweet. And I know . . . you too well. No good to . . . argue.

Damned straight.

Maybe it would help to get her mind off it. How's the remodel of the apartment going? I'd left it totally up to her, since she'd never really gotten to decorate before without having to please someone. I could live with just about anything, so long as she kept my recliner as is. But it was tan, so it would blend.

She knew what I was doing. I could tell, but she played along. Sometimes it takes two to ignore reality in a crisis. Frustrating. The accent wall they painted . . . with the red I showed you . . . mixed wrong. It's . . . a weird mauve-y burgundy, instead of the lipstick color that matches . . . the flowers in the . . . drapes. She was starting to wear out, so I threw some more of my own power into the thread of her mind. Yeah, I knew it was going to probably speed up the process, but it was all I had to keep her mind with me. Lose that, and the body doesn't much matter.

It's okay. We'll just paint over it.

Do . . . favor. 'Kay? Finish it . . . for me. Lelya has design. Even . . . if something—

I let out a small growl. Nothing's going to happen to you. I won't let it.

Now a small laugh. Nobody . . . to shoot . . . this time, Tony.

The thread started to fade away and I panicked. I grabbed it before she could react. Fine. If magic wouldn't work, what about life force instead? I'd had to do this once before—pull from my own body to give to her. It wasn't magic, per se. I just used magic to deliver it. Of course, if I gave her too much, I'd die. But them's the breaks.

The thread brightened just a little but before I could speak, a whispering started. It was faint at first, but then it began to echo and peal like bells in our collective mind. *Krhlow plihep . . . krhlow plihep . . . Krhlow plihep!* They weren't words in any language I'd ever heard, but they had an immediate effect. The sound wrapped around our collective head, pulling, tugging. Demanding we rise up to meet them.

More noises, but they still weren't words. *Rghnl olpnst nbwiq! Hoplez requay.* Now I could hear more voices and I could make a few of them out. Amber's soft alto and Ahmad's smooth, but angry baritone. A third female voice was mixed in, but I didn't recognize it.

Blue-tinged fire, the color of an oven pilot light, started to crackle at the edge of my vision as the words were repeated over and over. A chant. Was this the ritual Sue had mentioned?

Her voice was filled with relief. Yes. They've decided. I'd . . . hoped to keep . . . you separate, in case . . . goes wrong. But . . . too late now.

No big deal. We'd deal with it as it came. Sorry. You're stuck with me.

A light laugh that warmed me. I can . . . live with that.

The fire danced and crackled, higher and higher until the blue filled the landscape of our mind, covering it in light and shadow like mist over a moonlit English moor. Now more colors joined the blue in tiny pinpoints, blinking, sparkling, twirling. It was a Hubble photo, or the Aurora Borealis.

I've never seen the Aurora. Have you been to Alaska?

Sue's voice was stronger, drowning out the voices in the background. The abrupt change startled me. She sounded almost normal and the lift it gave me was astounding. Go ritual! Yeah. When I was eleven. My dad took me on a cruise up there. Said I could still be amazed, and it would be too soon that nothing would, so he wanted to let me have a few memories of awe. It *was* a pretty amazing year. We did the Grand Canyon, Old Faithful, and Mount Rush-more and then to Alaska before we set sail for China and a grand tour of Europe. Missed a whole year of school for it, and had to make it up the next summer. But it was worth it. We bonded at a time when I was still angry I was an orphan. Mom had only died a couple of years before and I'd just found out that Dad wasn't my *real* father. It was a rough time. Later I realized getting tight with him was more the plan than being awed. He was a pretty bright guy.

Long diatribe, and pretty useless information. But it was keeping her entertained. Her smile added a bright glow of orange and yellow to the landscape. He sounds like a good dad. I wish I could meet him sometime. I had a good dad too. I miss him.

Yeah, it'd be good to see him again. Except we're both dead.

I immediately winced, considering the circumstances. It wasn't how I meant it to come out, even though it was the truth. To the rest of the world, Tony Giodone and Suzi Quentin *were* dead—killed in a rival mob massacre at an airport a year ago.

Right now I feel *alive!* Like I could do anything.

It was the truth. Energy seemed to be swirling all around us in a heady rush that was like the adrenaline high of winning a race. We could probably figure out a way with Carmine's help.

Ooo! And we could see Linda and Babs again. I haven't talked to them in forever. I don't even know if Babs had the baby. It's been so busy and then . . . well, *this* happened and I sort of withdrew.

I'd noticed. She'd always struggled with depression,

which is why I suggested the decorating. It worked for a while, but I didn't realize there was an underlying cause of her anxiety. Stupid. I know better than that. I should have dug when I'd first realized it.

"What in the hell is going on up there? Tony's had some sort of collapse. He's mumbling Sue's name and he's bleeding from his mouth." It was Lucas's voice I heard and for a brief moment, I could see the inside of the living room, from the bottom up, and in black-and-white. Lucas had a cell phone to his ear, while the girls were helping Paul from the room. Apparently, I'd gone wolf at some point. I always see in monotones after I've shifted. I didn't like that I was bleeding, but there wasn't much I could do about it. I didn't really feel any pain, so I couldn't imagine it was too serious. Or, it was *really* serious and I'd completely left my body and was trapped inside Sue's head.

The living room faded to black and the beeping started again. I could hear a reply from Sue's right, so he must have called the clinic. But I didn't recognize the voice. It was female, though. It must be one of the nurses. "This is Sarah. They've started a ritual, Alpha. One of the ones from the book of Dr. Wingate's sister, Aspen Monier. The human woman was dying, and—"

Lucas growled, low and deep, and his voice held not only anger, but *fear*. "Who authorized that? There aren't enough people there to approve such a risky venture. We don't have any idea what could happen."

The woman's voice turned tremulous. "I . . . I'm sorry, Alpha. I don't know anything other than what I was told. Dr. Wingate, Councilman al-Narmer and Holly Sanchez are in there now. The door's locked, so I can't ask."

"What in the hell is Holly Sanchez doing there? She's just a child."

Now the woman's voice turned from afraid to matter-of-fact. "She's twenty-seven and she's turning into a really good healer. She's all we've have since June, when we lost all our doctors here. I had to take two children to the emergency room in Boulder in May to set broken limbs because we didn't have anyone to treat them. All I could do was pray that nobody did blood work or called Social Services." She paused when Lucas started to growl again. "They didn't. Between their parents and me, we convinced them the kids were playing in a tree and fell. It explained the scratches and bruises from their dominance fight. I'm sorry, Alpha, but I'm doing the best I can." The tremors were back in her voice again, but they were from anger, not fear. "We've called and called, but nobody's listened. The clinic has gone from a staff of six to *me* in a year and nobody has *bothered* to check on us. And I'm only an R.N. with no healing magic. What did you expect to happen?"

His reply was interrupted by an angry hissing sound, so I couldn't make it out. Something was happening and it didn't sound good. The noise finally drowned Lucas out entirely and I could sense Sue's fear. It was hard not to, since I was sharing it. I didn't have any warm fuzzies about the situation either.

Tony?

I hear it too. Ignore it and talk to me. No sense in getting worried. Might be a normal part of the ritual. Tell me about the Chicago pack. How are Yurgi and Pam?

They're— She paused and I could tell she was listening to the noise, which was getting louder, seeming to come from above. It wasn't the sound of a snake. I've heard them. This sounded like bacon sizzling in oil. Hot enough to burn. They're good. She seemed to get her feet under her, so to speak, and was able to continue on like the hissing wasn't growing like an approaching storm. They finally found a house they both like. It wasn't easy. Pam wanted a big kitchen and two bathrooms for when they have kids, and Yurgi insisted on a real backyard, with a patio big enough to hold barbeques. He's seen them on television and has always wanted to have one. Those are hard to come by in the price range they could afford.

I couldn't help but chuckle. Yurgi Kroutikhin was a Russian immigrant, exiled from his former wolf pack in Siberia and sent to live in America with our pack leader, Nikoli, as the omega—lowest wolf. Yurgi wound up saving the pack leader's life and Nikoli decided to reward his sacrifice by helping him buy a house—the second biggest thing to Yurgi you could imagine. The first biggest thing is having kids. Apparently, in the Siberia pack, he wouldn't be allowed to breed. Nikoli doesn't care and, in fact, thinks kids keep the pack strong.

They're the closest things to friends that Sue and I have in Chicago. Yurgi thinks I'm a god in wolf form, because I keep the others from picking on him too much.

They decided—*ow!* I flinched too as a small stinging sensation came from somewhere on our left side. It wasn't an arm or shoulder. It was inside our mind. Then another one made me wince and suddenly it was raining little sparkling bits of color like meteorites. Everywhere they landed they stuck and burned. At first it just made you yip, but after a few seconds it started to feel like a hailstorm pounding on our collective mind, except with bits of lava. There was nowhere to hide and no way to stop whatever was happening. All we could do was yelp and finally scream.

Fire filled the landscape of our mind. Pain erupted from places I didn't know could *feel* pain until our entire reality was never-ending pinpricks of searing heat—death by a thousand cuts. If the ritual was supposed to be helping, it wasn't. I fought back with the only thing I had, my Sazi magic. I raised a shield, pulling on what little I could feel of my body. In the process, I realized that Ahmad was still somehow attached to me. Whether or not he was aware of it really didn't matter to me. What mattered was that there was extra energy in my head and if I could harness it, I could keep the fire from burning us up.

Borrowing someone's magic for your own use isn't like grabbing a rope out of your neighbor's garage. It's more like asking to borrow their hand, taking it off their body, and then expecting it to grab something at your command. Sure, with the right stimulus at the right nerve endings, it *can*. But you have to know what you're doing.

I didn't.

But Sue's screams had turned to whimpering and it made me crazy. That's a weird thing about wolves. We literally can't stand to sense our mates in pain.

I reached out and grabbed that black-red stream of the snake king's power, not even caring that it would be like touching a high-tension electric wire. The tiny bits of pain became one massive wave that drove me right to the edge of sanity. But slowly, as though dogging the head of a charging bull with sheer brute force, I turned Ahmad's energy until it was not only connected to me in Kansas, but Sue in Boulder. Or maybe it was vice versa. An immediate change in our collective head happened. The mist on the ground turned red and an odd scent rolled across my nose . . . or was it Sue's nose? It smelled of nuts but sweet—heavy yet somehow delicate. Most importantly, though, the bits of fire fell into the red mist and dissolved. No more pain.

I had no idea what Ahmad might do to me once he figured out that I was stealing magic from him. But I didn't figure it would be good or pleasant.

You hanging in there?

The pause was too long. forcing me to ask again. Sue? Are you okay?

Her voice sounded a little . . . odd, but seemed okay overall. I've been trying to decide. But yeah, I think I'm okay. I feel a little strange, but strange is better than *bad*.

"Sue, we've finished the ritual." It was Amber's voice and it wasn't echoing like she was intruding on Sue's mind. We were hearing it with ears. "I'm going to give you an injection—try to bring you out of this coma. But I'm going to need your help, so really concentrate on waking up. Okay?"

What the hell? How do you *concentrate* on waking up? I hate it when doctors say bullshit stuff like that.

Sue chuckled. It means the alarm just went off and I can either hit the snooze or drag myself out of bed. I think it'll work better if you go back to your body and I wake up to see if the ritual did what it was supposed to.

What exactly was it supposed to *do*? Was it some sort of healing chant, like shaman stuff?

I could feel her shoulders wiggle a little as she tried to describe it. Not precisely. The goal was to bind me with magic. Make me something . . . different. Not a shifter like you, but not entirely human either. If it worked, being your mate won't hurt me anymore. I'll have magical blood.

Um . . . huh. That wasn't exactly what I expected to hear. You're okay with that? Does it have side effects? Because really, what doesn't? Even medication can give reactions.

She gave the equivalent of a mental shrug. Time will tell. A chance at living is better than the certainty of dying.

Tough to argue with that. And you're sure you want me to go?

Yep. I'll handle things here. But hurry back soon. We'll have things to talk about, either way. I felt a push that moved me toward the void that separated us. I was being shown the door and I couldn't say I liked it very much.

You're keeping something from me, aren't you?

The sunshiny light that filled the landscape should have warmed and comforted me, but all I could feel was suspicious. Oh, probably. Guess you'll have to come back and find out what, huh?

It wasn't like Sue to play games and I was starting to get worried that something strange had just happened. But I wouldn't be able to tell until I got back and saw her face-to-face. I'll **see you later tonight. Stay safe until I get there.**

Looking forward to it. At least that part was true, so I grudgingly slipped from her mind and closed the door again. But first I made it back to the normal kitchen door that we were both familiar with. I couldn't seem to sense anything from Ahmad, so I was hoping that ending the ritual had ended our connection.

I came to in a twitching, screaming rush that came out as a howl of fury. Lucas was the only one in the room and he'd clamped down such a tight hold on me that I'd apparently pulled several muscles struggling against it. Once I had my head about me, though, I was able to slow my breathing and let my legs relax. It was only after staring at me for a long moment that he realized I was back to *me* again.

"You ready to be let go now?"

He eased on the magic holding my head so I could talk. My tongue was dry and the metallic taste was probably the blood Lucas said I was frothing with. "I think so. It hasn't been a fun few minutes. How long was I out in real time? Felt like a century in Sue's head." Now the pressure holding me down released completely and I was able to shakily get up onto my four paws. "What's the situation here? Are you going to change me back, or have you gotten everybody out of the house and I'm going to stay a wolf for the time being?"

Lucas stood and walked toward me carrying a pair of jeans that would be far too big, along with a nondescript gray T-shirt. They weren't going to be enough to leave, and I really, *really* wanted to get the taste of blood out of my mouth. "You've been this way for about an hour. The girls drove to the store for more meat and to the motel to get your duffel. Since we hadn't even unpacked, you'll have everything you need to make yourself presentable again. I sent Paul to visit his neighbor, just in case anything went wrong."

I felt a brush of magic that increased in strength to the point of pain and then I felt my body starting to shift. It's hard to describe the sensation of changing from wolf to human. My legs broke and re-formed, lengthening and changing how the muscles attached. The fur pulled back inside my body until there was just a soft coating of dark hair on my forearms, legs, and chest. The mouth changing back is the weirdest. People like me who have had braces would understand the sensation. It's like right after the screws are tightened. It hurts, right at the site, but there's pressure everywhere.

Then I was human again, but one who felt like he'd just been hit by a bus. I got to my feet with the help of the built-in planter next to the door and my hamstrings told me I'd be limping for a week. Pulling on the pants was something of a challenge, because my legs really didn't want to raise up without a screaming fit. More planter holding got the job done, but I do hate pulling up a zipper without underwear. It takes patience and extra attention to detail to prevent . . . accidents—neither of which I have tons of lately. "Well, that was an interesting ride. I think I'll stick to the carousel next time, or maybe cut off the wrist band altogether."

"Tell me about it. Nobody's talking to me in Boulder, and it's starting to piss me off."

I shrugged as much as I could without wincing and then lifted my arms to pull on the T-shirt. "Not much to tell. I could hear you talking to some chickie named

Sarah at the clinic, but Sue was in a coma, so all I could see was lots of black. At first, whatever magic they called up was pretty, but then it turned deadly—like most everything else in this fucked-up supernatural world. Lots of pain and torment, so I had to take matters into my own, albeit virtual, hands."

"Like *how*?" Lucas is naturally suspicious of everyone, but he's always saved special levels for me. He crossed his arms until muscles bulged and he centered his stance.

I put one hand on my chin and the other on top of my head and cracked my neck before I replied. "Oh, I learned my lessons well when you sent me to spend time with Aspen and her new hubby. She taught me how to channel energy so that when I get into hindsight mode, nobody I'm attached to can hurt me. Sort of like judo—I use their own strength back against them. But I can also grab it and use it to defend myself, so I did. I'm thinking I used Ahmad's power to make the hurting stop, but I could be wrong." More circling of my head made the pounding in my temples ease and the nifty accelerated healing was making it so I could almost breathe without pain.

A car door slammed outside, and then a second one. The girls must be back. That's when I noticed there was still a slender thread of magic flowing out from Lucas. "Geez! You can't even let the girl go to the grocery store without a tracker?"

"No. She might bolt. Hell, if I could figure out how to put one on *you,* I would. But you don't even have to be out of my sight to leave and get into shit. *Trouble* has your picture next to it in the dictionary."

"Don't forget perturb, disquiet, and pain in the ass. I

specialize in those too. My mug shot is all over the the-
saurus." I couldn't help but laugh and that's how the girls
found me when they walked through the door. Laughing
my ass off on the couch with Lucas shaking his head
sadly at me, even though the room was filled with the
scent of oranges.

Chapter Seven

I WANTED TO stick around town longer to figure out what Stuart and Ricky were up to. Lucas refused, saying we needed to get back to Boulder—both to get Liz to safety and to check on Sue and Angelique. I couldn't argue, I wanted . . . no, *needed* to get back to Sue. Especially since Amber was actively blocking our link. I didn't know if that was good or bad, but I didn't like it. Still, I *really* didn't like leaving with a possible hit hanging over my head. Who's to say that Ricky was the *only* one hired to search?

I spoke softly even though nobody around us was listening. I've always found it odd that it's easier to have an ultra-secret conversation right in the middle of a group of people. We're taught from childhood not to listen in when others talk. "Couldn't we have just hijacked them and done a hindsight on Stuart real quick? Something has made Vito Prezza think I'm still alive, and that makes things dangerous for all of us. I can't afford to be alive in my old life right now."

"Do you mean those guys at the motel?" I'd almost forgotten that Liz was trailing behind us in the Denver

Airport, following the stream of travelers toward the shuttle stop that would take us to the long-term parking lot. She'd stayed so quiet in the back of the extended cab truck in Hansen, keeping her head below window level, so that other than her scent and breathing, she'd been invisible. Same with the flight back. She smelled afraid, of course, but I'd gotten used to that after a while. She'd also smelled determined—the scent of cold iron. She'd made her decision and had chosen the safety of her family and friends over herself. That boded well. "Don't worry. They weren't looking for you. They're looking for some East Coast hit man named Tony Giodone. Heather and I heard them talking in their car when we were grabbing the duffel bags. But nobody like that ever comes to western Kansas." I turned my head, raised my brows, and gave her a *look*. She was bright enough to get it in one, and paled visibly. "Oh. Um . . . I think I'll be quiet now."

"We'll have someone look into it. That's not important right now." Lucas wasn't rising to the bait of my argument, which was frustrating. Apparently, no amount of pushing or squawking was going to get him to budge.

I gave a little snort. "It's important to *me*."

Liz's snort sounded almost like my own. "Welcome to my world."

"Heeey, you!" The voice that said the words carried over the top of the several thousand people going about their business. A dozen years rolled backward from déjà vu. Not only did I know the voice, it came from the same world that Stuart and Ricky did. While the words were completely innocent and could have been said by anyone, there was a certain tone to the words, a particular cadence that only I would recognize, because we'd only said it in the privacy of the house we once shared.

Like, anybody can say, "Wild and crazy guy," but only Steve Martin really *says* it.

I turned so abruptly I nearly tripped the kid. She managed to jump out of the way, but her roll-along luggage did a triple flip until a bank of chairs stopped it.

I struggled not to show recognition on my face. I scanned the faces like I was looking for something, but not finding it. Because Lucas and I were still under illusion. There's no way she should have recognized us. Unless—and then I saw her, the second woman, a visibly pregnant alpha wolf. The woman who turned me and could smell me anywhere.

Lucas and Liz stopped when I did. Lucas raised brows, clearly interested and a little disturbed, if his smell was any indication. The girl just plain gawked, as did most everyone else around. Linda Leone is worth gawking at. I have to give her that. She was decked out in a low-cut designer outfit in cobalt blue that hugged every carefully toned curve and made her sapphire eyes jump out at you. But the hat adorning her shining crown of hair was more suited to Derby Day than an airport in Denver, in my opinion. Still, if Linda was wearing a hat, she was clearly on the cutting edge of the fashion that would hit here in Denver next spring.

She dripped with diamonds, just like always, and there wasn't a man alive who wasn't turning to watch her move in a way that probably hasn't been seen since Marilyn Monroe left this earth. Linda glanced to her left, trying to get confirmation from the wolf's nose that we were who she was looking for, even though her eyes were lying to her. After the brief nod from the auburn-maned Babs Herrera, her heels ticked against the marble floors rapidly as she raced toward me.

I knew her initial desire was to throw her arms

around me to give me a big hug, I'd let her too, completely unafraid that Sue would be concerned if she watched. While Linda and I had dated for a time, we split long before I met Sue. She was currently Carmine's wife and decidedly off limits—even if I had the inclination, which I don't.

The problem was that she didn't know who was who and with Lucas still wearing the cologne, even Babs couldn't be sure who was with me. She bit at her lower lip, looking from one to the other of us, waiting for some sign. Finally, I had to end the suspense. I smiled and leaned forward, then spoke softly, just next to Linda's ear. My voice should still be the same. I think. "Good God, woman, are you three planning on a houseful?"

She seemed both relieved and suddenly tense. She flinched visibly and probably only Lucas and Liz could see whatever facial expression she wore. But her scent was nearly as blank as Lucas's, which meant something was *really* wrong. Linda reacts to stress by internalizing. She can be a stone-cold bitch when she's totally freaked out. "Thank God it's you, Tony. Barbara lost the first one. Please don't mention it. It's hard for her to remember . . . the spider still gives her nightmares."

Crap. I hadn't known that. The last time I saw her, I'd just rescued her from a Sazi were-spider at Carmine's command. That's the problem with not keeping in touch with people. I'd have to warn Sue before she saw them and made a similar screw-up. I didn't know how to deal with that level of pain, and suddenly didn't know what to say. The problem is that I don't really *like* Babs Herrera. She's the one who turned me. She ripped out my throat and left me for dead. Of course, that was before she hooked up with Carmine and Linda. They're a three-some now, and I know either or both would marry her if the law permitted. The trouble was, a part of me was actually pretty happy she was hurting, because I hate her guts. But Carmine and Linda, and Sue to boot, would never forgive me mentioning it.

So I fell back on my normal tool . . . sarcastic humor. I pasted a smile on my face, but let the sorrow remain in my scent for her nose. I grabbed Linda's hand and gave it a firm shake, like you would when meeting a colleague from out of town. It shouldn't give anyone who might recognize Linda any clue who we were to each other. I didn't dare glance at Lucas, since he might be annoyed that I even acknowledged the pair.

I motioned to Babs with my thumb, shook my head, and whispered out the corner of my mouth. "That is just *sick*. You know that, right?" It was the perfect thing to say to her, because she smiled broadly. It told her we were back on the same old uneasy ground. She looked down at the shirt that was stretched over her big round belly and the smile turned to a grin. It was covered with baby animals, from fawns to tiny bunnies and even little fluffy skunks. On a normal woman, it would be cute and cause a lot of *awww* . . . comments. But I knew what it *really* meant, and it said she was laughing inside every time a human gave that response. Because right on the shoulder was a wolf paw print, painted in bright red. Hell, it could even be that she stepped on it in wolf form after dipping her paw. She's an alpha and keeps her full human mind in her animal form. "Training the kid to hunt before he or she is even out."

Her voice was all innocence when she replied, which told me I was right. "Why, I have no idea what you're talking about. Besides, all the psychologists say it's important for children in the womb to be exposed to basic food shapes, colors, and sounds."

Lucas couldn't help the guffaw that snuck out while I just shook my head. Linda looked embarrassed. She never has quite gotten into the wolf humor that Babs and I have. But poor Liz. She was just flat appalled. On the plus side, she was bright enough to get the joke. She just didn't know what to make of it—it's a lot like talking to Morticia Addams.

"Just please tell me you aren't playing tapes of predator calls for the kid. He'll wind up seriously messed up in the head if he never turns."

Babs had the good grace to blush. "Only once. He said the same thing." The *he* would be Carmine, and he'd probably be a little freaked out—being as it's his first kid.

Linda grabbed her arm just then and both of their scents turned to panic. They looked at each other and then at me. "Crap! That's what we're here to tell you. I can't believe we got so distracted. You have to come with us right now. He needs you."

Lucas picked up on the same things I did, but he spoke first. "You came *here* to tell him something? Why did you think we'd be here right now?"

But Linda can evade with the best of them. "That's not important right now. Besides, this doesn't concern you. It's just To— *him* we need to talk to." Babs winced when she said that, because she's well aware that if we're under illusion, names are a bad thing. Of course, it might also be because she caught the glimpse of Lucas crossing his arms and letting out a low rumbling growl. It was so low that I doubt anyone other than a

Sazi could pick up on it. Liz did. She took an abrupt step sideways from him and her eyes were showing too much white.

I had a solution that would get us out of the public eye and give us some privacy to talk. "You've got a car here? Great. How about giving us a ride? We're way out in the long-term lot." In Denver, the long-term parking lot is like three or four miles from the airport. That should give us plenty of time and if it worked out I needed to catch another flight, we could just turn around after dropping the others off.

It was acceptable to Lucas, because he waved Linda and Babs ahead. "Good plan. Lead the way, ladies."

Liz did the polite thing, which was offer to carry Babs's heavy bag. The rest of us tend to forget to offer, because even in her current state, she could lift a truck or chase down a full-grown elk and gut it before a normal pregnant woman could get herself standing from a comfortable couch.

At least, that's what I noticed with Bobby's wife, Asri. In fact, the more preggers the tiny Indonesian woman has gotten, the more *dangerous* she's become. Komodo dragons, of which Asri is the last, carry over a year. He'd expected seven months, since that's a normal snake term, but not dragons. It's been a rough time for Bobbo, and there's still a few months to go. He's a powerful alpha python—also the last of his kind, but he's no match for a hormone-crazed dragon. In the first trimester, they were still too busy having sex to notice her getting rougher about it. Then she started snapping at him . . . *literally*. Took a chunk out of his shoulder when he was handing her a cup of coffee at breakfast one morning. Currently, he spends most of his time at

Wolven headquarters, wherever that might be at a moment, and they talk on the phone. She stayed on Komodo Island for a while, wanting to give birth in her homeland. But the tsunami took an awful toll and the birthing places she remembered aren't there anymore. So, she's back in Chicago, where she was Nikoli's enforcer long before she and Bobby hooked up. The wolves are keeping a *really* low profile, because boy—they don't want her angry. Nikoli and his mother are capable of keeping her in line, which is the reason she went back. She was afraid she was going to do something stupid that involved humans and wind up getting put down by Wolven before she could deliver.

Linda had double-parked the Cadillac Escalade in the arrivals section. There was no ticket on it, so no doubt she'd sweet-talked some poor cop to manage it. Heck, he was probably *guarding* it. A man in blue headed our way as we exited into the warm late-summer air and Babs immediately tucked her arm underneath Lucas's. He let out a little sigh, realizing just as I did that they'd used the pregnancy as their reason. She started to do the pregnant woman waddle, putting a hand on her lower back in fake discomfort that she hadn't had moments before. Even Liz finally rolled her eyes and sighed. Linda waved and smiled brightly to the young cop, who couldn't be more than twenty-five. He tipped his cap in return before returning to flagging vehicles through the orange security cones, with frequent tweets on his whistle.

The size of the vehicle made short work of the luggage and everyone had plenty of space to sit. But I'll bet the mileage was hideous. Once Linda was behind the wheel and we were on the ramp leading to the entrance, she finally looked in the mirror. "So who is this pretty young lady?"

Liz started to answer with, "I'm Liz—" before Lucas cut her off.

"New turn from Kansas. She's got to be in Boulder before sunset, so let's speed it up." Granted that it was probably only an hour or two to get there from here, and it was still four before the moon rose. Mostly, I thought he was trying to keep on topic. He's heard a little about Linda from me and Sue, and realized she can get off on tangents. She did shut up and the digital speed display moved up a few more numbers.

I added a little more detail, so she didn't dig too much. "Liz Kendall. Twenty-three, new graduate of School of Mines."

Babs broke in with polite interest. "From Kansas? Will you be a cat then? Not too many wolf families in that neck."

"Badger," replied Lucas, obviously trying to keep it short.

But that only spurred Babs on. "*Really?* I thought the only badger left was Nigel Sutton."

"Granddaughter." This time Lucas's staccato reply was accompanied by a light growl that told people to drop it.

Babs got the hint and kept her reply to a simple nod and polite reply. Even Linda's mouth stayed closed. "A pleasure to meet you, Lady Sutton. Enjoy your visit to America."

It was logical to assume that we were there to pick her up, and I could have probably left it there. But what the heck. "Other way around." I ignored his hint, and it made him turn in his seat belt to give me a glare. I held up one finger, only because it's something we hadn't mentioned to Liz. "She's *from* America. Bound for England. She and Gramps have never met, so she

probably doesn't even know her grandfather's *titled* . . .
Lucas."

That stopped him. He reared back briefly. We'd been
so caught up in other things that we hadn't really paid
proper attention to the girl. "Oh. You're right." He
turned even farther, until his shoulder belt was touching his right elbow. "Liz, your grandfather is an English
lord—the tenth earl of Suttcliffe. Even though you
probably won't ever have a title—it doesn't pass to
grandchildren—you're probably his only heir. You'll be
staying at his estate south of London to train and the
servants will probably fawn over you. Come to think on
it, it might be a good idea to send someone along with
you so it's not such a radical change. His estate is far
out in the countryside and there's not much contact
with civilization. Would your friend, Heather, like to go
along with you? I can have Antoine Monier, head of the
cats, arrange it with her family and have someone pick
her up and meet you for your flight."

"I . . . oh. Well—" Poor kid. This was a bit much to
swallow all in the same day. "Would she be *safe*? That's
why I decided to do this, after all."

Lucas nodded and turned back forward. "Nigel's
staff can handle anything that might happen. You'll both
be safer than you would be in Hansen." He pulled out
his cell phone before she could even reply and clicked
the down arrow several times before punching the send
command and raising it to his ear. Her eyes were still
blinking a mile a minute and her scent was such a confusion of emotions that both Babs and I got a sneezing
fit.

My hearing was still acute enough that even over the
sneezing I heard Antoine speak and the French annoy-

ance was thick in his voice. "*Oui?* 'Ave you any idea what time it is here, Lucas?" He checked his watch, but his look was more embarrassed than his reply.

"I need a favor, Antoine. You know Nigel Sutton pretty well, right?"

A deep sigh now from the massive cougar that spoke volumes. "Oh, yes. Better than I would care to." Liz's ears were as perked as human ears can get, so she was definitely listening in. That Lucas made the call in the car, and stuck to speaking English, said he *expected* her to.

"I've got his granddaughter in the car with me, Elizabeth Sutton-Kendall. She's twenty-three, a new turn, and middle-class *American*. She's going to have to train with him."

Now the big cat was fully awake and had lost most of the French accent, which I knew he could turn on and off at will. "*Merde!* Someone actually *mated* with him once, and survived to give birth? Good lord. And you would inflict him on some poor schoolgirl? That's cruel, even by Sazi standards, Lucas."

Lucas laughed, even as Liz winced. "Hardly a schoolgirl, *mon ami.* Only two years younger than your *new wife,* if I recall." He paused long enough to hear the slight cough on the other end and then I could hear a light squeaking as he apparently walked on old boards into another room. Possibly to escape the glare of said wife—the very American, via Turkey, Caspian tiger named Tahira. "And yes. I have no choice. Who else would train a badger? Me? She's already alphic. Tony can see the aura, and she's already destroyed part of her hometown on her last turn."

Liz blushed a dark beet red as both Babs and Linda

turned to stare at her briefly. But Babs patted her hand in a warm way, and the blush turned into a relieved smile.

Antoine sighed deeply. "What would you have me do? Have you told Nigel yet? Is that what you're asking of me, because I *am* at my estate in France. It's only a few hours drive to his place if you need her to be guarded for the first meeting."

Lucas pursed his lips, thinking. "Actually, that wasn't what I had in mind, but it might not be a bad idea. And bring Tahira with you, in case we need to pull some of the fight out of him. No, I was actually calling to ask if you could phone the parents of a friend of hers, named Heather Marshall. They're cougar family members from the Colorado mountains, so I figured you'd have their number somewhere. The girl's full human, but they're close and she's been exposed to Sazi her whole life. I thought it would be good to let Elizabeth have an American friend stay with her, considering how isolated his estate is. Nigel's staff would ensure she stayed safe."

"*Oui.* I agree. They're accustomed to defending visitors from his wrath. She would be quite safe, so I have no problems guaranteeing her healthy return to her parents. Hopefully, they'll watch over the new turn as well. But that will be harder. His lessons will be quite difficult on her."

"But necessary." He glanced back over his shoulder to see the concerned look on her face. "She's tough, though. I think she can handle the old digger."

"Indeed? Then she and Tahira should get on famously. I doubt Nigel could object to a girl's day out on occasion—especially considering the tenuous relations with the Hayalet right now. He is nothing if not a political animal." I could hear paper crinkling in the background and Lucas waited patiently. "Yes, yes. I have the family on my roster. I'll call them straight away. Perhaps even include a trip for their family to my home in Arizona as a bonus. The cats in my show always get along famously with family members. They smell like cats, but don't present the threat that actual Sazi do." He paused and then sighed again. "Shall I break the news to Nigel, or are you going to rely on Charles for that? He's really the only one who can *order* Nigel to do something and have it stick."

Lucas nodded. "Definitely Charles, but you'll be the face of the council when she arrives. Oh, and has anyone talked to you about Angelique yet?"

A light snarl erupted in his voice. "*Non.* What is her problem this time? I will not change my vote no matter how much she harps, Lucas. She gets no more mountains in California. Her birds already have more than enough hunting ground. Hers is not the only species in the state, after all."

Lucas was tapping his fingers on the armrest now, and I knew why. But we didn't have any answers yet, and maybe Amber and the others had managed to make the ritual magic work on her too. "We'll talk later. Plan that you won't be going back to bed tonight, I'm afraid. If Charles hasn't already called you, he will be soon."

"You do know how to ruin my day, old friend. Very well. I'll start coffee and begin to make calls. We'll talk more soon, I'm certain. *Bon chance.*"

"And to you." Lucas flipped the cell phone closed. "It's a done deal. Antoine will make sure it happens. We'll work out the details later, but plan on her accompanying you or meeting you there." Then he turned to

Linda, who was just slowing to enter one of the lines at the exit toll booth. I was betting they hadn't been here long enough to owe anything, but it reminded Lucas again that they were here at *all*. Liz opened her mouth to say something, but he didn't notice, so he spoke directly to Linda. "So . . . you were about to tell me how you came to be here to find Tony."

Babs opened her mouth to reply, but I shushed her with a warning look. "You know he's going to get it out of one of you. He'll be nicer to *her*."

She sighed. "We might as well tell him, Lin. Tony's right. He'll make one of us tell him and it won't feel very good. And it's not like he swore us to secrecy or anything."

"Fine," she said, raising her one hand off the steering wheel to yank down the button to lower the window with obvious annoyance. "Fine then. Nikoli told us. Once we explained the situation, he understood how important it was we find Tony, and he made some calls."

Well, *that* didn't sound good at all, because there isn't much that will move Nikoli to share information, much less go out and *seek* it. "What situation?"

Linda clutched at the steering wheel and the wet fog of sorrow filled the car. She passed her ticket to the cashier silently, but not because she was afraid the old guy behind the glass would hear, but because she suddenly couldn't talk. Babs took over the story. "Carmine's in the hospital, Tony. He's in really bad shape."

Crap. Ricky's words in Hansen took on new meaning. There *was* a hospital, with someone important enough that I would normally go visit. And the room was being watched for any sign of me.

Linda kept talking and I had to force myself away from trying to figure things out to hear the story. "We were staying up in a condo in Vail, enjoying the fall colors, when he was attacked. He's been having a lot of trouble with a group from the East Coast, newcomers from South America that took over one of the families there. It's like a drug cartel, but they're shifters and they're really pushing their weight around Atlantic City. More than one casino has had a *hostile takeover,* if you know what I mean. I don't know what made them think they could muscle in on Carmine's turf, but we sent them packing, and without even a hint of it in the papers or on the police blotter. We thought it was all done, but they tracked us down."

Lucas and I both stared at Babs open-mouthed, because I hadn't heard even a whisper about this, and I should have, from one side or the other. I was thinking from the look on Lucas's face that it was news to him too. "Just how long ago was this?"

Linda sped up as soon as the gate opened for her and we were up to highway speed in a matter of seconds. But it was Babs who kept talking. "The attack? Just day before yesterday. They airlifted him down to Denver from the hospital up there because his kidneys shut down briefly and their dialysis machine was giving them fits."

Linda broke in, her voice steadier now. "Mom saw the whole thing happen, but they didn't notice her. She was in her whirlpool and it probably smelled too much like chlorine, plus the oil from her chair. She swore at least one of them turned into a snake and she was really freaked out. We told her she was hallucinating from the heat and stress, because . . . well, we haven't exactly told her that you guys exist." She turned to look at me then. I couldn't help but be surprised that Lissell, Linda's mom, would say something like that unless it was true. But no time to mull. I had to point back out the window because her hands always follow where her head goes, so the big SUV was veering toward the shoulder at a rapid clip. She jerked it back straight. "I've never seen anyone cut up like that, Ton. It was worse than when Barbara was disciplined for bringing you over. But we knew she'd heal. We . . . well, we *don't* know with Carmine."

Double crap. "Of course. As soon as I check in with Sue, I'll head down to visit him." I didn't look at Lucas. He was probably glaring at me, but that didn't matter. I would see him somehow, even if I had to take Bobbo with me to cast an illusion over me.

Linda shook her head so hard the hat nearly came flying off. "He don't want to see you, Tony. Not when he's like this. You visit him and it'll only piss him off. He just wants you to make it right. You need to keep things going back home, without anyone knowing about him, and make it right. You're the only person he trusts right now, because *someone* had to have squealed about where we were. We kept it out of the papers, mostly, with a fake name. It should be a few days before anything hits the press back home."

I knew what that meant and I was betting Lucas did too. I started to quietly beat the back of my head against the thick, leather-clad headrest, eyes closed. Fuck. But something sounded squirrely too, the longer my brain stewed. No way would Carmine have Linda order a hit. No way in hell. He wouldn't even let *me* do that. I don't care how close to death he was.

"I have to tell him you agreed, Ton. He made me swear I'd get you to do the job."

Now Lucas was shaking his head. "He can't."

Linda turned all of her worry and pain into blind fury, directed straight at the alpha wolf. Her voice was raw and harsh with recently shed tears and Lucas was taken aback at the intensity. "*You* stay out of this. It's family business. If you get your kicks beating up women, then go ahead and get it over with. But Tony's blood. You can't tell him no and make it stick forever unless you kill him. And you can't tell *me* shit. I know the rules you guys have to play by. Nikoli said I could ask, said he'd let Tony make his own decision."

Nikoli understands both sides, and I honestly didn't know which side he favored—Wolven law or family honor. He might be giving me enough rope to hang myself, or could actually be encouraging me to go to New Jersey to kill the attackers—to make it right. I only had one hope to satisfy both sides without directly refusing one or the other. "It's technically a Wolven matter if there were shifters involved in an attack on a human. Right?" I didn't wait for him to reply. "And, if there are South American snakes that have forcibly taken over a human enterprise, isn't that for Wolven too? Could we send *someone* to the hospital to investigate? Bobbo knows Carmine and could tell if any snakes touched him, and could detect any venom in a wound." Plus, if Bobby was the person sent, he'd take me along. Grudgingly . . . but he'd do it. After I got Carmine's orders, I could get started elsewhere—like back in my old hometown, leaning on the locals for information.

The low growl from the front seat said Lucas wasn't liking this. It made me shiver this close to the moon.

Linda was drumming her fingers on the wheel nervously, but other than the scent of hot-and-sour soup that was bleeding out of her like a broken pressure line, she gave no sign of fear.

We were nearing the turnoff to the parking lot and as Linda put on the blinker to move into the next lane, Lucas finally spoke. "I'll think about it on the drive up the mountain. Tony, Liz, you're with me. He looked at Babs and gave a small nod. "Give me a cell phone number and I'll call you with my decision after I've talked with some people."

"Oh *hell* no!" Linda slammed on the brake so hard the tires squealed and the back end fishtailed before straightening out on the gravel. Lucas had to throw out his hands to keep from slamming into the dashboard, and I had to put a hand backward so I didn't get beaned by a flying suitcase. "I ain't putting up with this 'I'll call you' shit. Tony's his own man. He drives with us. I'll follow you there and he can tell me what his decision is. I'm not going to have you go all official on him and make him say no when he means to say yes."

Okay, I'd had about enough. I raised my voice to be heard over their argument, both of them talking so fast and loud that their words were unintelligible. "Knock it off—both of you! Linda, you're right. I'm my own man. And Lucas is right that I'll ride with him. I'll make my own decision and it won't matter what *either* of you say. I know the stakes and I'll take the heat either way. So just *zip it* while I think."

Linda shut up, and Babs and Liz hadn't uttered a word. They just looked at each other, raised brows, and stayed thankfully silent. But Lucas responded by raking a whip of power over my skin until I ground my teeth to

keep from screaming. It was a completely silent ex-
change and only I could see it, but I got the point—mess
with him, or yell at him again, and I could expect more.
An alpha Sazi can do a lot of damage without ever
killing me. I've learned that over the past year. But *he's*
learned pain only makes me more stubborn and irritat-
ing. He'd have to kill me outright and for some reason,
that was always off the table. One of these days, I was
going to find out why.

Chapter Eight

THE TINY CLINIC held a surprising number of people, when it came right down to it. Linda and Babs insisted on following us up—ostensibly for a prenatal exam from a real Sazi doctor, which Lucas couldn't very well refuse. The patients were still there, as was Ahmad, Charles and his bodyguards had arrived, plus me, Lucas, and Liz. A pretty full house.

While Lucas pulled Charles and Ahmad in for a powwow, and Linda and Babs went with Amber for an ultrasound, I looked in on Sue.

The change in her was not only remarkable, it was slightly disturbing. She wasn't in a regular room anymore. She was in a private one, with a regular bed, and was sitting in a recliner reading a novel. It said how deeply we weren't connected in the head because I startled her when I spoke. "Wow. You're looking good."

And I wasn't kidding. The bruises were gone, as was the tired, worn appearance. Even the haircut did her proud. Most people get a haircut and it's not a big deal. But with her, it changed her entire appearance. She'd gone from pixie-like with a shoulder bob to a rowr-rowr siren with the wedge cut. No idea why. I think it helped that she was wearing an off-the-shoulder burgundy shirt that showed off both her chest and neck. She's got a terrific neck, and the shirt made her look nearly skinny. I got the feeling that she'd been losing weight from her illness anyway. She seemed pale and too thin when I'd seen her in the bed before.

She looked up from the book and the open-mouth surprise turned to delight. She dropped the book and slammed down the handle to lower the recliner footrest before racing toward me. I met her halfway.

There's nothing quite like a reunion after a long absence anyway, but to have her whole and healthy—well, that was just a bonus. I pulled off the gloves and gathered her into my arms. I held onto her until I could feel my racing heart start to relax. "Thought I lost you," I whispered into the melon scented hair and she responded by tightening her fingers in my back.

"You nearly did. It was touch and go. But, as you can see—" Sue pulled away and spun around, her hair flying into the air with the effort, "I'm as good as new. Actually, I'm *better* than new." She wiggled her hips and my groin did a little leap. She noticed and snuggled in against my chest again. "I asked Amber to keep us separated until we could be sure the magic was going to hold. So far, so good, and now I think it might be time to try the next test—a little conjugal visitation with my mate."

She grabbed my head and pulled me down into a kiss. I didn't argue a bit as her lips nibbled at mine and then slowly opened my jaw. The frustrations of the day were swept away by the sensations that flowed through me from just a simple meeting of our mouths. Whatever the ritual had done to her was making my magic go into overdrive. My skin began to heat, then burn, and it was only when she touched me that it cooled. She apparently felt the same, because the whimper she let out when I slid my hand up her shirt to cup her bare breast was enough to make me growl and push her farther into the room before kicking shut the door with my heel.

I wanted to taste her skin, run my tongue along her neck until I could feel her pulse beating under it. So I did. She responded by nipping on my ear and running her fingers through my hair.

Nice. Very nice. My body approved wholeheartedly.

While I recognized that this wasn't the time nor the place for sex, it had been a rough day already and frankly, I couldn't seem to help myself. The need to touch her was nearly as strong as it had been the very first time we were together. Sparks literally flew as I pulled down one side of her shirt and flicked her nipple with my tongue. Tiny charges of electricity danced into the air. Soon my hands dropped to her hips and pulled her tight against my growing erection. She moaned and squirmed enough that I nearly . . . very nearly, threw her to the bed. I wanted to tear off her clothes and take her. Right here, right now, and I didn't care who watched.

It didn't help when she groaned, "Take me, Tony. I want you inside me."

It took every ounce of willpower I had to pull back and shake the scent of her arousal out of my mind. "Soon, sweetheart. Soon. But there's waaay too much going on right now. Shit's hit the fan all over the place, and as much as I'd like nothing better than to ravish every inch of your body, we just don't have the kind of time I want to spend on you."

She looked disappointed and a little pouty, but there

was no helping it. All I could do was try to change the subject and hope it was exciting enough to get her interested. "Linda and Babs are here, and Babs is pregnant. Does that help?"

"Babs is having another baby?! Ooo! Yes, that helps!"

I winced and grabbed her arm before she could rush out the door past me. "Not *another*, sweetie. She lost the last one. The venom was too much for it." Her hand flew to her mouth after a loud gasp, and she closed her eyes. The thick wave of sorrow pretty much took care of the any remaining arousal that might still be in my system. "But this one seems to be okay, so we're happy for her today. Right?"

Biting her lip and nodding seemed to help her get back to a good place. "Yes. Yes, of course. Today's a good, happy day. Do I smell happy?"

I waggled my hand. "Mostly. You smell a little sad, but you can blame it on being sick, or just be honest. I think she'd be happier that you're sad for her than a blank slate. And complete joy would be a lie too. She'd smell right through it."

The sigh she let out was a little frustrated. I knew the feeling. "You know, life was a lot simpler when I didn't have to worry about whether my face matched my emotional scent. That's *hard*."

I snorted and pulled the gloves back on. They were starting to fit really well, like a second skin. "Tell me about it. I've got a tough decision coming up and someone's going to be pissed with me no matter what I decide. I'd love to be able to lie to one or the other."

Now her face and scent matched. They were concerned for me. "Anything I can do to help?"

"Sure!" I lied. "Just tell me whether I should let the men who sliced the crap out of Carmine get away with

it, or whether to violate Sazi law and go kill them."
She gave a little laugh until I didn't return it. It took a
few seconds of staring at my hard, angry eyes before
she realized I wasn't kidding.

"Carmine's been hurt? Will he be okay?"

I shrugged and had to turn away to stare out the window. "Dunno. Nobody knows. His kidneys failed and
Linda says he's been cut up worse than she's ever seen—
and she's seen some pretty awful things. He's in a hospital here in Denver apparently, but she says he doesn't
want to see me. He just wants me to go *make it right*.
There's only one thing he means when he says that."

Her hand flew to my arm and her fingers dug in tighter
than I'd ever felt them manage. Was this part of the new
stuff, or was she really that worried? "They'll kill you,
Tony. Wolven will track you down and kill you."

"And so will my old friends if I *don't*. Louis and Sal
know I'm still alive. If Carmine dies and I let it go—"

She buried her head against my chest, and this time
it wasn't with sex on her mind. "Oh, God. Tony, what
are you going to do?"

I shook my head and ran my fingers through her
cropped 'do, getting the feel of the new length. "I don't
know. I really don't. It was my life for a long time, Sue.
I can't let it go that easily. Linda's hurting and so is Babs.
No doubt the guys are in limbo, waiting for Carmine to
come back from what they think is a vacation. If he
doesn't, and this new gang moves in—" I let the thought
trail off. It used to be her hometown too. I knew she
didn't want it to go to war any more than I did. "No easy
answers, just like everything in my life."

She looked up and I didn't know what, or who, the
tears rolling down her face were meant for. But they

glistened and made her green eyes seem eerily bright. "Well, there's at least *one* easy answer. I love you, and I'll stand by you. I know I've always hated what you did . . . that you took lives. But those were choices, plain business. Carmine and Linda, though . . . they're family. At least as close as we both have now. Even the Chicago pack is a distant second. You do what you need to do, and whatever happens—"

I nodded, once. She was sounding strong and confident, which wasn't really like her. But I couldn't deny I liked it. "Happens." I kissed her again, just a light brush of lips to seal the deal. Talking to her had pretty much made up my mind, but I didn't think Lucas was going to like the answer. In fact, he might just put me down before I could even leave the clinic. But I had to try to avenge Carmine, and that's the best I could do.

We left the room hand in hand, her grip tight in mine, and everything sort of happened at once. Linda and Babs were just leaving an exam room, and Babs was tugging down the shirt over her belly. She and Linda spotted Sue and they did a double squeal and raced forward. Sue's joy wasn't faked as she released me and headed their way.

At the same moment, Lucas, Charles, and Ahmad opened the door to an elegant office that I'd seen in my head before when I got a hindsight flashback from Lucas. It was either his office or the person who owned it had remarkably similar taste in furnishings. They spotted me and Lucas twitched his finger for me to join them before entering the next room over to grab another chair. But Amber stopped me before I could reach the room. "I need to check you over before I remove the shield over Sue." Lucas started to protest, but she raised a hand to stop him. "No. This is medical. It comes before enforcement and you know it. I'll be five minutes. No more."

Then she walked away and expected me to follow. Sometimes it's better to go with the devil you *don't* know, so I tagged along after her.

I'd never actually been examined by a Sazi physician when I was *conscious,* so I didn't quite know what to expect. She wore a stethoscope, but apparently it was ornamental. Instead of tucking the pieces in her ears, she just placed a hand on my chest. A weird sensation flowed through me. It wasn't erotic by any means, but it didn't really hurt either. "Okay, so am I supposed to cough or something?"

Amber let out a frustrated sound. "You're supposed to stay quiet, so I can listen." I shrugged, still not sure what she was listening *for.* After a few seconds, she moved her hand to my forehead, like she was feeling for a temperature. The same weird sensation made my scalp tingle. Several smart-aleck remarks like *So, do I feel as hot as you look?* came to mind, but I kept them to myself. She didn't seem like she was in a mood for banter.

She blew upward to move the red-gold hair from her eyes in a practiced motion. "Look, I know you're getting frustrated that I'm not talking, but I told them five minutes. Charles is testy enough today without me wasting their time. I just need to be sure that you're capable of doing what they want before I let you go talk to them. But you seem remarkably healthy for a three-day. Most aren't as sturdy as you seem to be. But Lucas said you were bleeding from the mouth earlier. What was that about?"

I shrugged. "Not a clue. I was here, not there."

She lowered her hand, along with her eyebrows, and leaned against the wall next to the exam table where I was sitting. "Explain."

So I did. It didn't take long. I'm good at brevity. "So I pulled on Ahmad's power to stop the stinging. It worked, but I don't know if it screwed up your ritual. She seems fine, so I'm guessing not."

"Actually, she's better than fine, which has been confusing all of us. Her healing ability has gone through the roof, her blood seems to have similar magical properties to a Sazi, and she's had a slight change of personality—for the better. More confidence, stronger will, more cheerful. You have second sight, right? Did you by chance notice if she has an aura?"

Did I even look? No, surely I would have remembered that. "I was paying a lot of attention to her appearance, so I definitely would have remembered. She didn't."

Amber nodded. "I'll have to think about what you did, try to figure out how it changed what we were attempting." She scrawled some illegible notes on a pad and then tucked the pen behind her ear. "Okay, I'm willing to give this a try. But I want you to call me *immediately* if you start to feel strange or if you can't remember periods of time."

I considered asking the obvious question about how I could call her to report a loss of memory, if I *didn't remember*—duh. But I didn't, because I was just anxious to try out the new Sue in my head. If one ritual could manage what a year of therapy couldn't I'd be ecstatic.

"For the moment," she added with her hand on the exam room door. "Keep up your shields. Let them down *slowly,* over the course of the next twelve hours or so. I'm going to keep her here, under observation, for another day. I know you'll be elsewhere, but I want you to check in. On the phone, please, and personally. I want to hear *your* voice answer intelligent questions before I release her."

"Particle physics or simple chaos theory? Will I have to study first?" I couldn't help it. She left herself wide open.

She wrinkled her nose, making the few freckles scattered on it more obvious. "Cute. Let's just stick with your name, the date, the current president—that sort of thing. We can always make it more challenging later if you think you're up to sparring with me."

"Can I answer the last president instead? It's less painful."

She just rolled her eyes. "I think you're fine for now. Just don't try to remove your shields until after they're done talking to you. You'll need your full attention for that. I don't want you distracted. If you decide you want to go ahead with their plan, we'll talk more."

That got me curious, so I skipped any more banter and just nodded. We left the exam room and I headed down the hall to the closed door where they were waiting for me. But a whispered, "Psst. Mr. Davis?" made me turn my head as I was passing one of the room doors.

It was Liz. She was dressed in a hospital gown, but it wasn't one of the ones that tied in back. It was more like a caftan or housedress, so she was fully covered. "Yes?"

"A couple of people were talking and I think I heard that you were once just a regular human, like me. Is that true?"

I nodded and walked a little closer to her room, but

made sure to stay well out of range of what might be considered improper. Yeah, she might be of age, but she still felt like a kid to me for some reason. Maybe it was her scent, which was similar to baby powder with cornstarch, or maybe it was that pearlescent pink aura. "Yep. You heard right. I was attacked by a werewolf and got brought over to this by force. But that's not quite like you. You actually have the genes. You just didn't turn until late."

"But I've never known any other life. This is all confusing me, and I don't know what to expect. What's going to happen to me when the sun goes down?" She didn't smell afraid, per se. More curious and a little excited about the prospect of something entirely new.

Wow. I didn't know if I was the right person to answer that question. "Geez, Liz. That's a tough one. It's different for every person. But for me, it hurts. Shifting forms hurts a lot. But then, I'm not one of the powerful ones. I think you are . . . or will be. For alphas, it doesn't hurt at all. They just think about it and it happens. No fuss, no muss. After that, you'll do what your animal *wants* you to do."

She was nodding, taking it all in. I couldn't imagine why she'd trust me, except that I tend not to lie . . . except when I do. But there was no reason to lie right now. "That's the toughest part, because animals don't have morals or regrets. You'll find that things seem very simple when you're in animal form. You have a need, you fill it. But it's the memories you have to deal with— especially if you wind up an alpha. I think I was happier not remembering the stuff I did. I didn't for the better part of a year, before I met my wife. Mating with her made things a lot better, but more difficult too. But I was always a hunter, so stuff hasn't bothered me as much as it does others. Like, can you look at a packet of hamburger in the store and think about, really *think about* where it came from?"

Liz shrugged and leaned against the doorway, tucking one bare foot behind the other. "Sure. I grew up around ranchers. I've watched the slaughter process. It's not pretty, but it's necessary." No black pepper, so she wasn't fibbing.

"Then you'll do better than most. The thing is, you're going to have to keep an open mind and not blame yourself for things you do while you're learning how to control yourself. If you really did take out the water tower . . . and it's a good bet you did, you can't beat yourself up. Even if someone dies in the process. That's the real trick with all this supernatural stuff. Things die so we can live." I put a gloved hand on her shoulder. "You come to terms with that, and you'll be fine."

She looked at me for a long moment, deep in thought. "And you really were a hit man? You don't seem the type. You seem . . . *normal,* and pretty smart."

I couldn't help but smile, even though it was probably darker than she expected. "I am. Both. Most of us tend to look normal . . . average. Someone you'd completely forget in a crowd. And it's not 'were' a hit man. Present tense, kiddo. Always present tense." I ruffled her hair on the way past and caught sight of her in the convex mirror at the end of the hallway. She was staring after me with a cocked head and confused expression.

LUCAS'S OFFICE DOOR was closed, but I could hear the three of them chatting about the weather in various parts of the world as I raised my hand to knock, but I didn't have to. It went silent before my knuckle hit the wood and Lucas spoke quietly. "Come in, Tony."

I walked through the doorway and as I closed it behind me, there was pressure against it that made it hard to close. I hadn't noticed it when I walked through, but apparently there was a shield of magic that swallowed the entrance. It was clear and shimmery, like the finest crystal, but cool to the touch. I'd never noticed that Charles Wingate, the Chief Justice of the council had much of a glow about him, and maybe this was why. It's not that it's not there, I just can't see it. But that's okay, because the other two were bleeding enough energy that it felt like standing next to a generator station. The air felt . . . heavy, thick enough with power to make my skin crawl and burn.

Charles looked just the same, sitting in the chair farthest in the corner. He has that serene confidence of someone who doesn't have anything to prove to anyone. On most people, the tiny dark eyes over a large nose would look odd and out of proportion. But it really doesn't on him. The eyes hold so much intelligence, so many *years,* that you just sort of forget to notice anything else. I'm told that in his animal form, which is a polar bear, he can stand flat-footed and look in a second-story window. I'd sort of like to see that, because it was hard to imagine from looking at him. He's broad across, built as solid as a tank, but he's not all that tall. Maybe six foot one.

"Good to see you again, Tony. How have your lessons been coming?" Charles is the one who set it up for me to train with Aspen. He's another seer, like me and her. I presume his talent is foresight, but he might be able to do other stuff too. Like Lucas, he doesn't give much away.

"We both got interrupted, so we agreed to meet back up after the holidays. But my shields are stable, and I'm able to manipulate a hindsight vision enough to extract information. So, that's something."

He nodded, his hands clasped over his tailored vest like a modern Buddha. A statue with a highbrow British accent. "Excellent. Hopefully you've been of use to Lucas in closing out old files?"

Lucas spoke, his voice filled with dry humor. "He thinks my handwriting on old files was sloppy."

I shrugged and planted myself in the empty high-back chair with tooled red leather upholstery. It put me right next to Ahmad, but there wasn't much I could do about that, and so far he was ignoring my existence as he scanned through a file folder thick with papers. "It is. Tough enough to go through cold cases without having to decipher every other word."

Lucas snorted and rolled his glowing dark eyes. "Next file you work on, you'll get the same quill and ink bottle to work with . . . by candlelight, without a smooth surface. If *your* handwriting's legible, you can complain all you like."

I shrugged again, not disagreeing, but not accepting the challenge either. It was enough that he felt he proved his point, although I wouldn't be at all surprised to find a quill and bottle on my desk, with all my ballpoints missing, next time I sat down. I should probably practice. I'd love to see his face if I could manage it.

"Can we get *on* with this, gentlemen? I have to get back before they have too much time to think or compare notes." Ahmad's tone was unusually respectful.

Maybe it was because Charles was in the room, but I hadn't noticed that it had ever stopped him from being an asshole before.

Lucas waved him on. "This is your show." Then he turned his eyes to me. "Tony, this is your official debriefing of the rescue operation. Just answer all the questions as honestly and completely as you can and this will be short."

I raised my brows. I'd never had a debriefing done before with this many council members. I didn't mind, exactly, but I was getting the impression that there was something big going on. "Are we being taped?" I'm not big on recorded conversations.

Ahmad looked at me like I was an insect that needed to be squished and opened his mouth—probably to say something offensive or insulting. But Charles raised a placating hand. "No. Nothing will be taped. Only the three of us will be privy to your answers. There's also no question of punishment, before you ask. We only need information and it seems to reside strictly in your memories."

He was right. That *was* going to have been my next question, but since we were just chatting, I leaned back and rested my elbows on the cool padded arms. "Fine. Fire away."

Ahmad flipped to the first sticky note tab in the sheaf of papers. "When I arrived on the scene, you were saying you were surprised, and you were looking down at the prisoners being taken to the helicopter. What surprised you?"

I dipped my head in acknowledgment. "First, that there were *two* prisoners—we were expecting one. Second, that the second prisoner was the councilwoman for the raptors, Angelique Calibria. We hadn't been in-formed that she was anywhere in the area. For that mat-ter, we didn't know you'd be there either."

Another flip, another sticky. "And how did you rec-ognize the councilwoman? Had you met her before?"

I nodded again. He, Charles, and Lucas knew full well where and how I met her, since they were there too. But I answered anyway. "Yes. At the winter coun-cil meeting in Chicago. I was working outside security when she arrived and Lucas identified her to me."

The conversation went on the same for the next half hour or so, every question wrapping just a little deeper into the situation than the one before. At last we finally got to the meat of why I was in the room when Ahmad said, "Explain the circumstances that allowed you to see my actions after we parted."

"Not just your actions. Your thoughts and memories too. I *was* you."

He looked sharply at Charles, who raised brows high enough that they shouldn't even be on his fore-head anymore. "Why would you believe that, Tony? Were you able to actually hear him speaking while you were in the hindsight vision?"

I shook my head. "No, no. It wasn't a hindsight vi-sion. It was in real time. That was the screwy part. I don't know . . . maybe it was because I was dying. Maybe it was that weird cave. But I was getting a depth of immer-sion that I've never had before."

Ahmad's voice sounded haughty, but underneath it was a light thread of fear. Something about the situation was really getting to him. For both our sakes, I hoped we could figure out what it was, because I certainly didn't want it to continue to happen. "Tell me something that you couldn't have learned if you were simply eaves-dropping."

My sigh wasn't aggravated. It was an admission that I hadn't a clue where to start. "Tuli called you Rimush, but that was out loud, so that's no good. She was surprised to see you and wanted to know if you were there to claim the right of succession . . . oh, wait. *There's* something that was internal. You were trying to remember what that might mean to her tribe. The Hurnans? Hurrians? Something like that. She got annoyed when you paused and apparently thought you were releasing her from her slavery. You reminded her that you wouldn't have saved her life when you were kids if you were going to release her and that satisfied her. But you were *remembering* some prince-and-the-peasant-girl nookie in the back of the kitchen, and—"

"Enough!" The word was sharp enough to cut and I was surprised to see his face darken. Was he actually *blushing*? Okay, this chickie has got some power over the guy. "Very well," he continued, and ignored the carefully blank looks from both Charles and Lucas. "I will accept that you had some sort of access to my mental process. Of course, nothing you saw or experienced during that time will leave this room or I will make sure you never live to repeat it a second time."

"Suits me. Consider it forgotten."

He looked away from me, his eyes strangely uncomfortable. He locked eyes with Charles and struggled to keep his composure, if his aura was any indication. "I suspect it was the cave where I had instructed them to go that aided in the connection. It was once a sacred cave, and numerous rituals were done there. Perhaps some residual magic activated his hindsight in an unusual way."

"That wouldn't surprise me." I was starting to re-member the other bits of the dreams I had. "Part of the vision involved shifters in furs walking through the cave with torches. There was a book they were hiding, and then someone else stole it later. Looked kind of like you, but not you."

Now Charles leaned forward with interest and spoke to Ahmad. "Was this the cave where the second book was hidden? The one Sargon recovered before we could get to it?"

Ahmad looked more than a little surprised. "I didn't *think* so. But we had traced it to that general area, so it's possible."

"Of course," I amended, "the cave's a nice theory— residual magic and all that, but it doesn't really explain the other times."

Apparently, Lucas hadn't mentioned the two times in Kansas, or he forgot, because both Charles and Ahmad nearly came unglued. "What are you talking about?" and "Explain yourself!" came out nearly in unison.

Lucas had the good grace to look embarrassed be-cause apparently he should have remembered. He leaned back in the chair and put a hand over his eyes for a second. "I'd forgotten that, but Tony's right." He paused and then looked at me curiously from under-neath his hand. "But in the restaurant, was that an ac-tual connection?"

"Tough call," I agreed. "But I don't know many snakes, outside of Bobby. I can't figure out any other way that I could have had a flash of knowledge that a cobra named Mustaf gets violently ill from the scent of cherries."

The file folder nearly slid off Ahmad's lap and was

only stopped by him slapping an abrupt hand onto it to hold it in place. "Mustaf Karzad? Is that who you mean? What would *he* be doing in America, much less *Kansas*? The last time I saw him he was working as a policeman in Kabul, Afghanistan."

Lucas shook his head and let out a deep sigh. "Not anymore. Now he's a bounty hunter . . . hiring himself out to the highest bidder to track down other Sazis."

"What?!" Charles was suitably appalled.

"And," Lucas continued, "when I told him Wolven didn't sanction freelance assistance, he was kind enough to remind me that only the *council* could make such a decision, and has requested the right to stand before a full meeting to defend his business. Apparently, he's not the only one, either—which doesn't make me very happy."

The big man in the corner shook his head with frustration written plainly on his face. "We'll have to nip this new kind of *enterprise* in the bud. It will most definitely be an agenda item at the next meeting."

"But back on topic," I interjected because I really didn't want to be here all night, despite the fact that whatever sort of magic Charles had over the area was completely blocking the moon's effect on me. I felt pretty much normal for the first time in a couple of days. "I had one confirmed attachment after the jungle. You were here at the clinic, arguing with Amber about whether to do the ritual on my wife." I paused and looked him right in the eye, but didn't hold out my hand. I knew he wouldn't take it. "Thank you, by the way. I'm grateful for your help, even if you didn't feel she was worthy to live."

He shrugged. "Testing the ritual magic in the text

seemed prudent before we tried to heal the council-woman. A human subject was more expendable."

I shouldn't have bothered. I just let out a small snort and shook my head. "Be that as it may, we should prob-ably try to figure out *why* we're attaching. It had better not be some sort of weird mating thing, because I don't swing that way. You're *really* not my type."

He looked at me for a long moment before shudder-ing in that fluid, wiggly way that snakes have . . . like they're getting rid of an old skin. "I prefer to believe that errant ritual magic may have attached to you for some reason. But either way, it will be useful for our purposes today."

That raised my brows. "And what *are* our purposes today?"

Charles took over the explanation. "We're going to be unusually frank with you, Tony, because we're go-ing to expect your full cooperation. Ahmad has discov-ered a way to infiltrate whatever operation Sargon was planning."

I nodded, and now the conversation at the helicopter was starting to make sense. "Tuli. He's going to play on her affection."

"She remembers him of old, and has no reason to believe that he wasn't working closely with his father."

Ahmad steepled his fingers just under his nose. His eyes glowered a deep red, making it that much easier to believe he's been one of the bad guys all along. "Thus far, I've learned that whatever he was planning involves a pyramid they've discovered near the cave. Tuli was going to take me there, but I told her I had to wrap up some business first, and then I would come down to take over for my father. Unfortunately, Nasil is already there. It will take some effort to get him to believe I'm on their side, so I'm going to have to go undercover."

Lucas offered a little more explanation when he caught my frown. "Nasil was Sargon's right-hand man. You might have met him when he was undercover himself, as Antoine's animal trainer, Bruce. He was actually spying on the council for decades . . . reporting back to Sargon about our movements. But, he wound up deserting Sargon the night Ahmad, Antoine, and Tahira destroyed him in Germany. We don't really know why. It could be he planned to take over the operation and reap the payoff, or he might have switched sides and is actively working to dismantle what Sargon planned, fearing the result. That's what we need to find out."

I threw up my hands, probably looking as confused as I felt. "I'm thinking somewhere in this play is where I step on stage, but so far I haven't figured out my role."

"To put it simply," Charles said, his eyes lightly glowing so that it looked like they were watering. But the magic was so thick it was like seeing his pupils through the bottom of a pop bottle. "You're going to listen in and report back. We need you to be our eyes and ears."

I looked at all three of them, but it still wasn't clicking in. Or maybe I just didn't want it to click in. "Huh?"

Ahmad closed the file folder and finally deigned to look right at me. "They'll search me for wires. I'll be stripped bare and probably be kept separate from the operation until I can establish my trustworthiness. But the one place they can't search me is inside my mind."

Ah. Now the bolt was sliding home. I was starting to think that this was one of those assignments I wasn't really going to like at first. And then I'd learn to hate it. I addressed my concern to Charles, because he was ultimately the one who was going to make the decision. "Not to throw a wet towel on this plan or anything . . . but I don't really have any control about when I attach to him. I can't see how it's going to benefit you."

Lucas nodded, but apparently my concern meant little. "You'll have more control after the binding ceremony."

Binding ceremony? Um . . . so no. That sounded way too dangerous . . . and *permanent* for my taste. "I'm thinking you've got the wrong wolf, gentlemen."

Ahmad's voice was a smooth hiss that made the hairs on my arms stand at attention. He's never liked being told no. Fortunately, though, whatever Charles had done to the room made it so that he couldn't sting me with magic. "It'sss not as though you have a choiccce in the matter."

I shook my head once, firmly. "There are always choices."

"Not if you want to live." He wasn't backing down, but I wasn't either.

I smiled grimly. "That's one of the choices."

Lucas cut in. "Tony doesn't respond to threats well, Ahmad. He's got a similar background to your own, and reacts to pain and death about like you did with your father."

That stopped him cold and it told me more about him than I really wanted to know. "I see. How attached is he to the woman we saved?"

The growl that erupted from me at the threat to Sue made him raise his brows, realizing he'd hit a nerve. But before I could do much more than lean forward, Charles let out a sigh. "That's quite enough. We're not going to threaten him, Ahmad. There's no need. All Tony requires to cooperate is for us to make it worth his while."

I had to shake my head. "Not this time, I'm afraid. I can't think of any amount of money that would convince me to be bound to *him*." I jerked my thumb toward the snake king. I was pretty sure from his expression that if Charles hadn't locked down the room to prevent magic, he'd have sliced and diced me without ever leaving his chair.

"Money's not the only thing we have to offer." Lucas apparently still had some cards up his sleeve, because his tone was enough for me to turn to him with interest. He had his hands clasped on the desk in front of him, with that absolute poker face that good attorneys can manage. "We also have *permission* to put on the table."

That piqued my interest. "To do what?"

Charles also leaned forward slightly and rested an elbow on the desk. "To find out what happened to your old boss. *Carte blanche* to investigate where the trail leads."

I let my body drop back into the chair and tapped a finger on the armrest. It wouldn't do any good to try to hide what I was thinking. All of them could smell where the emotions led and it was even money that one of them could probably read thoughts—though I'd probably never find out which one. "And when I find the person or persons responsible?"

Lucas blinked first, so the permission didn't extend as far as I needed it to go. "Then we'll talk."

Now I shook my head, but not so much that it said

an absolute no. Just enough so they knew that there had to be more in the pot. "Not enough. I have to finish it. I owe Carmine at least that, a dozen times over."

The old wolf merely shrugged. "Then I guess you'll need to turn in a compelling report, with all the I's dotted, so I can justify any *finishing* to the council."

There it was then. I was being offered a sanctioned kill of the men who put Carmine on life support, provided I could make the reason sound legitimate enough for Lucas—the former trial lawyer—to sign off on. And all I had to do was be a tape recorder for Ahmad while he went undercover for—"For how long? How long is this undercover thing going to last?"

"Unknown." That from Ahmad, who wasn't liking this any more than I. "I would prefer to have it over in a week or so, but it's impossible to judge. Obviously, my goal is to only involve you when something critical is occurring . . . a meeting or event that's worth the council knowing. My mental shields are formidable, so I can't imagine either of us will be inconvenienced very often or very long."

So, he didn't want me attached to him any more than I wanted to be attached, and I didn't doubt he had good shields. He's had centuries to practice up. Now it wasn't sounding like such a bad thing. "And if . . . *if* I agree to this, when would this ceremony happen? I've been on four assignments in a row, and could use a day or two break before I start anything. You know, meet and greet with the wife, have a dinner that's not out of a can or wrapper—that sort of thing."

Ahmad shook his head. I was afraid of that. "I must return tomorrow evening at the latest and it's a long flight. If we're to do the ritual at all before I leave, it will have to be no later than tomorrow morning. But tonight is the full moon, and while any ritual would have considerably more power, it would also hold a greater risk, for both me and the healers."

No mention of concern for me. Gee, what a surprise. I just knew this was going to be another one of those things I was going to regret, but—"Okay, I guess I don't have much choice. I don't much like the idea, but so far it hasn't been worse than a hindsight, and I've gotten used to those. Just let me go hunt and I guess we'll do this tomorrow."

He nodded once, about the only acknowledgment or thanks I was probably going to get. "Until then." Before I could even reply, his face was buried back in the file, leaving Lucas to shake his head and Charles to roll his eyes before speaking.

"We appreciate this, Tony. It's vital that we learn what Sargon was up to in the jungle. This might be our best chance to find out without sending in a strike force and risking them scattering for months or years."

Since I'd spent the better part of six months moving from state to state, trying to track these guys down, I wasn't going to argue it was time to find out their plan. "Yeah, he has some real sickos working for him. Glad I never had the displeasure to meet him in person."

Ahmad spoke without ever looking my way. "It would have been a very short meeting. My father loathed wolves."

"And cats, and bears, birds and humans . . . pretty much everything other than snakes was beneath his notice," Lucas added. "But one thing nice about Sargon was that his goal was always simple—snakes should rule the earth, and he should rule the snakes."

Ahmad looked up then and let out a little sigh of frustration, which didn't seem like him. "But as simple as the goal was, the plan to get there was intricate beyond belief, and could easily survive his death. That's why we have to learn what we can, *while* we can. Now, if you'll all excuse me, I need to finish reading this report if Charles is to take it back with him."

That was my cue. It was time to go find Sue and spend some quality time getting to know her again.

"And you and I should talk, Lucas, about this *bounty hunter* business." Charles half stood from his seat and Lucas did the same. He reached for the doorknob to what I presumed was an adjoining office. I didn't think I was invited, so it was time to make my exit out the main door. I only hoped that it wasn't going to be another frantic series of people grabbing at me.

Chapter Nine

PFFT! NO WORRIES about that. There wasn't a soul in the place. I wasn't sure what Charles had done to the room, but when I walked out the door into the darkened, deserted hallway, it was nearly a dozen steps before I could hear again. It was like a vacuum seal popping and then sound returned in a crash of thunder and staccato phone rings behind the nurse station—so loud it made me jump.

Where in the hell *was* everyone?

The steady drumbeat of rain on the metal roof, combined with a second immense boom made me realize the weather had gone to hell. I shouldn't be surprised. I remember someone in Chicago being amazed that the skies were clear because having too many powerful Sazi in one place tended to wreak havoc with the weather.

I got a general sense of joy and contentment from Sue, so I was assuming she was still with Linda and Babs somewhere in the clinic. I started poking my head into doorways but there were no people. What had happened while I was in the room with the others? Another crash through the pounding rain hurt my ears. It occurred to me that the power had probably gone out. Everyone likely retreated to somewhere in the clinic with lights. Most every hospital I've encountered has some sort of generator to keep vital equipment going in critical areas, so I just had to find that place.

The easiest way was probably just to ask, since this was Lucas's stomping grounds. I turned around to go back and check with the others, but the way was barred. I raised my hands and felt around, but all I found was a smooth wall of nothing—like a bird trying to find a way through a plate-glass window. Even when I took off the gloves and tucked them in my pocket, there was nothing to feel. I could *see,* but there was no walking through it. I was also betting they wouldn't hear me knocking even if I did, since I hadn't noticed the storm while inside.

When I reached the nurse station, I stepped behind the desk and looked around on the counter and work area for a note or message for one of us about the situation. But there was nothing. At least, there was nothing until I turned around to the computer station. That's when I saw the smear of red on the keyboard during a lightning flash. My Taurus five–shot sort of appeared in my hand without my conscious recollection of pulling it from the holster at the small of my back. Even as I was reaching to check whether the blood was fresh or old I was scanning the area, looking for a target. Yep, it was still wet, slick, and warm between my thumb and forefinger. I searched around, now looking under the desk, inside cabinets, and behind doors. But there were no bodies, and no other bloodstains.

I moved to the pale cream wall and flattened, moving sideways smoothly. I slid through the shadows where the flashes of lightning didn't reach and used the moments of light to keep watch around me. It might be that nothing was wrong and I'd wind up scaring the shit out of the nurse, bandaging her own nasty paper cut. But better safe than sorry.

Room after room was deserted. It wasn't until I reached the next hallway that I realized just how far Charles's power bubble extended, because the moon struck me with the force of a speeding bus. I dropped to my knees as pinpoints of too-bright magic erupted from my pores. That had never happened before and I could only hope that I was the only one who could see it. The gun clattered to the tile seconds later and my scream became a howl of pain as bone after bone broke and re-formed.

So much for low-key.

It's hard to describe pain that intense. Your mind tries to block it and when that fails, you're pretty much helpless until it ends. Thankfully, it didn't last long, but even a few seconds can seem an eternity. I came back to my senses on my side on the floor. My breathing was labored and I was still seeing stars.

The world became a kaleidoscope of black, white, and a thousand shades of gray. The only colors were the scents that hung in the air like twinkling fireflies. I got to my feet and pulled off the tattered remains of my clothing with my teeth. They would eventually fall off my furred form, but there were still enough seams to prevent easy movement right now, and I needed to be able to move quickly. The ankle holster I'd been wearing slipped right off my leg and I couldn't help but sniff at the gun, taking in the intense chemical scent of oil and residual cleaner. It made me stop to think. It used to be that I'd just move on and not even worry about the mess I left behind, but I really didn't want someone to happen along and find my billfold, keys, and guns. Especially the guns.

It only took a few seconds to find a hidey-hole in a nearby patient room, but it took three trips to get the stuff there. No hands occasionally sucks.

Then it was back to the nurse station. I couldn't seem to remember why I hadn't sniffed around before now. I was a little surprised I hadn't noticed the scent of the blood in human form. In fact, I hadn't noticed any scents at all. Maybe there had been some sort of aversion magic tied in with the bubble around the room. But why would that be different now that I'd changed forms?

Weird.

Still, now that I could sense smells more strongly, I was able to find a trail that led away from the keyboard—tiny droplets that blended in with the red specks in the floor tiles. I could also pick up the lingering scents of the people who'd been here, and the particles of algae and dirty metal made all my senses go to full alert. How the hell could Ricky and Stuart have managed to track me to a private clinic in Boulder—especially when I've been traveling with my appearance altered?

I didn't have any time to mull, though, because the sound of screaming and frantic splashing outside managed to catch my ear over the pounding rain and thunder.

It took only seconds before I was resting my front paws on a window ledge on the west side of the building. I could hear, but it took another flash of lightning before I could see the situation. There was a body lying in the mud. It was hard to tell, but it looked like about the right shape for the nurse, Sarah. But my eyes were drawn toward movement on my right, before I could make a positive ID. Ricky was running like mad away from something, his body moving in that sort of stumbling, sloppy gait that only life-or-death brings. Blood splattered his clothing, which was ripped enough to show skin at thigh and chest. I also noticed he was dragging one leg. Then I spotted what he was running from and I couldn't say that I wouldn't be doing the same thing in his place.

The beast following him was broad and low-slung, but at least thigh-high. It was chasing with a sort of loping motion like a ferret. Each leap forward showed off front claws probably eight inches long and bared teeth to match, if the light wasn't playing tricks on my eyes. But it was the brilliant white stripe of fur that ran up the side of one eye that told the tale.

Liz was loose and she wasn't happy.

In a sudden movement, she leapt into the air and I fully expected that she was going to pounce down on him. But instead she dove downward, her claws leading the way and those short little arms started moving in a blur of motion. Dirt and rocks flew into the air so high it look like a tornado had hit. She was underground quicker than I could follow. While she might be slow and clumsy on the surface, she moved like a dolphin underneath the ground. A smooth line of dirt and rocks appeared as she started to catch up to Ricky. I could tell he was trying to reach something to climb up on, like you would from a pack of dogs. But she was going to catch up with him before he could reach the nearest tree with a limb low enough to swing up on.

Now, I didn't really mind if she killed him eventually, but not until after I did a hindsight on him to find out how they got here. Someone squawked, and loud, or they never would have found their way here from Kansas.

While prudence suggested that I wait until I figured out where Stuart was, there wasn't much time before that burrow caught up with Ricky. Luckily, the Boulder clinic is outfitted with magnetic flaps in the exits on the west side. I refuse to refer to them as *doggie doors*. The nearest one was on the next hallway and I sprinted there as fast as I could, Ricky's screams growing distant as I raced away from him.

Stuart was guarding the door I needed to go out, and it only took one second to figure out why he hadn't already killed me and why he wasn't helping Ricky. The stupid piece of shit was wearing earbuds, blasting some sort of weird techno beat with a Latin edge. He was happily watching the storm from behind the reinforced window, thumping his gun against his leg in time to the beat. I should kill him just because he was too stupid to live, but I really didn't have time to deal with him. Fortunately, I was moving fast enough that I took him by surprise. He dropped the gun and didn't even have time to finish fumbling on the ground for it before I dove for the flap and was outside.

The rain assaulted me and I had to blink repeatedly to stop my eyes from stinging while I oriented myself. I hadn't expected that Stuart would follow me, so when I heard the zing of a bullet past my head, followed by a loud pop, I admit I was startled. I started to duck and weave to make it as difficult as possible to hit me. I had no idea if they'd been instructed how to kill a Sazi, and I wasn't waiting to find out.

I raced after Ricky and Liz, hoping I'd reach them before Stuart managed a lucky shot. It would *have* to be lucky, because so far, he sucked as a shooter. I would have grazed me at least a couple of times by now, even back when I was human.

What I couldn't figure out was where the hell Charles, Lucas, and Ahmad were. Three gunshots should have brought them storming out, which told me that either they were overly confident of the clinic's remoteness, or that damned barrier was just too good.

I reached Ricky's side just as the shooting ceased. Apparently Stuart had to reload. But then Ricky disappeared down into a massive sinkhole that suddenly appeared. His scream should belong to a six-year-old girl.

Crap. What to do? He was trying to climb up out of the hole while Liz's claws raked his back. He started crying openly when she let out a fierce snarl that would do a wolf proud. I didn't dare jump down in the hole because she'd have me for dessert before I could get out. But I also couldn't turn back because Stuart had finally reloaded on the fly—unless I killed him, and I really needed him alive. Of course, that didn't mean I couldn't take off his shooting hand. *One Paw Prezza* had a certain ring to it.

Hungry. Meat close.

Double crap. Apparently, the real problem was that the scent of Ricky's blood was finally getting to me. My vision started to bleed red and my human mind was having blackouts. I bared my teeth and didn't even realize it until I felt rain splattering on my gums. Or maybe it wasn't rain. Maybe it was drool.

Pain erupted in my shoulder and I howled . . . not in pain, but in triumph. I realized I was several feet closer to Stuart and he was afraid. Thick Chinese spices roiled over the rain, turning the very ground into a pool of spicy flavor. He was standing his ground, which wasn't bright of him. His little pop gun couldn't help him anymore. He was shaking too hard to aim it.

I advanced again as the skinny human in the pit screamed once more. He was afraid too and that was good. But he was the little bear's food for now. The big one was mine.

Shit, shit shit! I really had to get help out here—not so much to protect me from Stuart, but to keep me from eating him. I don't eat humans.

No matter what Amber said, I had to get word to them inside and the only thing I feared would work was a direct call to Lucas's private phone, which was a landline. I didn't *think* it would be affected by magic like digital systems were. Sue had called him here more than once to talk over bookkeeping questions, and she was really good at remembering numbers.

I flung open the door between my mind and Sue's, then threw myself into her body. She was in a restaurant, a nice one with paneled walls covered in heavy satin drapes. I grabbed onto her mind and spit out what might well be the last human thoughts I had. Call Lucas! West side of building. Assassins. Liz is out and so am I. Losing . . . the fight.

I could feel her lips move, hear the words come from her mouth. Linda dropped her knife and it hit the plate with a clatter, spraying bloody juices across the nice white tablecloth. Babs immediately reached for her purse and, I hoped, a cell phone. But then I couldn't see anymore. The normal spark when our minds meet flickered and then caught fire. Red and black flames crackled over my brain, and then were joined by golden and white light. The pain was sharp and immediate and made me lose the little bit left of my senses.

The human went down in a tangle of limbs. Another flash of pain came from my back leg and I yelped. But I bit down hard and felt a satisfying squish as my teeth sunk home into warm, fragrant meat. It tasted bitter, but I was too hungry to complain.

The prey threw me off and scrambled to his feet, his shoulder dripping, sweet and red. The scent filled me, completed me and my growl told him I wasn't done. The roar I heard in response wasn't the metal thing in his hand that spit fire and steel. A white wall of fur filled my vision and then there was a blur before the prey's head disconnected from his body and sailed past me.

I lowered my front legs into a fighting stance. The new bear was big . . . *huge,* in fact. But it was *my* dinner and I'd fight for it.

"Not this one, Tony. Not tonight." The rumble of the voice struck something in my memory, and I struggled to place it. But then something was flying through the air toward my mouth. Something soft, furry, and succulent that smelled like food. I jumped up and grabbed it from the air with my mouth and tasted the sweet flavor of fresh rabbit—much better than the other meat. I dropped to the soggy ground and let my jaws clench down until I heard the satisfying crack of bone. The screams in the pit had ceased too, even though I didn't hear the little bear feeding. Still, she wasn't trying to take my rabbit, so I didn't care.

Tony? Can you hear me? Are you there?

My mate! My mate came to hunt with me. I wagged my tail at her voice and let her taste the rabbit along with me. She was eating meat too—warm deer, and she chewed slowly, both of us savoring the blended tastes.

It took a few moments, but my head started to clear. I really *was* tasting both rabbit and deer, which confused me for a minute. You're eating deer? Where are you?

The warmth of her smile filled my mind and beat back some of the black fire that scorched the edges of my thoughts. I wanted to surprise you. I'm down in Denver with Linda and Babs. They had venison on the menu, so—

"I need you back here with me, Tony. Can you hear me?" The deep rumble I'd heard a moment ago filled the air again, but now I could recognize the voice. I looked up, and up, until I could see a pair of dark eyes swimming in a sea of dirty white. Here, then, was Charles Wingate's animal form. He was the size of a house . . . or at least a good-sized cabin. His feet were so deep in the wet soil that he must weigh several thousand pounds. Yet, that's not possible . . . physics being what they are.

Or was it possible? I can't honestly say I've ever weighed myself in my different forms. Did I have a different weight as a wolf than as a human? If so, where did the weight go? But that was a discussion for another day.

"Yeah, I'm here. Mostly. Thanks for the rabbit. Or was that you?"

He nodded and I could feel air whoosh against my face from the movement. "It was me. Can you use your gift in this form? The man Liz attacked is almost gone. He's alive, but I don't know whether his mind is still there."

Could I get a hindsight vision in animal form? I hadn't a clue. But I stood anyway. My back leg hurt and I looked back to see blood painting the brown and gray fur and a rapidly healing hole. Did he shoot me? I couldn't remember. But I padded slowly over to where the second man lay in the mud. He was lying faceup and really didn't look that bad. But from the red smears on the edges of the hole where Charles had apparently pulled him from, I could imagine what his back looked like. Probably like mine did after Asri ripped me open. I pushed Sue into the background with effort. She tried to help separate us, but it was like the door was stuck open. I try not to force the visions on her, but I might not have a choice this time.

If you can handle it, so can I.

That surprised me, because she was normally really adamant that she not be involved. But it was nice, because I'd really hate to have to tell the nice white bear *no*. He might not be as nice if I did.

Liz crawled up out of the burrow she'd dug and glared at the man on the ground with undisguised anger. Her small dark eyes glittered and she thumped one paw on the ground like she'd rather be digging her claws into him again.

"He . . . hurt her."

"You have a mind." Charles nodded his head and it was just then that she realized he was there. Sometimes something is so immense that you sort of ignore it. But he's hard to ignore once he starts talking in that bass rumble. "That's good. It's all that's saving your life right now. Can you tell me what happened?"

Liz shook her elegant white-striped head and I could see the wheels turning as she tried to figure out how to respond. I could probably hindsight her to bring it to the surface, but she wasn't damaged. Ricky was and he would probably give us better information.

His eyes were closed and his breathing shallow as I put a paw directly on his forehead. Skin to skin works best, but a paw isn't really skin. Still, it was the best I had at the moment. I could only hope it was enough. Normally I try to center people and take them back to the place I need them to be. That's because the most important thing on their mind will be what shows up first. Given no suggestion or stimuli, the *important thing* is usually one of the big four—hunger, thirst, survival, or sex.

I could pretty much rule out three of them in this case. The trick was going to be to get him to think of something *other* than survival. Like how he got here, or why he attacked the nurse, or even why they were hunting me. At first, all I could feel was blinding slashes of pain. The wounds enveloped me, became me, and it took everything I had . . . and more, to step outside of Ricky's injuries to be able to control his thoughts. I honestly didn't know where the *more* came from. I pulled and it flooded into me. I was really hoping it wasn't from Ahmad. He wouldn't be a happy snake.

"Can you see anything?" Charles was trying not to sound impatient, but I did understand the urgency. Ricky wasn't long for this world and we really needed information.

"It's hard to get him past the attack." There was a flicker of motion in his mind when I said that and I grabbed onto the thought like a lifeline.

It began to replay in my head and I threw more magic at it until the thoughts made sense to my animal mind. I was thinking differently, and that wasn't helping matters. My wolf mind kept trying to take him back to his last meal . . . another of the big four. I needed a time between the major events of eating and dying. He kept coming back to the sensation of claws in his leg, teeth in his side, when . . . when—

Flight, run. Run from where? Water, storm, voices yelling. Yes, there. Start with yelling voices.

And suddenly the picture cleared. I was in Ricky's body as he entered the clinic. Sarah was sitting at the nurse station and she was immediately alarmed. Of course, Ricky couldn't know that she would know every person who walked in the place. "Okay," I said out loud and presumed Charles was listening, because I could only see what Ricky was seeing. "I'm in. They'd made plans to pretend to be friends of one of the patients. But Sarah confronted them immediately and told them to leave. She reached for the phone. He—" I felt Ricky reach into his pocket but it wasn't a gun that flashed into his head. "Hmm . . . sharp. Round. He flicked his wrist and then she was coughing. Oh!" I would have slapped my head if my legs would have bent that way. "Throwing star. She reached up to pull it out and then started to fall backward so she grabbed the keyboard. That's the blood I found."

"Go on," rumbled the big guy, even though I couldn't see him. But at least I knew I wasn't talking to thin air. He was listening. I concentrated, trying to sense what he was thinking and feeling and trying to keep him alive long enough to reveal what I needed. His heart was trying to stop and I'm not a healer, or a doctor.

"I don't have much longer. I have to speed this up. Hang on." I pushed forward, which is usually a bad idea. Point A to Point B isn't always a straight line. Fortunately, in this case it was. "Stuart grabs the woman before she hits the floor and they carry her to the back door. Ricky's going to go dump her body in a hole he saw out back and Stuart was supposed to keep watch for Giodone—for me."

Why? C'mon Ricky. Give me a reason. But he wouldn't turn backward. All I could do was keep moving forward and hope I learned something. "He passed a series of window wells and heard growling coming from one of them. But there were bars and he didn't see a door, so he didn't worry." His arms started flopping and I realized the nurse wasn't dead yet. She was starting to struggle. Now I understood what Liz had meant. "Sarah started to struggle and he hauled off and punched her in the temple. It was in clear sight of the window wells."

I could hear Charles in the background asking questions at the same time that Ricky was remembering a rumbling sound underfoot. "Did you witness this man hitting Nurse Franklin?"

"Yes." Her voice was steadier now. Maybe she'd figured out the talking stuff all on her own. Another good sign she'd be alphic. "Hurt her." She let out a hissing growl. "Not supposed to hit women."

Well, I couldn't disagree and in her altered state, I understood why she attacked. I'd paused Ricky's memory, but it was starting to fade at the edges. He was nearly gone. I figured I'd better speed it up so I had some memory of the events. "Going to have to go internal now so I can play this out. You guys have fun chatting."

I let loose the figurative reins and I was suddenly along for the ride as Ricky played out his final minutes again. The ground rumbled underfoot and it was hard to keep his balance all of a sudden. He dropped the woman and pulled his gun, spinning around like I would, looking for a target. The speed that the hole opened was astounding and then Liz was on him with a shout. "You hurt her! Asshole!"

Wow, that was pretty good for her first words, if they were, in fact, her first. It occurred to me then that she'd tunneled out from the basement. I'd visited once before with one of the former residents, and had gotten the grand tour. The basement was composed of individual concrete cells with silver-clad doors and alarms on the doors and windows. They're normally only used in case of feral turns or as makeshift jail cells. I was starting to see the scenario that happened. Sue begged to go to dinner with the girls and Amber probably let her go with the condition that she call in if she felt anything weird . . . the same orders she gave me. Then Amber probably went to hunt and took the local healer with her. I remember the girl saying that she wasn't hunting with the pack anymore, since they kicked her best friend and uncle out of the pack. That left only Sarah watching Liz, but Amber probably wouldn't have allowed that, unless she was in one of the cells. I was betting she was in the second cell. I seem to remember that one was unusually plush— wide-screen television built into the wall, kitchenette, recliner, and a double bed. The animal side wouldn't care, but the human half would appreciate the comforts.

I witnessed the chase again a second time, from Ricky's point of view. But what surprised me was that it wasn't Liz who put him in this state. Oh, she tore him up pretty bad, but no worse than a guard dog might have. And she'd stopped short of killing him. It had been his own hand that had reached into his pocket and pulled out a thin push dagger. He'd closed his eyes, placed it over his heart, and waited. Technically speaking, she *had* pushed him into the dirt wall again, but without claws, and he was holding the blade. Oddly, it wasn't because she was slicing him up. He had no fear of being eaten alive. It was because he feared he would live and wind up in jail because he couldn't run. The memory faded at the edges. Little pixels of the last sight he saw froze and dissolved as he gave one last shuddering breath and died. It was an earthworm wiggling in the dirt. Ironic, that. "Okay, verdict time. He killed himself. Case closed."

Charles swung his shaggy head my way and peered down at me. "Pardon me?"

I let out a short bark when my eyes focused again. It's really hard not to laugh when you hear a massive polar bear excuse himself with a British accent. Sort of an *America's Funniest Supernatural Videos* moment.

"He killed himself." I repeated it and then tugged his shirt aside with my teeth to reveal the narrow hole that could have been mistaken for a claw hole if not for the hindsight. "Check the bottom of the hole. You should find a bloody push knife with a wooden handle that he used to stab himself in the heart. He probably would have recovered if not for that. He didn't want to go to jail. Just that simple."

Liz blinked at me with those little brown eyes and

then looked down at the dead assassin. "You're not lying, are you?"

I shook my head. "I never lie about this crap. It's not worth the pain. Everybody can smell it and punishment is rough on the body."

Now she cocked her head, and the straight white lines of fur down her neck turned to zigzags. The pretty pink aura was quite striking with the black and white of her fur. "So I really didn't kill him? I was actually doing okay with it, but I like it better that I didn't."

It was worth repeating in front of witnesses that mattered . . . like Charles. "You really didn't kill him. And you protected the nurse." I turned my nose toward where the nurse had been, only to find her gone. Then I looked at the white bear and got a face full of rain for my trouble. "Will she live?"

His shoulders twitched, which was the equivalent of a foot on a normal scale. Another lightning strike shook the ground and raised my undercoat to attention. Yow. That one was close.

"Difficult to say. If Amber returns from her hunt in time, she should. I've tried to convince her to take a Bluetooth along on hunts, but she says things clipped to her ears are distracting. So all we can do is wait and hope. I have no healing ability to speak of and Lucas is likely . . . past his reserves."

That reminded me. It wasn't like the Wolven chief to not be in on this sort of action. "Where *is* Lucas?"

Charles sighed and turned away from the pair of dead bodies. We'd have to clean them up later, but for now, I was curious enough to follow him. "It should be safe to go back in now, but stay away from any viscous wet spots you might see on the floor or walls. Ahmad seems to have gone bloody insane, and Lucas has been trying to keep him from killing us all."

I TRIED TO decide whether I should claim any involvement in that, but it would probably be better if I kept quiet until I learned more. Charles's scent wasn't giving me any impression he was blaming the connection I'd mentioned earlier, so neither would I.

A powerful scent was coming from inside the clinic as we approached the doorway. Liz stopped cold in her tracks and reared back her head, clearly unwilling to go farther. I couldn't really blame her. It was a noxious blend of chemicals, but I couldn't identify any individual scent that told me it was dangerous. Yet something in the back of my wolf brain knew it was.

Charles listened at the door for a long moment and I tried to tune my ears to hear whatever he was listening for. I could hear hissing, like a broken steam pipe, and something that sounded like a whole wad of jingling necklaces. "Good. It should be safe now. I understand if you'd rather not come in, Elizabeth. I can't guarantee your safety if you do. But I would like you to come inside, Tony, and see if there's any possibility of a hindsight to tell us what happened to him."

I wasn't really sure I liked the idea of doing a hindsight on someone who might have gone insane. That could be a maze I wouldn't be able to find my way out of. But right now Charles was *asking*. I saw what was left of Stuart Prezza's neck and those bear claws weren't to be taken lightly if he decided to insist.

Charles went through the doors first. I couldn't go with him because he took up the entire space. When the doors finally closed behind him I eased inside only to find that he'd changed back to human form and had either put on a suit and tie lickety-split, or was completely nude and only looked like he was wearing clothes. I didn't particularly care either way but I thought I should warn him. "The girl can see through illusions. That okay with you if she wanders in?"

He looked at me, startled for a moment, then held out a hand to stop me and pointed down. "Careful of the venom. Don't move until I come back."

He disappeared into an adjoining room and I got the chance to look around. I saw what he meant. The clean painted walls and floor weren't so clean anymore. The place looked like a hundred years had hit it—just without the cobwebs. There were holes in the surface now, but not like someone had put a fist or knife through the drywall and marble tiles. No, it was more like they'd . . . *melted.* Pockmarks were scattered all over, like someone had come in and sprayed acid with a super soaker.

Moments later Charles came back to where I was standing, wearing pale blue hospital scrubs and carrying a second set. I shook my head in disbelief. "Jesus . . . and this is from Ahmad? Are all the Sazi snakes like this?" Because suddenly I wasn't really liking the idea of confronting a bunch of them in New Jersey.

He shook his head. A line of magic began to flow from him and wrapped around me. It felt different than when Lucas shielded me—like the finest, thinnest leather versus rawhide. But it didn't change the fact that all of my skin and bones needed to fit back in their original shape, and it still felt like being swarmed by wasps. I keep hoping it'll get better with time, but I'm betting not.

"No. Just Ahmad," he said while I was pulling on

the oversized cotton pants and pulling the string tight. "He gained some unusual powers during his father's death. Most Sazi venom burns and is highly neurotoxic, but unless it's injected through a bite, it's like scalding water, not acid. This is new. Lucas said he was prepared, but I admit to being a little concerned."

The jingling increased to our left just as a female voice came from the distance in the other direction. "Charles? What's going on in here? Where is everyone and why are the lights out?"

He raised his voice until it boomed through the corridors. "Don't come down here, dear, until we have the area secured. You have a patient in Five-B. Sarah was gravely injured. See to her first and I'll call you when we're ready down here."

The footsteps stopped even as we kept inching forward, continually watching the ground and ceiling for venom. There was a long pause and then Amber's steady, determined voice. "Holly can manage Sarah. I'm coming your way."

Lucas's voice made me feel a little more relieved. "It's okay. I've got him secured. But we'll need more chains if we can't turn him back."

Charles sighed and repeated the advice he gave me down the hallway toward where I could see Amber's shadow moving. "Watch out for the venom."

We rounded the final corner and I had to blink a few times before I could come to terms with what I was seeing. I'd seen Ahmad in snake form once on the Wolven training course. He's a king cobra and had the traditional markings and hood—just a lot bigger than one you'd see in the wild. But something about him had changed. He was broader across at the neck than I remembered and the yellow and brown markings had become gold and black. He was thrashing about on the floor, his tail whipping around like an unattended fire hose. But what I found interesting was how Lucas had "secured" him. My comparison to a fire hose was because that's what he was wrapped in. Lucas had not only tied him to the wall with the canvas fire hose from a rack on the wall, but the rack had been devised to drop down and hook to a ring set in the floor. Behind the hose was a set of silver chains that were anchored to some part of the building's structure.

It sort of looked like a dog collar, and maybe it was—considering this was primarily a wolf clinic. But it was high around his neck, just below his fully extended hood. His eyes were glittering angrily and I had no doubt he wanted to spit at all of us. But he couldn't open his mouth past the duct tape. Ah, duct tape. A tool for all seasons and occasions.

"Good Lord!" Amber's voice was shocked and appalled. "What's been going on down here? I was only gone an hour!"

Lucas stepped into the light and I winced. The massive white wolf looked like he had mange. Big honking chunks of his fur were missing and there were reddened welts where apparently the venom had landed. That had to hurt. Even Amber and Charles pulled in a sharp, hissing breath. "An hour can be a really long time some days." He pointed to the floor just before Amber stepped directly in a puddle of the creamy white acid. "Careful!"

That's when I noticed we had a visitor. But I wasn't going to rat her out. Amber rolled her eyes. "I'm immune to venom. Remember? Handy part of being a healer." She stepped forward and went to Ahmad's side.

He looked at her warily, but his tail stopped thrashing. "I'm going to put you into a healing trance, until we can figure out what happened. Will that be okay?"

He nodded gravely and blinked his eyelids closed. I read in a book that most regular snakes don't have eyelids. But the Sazi do. Only they flick upward from the bottom. Weird to watch. Amber's golden light flowed outward and surrounded the serpent. He slumped against the thick silver chains and went still.

Charles turned to look at me and raised his eyebrows when he also noticed that Liz had joined us. "Can you do a hindsight, Tony?"

"Absolutely not. I refuse to allow it." Amber stared him down with hands on hips. "We don't know a thing about what's wrong with Ahmad and they're not even the same species. I'm not going to risk either of their lives until I know more. In fact, I'd rather everybody left the clinic except you, me, and Lucas."

Charles let out a little rumble. "Elizabeth can't be alone tonight. We don't have any cells to contain her."

Apparently, Amber hadn't noticed her hiding in the dark shadows near the doorway. After all, who can resist the call of *don't come down here*? It just screams *ooo, look at this!* "But she *was* in a cell. I put her there myself. Who let her out?"

The big bear let out the equivalent of a chuckle, but it sounded pained. "It's been an *eventful* hour, my love. But for the moment—" He paused and then looked at me. "Tony, why don't you take our car and find a hotel in town with your wife. I don't think we'll be doing the ritual tomorrow, considering the circumstances. But I do think I'm going to make some calls. It's time that Nigel came and collected his relative. I'm not going to have her flying over an ocean without an escort, so he'll have to manage to control his emotions about visiting this country. I'll want you to take her to meet him. After that, you can begin your investigation as we agreed. But if I ask you to interrupt to finalize the other part of the bargain, I'll expect you to comply."

It was hard to argue with that logic. "Have granddad arrive in New Jersey instead of New York to get her and we can kill two birds with one stone."

While I didn't mean for it to come out like that, I couldn't deny it was appropriate.

Chapter Ten

I WAS SITTING in the only recliner in the room, having a scotch, when Sue arrived at the hotel. I could feel her in my head, sliding out of the rented limo, to giving Linda and Babs a quick hug each. I closed my eyes and could see through her vision as she walked through the door of the hotel. She was excited and strangely nervous to be here—and I could see why.

She'd changed.

It wasn't just that she had a little magic in her blood now. The ritual had changed something really fundamental inside her. Her entire thought process was different. Decisions were quick and final, with none of the *what if's* that had plagued her since we'd met. She was reveling in men looking at her, from the valet who tried to peek down her shirt when he was helping her out of the limo, to the doorman who leered instead of smiled. That was closer to a Linda reaction than a Sue one. I wasn't really minding it, but it was startling after having been bumping around in her head for a year.

I heard her arrive at the room, and I didn't move to open the door for her. She should have a key and I found

I was enjoying the anticipation of her arrival too much to end it abruptly. Something that hadn't changed was her scent, which flowed under the door and caught the air-conditioning draft to brush my nose. She smelled of fresh flowers in a summer forest and it was still a scent that pulled at things inside me—made me think of home and permanence. But she also smelled as aroused as the day I met her. The thick, earthy scent made me stare at the door with suddenly tight fingers around the crystal glass, and a rapidly tightening groin.

She slid the card in the lock and I heard it click. The handle turned slowly, in a twitching movement that was nearly teasing. Apparently, I wasn't the only one aroused. The door opened and the image of her, framed by the hallway lights, made me suck in a slow breath. She was wearing an outfit I'd never seen before, and never dreamed I *would* see on her. I hadn't realized the burgundy blouse had buttons and they were now undone to where both milky breasts strained against the fabric and both shoulders were bare. She must be wearing a push-up bra to get the level of cleavage I was seeing. The lowest button was also open, leaving just three buttons holding the shirt on her body. It draped over a skin-tight black miniskirt that hugged every curve and revealed just the barest hint of garters. My eyes raked down and down to the shiny patent pumps with the four-inch heels

Oh, baby.

"Hi, lover." Her voice was thick and husky as she stalked forward and I found I had to shift my hips to move the zipper from pinching the suddenly tight skin underneath.

I had to clear my throat and take another sip of liquor

before I could talk. "Hi, yourself. Did you go out like that?"

She smiled with those perfectly matching burgundy lips and nodded. "Uh-huh. You like?"

I'd be lying if I said otherwise. "Oh yeah. I like."

She stalked forward, her hips twitching in time to the throbbing of my dick and when she reached me I started to stand. She didn't let me get that far. Instead, she crawled into my lap until she was straddling my hips, knees bent and tucked neatly into the space between the seat and arms. Her makeup was absolutely perfect, meaning she'd either taken lessons or Linda had done her up. I was betting on the latter, but I might be wrong. Still, when Sue got dolled up, she looked great. When she didn't make the effort, she tended to blend in and be invisible. Completely average, just like me.

"Missed you." She leaned forward and put manicured hands on either side of my face. I'd taken the time to *doll up* myself, meaning that I'd showered and shaved, brushed my teeth, and splashed on some of her favorite musky cologne. She let out a little moan of pleasure when our lips met.

Magic flared with the intensity of a wildfire and I got lost in the sensation of her lips and tongue and hardened nipples pressing against my shirt. I didn't stop her when she reached down and grabbed my hand. We interlocked fingers for a moment and then I got my next surprise. She guided my hand down between her legs and I realized she wasn't wearing underwear under that tight mini.

It took, *Did you go out like that?* to a whole new level. She was sopping wet, slick enough to make me moan. I began to thumb her clitoris and she whimpered around the tongue I had stuck deep in her mouth. She reacted by unbuckling my belt and pressing my erection tight against my stomach to unzip and release it.

This wasn't at all what I had in mind for the evening, but damn, I wasn't about to stop it. My dick jumped out of the underwear so fast it slapped her between the legs and made us both jump. Magic was flowing so fast between us that I could barely breathe as Sue guided me inside her. I shoved my hips hard against her and she arched backward, causing her breasts to pop out of the shirt and bra altogether. The thought that the same thing might have happened out in public turned me on to no end. But then I happened on another new thing. I suddenly realized that I wasn't the only one turned on by it. Walking around nearly naked for other men to ogle her . . . noticing their sudden erections and pretending not to . . . flat got her hot. That was totally unexpected and was really, really not Sue. But it was driving me mad with desire. I grabbed her hips and started pumping into her as she leaned close enough that I could suckle one breast and then the other in rapid succession.

"Tony, *yes!*" She let out a growl from low in her chest and bucked against me as fast as I hammered into her. I could feel the magic building with each squeak of the tortured chair springs until there was nothing but sweat and roiling power and the scent of sexual perfume. She wanted to end it, wanted to climax, but I wouldn't let her. Each time she pushed against me and dug her fingers in my arms, I slowed—held her legs so she couldn't move and rocked so slowly that it was pure torture for both of us. Then I lifted her up until I was nearly completely out of her, with just the barest tip teasing her entrance. She struggled and squirmed, but she was no match for my strength. All she could do was moan again and try to shove herself downward. "God, you're killing me."

I smiled at her and the near panic in her eyes made my heart beat faster. "Beg me for it. Ask me, pretty please, to let you come."

Her shirt was splayed open, framing the heavy breasts, her nipples as dark as her shirt. I could feel the warmth of her juices running down her legs and I wanted her more than I ever had in my life. This game wasn't one to finish lightly.

She paused, realizing as I did, that something new and special was happening. Just to keep the tension going, I dropped her down, burying myself to the hilt and then lifting her off so quickly that all she had time to do was open her mouth in shock and catch her breath before her head flopped back and her fingers dug into my arms.

"Say it, Sue. Beg me to screw you."

She gathered herself together after another drop filled her tight, wet hole. Her head flipped back down, making her dark hair sparkle in the lights. Her eyes were as cold and sure as the ones I've seen in the mirror all my life and it grabbed my gut and made it do flops. The moment turned from teasing to deadly serious and I suddenly realized why. It was in her bearing, in her face, and in the mind that brushed mine. Confident, independent, proud . . . yet still caring and loyal. This was the woman I've wanted . . . the one I've waited for her to become. "Do it. Screw me until I come, killer. Just for you." She paused and caught my smile, only to give me one of her own that was filled with hope and love. The scent of love was unmistakable. It didn't throw away the other scents. It just blended and made our lust more profound. "Always for you. Make us more than just one, my mate."

Reality seemed to shift when she said that, just a fraction. Some sort of weird magic tightened my skin and made all my hair stand on end. I felt off-center, yet clearer headed than I ever had been in my life. Some men want a soul mate, the part they're missing. A yin to their yang. I realized I wasn't one of them. I want two yins, or two yangs, but not half of each. I want a woman who will *share* my soul, not compliment it. Somehow, whatever had happened in that ritual had done what love hadn't, and no amount of therapy ever could. It was more than acceptance, more than need. I sensed a joining that would make both of us stronger, yet allow us to be individuals who could stand alone. Not two halves of a whole, but two wholes who could stand against the world together.

"You got it." I closed my eyes and let myself slide into her body, and into her head. I let her feel the sensation of tight warmth that made my nerves dance, at the same time I felt the intrusion, and stretching, that made our stomachs ache with need.

Now I eased slowly in and out, letting the tension build again. She began to moan and whisper my name. Over and over, in my ear and in my brain, like a mantra that made me want to slip inside her skin and never come out again.

She took control away from me and I let her. She started to rock over me, kept my hands pinned to the chair arms so tight it felt like another Sazi, not just a human. I remembered then what Amber had asked and opened my eyes. No, she didn't have an aura, but how was it her eyes were glowing with a deep emerald fire? I wanted to dwell on that more, try to piece together whatever clues I was seeing, but my body wouldn't co-operate. The intensity of the sensations was too much. All I could do was pull loose from her grip and grab that tight leather-clad ass and pound myself inside her until the rumbling in my stomach became a wave that crashed over me so hard I yelled out loud. The climax was so intense it was like I hadn't had sex in years. Sue followed soon after and it doubled my pleasure, nearly making us both pass out.

It was nearly a minute of pounding hearts and heavy breathing before either of us could talk. I chuckled and gave her a little slap on the thigh. "Anytime you decide to drop by and visit me in a hotel, feel free."

She laughed brightly and leaned back until she could see my face. Then she kissed the tip of my nose. "It'll be more often than before, I assure you. The clothes aren't the only thing that's changed about me."

"I'm starting to figure that out." I let her get off me, not really surprised that her legs were a little stiff and one foot was asleep. I definitely got the better end of the stick on comfort. "I'm up for a shower. How about you? Do you have any other clothes with you?"

Her response started with a sexy, knowing smile that tightened parts of me that should be unable to respond. "I asked the front desk to have my things sent up in an hour. I told him we might be too busy to answer the door until then."

I got to my feet and took her into my arms. "Might be even longer than that. We'll have to see." I kissed her again and let my hands follow the slender curves that might last or might not. I didn't really care about her weight, so long as she was healthy and happy. I pulled away briefly, before my head started being ruled by a different part of my body. "Have them send up food with the bags. I think you're going to need your strength tonight."

The laugh made me smile and she winked as she reached for the phone. "Maybe some whipped cream and chocolate. I've always fantasized about licking whipped cream off a man."

"Hey, it's a night for fantasies, apparently. I'll try to remember what some of mine are. I think one involves a little maid's outfit. But the one you just did has always been a particular favorite."

I started to more to go into the bathroom to turn on the shower when her voice stopped me. I turned my head when she said, "Tony?"

"Yeah?"

Another little smile. "That's why I did it."

Chapter Eleven

I WOKE WITH a frantic slapping of sheets for the third time since Sue and I had finally drifted to sleep. It was still dark outside, but wouldn't be for long. I should feel content and satisfied after a night of having a good number of my fantasies come true—even some of the kinky ones, but instead my heart was pounding a mile a minute and I couldn't seem to breathe right.

I was choking and the more I struggled, the worse it got. Worse still, I couldn't raise my hands to relieve the pressure.

Pain. Bound and in pain. What had I done this time to anger him? I was smelling something that raised old, nameless fears in my head, but I couldn't remember what or why.

As soon as I opened my eyes again, I realized what was happening, even though I couldn't stop it. I could see the tasteful wardrobe across the room, highlighted by the bathroom light that we'd forgotten to turn off. But superimposed over it was a silver door that glinted every time the moon came out from behind a cloud.

I was stuck in the snake king's head again. The sensation of pain at ankle, wrist, and neck, combined with metal tinking and rasping against concrete told me he was probably in cell four. That one has a bed, but also has thick chains—the size you see holding loads on big rigs. They're bolted to the concrete and have a high silver content. Now, silver's not really a strong metal, but it hurts like blazes to a Sazi. Left on long enough, it can scar, and it weakens us pretty quickly. It's not like it saps our magic or anything. It's not Kryptonite. But pain is wearing after a while. It sucks out your fight and makes you easier to manage.

I was frankly pretty surprised they did that to Ahmad, him being a council member and all. But I was also noticing that he wasn't quite in his right mind. It was hard to concentrate on anything but the fear that was pounding his heart. Chains, and the scent of venom was pushing him into a frenzy that was dragging me down into the depths with him.

While I wanted to tell him to get his shit together and relax, that was like telling a little kid there was no monster under the bed. Whatever he was reliving was very, very real to him and I had to figure a way out of the delirium before there was no mind left to save.

Center. Who is hurting you? Maybe if I treated this like any other hindsight, I could pull him out of this. *Show me his face.*

A snake, the jaw open wide to strike, appeared in my vision so suddenly that I slapped out with my hand to knock it away. I had to shake my head and fight off the cold sweat that threatened to make me panic too. Sue was starting to get restless beside me, not quite awake, but nearing it if I wasn't careful. I had no idea what would happen if she woke. We'd tied our minds so tight together over the past few hours that we hadn't been able to shut the door again. I couldn't imagine this would *help* any.

I carefully slid out from underneath the covers and found my way across the room to the recliner. At least I could *try* not to wake her. The snake led me, still fixed firmly in my vision, a monster in the dark.

Maybe it was important to know what kind of snake it was. With the image frozen, waiting the next command from me, I studied it and tried to recall my very basic knowledge of the serpent family. The teeth were long, so I was thinking it was part of the viper family. Hard to tell if the head was triangular from the image, but I could definitely see a deep pit between the eye and nostril, so I was betting it was a pit viper. And, it was coal black with the mouth a pinkish-white. Um . . . a black mamba? Was that a viper?

I was guessing the answer was yes, because the image fast-forwarded, the snake striking fast enough that I couldn't quite separate the vision from reality and backpedaled into the depth of the chair so fast the footrest shot into the air.

The snake can't hurt you. It can't reach you while I'm here. It seemed seriously weird to be telling the snake king that a snake wasn't going to hurt him. But nightmares aren't terribly logical, and I presume that there are bigger and badder snakes than him out there somewhere.

I repeated the words again. It took a third time before the snake retreated back to the depths of his memory. I felt his muscles start to relax. The chains loosened when he did, and some of the pain eased.

Now he was coming back into his mind and starting to figure things out, but for some reason he didn't know

I was there. Most of my hindsight victims know I'm pulling at their memories. They just can't stop it. But Ahmad really didn't seem to know we were attached.

That might not be a bad thing, because it could be more useful to Lucas than a knowing link where he was in control. There wasn't much to see right now, since he was just figuring out where he was. Bits and pieces of memory were still there, from meeting with the new wolf (me) and then having a severe headache soon after he left. But the cause of the abrupt pain that had driven him past the point of sanity was a mystery. Ahmad lifted one arm, then the other, and yanked on both simultaneously with as much strength as he could muster. The wristbands and chains stretched but held. The pain the silver produced wasn't as bad as the headache had been but wasn't worth repeating, either.

What part had been reality? Had he truly attacked both Lucas and Charles and tried to destroy the clinic? For what purpose?

Still, judging by the number of chains on me, the up-stairs must be quite a wreck.

It was dark outside if the image through the bars could be trusted, but was it even the same day? *Have I missed the one opportunity to infiltrate the Order, or is there still time?*

The superimposed cell in the darkened hotel room was odd, but try as I might, I couldn't shake the image from my brain. Ahmad thought about calling out to see who answered, because surely, with this level of security, there would be someone standing watch. But to what end? Amber might be considering whatever Angelique had to be contagious . . . and who was to say it wasn't? No, it was better to try to get some sleep for now, despite the discomfort of this horrible slab of concrete. Morning would come too soon and there would be questions to ask on both sides.

As Ahmad let his mind drift, mine starting working overtime. Where had Angelique *been* during the whole episode? Was she back to normal and released? Was she unconscious, or even dead? I hadn't thought to ask, which wasn't very bright of me.

I'd also like to find out more about this *Order* that Ahmad was thinking about. It might be that he simply didn't know and was flying blind, or he absolutely knew I was in his head with him and was feeding me misinformation.

He's sort of like professor Snape in my way of thinking. He might be trustworthy, but he's definitely suspicious and it might not take much to turn him. Frankly, if he was in Carmine's group, I'd suggest sending him far away from anything important or sensitive.

Of course, thinking Carmine's name got me back to planning my strategy for New Jersey. I needed to decide how to approach the whole thing. Not only was I a persona non grata in the state by the mob, but I was also wanted by the cops and presumed dead. I could take Bobby along to do the illusion thing on me, but he's too well known as my normal partner in crime. It might be better to simply try my hand at a disguise. I used to be pretty good at makeup and hair coloring. Going back to basics might be just the trick to fool a bunch of snakes. Then the only thing left would be my scent. There was no mistaking I was Sazi . . . or *was* there?

I wondered if there was a way to actually start a conversation with Ahmad mentally, like I could with Sue. It didn't seem like he knew I was there, but I wondered—

Searching with your mind is a lot like standing in a pitch black room with your feet strapped to the floor and trying to find a particular object by bending and reaching to feel around. If you know what you're looking for, it doesn't take long. But when you're just reaching to find out *if* something is there, that's harder. Now, I knew that Sue's mind was there because in my head it was like a bright, warm spot of sunshine through a window. But if Ahmad's mind was out there, it was either hidden or dark by nature.

Of course, about the time I gave up and decided to go back to bed, I fell through the looking glass with a suddenness that took my breath away. The hotel room disappeared behind the new reality of concrete walls and a silver door that was sparkling around the edges.

No, wait. Not sparkles. *Sparks.*

I could smell metal burning. Someone was using a freaking welding torch to cut away the hinges of the door. Either someone upstairs forgot the combination to the high-tech lock I knew was outside, or something really interesting was about to happen.

The scent and bright light brought Ahmad fully back to his head. He began to carefully spit toward his hands, which seemed a sort of strange thing to do under the circumstances. Except . . . ah, I realized what he was doing. He was cutting apart the bindings with his own venom. Pretty slick.

But he apparently hadn't had anything to drink since they brought him down here, so spit was in short supply. Still, he was able to get enough onto one bracelet and the other chain that he was able to pull them apart and sit up before the cutting stopped.

I was curious to see what the visitors would do next, since the door wasn't made of balsa. It was meant to withstand a feral, insane, magical creature of unknown ability. Raven and I couldn't manage it alone when I visited, and he's one of the more powerful alphas.

Whoever was on the other side of the door was no lightweight either, because dark-skinned male hands appeared around the bars near the top. The door hesitated and then began to move inward, an inch or so off the floor. Ahmad flicked his tongue out repeatedly, trying to catch the scent of the person through the scorched metal. Just before the door swung to the side, he apparently did and his reaction was telling.

I was catapulted inside Ahmad's head, no longer an outsider watching, as I felt our tongue frantically move around in a dry mouth, trying to find enough fluid to make the venom sacs work. If Nasil found me helpless and in chains—

But it wasn't the man I'd spent my entire existence loathing and fearing who first came through the door.

I felt my brows raise and a hoarse croak that hurt my throat. "Tuli?"

Her entire face lit up and her taste was filled with both relief and joy. It carried over to the word that was barely loud enough to hear. *"Rimush."* She flung herself at me so fast that all I could do was catch her so I didn't get knocked onto my back. Her lips were on mine before I could react and the taste of her sweet, almost salty venom was enough to make me clutch at her arms desperately. No. I had to push her away before I took leave of my senses the way I used to in the palace. She hissed from the sting of the silver in the cuffs and looked down at the burns struggling to heal at my wrists. She turned her head and whispered. "You see? I *told* you he was a prisoner."

"You did indeed." Now I raised angry eyes and pushed Tuli the rest of the way from me, preparing to fight. Nasil looked just the same, except his hair had grown to shoulder-length, the way he'd worn it for so many centuries. He let out a small smirk that could mean nothing, or everything. His voice was likewise quiet, the tone amused. "It appears you could use some help, my prince."

What in the name of Anu was he doing here? Should I whisper or raise my voice and alert everyone in the clinic? I had to presume they arrived alone or Tuli wouldn't bother speaking softly, so I followed suit. "I hardly need help from the likes of *you*, Nasil. As you can see, I'm nearly free on my own."

He glanced at the solid steel-and-silver door, still smouldering lightly from the torch cuts, then raised a brow at me. "Oh, without question, *my lord*. Shall I return the door to its place so you may escape under your own power?"

"Stop it, both of you." Tuli was in no mood for our banter, which was reasonably friendly at this point. There was no purpose antagonizing him until I had full freedom of movement. He was too fast and too deadly to risk that. "Of course we're going to help you, my prince. It's why we came."

It *was*? But that journey takes nearly a day, and I haven't been back long enough for anyone to grow concerned. Or had it been longer than I believed? "I've only been gone a day. I told you I would return in several."

Tuli blushed and stared at the floor, which confused me. I thought at first that the traitor Nasil wasn't going to answer me, but he raised that single brow again—probably because he knew how much I hated it. "We left only a few hours after you did. Tuli seemed to believe it was critical we reach you before . . . something happened. I have to admit to a certain amount of surprise we found you in chains. It does seem to support Tuli's . . . *feeling.*"

I stared at her, but she wouldn't meet my eyes. That wasn't like her. "Explain."

I reached out to grab her arm to make her look at me but she slipped out of my grasp with a speed I hadn't known her to have before. "We really don't have time for discussions, my lord. We have little time to get you to safety before they find the cat."

Had they harmed Amber? Charles would tear the world into bite-sized pieces to find them . . . and *me* if they had. "What have you *done,* Nasil?"

He was busy dripping a strong chemical acid on the cuffs on my ankles, and looked up at me with the sort of disdain I expected from him. "Please give me *some* credit, Ahmad. Do you really think me foolish enough to kill anyone here—much less Charles's *wife?* I merely hit Amber with a tranquilizer. But I only used enough for an elephant-sized target, so we probably only have five more minutes before a healer of her stature wakes up. And she'll have a nasty headache, which won't make her a pleasant kitty to encounter if she discovers us walking off with a Wolven prisoner."

Nasil knew Amber nearly better than anyone, so I believed that he'd used a sufficient, but nontoxic dose. He'd been the supposed *friend* of her brother, Antoine, for more than a decade and had been spying on the council for Sargon without my even knowing. I didn't trust him, but I couldn't argue he knew his job.

While Charles would no doubt be displeased that I left custody, I could think of no better scenario for

Nasil to find me in than this one. If I truly had been in league with my father, and Wolven discovered it, I would be in this exact same location awaiting trial before the full council. "I presume you have transportation waiting outside? Are there others with you?"

Nasil shook his head as he pulled apart the two pieces of the inch-thick cuff around my leg with a sizzling of flesh that made us both wince. "We came alone and while we have a stolen car outside to take us away from the complex, we flew commercial to get here. We'll have to figure out some other way to get back before we're discovered."

I couldn't help but smile darkly. It would serve him right for putting me through this level of hell. Nasil looked at me with interest when I swung my legs from the concrete slab and chuckled. "Actually, I may have a solution."

Chapter Twelve

I CAME BACK into my head with a start as the scene went black at the clinic. I couldn't seem to figure out why I kept getting these random flashes, yet had no control over them. Worse still, they were starting to make my head ache like I had a pinched nerve. I grabbed my chin and the top of my head to see if I could get my neck to pop and ease some pressure, but the muscles were too tight . . . probably from Ahmad's struggle against the silver chains.

"Tony? Is something wrong?" Sue's sleepy question was accompanied by an increase in the warm light in my head and it shook away some of the cotton in my brain.

"No, I—" I paused and reconsidered. Sue's a smart woman. More than once she's come up with an answer that had been eluding me. She's been spending a lot of time reading through old records at Wolven headquarters, trying to figure out what was stolen by the mole. "Y'know, actually, yes. There is."

She patted the bed and pulled back my side of the covers. "Come tell me about it."

So I did. The trick was not to let the warm press of her skin against me lull me back to sleep. There's just something about when she's got one leg curled over my hip, with an arm around my waist and her head on my chest that makes everything right with the world and reality fade away. While I really *needed* the sleep, I also needed to decide what to do about Ahmad. I didn't know what his *solution* was and without that, there wasn't much to tell anyone if they asked where he went.

It took the better part of an hour just to tell her the *highlights* of the last few days. "And now I'm back here with you."

"How weird," she said. Her brow wrinkled under the fingers I was using to stroke her hair. "Well, let's go through this. Ahmad thought it might have been the cave that did it, and I've read about that sort of thing happening in some of the really old books I've found. But why you, and why *him*? If it should be anyone, it should be Will Kerchee. That would make sense at least. He's the one you were in contact with in the cave, or even Councilwoman Calibria or the other agent. But *Ahmad*?"

I shrugged, which moved her head and she had to readjust. "Precisely. But it is what it is. I just need to figure out how to make it work for me. You know Lucas and Charles are going to grill me about what happened now that they know I'm in contact . . . even occasionally, and they're not going to let me leave to go deal with my job for Carmine. I have to at least get them started on something."

She let out a slow, "Hmmm" and tapped one fingernail next to my belly button. "What did he think again right at the end? As exactly as you can remember."

That was easy, so I repeated it. "*It would serve him*

right for putting me through this level of hell. But I don't
know who *him* is, so I don't have any idea what it might
mean."

She paused long enough that I felt my eyes starting
to close. But I woke up again with a start when I felt
her smile against my skin. A moment later, a flash of
color jumped into my mind and the scent of triumph
filled the air—sort of like bitter orange marmalade
to my nose. "I think I know, and you've got a call to
make."

A SLEEPY, GRUFF voice answered on the fourth ring.
I was already showered and dressed, which I did while
Sue explained what she believed happened. I tried to
push through an image into Ahmad's mind. I'd managed a sound while I was standing under the hot water,
but no image. Still the loud, whining roar I'd heard was
probably enough to ask the question. "Go ahead."

"It's five A.M., Lucas. Do you know where your plane
is?"

I could hear the confusion in his voice, which told me
that either they'd given Amber a bigger dose of tranq
than they thought, or he hadn't answered his phone from
several earlier calls. "What? Tony, is that you? What the
hell are you talking about?"

He sounded too tired for the long explanation, so I
opted for the short one. "I'm pretty sure Ahmad escaped
the cell in the basement this morning with some help
from Nasil, and is on his way back to the jungle . . . in
your jet."

I could hear sounds of abrupt movement in the background and then his voice wasn't so sleepy anymore.
"Nasil's captured Ahmad? Did you have another hind-

sight from him? Was he . . . lucid when they grabbed him?"

I shook my head as I tried to reach my other shoe where it had bounced during last night's romp. But the landline cord wouldn't reach. Sue noticed and walked across the room to pick it up and hand it to me on her way to the bathroom with a cosmetic bag tucked under her arm. I made a kissing motion at her before I replied. She smiled and winked. "Lucid, yes, but not captured. He went willingly. In fact, he suggested it. I think he's ticked at you for putting him in chains and thought having to track down your plane would serve you right. And I'm still not certain whether to call them hindsights. These feel different. I still think they're real-time."

I could hear tiny little blips over the phone line. Probably checking his cell phone for missed calls. He must have a high-end model. I can't do that with mine when I'm talking on it. "Nobody's called me. Are you certain about this?"

I let out a chuckle. "Oh hell no. I'm not certain about a damned thing lately. But so far, these images have been dead-on, so I figured it was worth calling you. I'm already dressed, so I figured I'd wander back to the clinic with Charles's car to check it out. Thought you might want to come along. Are you in Boulder or Denver?"

"I'm in Boulder, at my house. But I don't want you coming up here. If things went badly . . . no. I don't want you up here."

I pulled the phone away from my face to stare at in disbelief, like I could make him see my expression if I just looked hard enough. "Afraid I'll faint at the sight of blood? Uh, *hello?* Besides, I've got Charles's rental.

I presume he's going to need it if I'm *wrong* about the vision."

He paused and then sighed. "Fine. Bring the car back. Maybe you can help figure out what's happening. But leave Sue there where it's safe."

I couldn't disagree, but apparently Sue did. She walked up, hand on hip, and motioned for the receiver. She could hear him talking from across the room? That was new. I shrugged and handed her the plastic handset and backed away.

"Lucas, it's Sue. Look, I appreciate the thought, but really . . . I'll be fine. I've been spending a lot of time at the Wolven facilities. I've gotten pretty jaded about blood and gore."

That raised my brows. She had? I didn't mind her tagging along, since it wouldn't do any good to say no anyway—I mean, where would she go? But maybe it's not just since the ritual that things had changed. I wasn't kidding about being gone on four assignments in a row. I hadn't been home for more than a few hours in nearly three months, and have been trying to keep Sue out of my head during the interim. Maybe I needed to sit down with her and find out what she'd been up to on this end that hadn't made it into the nightly conversations.

His voice sounded tired and determined. But so was she—the chilled metal scent was stronger than her perfume. "I really think—"

"Don't, Lucas. Don't *think*. I'm growing up, okay? It's a shame it took twenty-six years to do it, but I'm finally becoming an adult. Shit happens. People die. People I *love* die. I can't fix it, I can't help it. All I can do is move on and do my damnedest to be happy. Isn't that the lesson you wanted me to learn?" She didn't wait for a reply, and I was amazed and proud of her for it. I found myself with arms crossed over my chest, staring at her with brows raised and a smile on my face. "So, yeah. I'm coming up. Whether or not Tony does. There'll be things to do whether Ahmad is there or not. 'Cause like it or not, that's what I do now—clean up messy things that nobody else wants to, because they have to get done. So see you soon. Bye." Sue hung up on him and it made me laugh. She wasn't shaking, she wasn't near tears, nor angry—so my laugh just made her turn her head as she was putting down the phone. "What?"

I raised my hands symbolically and clapped lightly. "Attagirl. But I probably ought to ask if you're planning on telling *me* to go to hell soon too?"

She looked at the phone, and the air was suddenly filled with the flurry of conflicting scents that confusion brings. "I didn't tell him to go to hell."

I took the two steps over to her and touched her face lightly. "Not in so many words, but yeah . . . you did. It's okay, and even though I admit I'm surprised, it's been needed. I probably deserve to have it said to me too. I've been keeping you out of the shit I do, and haven't even bothered to ask whether you *want* to be kept out." Whatever was waiting at the clinic could wait a little longer. I motioned toward the bed and sat down, reaching for her hand to have her do the same. "So, what *do* you want? I'd like to think that my life will be settling down soon, but I honestly don't see that happening. If anything, it's going to get busier. I'm afraid you're going to wind up alone more than I'd like, but short of flipping off the council and disa-damn-pearing to parts unknown, we don't have many choices. If this ritual really did work and you're going to stay healthy, what does Sue, Version Two-point-oh, want out of life?"

She looked a little taken aback. "Out of *life?* Wow. I can honestly say I haven't thought that far out. But I'm a little surprised that *you're* surprised. How could I not grow up? It was like throwing a pet dog into the wild to live with wolves. It learns to survive or it dies. I've been really grateful to all the people I've met at Wolven. They're really good people, Tony. Dedicated and hardworking, fearless and tireless . . . a lot like you. They're just amazing. It's hard to be afraid of *anything* when they're around. Serial killers? No problem. Terrorist threats? Piece of cake. Feral new turns? All in a day's work. Yeah, they come back bloody and exhausted, but they still manage to train and do paperwork. There really isn't much bookkeeping to do on a daily basis, you know. It's all on the computer and once I started to sort out all the inconsistencies and fix them . . . well, that took about two weeks. It's been ten months, so I've had to figure out other things to do. I know Lucas just took me on as a kindness, but I've really been trying to be useful, so I've sort of turned into an all-around secretary. Do you know how many reports I've had to Wite-Out splatters of blood and run them through the copier just so you could *read* them . . . including yours? How could I *not* learn from people like that?"

I listened, really *listened* to her ramble, because I really hadn't thought much about the other half of the business, or what she's been doing. Of course there have to be copies, and of course they have to be semilegible. The council members are demanding SOBs, which must mean she'd been busy.

She smiled and squeezed my hand. Her scent was a blend of everything good in the world and it made me return the squeeze. "Lelya in Chicago has been great as a sounding board, but Tahira has really been the terrific one to get to know. Even though she came over from blood, she was nearly an adult when it happened. So she started out a lot like me—human and clueless. Plus, we both wound up marrying tough guys who don't always talk about what they're going through. One night when we were alone and I was sorting out a bunch of files Lucas brought by, we sat down and started going through the cases you guys have worked on. It wasn't hard to read between the lines and combine the careful language with the little bits you've told me on the phone, and the bits when I got sucked inside you during a crisis. I've started to figure out what you're going through out there." She paused for a long moment and looked at her lap, her fingers nibbling on themselves, then tapping on her leg, her scent filled with indecision. I realized it wasn't that she didn't know *what* to say, but wasn't sure how I would react to it.

"Go ahead," I urged, because I really did want to hear it. Behind her, the sun was starting to light the horizon. The mountain backdrop and flickering streetlamps reminded me of our first conversation, in another hotel room far from here. But neither of us were the same people anymore, and I was thinking that was a good thing.

"I'd like to start doing fieldwork. I really think I'd like that."

Okay, I wasn't expecting *that*. "Fieldwork. Like as a Wolven agent?" She nodded and I had to draw in a sharp breath. I raised a hand to rest against my mouth and chin while I thought and let out the breath slowly.

"Wow. Um. I can't imagine that *anyone* would approve that, even if I did. Hell, they don't even like *me* working on cases because I'm a three-day. You're full human. You'd get eaten for lunch out there, sweetheart . . . *literally*."

She wasn't deterred though. Her scent wasn't disappointed or even afraid, still just determined. I couldn't decide what I thought about it. The wolf part of me was terrified, because she was my *mate* and could die. The old mobster in me was proud of her for asking, but still chauvinistic enough to want to say no . . . like Carmine would say no if Linda wanted to start running part of the business. Qualified or not.

And . . . like he'd probably said no when she wanted to order the hit. I'd have to talk to him. I knew that now.

Her voice stayed calm and sure. Apparently, she'd worked out her arguments long ago, waiting for just the right time to bring it up. "But not every case has needed a heavy hand, or even magic. A lot of them got solved with just information and the person turned themselves in voluntarily."

I held up an amending index finger, because she was only seeing half the picture. "Not quite. The information is often gotten because of the *threat* of the heavy hand that's doing the asking. And the person turned themself in to avoid being tracked and slaughtered."

"Not every time."

I nodded in agreement. "True. But you talk about the agents returning bloody. That's the norm, not the exception, hon. How many scars do I have now compared with when we met? The being-cut-up-with-claws-and-teeth crap never used to happen when I was working for Camine. Now it's nearly every day. How much time do you want to spend in the E.R.? 'Cause a healer's not always available and you won't heal for shit."

Her face shut down and I didn't have to be hooked to her mind to know she was frustrated. It's the opposite of determined, so it smells of hot metal, rather than cold. Sort of like wiring burning inside the walls. "So you're saying *no*."

I waved my hands in front of my face, starting to get a little pissed now. "Whoa, whoa. Don't make me out to be the villain in this play. I didn't say any such thing. I'm only stating the facts. If they don't play nice with the script you've been writing in your head, that's not my fault. I'd love to have you excited about something. Hell, if you want to be a policewoman, go for it. But Wolven? That's like showing up for the Olympics before your first amateur match."

Now her voice turned sarcastic and biting, but underneath it was the scent of sorrow, so I decided to listen really close. "I'm *dead,* remember? Nobody hires dead people. Don't you think I *know* I can't afford to have my background or fingerprints checked? Everything I've ever trained for is in finance, and they do intensive background checks. Every single company. Maybe Lucas fixed everything in my background, maybe not. But I don't dare check, and I would be too afraid to ask him if he did it *right.* Y'know?"

Crap. The reality of that hit me like a blow to the head. It wasn't just that I was stopped from doing my *illegal* job, she couldn't even apply for a legitimate one without going through the meat grinder of the post–9/11 system. "Shit. Look, Sue. I haven't even been thinking about your side of it and I should have. You're not like Linda and I should know that."

She sighed and leaned back against the headboard with a sad expression. "Sometimes I *wish* I could be like her. She can spend a full week just shopping and buying things, or lazing around the pool reading book after book. If she wants to start a new business, poof! It's opened, no expense spared and no questions asked by officials at any level. If it folds, then it's, 'Oh well. No great loss.'" She shook her head. "I just can't do that. I have to *do* something, and I want it to have meaning. Wolven has meaning. It's important . . . agents stop wars and keep people safe. I want to do that, and I think I could."

I was willing to listen, against my better judgment. Maybe this was a midlife crisis, or a near-death experience. Risk taking was pretty common after both. But to deny it now would only make it worse later, and this time I might be able to control enough that she wouldn't die. "Okay, tell you what. Let's go have breakfast downstairs and you can tell me what you have in mind. If there's any possibility of making it work, I'll try to come up with some buzz words that might win you a friend or two on the council to sponsor the idea."

She smiled and leaned forward, all tangerines and cinnamon spice that blended nicely with the vanilla perfume. "I knew you'd listen. Tahira said you'd scream and rant at me and say it was a stupid idea, but that's not you."

No. It wasn't me. Screaming and ranting come out of fear—whether fear of losing control over another person, or fear of loss. I wasn't afraid of either one, so there was no need to rant. I didn't want to control Sue, and I've been struggling with my fear of losing her for a year. Nothing new there. A light brush of lips sealed the deal, but it wasn't enough. I slid my hand behind her head and pulled her mouth against mine. Scent and taste rolled into one and I was lost in her body and mind. The door opened, if it had ever truly closed, and it was like our very first kiss was rediscovered. Soft lips, strong jaw, delicate, probing tongue.

She tasted minty and sweet and . . . salty. Yeah, salted cashews, or maybe walnuts. But where had she found walnuts in the hotel?

So sweet . . . like the honey from the bees that swarmed through the gardens behind the palace. Her venom danced across my tongue like bubbles from champagne, and made me just as giddy.

I pulled back from the kiss and stared into her eyes, those too-blue eyes, the color of the finest lapis stones from the quarries near her home. What had possessed me to pull her into my arms and kiss her? It was as though I couldn't control my own actions. While there was nobody to see us on the sofa in the back of the custom plane, Nasil would most definitely smell any arousal. And how could I not be aroused?

"Rimush." The whispered name struck my chest like a knife, but not for the reason she probably expected.

"Rimush is dead, Tuli. He died long ago. For better or worse, I am *Ahmad.* I chose my name when I chose my path. There is no going back."

She ran a slow fingernail across my neck, then farther and farther down the open neck of my shirt. When had it become unbuttoned to nearly my waist? I couldn't help the shiver that raced over my skin from the tingle of her magic, far stronger than I'd remembered it. I'd never expected her to be alive after so many centuries. She was a lesser princess, with no particular magic to make her a valuable commodity to her father the king. She should be dead by now.

But she's not. She's right here with me. And nobody is here. I pulled back my hand from where it rested just underneath the fold of her breast. They were still firm and taut under the tight green tank top, with no indication she'd ever nursed a child. Had my father never allowed her even that?

"Ahmad." She tried out the name. "It's a good name, I suppose. But I don't understand why you gave up your *true* name, your home, your . . . throne. You just disappeared, and we believed you dead for a very long time." A pause and then she shook her head. "*Ahmad al-Narmer.* It makes no sense. How can you be *from* a man, not even your father, instead of a place? King Narmer was a fine ruler, but he was no Sargon of Akede. Your very name is a slap in the face of your family."

"Yes," I replied, my voice once again dripped with disdain for the man and his ideals. "It is. It was intended to be. I didn't just disappear, Tuli. I was forced out, stripped of my title, of my name—banished forever for bringing shame to his throne."

Now she looked truly confused and reared back in her seat. I'd forgotten how her emotions showed on her face so easily, while I'd schooled myself for centuries to show nothing at all. "Shame? But you were an *icon* of the people. The hero of the northern war who turned back the invaders and brought us new lands. You were the emissary to the great meeting of shifters . . . even learning the languages so you could speak on behalf of the snakes. You brought glory to all Akede by securing your father a seat on the first council of leaders."

All true, which is why it had been such a shock to

me. "My shame had little to do with my *own* actions, I'm afraid. No. It was a small bobcat that was my undoing. We were to be a marriage between two great houses—the snakes and the lions. The girl was a half-breed, but a powerful seer and Father wanted her talents for his great mission. But she refused the offer, slaughtered the escort I provided for her, shunned the gifts of gold and slaves, and fled. I was forced to return home a failure. He cast me out quietly, in the dark of night, with a price on my head if I returned."

Tuli was open-mouthed, which was almost charming. The shock in her scent told me this truly was news to her. I should be surprised that Father had never told anyone. But I wasn't. Just like I wasn't surprised . . . *now* that Josette Monier, the cat in question, had refused me. She'd *seen* Father's goals and treachery even back then. I knew that now. But I couldn't imagine her abilities back then. I still hate her, will always hate her for the life she stole from me. But I couldn't blame her. Not really.

Tuli's voice made my muscles twitch and I felt a swelling of something like pride inside at the intensity of her outrage. "She *refused* you? A prince who might someday rule an empire that stretched across most of Europe? You should have *killed* her for that insult!"

My own chuckle caught us both by surprise. "Oh, I've tried. Trust me. She's not so easily killed. As I say, she's a seer with powerful foresight. It's difficult to sneak up on her, and there's no defeating her in a fair fight. The lion in her is strong."

She was silent for a moment and then asked quietly, "So Narmer took you in? Is that why you chose his name as your own?"

I felt my head nodding and realized my hand had crept over to where it was covering hers. The olive skin was so very soft and I couldn't help but trace my thumb over the pulse point of her wrist the tattoo of the order feeling slightly cooler than her skin. There was a frantic flutter as I did. And those blue eyes . . . they'd haunted me for so many years after I fled. "Rather than be publicly whipped and chased through the streets of cities and villages, I left Akede as Father demanded. He had that power back then, if you remember, with Nasil at his side to support his edicts among the populace. I wandered for a long time in the desert, a nomad filled with self-loathing and shame. But Narmer took me in when I finally asked to be allowed to settle—offered me a post as an adviser even though I was a man without a country, without a name. Frankly, I'd fully expected Father to send runners ahead of me to announce my banishment to the neighboring empires so I'd be forced to wander forever. But I wasn't even worth that much time and trouble. I was simply forgotten, left to fend on my own. We didn't see or speak for close to a thousand years, while I lived and served in the house of another. Narmer and his brethren taught me things that Father had no concept of—tolerance, patience, and leadership without the fear of the people. The man I became was because of him, not Sargon. I couldn't hold my seat on the council now without the skills I learned from a foreign king. While some of the deceit and violence that were my father's legacy have also served me, I honor Narmer instead. So in a way, you weren't lied to. Rimush *is* dead. He has been for a very long time." It was strange how little the recitation bothered me. I'd fully expected to feel anger and shame roil up again, even after this long. But it didn't. Maybe it was the satisfaction of knowing I'd had a hand in his death that had also exorcized the demons that had chased me.

I stared out the window of the high-tech jet, watching the blinking lights far below fade back to the blackness that had existed since the dawn of time.

We were quiet for a moment, each thinking our own thoughts, so it surprised me when Tuli lifted my hand and pressed it to her lips. There were tears falling from her face to land on my skin and I suddenly couldn't think what to say. All I could do was turn my hand in her grip to raise her chin and look into her eyes with a smile that said she didn't need to pity or feel sorrow for me. She reached up with her other hand to stroke the side of my face, and when she pulled me forward into another kiss, I let her.

With age has come experience, so each careful touch was meant to bring intense sensation. My magic could be feather or whip, and I really didn't care whether Nasil heard Tuli's moans as I refamiliarized myself with the taste of her skin, the curves of her body, and the delight of her cries. I wasn't quite willing to go so far as to remove my clothes and bed her right here, but a great many pleasures can be had without revealing skin.

I could tell she was fighting her desire. She also hadn't planned on going this far, but something about letting me proceed was both terrifying and deeply arousing to her. When I unbuckled her seat belt, the muscles in her stomach twitched under the camouflage trousers and her fingers convulsed in my hair. Pushing her backward into the soft leather cushions and tracing my hand heavily along her muscled thigh caused a whimper and made her come up for air from the kiss.

"Ahmad, I *can't*."

That widened my eyes and forced me to ask, "Why? Are you married? Betrothed to someone?"

She shook her head and bit at her bottom lip while staring carefully at my neck. But her protests weren't quite enough to keep her from sliding her hand across my chest under the shirt and flicking my nipple with her fingernail. I responded in kind and felt her shudder.

I dipped my mouth to her ear and let out a slow, rolling hiss that brought a new tightness to her nipple, slowly being tormented between my thumb and forefinger. "Tell me, Tuli. What would happen if I took you again after all these years?"

"It's . . . it's not something I can talk about right now. I just can't."

I waited for a long moment, but there was no elaboration, so apparently that was all the answer I was going to get. She fought through her attraction until all that was left was confusion and embarrassment. I rose up off her, reluctantly letting my hand move away from her silken skin. "Very well. I've no need to force myself on a woman. If the feelings we once shared are gone, there's nothing more to say."

She opened her mouth to reply, a startled look on her face. But then she closed her mouth again, tight-lipped to avoid speaking whatever had tried to rise to the surface.

I moved away from her, buttoning my shirt as I did. "Perhaps it's time I checked on Nasil. He'll probably want a break from flying soon. I'll leave . . ."

. . . *leave, Tony?* I shook my head, pulling myself

away from what Ahmad had been doing to the woman in the plane. Can you hear me? Don't we have to leave?

I pressed fists to my eyes, trying to scrub away the image of the plane floating in front of me. It had at least frozen in place, so I wasn't hearing and seeing them.

When I could finally open my eyes back to my own reality, Sue was lying under me on the bed, looking rather disheveled and hazy. The digital clock on the nightstand said another half hour had flown by. I had a raging hard-on, and she looked like I'd been doing to her what Ahmad had been doing to Tuli. Just great. "Goddamn it," I muttered. "I'm getting sick and fucking tired of being trapped in someone else's wet dreams."

I rolled off her and raised a finger and then made shooing motions to make her leave while I tried to think of things that would get rid of this erection without having another round of sex. Not that I *minded* the thought of sex again, but I had to beat this without giving in to it every time. My only consolation was knowing that Ahmad was probably going through the same thing at thirty thousand feet.

Fortunately, the usual things worked to bring my libido to a standstill: mental images of my high school gym teacher, a creepy old guy who spent way too much time in the locker room showers watching us. And then there was the horse-faced nun who'd slapped my wrist with a ruler every time I asked a question in Sunday School. Finally was Carmine, slashed and bleeding on the floor of a condo.

Okay, that did it.

Sue had done as I asked. She stayed quiet and left the bed to go comb the tangles out of her hair and touch up her makeup. Once I'd thrown down the rest of the lukewarm coffee from the four-cup maker on the table, I was just about back to normal.

We didn't really talk until we were almost out the door. Then she made a comment, real casual-like, that made me want to pound my head on the wall. "For what it's worth, you're a really good kisser when you're Ahmad."

But a second later, I stopped cold, right in the hall-way, and pointed the car key at her chest. I hadn't said his name when I shooed her away. "Why did you say 'Ahmad'? What was I doing while I was kissing you? Was I talking?" That would be something entirely new, as would Sue being along for the ride into his head. Would that mean she could also *see* hindsights now when I was doing them?

The question made her freeze, brows raised and mouth open in a small 'O'. She stared at me, and then the floor, and she finally wound up tapping her foot on the carpet, hands on hips. "I don't really know. Let me think about it for a minute."

Fair enough. I turned to walk and she did too. We got in the car, breakfast forgotten, and drove silently until we were nearly at the clinic. Time was ticking by way too fast and I knew Charles wanted me to drive the kid to the airport. I didn't know how many flights there were per day to New Jersey from Denver, but I was betting it wasn't many.

There were a ton of things rolling around in my head, but seeing a narrow cutoff at the edge of the Sazi land made me remember our earlier conversation—

before the whole Ahmad-nearly-getting-laid episode. I turned down the road and had to slam on the brakes to avoid a big pothole.

"Where are we going? This isn't the way to the clinic."

I nodded once. "You're right. We have something to do real quick." She stopped talking and grabbed the strap next to the visor when I made an abrupt left to go around a rock big enough to take out the oil pan. The Lexus really wasn't the car for this terrain. Raven had taken me up here in a Jeep. But I needed to see something for myself before I had any talks with Lucas that involved Sue.

Fortunately, it was only another few hundred yards and then we came down a slight hill into a basin where a row of wooden stands faced a hillside. The Wolven agents had to train somewhere, and having a private gun range on the land was a pretty good solution. While I wasn't outfitted as well as I'd like, I did have the Taurus and the Ruger, both of which I had an extra box of ammo for in the trunk. And according to Lucas, there was plenty more at the clinic.

"Ah, gotcha. No problem."

I flicked my gaze toward her as I shut off the engine. "You just intuitive today, or reading my thoughts?"

She shrugged and her scent was pretty much normal. No particular emotion. "Intuitive, I guess. It's a shooting range. We were talking about me becoming an agent. You're an *I'll believe it when I see it* sort of guy, so I presume you want to see it. And hey, I've been practicing really hard, so I'd sort of like to show off a little."

She would, huh? "Okay, let's see what you've got."

I walked her toward the first table in front of the bar and pulled both guns from their holsters . . . one at the small of my back and the other at my ankle. "I'd love to give you earplugs, but you won't get any out in the field in a crisis. Better to know now if you're not going to be able to hear afterward."

I stepped back and waved a hand toward them in invitation. I wanted to see how she'd approach them. Had she been taught proper handling, and by who? Shooting's not about just picking up a gun and pulling the trigger. It's a process. Was she looking down-range to check her target? Did she open the cylinder to check the ammo? Etc., etc. But I didn't want to coach or reprimand. I'd heal if she shot me, and we were next to the clinic if she shot herself. So I leaned back against the nearest pole support and decided to just zip my lip, lock my head to our mental link, and observe.

She took a deep breath and let it out slow, knowing my eyes were watching her every move. Her scent was a blend of fear, determination, and worry, which is a really weird combination—sort of like soggy stir-fry left in the fridge too long. It doesn't smell *bad,* per se. But it's odd.

It didn't take long to tell me what I needed to know. She picked the guns up with a level of comfort that said she hadn't been bullshitting about practicing. She checked the gun and the ammo, and found an unmarked portion of an old paper target at the fifty-foot line to fire at. The caustic, familiar scent of burned smokeless powder filled the air as she squeezed the trigger. God, I love that smell. I'd like to say that the noise didn't bother me, but it did. Guns are hideously loud near the full moon. But I managed not to wince.

Her stance as she shot told me she'd been using target loads in her practice sessions. She made a little stutter backward in her steps and stared at the gun like it had bit her. I load my shells pretty hot, even for hunting rounds. She glanced at me as a question, but I didn't so much as blink. Not accusatory, nor comforting. But when she looked away, I noticed that she'd hit about an inch below the black dot on the target. It wasn't a bad shot, but since I know it's *not* the gun, it wasn't that great either. Still, it would put down a deer, or a charging wolf at that distance, so I couldn't bitch much. Perfection takes practice . . . and lots of it.

Still, the second shot, once she'd adjusted her footing and rubbed her hands against her pants to get the feeling back in the palms, wasn't half bad. It moved up closer to the dot, as did the third. "Try the other one."

The Taurus fit her hand pretty well, and it was a .38, so it would be an ideal gun for her. The Ruger was bigger, a .44 Magnum. If she thought my little ankle pop gun was a challenge, let's see what she made of its big brother. Several of of the Wolven agents carry Blackhawks, although most prefer Colts or Sigs.

She stared at the gun for a long moment, and I could tell she knew what she was in for. It was going to hurt. Not a little hurt, like a papercut, but a big hurt, like your skin is being ripped from your bones. The Pachmayr grips are dandy for keeping ahold of the thing when you're wet or bleeding, but those little diamond cuts in the rubber are like freaking razor blades with enough force behind them. But she didn't argue. She nodded once and picked it up, steadied herself, and held it firmly in front of her in a modified Weaver stance. I approved. Good choice for lessening the kick. She squeezed the trigger, meaning she was taught right. Too many new shooters *pull* the trigger. That tiny motion yanks the whole barrel upward. Not only will you miss the *center* of the target . . . there's a good chance you'll miss the target altogether.

Fire blazed from the barrel and I couldn't help but smile a little. She very nearly hit the center of the dot, which would take down anything in her way. But her composure was finally lost. She put the gun gingerly back on the table and shook both of her hands, the palms red even from where I was standing. "*Owwww!* Damn it, Tony! What do you have in here?"

I finally stepped forward and picked up the Ruger. "Silver's not heavy enough to go the distance and keep the trajectory, and Wolven uses all silver rounds. So you have to have a lot of powder behind it to get it where you need it to go. It's not perfect, but I tried silver-jacketed and they didn't work worth crap. So, we have to make do. I'm not saying you'd have to have this level of round in your own sidearm, but if you have to grab a random gun in a fight, you need to be able to handle it on the fly."

She seemed to take that in. "So in other words, practice with hot loads and then be pleasantly surprised in a crisis?"

I bonked her on the nose with a finger. "Exacta-mundo, sweetheart. Ever see the movie *Chariots of Fire*?" When she nodded, I added, "It's like the guys learning the shotput. They practiced with one way too heavy without realizing it and wound up winning because the regulation shot was lighter."

I tucked both of the guns back in their holsters, reminding myself to reload when we got up to the clinic.

I'd probably have to leave them here anyway, since I couldn't take them on the plane. But I'd seen all I needed to. "Nice job, by the way. Every one of those would have put down the target for the count."

"Thanks. But . . . um, before we go, could you—" She motioned toward the target. "You know, I've never actually seen you shoot."

Oh. Well, actually she had, but I wasn't going to remind her that she was in my head during a couple actual jobs, like when I killed a rival boss back home, and a hit man hired to take me out.

Well, heck. If I was going to show off, it should be a show. I dipped my head and sure enough, there was a wad of chewing gum stuck under the table. It's not a perfect glue, but plenty for what I had in mind. A quarter came out of my pocket and I stuck it to the wood, slightly lopsided, but firm. I backed up a dozen paces, until I was actually behind the covered shooting stands, near the car. There were tables and railings in the way and I was pretty sure Lucas would kick my ass if I shot them up. So I'd better not miss. I motioned her to come back to where I was standing. I still had four shots in the Ruger, since I always keep the barrel chamber empty when I'm driving.

Before she could react, I took off running away from the car, parallel to the benches. I then spun and headed back, pulling the gun when I was a dozen feet from the target. I threw myself sideways on the gravel and skidded until I passed the target stand. I fired four times in rapid succession, adjusting my aim around the various supports, benches, and metal sheeting as I moved. I was dumping the empties from the chamber as I slid by in front of her feet and then rolled back to standing before

I completely stopped. The whole operation took less than five seconds . . . barely enough time for the movements to register in her brain. "That what you wanted to see?"

Her eyes were bright and her mouth open in awe. She raced forward, completely forgetting the rule that you don't run down-range while there are still guns in hands. I wasn't going to shoot her, but it was still a bad habit we'd have to break.

"My God!" she exclaimed when she reached the target. "You hit it three times!"

I smiled and holstered the gun as I walked toward her. I could see the quarter from where I was. "Four, sweetheart. Look again. Two went through the same hole."

There wasn't much left of the quarter. Just a frame of twisted metal around the big slug holes. It took pointing out that one hole had a second dip on the top rim for her to believe it. I tucked it in her front pocket. "Keep it as a souvenir of what you'll be able to do in the future if you keep it up. There are plenty of perfectly human exhibition shooters, including women, who can do this same thing—just not as fast. Shooting's all about practice. Keep it up and it won't matter if you're a Sazi or human agent."

Her scent turned to the light, fluffy fragrance of hope and tangerine happiness. "You really think I can?"

"We'll see, but *I'm* willing to give you a try. I just can't speak for Lucas."

WE UNANIMOUSLY, AND silently, decided that discussing *anything* with Lucas would be a bad idea today. Apparently, my vision had been right on, but I'd sort of forgotten to mention the blowtorch to the door hinges. Oops.

Nasil had been right in my head that Amber would have a headache. Apparently she was out for almost four hours and Charles was *livid*. I caught the tail end of an argument between them as I walked down the stairs to the basement.

"I told you someone else should have stayed here with you! Dammit, Amber. What if he'd used poison instead of a tranquilizer?"

Her voice got to a similar shade of red. "Oh, and this is all *my* fault now? You were with Liz, who absolutely needed to be watched. Holly absolutely needed to hunt and Lucas absolutely needed to sleep. Tony and Sue absolutely needed to not be here in case Ahmad went berserk. Angelique is still unconscious in her room and so is Sarah. Which *someone* should have stayed to guard me? How exactly was I supposed to have avoided this situation, oh great and wise seer? And by the way— couldn't you have predicted an *elephant tranq*? I'd think that would stand out in a vision."

"Now *look*—" Charles's voice became a rumble, and the sting of magic shot up the stairs like a back draft in a house fire. I had to back up just to keep my skin from smoking from the force of it.

Oookay. Probably best to let them sort things out privately. I'd technically already seen the door. If I missed seeing it again, I could live with that. More on point . . . I could *live*.

Liz was upstairs, learning a valuable lesson about the sting of high-octane magic. Her scent was actually that level of panic where you're too terrified to move—like a deer in the headlights. She was swatting at her arms like there were bugs crawling on them, while Lucas slammed doors and dug through papers on the desk, cell phone to his ear. I couldn't hear what was being said, so either the person was whispering, or he was on hold.

I was pleasantly surprised that Sue wasn't flinching from all the negative energy in the place. She patted Liz on the arm as I walked up to them. "You'll get used to it. Honestly. Most of the old ones really have excellent control. It's the magic you're feeling. I'm happily immune to the crawly skin because I'm human, but I know it's a struggle not to take off like a bat out of hell and run."

Liz shook her head and tears threatened. "I don't know if I can do this. I mean, snakes and bears and wolves—"

"Oh, my." I added the last bit, since she seemed at a loss for words. She let out a sad little chuckle. "But don't forget badgers. You've got it all over several species if zoology is any indication." When she looked up at me, her eyes were filled with disbelief, as was her scent. I crossed my arms, settled my stance, and nodded. "I'm serious, kiddo. Animals in the wild are *terrified* of badgers. Go look it up. There's hardly a species out there that will take one on, even up to the big cats and wolves. Spend some time online. Learn about your animal. What it can do, you can. What it *must* do, same thing. Heck, you might even find some footage on YouTube of how they fight or hunt. It's handy shit to know when the moon comes calling." I motioned with my head toward the doorway to the basement. "Now, before old big, white, and furry comes back upstairs, what's the plan? I've no doubt he told you and remember . . . I'll know if you're lying."

Her eyes darted away for a second, so when the burst of black pepper into the air preceded her mouth opening, I wasn't surprised. I lowered my chin and let out an amused, "Uh, huh. You sure you want to go there?"

She opened her eyes wide and looked at me with an expression of indignation. But her scent was the dry desert heat of embarrassment. "I didn't even *say* anything!"

It was Sue who responded, with another pat on her knee. "You don't have to. That's the problem with dealing with these guys. Scents happen at the same time as the *thought.* Most Sazi will give you a chance to change your mind, or think things through. But you have to be really careful of what you say. Everybody will know what you're *thinking* because of the scent, long before words hit the air."

She let out a little huff of air and the pink glow around her swirled and danced in annoyance. "That is *really* not fair." I couldn't disagree, so I just shrugged and stayed silent, waiting. Finally she let out a sigh when she heard footsteps below our feet. "We've got a ten-thirty flight to Newark." I checked my watch. It was already past eight. With the drive and security and such—

"Crap. That doesn't give us much time. Did you already download the boarding passes online?"

She shook her head. "The plane was technically full. We have standby tickets. But Mr. Wingate said you'd know what to do so we can make the flight—whatever that means."

I smiled, and it had a dark edge. "That means a few people need to not want to fly today. Maybe quite a few, depending on how many standbys there are." She looked at me askance, but I just chuckled. "Don't worry, kid. Stick with me and you'll learn the games we play." But with the added time of going to the ticket counter, or logging in at one of the kiosks, plus probably getting extra attention from security for the late purchase, we really needed to get moving. "Where are your bags?"

"Still out in the car. Should I go get 'em?" The question was too abrupt and hurried. I didn't need my nose, or my degree in psychology, to know what she was planning.

It was still amusing, but would get annoying if she kept it up. "Nice try, but you need to stop telegraphing. Can you smell that sweet, cloying scent in the air, with maybe a hint of pineapple?" She stopped and sniffed a few times and then took in a slow, deep breath through her nose.

"Yeah. What is that? It's really faint, but smells like a tropical fruit salad."

I gave her a pointed look. "That would be *you*— planning your escape when you went out to the car. So no dice."

Now she looked annoyed, and smelled of it too. "You said *emotions* have scents. What kind of emotion is *escape*?"

I was getting tired of standing here answering questions, so I started moving. I snapped my fingers and motioned her to stand while I bent down and gave Sue a kiss on the cheek. "Most everything we do has some sort of emotion attached, Liz. I'd guess excitement, anticipation, and maybe that sneaky sort of happy when you pull something over on someone. I tend to call it dark glee to myself. You can call it whatever you like. But we have to get moving." I lifted Sue's chin and she smiled. "You going to be okay here?"

A quick nod was all I needed, plus the scent of confidence and the burst of warmth in my head. "I'll be fine. You go and take care of things. But you should probably leave your guns and get new ones there."

Oh. Good point. Instead of pulling them from the holsters, I started to unbuckle my belt. Liz raised her brows but I just rolled my eyes. "Gotta get the holster off somehow, kid. Ease up." The stretch slacks I was wearing had plenty of give, so all I had to do was reach down and unsnap the strap and pull it out from behind my back. Apparently, Liz hadn't noticed it was there, mostly because I tend to keep the grips down low so they don't show even when I'm not wearing a jacket. I rolled the strap around the holster and handed it to Sue. Then I reached for the ankle one. "Feel free to spend some time with them, but don't waste the silver if you can avoid it. Just get some hunting loads at Wal-Mart or somewhere."

Liz had picked up her purse and slung it on her shoulder. Lucas wasn't anywhere to be seen so I walked to the basement door. I hollered down, in case they were in one of the cells in the back. I didn't hear arguing anymore, but that didn't mean anything if the level of magic in the stairwell was any indication. "Hey, you two! I've got to get Liz to the airport. I'll leave the car in the short-term lot with the key in the wheel well." Rather than track Lucas down, I just yelled to the open air, figuring he'd hear me, his ears being what they were. "I'll call when I get to New Jersey!"

"New . . . Jersey. 'Ave to get—" The words were a

screech that made both Liz and Sue cover their ears. I'd heard the voice before so all I did was wince at the tone . . . like fingernails on a chalkboard. Angelique came racing down the hallway, her cotton gown flowing behind her from the wind she was creating. She hit me full force and we toppled to the ground. "New! Jersey! 'Ave to get . . . Atlantic!" She started slamming her head against me, as though she had a beak in human form. Her arms were flapping and her feet were clawing at my pants, but thankfully neither could do much more than bruise.

I grabbed her arms and rolled her over onto her back. Liz and Sue backpedaled hard and fast, and Liz's purse went flying. But there's a reason Angelique's leader of the raptors. Magic flew out of her in a greengold rush that was like being hit in the face with a blast from an air compressor. It would have thrown me off her if it wasn't for the fact that I'd wrapped my legs around hers. But it didn't do my back muscles any good. "I could use some help here, people!" I made the words even louder than my earlier announcements and I heard feet heading my way.

Angelique shrieked again, the sound of an angry falcon, and she beat at my sides with her fists like a hummingbird on steroids. It hurt. A lot. "New! 'Ave to fly!"

Another burst of magic sent me flying, and she changed forms in a flurry of cotton shreds and feathers. But she didn't get far. Lucas was there and tackled her out of the air before she could take a second flap toward the nearest window. I didn't think the glass would stop her like it would a normal bird, and I was betting Lucas knew that too.

I could see his blue-white light surround her green-gold, but he was in a battle royale to freeze her, an acid trip of colors tripping over themselves for dominance to my eyes.

Charles and Amber showed up a moment later. He changed to bear form in a flash and sent furniture flying from the sheer mass of the new furred form. Sue and Liz were plastered against the wall now, just trying to stay out of the way, but still watch. Sue had my Taurus in her hand and it was pointed at the bird on the floor. You go, girl.

She kicked the other holster across the tile toward me. I had to dive to grab it before it slid under the couch, but that was okay. Then there were two guns pointed, but they weren't really needed. Charles simply allowed Lucas to get off her and he froze her in an ice cube of shimmering air. Then he stood on her wings to keep her motionless and released her. That didn't seem bright, because she was quiet when she was frozen. Now she was shrieking again. He turned his head to me while Amber ran down the hallway for points unknown. "What happened here?"

"Good question. I was just telling you guys we were leaving for New Jersey when she came screaming down the hallway."

The words set her off again. "Jersey! Fly! Go!" She was struggling so hard I was afraid she was going to tear off her own arm . . . or wing. Charles actually had to take a moment to get his balance again. But then Amber arrived and she was carrying a syringe. I shuddered. I *hate* needles. Odd that I don't mind getting sliced and diced, but a little tube of metal makes me insane.

Charles looked at his wife with surprise, and it made her snarly again. "I'm a little too burned out right now to do a trance, okay? This sedative works fast and should keep her down for about four hours. I should know."

The big bear blinked once, at just about the same time as I got it and wisely closed his mouth.

Amber looked around his massive paw, either trying to find a vein or trying to find a spot that wasn't covered with paw. Finally she shrugged and muttered, "IM it is." Without further warning, she stabbed the needle to the hilt in Angelique's thigh and pressed the plunger home. I noticed that there was a growing stain of blood creeping across the tile and realized that while he had been holding down her wings, she'd been clawing up his back legs. Amber sighed. "You're bleeding, dear. We should get you cleaned up."

Charles and Lucas both moved their gaze to where she was looking and got panicked expressions. They simultaneously turned toward Sue and said in complimenting harmony, "Don't come any closer."

"I wasn't planning to." Her voice sounded odd enough that Lucas finally noticed the Taurus in her hand, held nice and steady. He raised his brows and his eyes flicked to me, where I had the Ruger in a similar grip.

"Who were you planning to shoot?" He wasn't asking me, even though that's where he was looking.

She didn't take her eyes off the target. I'd have to compliment her teacher. Yeah, you can do two things at once when you're concentrating with a gun. You can see things around you and react when needed. But when it comes to higher brain function, like answering questions, the tone comes out sort of flat and emotionless. "Whoever came any closer."

Lucas was still staring at me, and added folded arms to the cocked head and peculiar expression. I was just about ready to lower the gun, because Angelique was finally settling down. But I kept the gun in place until he asked the last question I knew he was going to. "Where are you aiming?"

I knew what Sue's answer was going to be because it was the only one she could give, considering her position. We also responded in chorus, my "heart" to her "head."

Charles finally took his weight off of the bird when her head lolled to the side and her little pointy tongue fell out of her little pointy open mouth. Her talons curled inward like she was grasping a branch and she slept. Charles looked at me again. "Are you quite certain all you did was say *New*—"

Amber slapped his leg hard enough to make him flinch. "Shhh. She's not quite under yet. Go somewhere else and talk to him. Lucas, give me a hand getting her into bed. She's hard to carry like this. Once she's fully under, you can change her back and we'll chain her down. I've got to do some more blood tests. There's something weird going on. First Ahmad running amuck and now her. That's two too many for my taste."

I lowered the hammer back to locked position and put the Ruger in the holster just as Sue was doing the same on her side of the room. It's when I was spinning the leather band around to secure it that I noticed my watch. Dammit! We'd lost another fifteen minutes. I fished in my pocket for the car keys and shook my head.

"I'd love to stay and chat, but we've got a flight to catch. Can we do this by phone?"

Amber and Lucas disappeared down the hallway, half carrying and half dragging Angelique's still form. Her wings were so long they brushed both sides of the hallway and I could hear them spitting out feathers as they pulled.

Charles peered down at my arm in a nearsighted fashion so I held the watch so he could see it way up where his eyes were. "Good lord! You're quite right, m'boy. Nigel is testy enough without being forced to wait. Thank you for keeping me on point." He turned back to human form, a dapper three-piece suit in dove gray covering him.

To everyone but Liz, that was. She let out a little gasp and put a hand up to shield her eyes, staring carefully down at the floor. The room suddenly smelled like a desert again. Charles swore, but tried to maintain his dignity by stepping behind the couch to block his more intimate parts from her superior view. I wasn't surprised he'd forgotten, considering the circumstances.

Sue bent her head close to the other woman. "You'll have to get used to that too, Liz. Lots of naked people in this group. You'll lose any sense of modesty you ever had a year from now."

Liz removed the hand, relieved, and shook her head—tiny little movements that spoke of both frustration and amazement. "I've always considered myself pretty liberal. I saw some weird stuff in college. But this happens so *fast*. Blink, animals. Blink, naked people. It's insane. Like Monty Python on crack."

I gave the comment the snort it deserved. "And with

that, we gotta go. Ten-thirty is going to be here way too quick."

Charles stopped and turned his head. "Why ten-thirty? Your plane doesn't leave until nearly noon."

I turned my whole body toward Liz with a very disapproving expression and a low growl from deep in my chest. What had she been trying to pull? "Ten-thirty, huh? Planning to ditch me while I was trying to figure out what our real flight was?"

Her expression grew panicked. "No! I swear. I saw it on the screen when Mr. Wingate was ordering the tickets. American Airlines to Newark at ten-thirty."

Now Charles reared back with a startled expression. "Oh! My humblest apologies, m'dear. After you went to bed, I cancelled those. Your grandfather and I talked again and his flight had an hour layover in New York, so I tried to make the flights match as close as possible. You're now on United at, I believe, eleven-forty. It's flight 874. The only seats left were first class, but you should get used to that anyway. Your friend Heather will meet you in London. She had to visit her parent's home to pick up her passport first. Your grandfather will have yours with him. Your father e-mailed him a recent photo to use." I wasn't going to ask how Nigel would manage to get a passport without the person being present. Money talks, even in today's world.

I held my holster out to Sue, who walked the few steps to take it from me and stared at me until I heard her thoughts in my head. I thought of the answer just now, by the way. She continued when she saw my blank expression. In the hallway, about how I knew it was Ahmad?

Oh! Sure. Go ahead.

You *move* differently. Quick and abrupt normally, but smooth and flowing when . . . well, you know. You use your tongue a lot more too. Um . . . try to keep that part. She blushed but managed to avoid my amused expression by coughing and beating a hasty retreat to get a drink. Like her, I didn't really want to broadcast the whole situation to Charles. He was going to find out soon enough. I'd just prefer it was over the phone, when I was far, far away. I nodded as she left. We could continue the discussion later—and we *would,* since I'm comfortable with my foreplay skills as they stand now. But that conversation was for when there weren't prying eyes to notice me blank out for long periods . . . like on an airplane.

Uh, huh. We'll talk more about *that* on the flight.

She didn't respond.

Liz and I both sighed almost simultaneously. But mine was frustrated, while hers was relieved. Still, the timing of the flight was actually better overall. "We'll have time to eat then. Can't afford not to have a full belly of meat on the moon and there's hardly anything in the airport restaurants with meat for breakfast." I didn't need to mention our other stop along the way.

Liz let out a little half belch and went to fish her purse out from underneath the magazine rack. "I don't know if I ever want to see meat again. The beef kebabs last night were awesome. Best I've ever had, but there were a ton of them. I still feel stuffed."

"Not beef, Elizabeth," Charles commented with a chuckle. "Rabbit and ground squirrel. I do try very hard to feed new turns their natural prey so they get accustomed to the taste and smell. The one you tried of mine later was seal. My favorite."

"*Seal?* Eww—" We left with Charles and Sue still snickering at the grimace on her face as she trailed after me.

Chapter Thirteen

"OKAY," LIZ SAID as she followed me down the hospital corridor. "I know I've led a really sheltered existence. But there's something really strange about all the men hanging around outside. The staff seems terrified by them, but nobody's making them move."

I didn't get a chance to reply because we rounded the corner and saw two more of the men I knew at the end of the hallway. They were standing outside the doorway, blocking the entrance. Marvin was one of Carmine's best bodyguards, big and tough-looking, and fully capable of killing on command. The other was Mike. He was tough too, but he was a real softy underneath for his family . . . and stray dogs. Lots and lots of yippy lapdogs at his place, and always more welcome.

I'd thought about getting Bobby to come with me to use illusion. But there's value in knowing you're being watched. I wanted to see who went squealing where once I was inside. We'd been careful to only go down empty corridors and I hadn't smelled any Sazi of any flavor on the trip upstairs.

"Wow," Liz said under her breath. "They feed better food here than at my school. That Italian dish smells amazing."

"You're looking at the *Italian dish* right now." I whispered the words from the side of my mouth, just for her. "That's what Mike smells like normally—the man on the left. It's his base scent. Everyone has a base scent. Yours is cotton candy, by the way. Matches your pretty pink aura. You're just a regular ballerina princess without your fur."

Her outrage was immediate, same as my amusement. She stopped to stare at me with hands on hips. I ignored her and walked right up to the boys, my highest *predator* magic pushing ahead of me by five feet. They were too stunned to pull their pieces. After all, not only am I dead, but I was damned close to Carmine's second in command. "I'm going in, and it'll be private. You have any objections?" They looked at each other in confusion but then shook their heads. I pointed to Liz with a flick of my thumb. "Keep an eye on the girl. She doesn't leave, she doesn't ask questions, nobody takes her, nobody hurts her. Got it?"

Marvin had been reduced to nearly a drooling dolt. His eyes were blinking almost too fast to be real. But Mike swallowed a big gulp of his own spittle and nodded. "Whatever you say, Tony." He picked up the lone chair from near the door and put it next to Liz.

I motioned her toward it. "Sit. This won't take long."

She tried to pull herself together enough to be aloof. She glanced at her little silver watch and adopted a haughty voice, carefully avoiding the chair. "It had better not. We're on a schedule."

That made me chuckle a little. I didn't worry about

her skipping. She might be tough, but Marvin and Mike are damned smart. If Marvin couldn't hold her down, Mike would charm her. He's quite a ladies' man while on the job, even though he's devoted to his Maria on his own time. "You've got it, your ladyship."

I walked through the door and was expecting to wince. But the docs had patched him up pretty good. Oh, he was still a mess, but he was a mess wrapped in clean white bandages. It makes it easier to bear. He still smelled of cigars, whiskey, and sex and there was no telltale glow that said he'd been attacked and turned. So, Mustaf had been right, and Lissell wrong. Maybe. But at least if a snake was present, it hadn't bit him.

There was a lot of equipment present and while I didn't pretend to know what they all did, I did grab his chart and flip through it. Most of it was mumbo-jumbo, a flurry of abbreviations and dosages that didn't help me much. But I did like the new sticker on the metal clip, labeled, *STABLE*. Much better than how Linda had portrayed it.

It's why I needed to come. Like Sue said, I have to see it.

"Hey, boss man. You awake?" I kept my voice low, but loud enough that if he was just dozing, he'd notice.

He did. His eyes opened and he tried to chuckle past the bandages. His voice was raw and slow, but he could talk. Another good thing. "Told Linda she couldn't keep you away."

I didn't want to keep him. I had no doubt even a few minutes was going to be tiring. "You up to telling me what happened?"

He nodded once and moved his chin slightly toward the chair. It was enough of an invitation that I sat. He could probably see me better this way too. "I'll keep it . . . short. New family out of Jersey . . . hit us. Central-American guys. Word has it they're heavy into the drug trade. Never seem 'em before. We fought 'em off, but they killed Ira."

Aw, man! Ira was just an accountant. He'd never even picked up a gun, and certainly wasn't someone who knew anything important. "Sorry about that. He was a good man. I'd send my regards but . . . well, you know. The whole *dead* thing."

He nodded, just a little. "It's been a pretty empty poker table for about a year now. Thinking I'll have to give it up if this keeps up." The *poker table* he was referring to was what had been a monthly tradition for nearly a decade. Me, Carmine, Joey the Snake, Ira, and Louis Perricone had played an all-nighter for high stakes. Now Joey was dead, and Ira and me. No shit, an empty table. "Louis says no, we go on no matter what. But we'll see. Not that many guys I trust to take the seats. Sal took your place, but he's not much of a poker player. And half the time we have to spot him part of the buy-in. It sort of defeats the purpose. Trust, y'know?"

I did. "Which is why I'm here. I need it from your lips. What do you want from me?"

He coughed, tried to speak, and coughed again. I motioned toward the water pitcher, a question on my face. He nodded, so I poured some in a glass and held it so he could sip some from the straw. I knew he didn't like that. He'd rather it was whiskey from cut crystal, held and swirled by his own hand. "It'll be scotch soon enough. You just tell me and I'll leave you to rest."

"Need you to make it right. Ton. See, when they killed Ira, I sent the kid calling." Ah. He must mean Scotty. So, he was giving him freelance work now. That was probably good. Scotty is a killer, no matter how you slice it. He either kills for money, or for fun. Carmine can keep him closer to the straight and narrow with jobs than with Social Services bullshit to "change" him. "He was supposed to take out just one guy—the man who killed Ira. He had the name and the address. I think he did it right. We got word back that the guy was dead with no leads. But then he went and took something of theirs. I only know because that's what these bastards came looking for. Some sort of ancient artifact. You know Scotty and pointy things, so it was probably an old knife or spear or something. I've tried to work with him, but he's still too impressed with *things*. Nobody called, though. Not one word or message asked for the return, which I would've done. No sweat. But they just came stomping in and beat the crap out of me, and wouldn't believe when I told them I didn't know what the fuck they were talking about." He coughed again and the heart machine started to dance enough that a nurse was going to come knocking soon.

I held the glass back to his face, but he waved it away impatiently. "Water won't cure what they did, Tony. I put the word out for Scotty to come back, but now he's scared. Someone blabbed about me being here and he thinks he'll be killed."

"Won't he?" I mean, realistically, that's probably what he was asking me to do.

He shrugged. "Maybe. If he'd taken the knife and I had to get it back and apologize—sure, I might'a offed him. But they started the ball rolling and then didn't play by the rules. The rules that the rest of us have used for *years*. Damned foreigners. I don't like that. It pisses me off. So here's what I want you to do—"

I heard a commotion outside and turned to go check it out, but Carmine grabbed my sleeve and held on tight. I'd forgotten how strong he is, nearly Sazi strong, so when he pulled, it kept me there. "No. You stay and listen. I want you to find the kid and get back the knife. Then you use it to kill the fuckholes who put me here and bring me the knife as a trophy. I want a message sent that *nobody* messes with Carmine Leone so you make it public, and wet. Front-page stuff. Oh, and you can slap the kid around a little if you think he's not got the proper respect, but don't mess with his fingers. I don't have a replacement for him right now. You got it?" It was unusual for Carmine to use so many swear words. It told me even more than the burned coffee and jalapeño scent that rose from him that he was well and truly furious.

The voices were getting louder, and it annoyed me I couldn't make out what was being said. The machines were playing hell with my hearing. Everything was high-pitched. It was knocking the midtones out of my brain. But you don't ignore Carmine, so I nodded and kept my eyes on him. "Got it. Get the kid, get the knife, take out the hitters . . . messy, and come back with the prize."

"You going to have any problem with your people?" It was weird hearing him talk about *my* people, an acknowledgment that I wasn't *his* people anymore.

I shrugged. "Already got it covered. There's a price, but there always is, and it won't come back on you."

He nodded. "Your usual rate."

I held up my hand and shook my head. "No charge. This one's on the house."

He let out a growl that would do a wolf proud. "*Your usual rate*. I'm not a charity case. I pay my bills, just like always."

I'd pricked his pride and hadn't meant to. But I didn't want to get into a situation where I was taking money on the side while working for Lucas. I had an idea, though. If it worked I'd be a really happy camper and Lucas might growl, but not too loud. "You want to pay me back? Fine. You get me back my car. I miss the old girl. Restored condition, but untraceable, and we'll call it square."

I knew where the car was, and so did he. My old '67 Mustang Fastback had been my pride and joy. It was black with a white interior, and had all original equipment. It was presently in the possession of my old buddy Jocko, who ran the bar where I used to hang out. He got it by default when I accidentally trashed his Lincoln while chasing down some kidnappers who'd grabbed Sue. But I hated giving it up. I wanted it back. And, I knew Jocko had torn out the front driver's seat to be able to drive it. Yes, he's just that tall, but it was *original*. It would need extra work to make it like new again.

He nodded and had a little smile on his face that he wasn't explaining. "Done and done." He offered his hand, which was attached to a variety of tubes. I took it and shook it as firmly as I dared without yanking off any tape.

"You can find them in Atlantic City, a new casino they're calling the *Quetzalcoatl*. I think it's a stupid name . . . way too tough for people to spell and pronounce. But it's easy to find. You can't miss it."

Yet another tie-in to the snakes. I thought I remembered my mythology that a quetzacoatl was a winged serpent that was the god of wind and rain. Or maybe it was lightning and storms. Something like that anyway. I winked at Carmine and gave him a small smile. "Don't tell Linda I was here. After all, you didn't want me to see you."

He rolled his eyes and leaned back heavily into the pillows. "I love the woman, but she just doesn't get me some days."

I was almost to the door, where things had quieted down outside when I snapped my fingers. "By the way, congrats on the kid. Have a name yet? Boy or girl?"

He smiled and there was no mistaking the orange-scented happiness that covered over the antiseptic of the room. "We decided to be surprised. If it's a boy, Vincent, after my granddad. Middle name's up in the air. Linda says Matthew, but that sounds weird . . . Vincent Matthew. She's coming up with some others from the baby book, but some of those names are flat strange. I mean, *Denim*? Who wants a kid named after blue jeans? If it's a girl, though, Barbara wants to call her Isabella Marie. I like that. Bella Leone. Yeah, that's the one."

I told him the absolute truth, my hand on the door. "You'll be a good dad."

He nodded, but then his eyes hardened. "You just make sure I'm around for that birth. I'm Barbara's coach, so don't make me have to go take care of business myself." Now that surprised me. I nearly laughed, if he hadn't sounded so fierce about it. Carmine in a Lamaze class making panting noises, stopwatch at the ready? That was almost worth pictures.

I left the room feeling pretty good about his future. I hoped I wasn't wrong. A figure stepped around the corner just as I hit the hallway. I recognized the scent as friendly, but I couldn't quite place it. Liz was in the chair, Marvin's left hand firmly on her shoulder. She was staring after him too, and I didn't like the look in her eye.

I took a slow breath, but the antiseptic covered over anything that might be a personal scent. I looked sharply at Mike. "Who just left and why were people yelling out here?"

The big guy shrugged and rolled his eyes. "Oh, it was just Louis. He wanted to go in and measure the room, but we wouldn't let him. You said private, so it was."

Louis. Yeah, that could have been him. But I hadn't seen him in long enough that I didn't remember what he smelled like. I squinted my eyes in confusion. "*Measure* the room? For what?"

Marvin let out a sarcastic little laugh. "What else? A poker table. Said he didn't see any reason why the game couldn't go ahead as planned. Even if it was just for fun . . . no money chips."

Man, that guy is a gambling *whore*. Liz opened her mouth to say something but I shook my head. She closed it again, but didn't like it. "Did Louis know it was me in there?"

Mike looked at me like I'd lost my mind. "Private meetings are *private*. You know that. Carmine said to let you in if you came by, but we thought it was the drugs talking. I mean, the papers said—"

I nodded once and motioned for Marvin to let go of Liz's shoulder. "And as far as you know, the papers were right. I'm laying so low right now I have to look up to see the devil's ass."

Marvin nodded just as Liz let out a guffaw. He pointed down the opposite hallway. "Then use the stairs around the corner. They come out the side of the building . . . an unmarked employee entrance. Louis said he'd be right back, and if you don't want to run into him—"

Good advice. I shook both of their hands solemnly and we wished each other a safe journey through life. It might be the last time we ever laid eyes on each other. They knew it too.

Liz was real quiet as we ducked into the stairwell and started to make our way down the six flights to the ground floor. It wasn't until we reached the underground parking garage, with enough time to actually do as I told Lucas and get some meat, that she finally spoke. "Those guys really respect you, huh? They said it had been an honor to know you. That's not real normal language."

I shrugged and pressed the button to open the door locks. "I like to think so. I've sure as hell earned a little respect."

She paused and then took a deep breath, her hand on the latch. She stared at me over the roof of the car, eyes intent and focused on my face "*Okaaay . . .* so it's probably none of my business, and you can tell me to shut up now and not answer this next question, but I have to ask it. Was that some sort of mob capo you were visiting? When that Louis guy showed up, he made my skin crawl. He smelled weird, pretty obviously had a gun under his jacket, and the guards sounded like a *Sopranos* episode talking to him. And don't pretend they weren't guards. If those were *friends,* visiting like you, I'll eat my hat. What kind of person are you to visit someone like him and have those guys respect you?"

Oh, sure, I could be insulted at the question. But she was a nice, white-bread girl who'd just gotten thrown into a harsh world without any entrance exam. My world. I'm not ashamed of it, and not afraid of defending my choices. It also wouldn't do any good to lie, but I couldn't tell her everything either. I got inside the car and she followed, still watching my face. Her nostrils were flared, probably watching for any sign of the emotions I told her she could smell. "There are lots of kinds of people in the world, kiddo. You just met one kind. Lucas and Charles . . . they're another. There are good people, bad people, and neutral. Me? I'm neutral—somewhere in between the two, neither fish nor fowl. But I can both swim and fly." I stuck the key in the ignition and fired up the engine. It purred quietly. Nice machine. I'd get one if Carmine couldn't manage to round up my old one. "I take lives, I save lives. Sometimes both at once. What you wind up being is entirely up to you. Just know that people can be happy in both roles, and miserable in both. I'm one of the happy ones, on both sides of the coin flip." I turned in my seat, put an arm on the headrest and raised my brows at her. "Now, let me ask *you* a toughie. Let's say you happen upon a man who has just attacked a young woman, wearing a wedding ring and with an empty infant seat in the back of the vehicle she was getting in. You know . . . absolutely *know* without a doubt from using those shiny new supernatural senses that he's going to rape, torture, and kill her. Would you kill *him*?"

She shook her head quickly and surely. "I'd call the police."

I met her indignation with a smile and a slow shake of my head. "Sorry. No police allowed. He's Sazi, she's human, and if the cops arrest him and hold him past the full moon, we're all discovered. Humans will panic and there'll be genocide on a worldwide scale of a kind you couldn't imagine. You're the only thing standing in his way. So, I ask again. Would you kill him? You can smell his lust and *need* for pain. It's a thick, oily, nauseating scent that makes you want to scrub down in a shower afterward. Her fear makes your jaw tighten . . . and his too. What will her blood make his animal want to do? Eat her, bit by bit while she's awake and feeling it? It's probably already occurred to you that we're *really* good at torture. And remember this is real life, not a movie with a happy ending. He's done it before and he'll do it again if you let him go . . . even if you get her to safety. Are her kids next? Her address is in her wallet. You can walk away, or you can kill him."

Liz looked sideways at me for a long moment, as I eased the car into traffic, bound for the airport. She started shaking her head, but her scent was cold-metal determination, blended with the slightest touch of fear. "Then yes, I suppose I'd have no choice. I couldn't just walk away and let her die. I guess I would."

I eased to a stop at the traffic light and turned my head to catch her gaze. I let my eyes fade to the blank, expressionless killer ones I've had for a really long time. She shivered abruptly, unable to ignore what she saw. "So did I." I let that sink in for a moment before I returned my eyes to the road. "Like I said . . . it's real life. What kind of person do *you* think that makes me?"

The wheels started turning in the girl's mind so fast you could nearly smell smoke. I liked that she didn't have good answers and was thoughtful. I figured eventually she'd get tapped for Wolven, being an alpha and an animal most Sazi would naturally fear. The cab was silent for a long time, until we were on the freeway headed east. That was fine with me. The sun was already long past hitting me in the eyes, and the day was perfect for flying—clear and cloudless. Denver's a pretty city, so I just enjoyed watching the scenery, trying not to sneeze. The blend of scents from her was pretty much every one in the book and it was like walking into a flea market where every smell imaginable assaults your nose at once. Finally, when we were less than a dozen miles from the airport, she shook her head again. "You're a very unusual man, Mr. Giodone."

It was the first time she'd called me by that name. I tried to remember where she'd heard it. I'd been *Davis* to this point. The traffic in front of me began to dissolve in favor of trees and vines. Crap, crap, *crap*! Really bad timing here!

Clouds began to appear like magic and I could taste thick creosote, like licking a railroad tie. I dove quickly onto the shoulder of I-70. So quick, in fact, that Liz threw her hands forward onto the dashboard, and luggage flew from the backseat to bounce against the headrests. We stopped in a swirl of gravel, horns honking all around us. "You have no idea, kiddo. See, I'm about to disappear from this car, so we're going to have to switch places. You'll have to drive and I'll be really annoyed if we wind up anywhere but the airport." At least she was unlikely to ditch me, being on the side of an unfamiliar highway.

She unbuckled her belt and opened the door, confused as all get-out. Rather than risk opening mine when I couldn't see clearly, I unbuckled and scooted over to the passenger seat. I was fading in and out now, the black hole in my mind threatening to eat me alive.

As soon as traffic cleared enough to open the door, she hopped in. "But I don't know where I'm going. I've always been a passenger coming out of Denver."

I reached for the lever next to the door that would lay the seat back. "You can't miss it. Just look for the Pena Boulevard exit. It's a two-lane exit to the right and only goes one place . . . the airport. Hopefully I'll be back with you before we get there. But if not, head for the Departures section and park in the covered lot near one of the United check-ins."

Now she was looking concerned, because the headache was back and she could probably smell the pain. "Are you okay?"

I let out a small chuckle and closed my eyes. "Not really, but it's a hazard of the job. As you learn the ropes, you'll probably hear a lot about this group of exalted people that the Sazi call *the seers*. I'm one of them. We have weird psychic shit happen—seeing the future, the past, and all points in between. Oh yeah. Real *exalted*. It hurts and it's annoying as hell because you can't predict when it's going to lay you flat on your back." I paused and opened my eyes, ignoring the pain so I could make my point. She glanced at me, blinker on, ready to leap back into interstate traffic. "I don't recommend it as a career choice."

And then I was out again.

Chapter Fourteen

NASIL LOOKED DOWN at the gas gauge and tapped it, hoping as I did it would rise above the red line just a fraction. "I've never tried to milk the tanks this dry before. The camp's just over the next rise, but it's a question mark at this point whether we'll make it."

I had no particular fear of plane crashes. I'd survived a dozen before. But I wouldn't relish telling Lucas the Wolven jet was scattered across the Honduran jungle. "You'll have to *find* a way to make it."

"We'll land." It was a solid mass of leafy green below us, with no flat surfaces, leading up to a high peak. Nasil apparently caught my incredulous look because he shrugged. "There really is a landing strip at our camp. I've no desire to walk out of the jungle either."

"Why are you *in* the jungle? You could have gone anywhere after I killed my father."

He raised his brows in amusement. "After *who* killed your father? I seem to remember a certain young female tiger who did most of the killing."

"Tahira couldn't have done it alone. You know that as well as I. She would have burned up from his power if she hadn't shared it . . . with *me.* You do know I gained a great amount of my father's power, don't you?"

He didn't reply for a long moment, but his tongue flicked out cautiously. There was nothing for him to smell, no way for him to dispute the facts—mostly because he left before the end. Deserted both my father and Antoine in order to escape with his lover. And I couldn't imagine he'd kept up with news about the council since then. He tried to keep his voice from showing any inflection, but he failed. "Have you? And what have you gained?"

Oh, no. It wouldn't be that easy. "Betray me, and you'll discover firsthand. I'm no longer someone to be dismissed as weak or impotent."

I used those words intentionally. I'd heard them from my father's lips to his ears, years ago. He stared at me for a long moment, eyes unblinking and cold. But a hint of surprise leaked out from underneath the unfeeling exterior at my lack of expression or scent. I'd never before challenged his authority, nor given any indication I was a match for him. I'd longed to track him down right after Sargon died, when the powers I gained were at their peak. That they were fading now said I'd probably eventually lose them all, which was frustrating. But I was fairly confident I was still Nasil's equal . . . or better.

Tuli poked her head in just then. I looked toward her, but she carefully avoided my gaze. "Are we nearly there? The terrain looks familiar."

Nasil turned his gaze from me to her. He had to get in one last dig before we landed. "Just over the next rise. You should both probably resume your *discussion* in the back."

If he expected me to flinch or show any embarrassment, he was disappointed. Tuli wasn't looking at either of us. She was staring out the front window and raised a finger to point. "Is that smoke on the horizon? Why would they be lighting the cans in broad daylight?"

At my questioning look, Nasil explained. "We fill oil cans with gasoline-soaked rags and burn them at night to keep away *el tigre*. It lets us get a few hours sleep since Sargon left. They never approached the camp when he was here, but now they've grown bolder."

"You have tigers in the jungle?" That did surprise me. Where were they imported from?

"Jaguars," Tuli answered. "But the locals *call* them tigers. They don't realize there's a difference. And the cats have gotten a taste for snake lately so they're a real problem. But we normally don't see them in the daylight."

As the hillside flowed under us, and the engines began to sputter and whine, my brows raised. "I don't think the jaguars are your biggest problem anymore."

It wasn't just cans burning on the wind. It was the camp. The smouldering remains of brick residences and elaborate wooden buildings were scattered across a broad area. I'd thought of *camp* as being just a few ramshackle storage buildings and some tents. I'd had no idea of the scale of the project father had been planning. It was a small city down there. Or it had been. I didn't notice any people around. At least upright ones. There were a number of bodies sprawled in openings between the trees and I could finally see the landing strip. I frankly didn't think it was long enough for the jet, but Nasil seemed confident.

"Eternal Anu!" Tuli exclaimed. "What happened?"

Nasil let out a hiss of frustration. "Federales, rival drug cartels, maybe even just an accident in the lab. Hard to say. I guess we'll find out. But let's see if anyone is still down there." He adjusted his headset and pushed a button on the console, as I digested that there was a *lab*. What had they been making? *"Cinco, Cinco, Ocho, Be. Bien?"* I supposed it wasn't surprising they had to speak Spanish down here. It wasn't a language I was terribly familiar with, but I could learn languages fairly quickly when exposed to them. Nasil repeated his call and then turned a dial. "Maybe they switched frequencies." He said the words again, even as he was lowering the landing gear. He listened intently and then turned on the speaker for Tuli's and my benefit. There was only dead air. Not even static. "It doesn't look good. It might be that the government finally managed to locate the camp. They've been trying for nearly a decade."

He started to lower the flaps. The plane hit a pocket of turbulence just as one of the engines stuttered to a stop. "I think it's time to buckle up. Will you need help up here?"

Nasil shook his head, concentrating on keeping the jet level. "I'm more worried about taking off again than landing. If all the fuel was burned or stolen—"

Tuli and I left him to the landing, hurrying back to the seats and buckling up. I wanted to ask her things, but she'd closed down from me, careful not to make eye contact—even though she made a point to sit right beside me. I could smell her desire every time we brushed hands or arms, which was often as the plane dipped and slid over the treetops.

Nasil's voice came over the intercom, making us both look at the ceiling. "Hang on. It's going to be bumpy."

He didn't exaggerate. Branches cracked against the bottom of the plane, making ripping sounds that caused Tuli to lift her feet from the carpeting. The entire plane shook and the oxygen masks dropped from above . . . not from lack of air, but just because they were shaken loose. Tuli finally spoke and it was accompanied by the taste of fear. "Have I mentioned I'm not fond of flying?"

It seemed an odd thing for any Sazi to be afraid of. I shrugged. "You'll heal if we crash."

Even if it was what she expected to hear, my matter-of-fact tone apparently surprised her. Her expression and scent turned to one of deep hurt and she looked away from me. Had she expected comforting words? And why?

She gripped the armrests and closed her eyes, her teeth gritted for whatever would come. I heard the slowing whine of the second engine just as we made a steep nosedive, still going faster than I could care for this close to the ground. But then the nose rose rapidly and we were thrown against our belts from the force of the air brakes slowing us. The wheels hit the ground with a bone-jarring thud that made my jaws slam together. We were thrown abruptly backward against the cushions and then forward again as the brakes were applied. Smoke rose from the wheels, invading the plane and coating my tongue. It would take days to get my joints back to normal. Even if I shifted now, I'd ache.

Loud scraping outside came from the front of the plane, with more branches breaking, as we went off the end of the runway. But we'd stopped. Tuli was still gripping the armrests with white knuckles and her breathing was rapid. I touched her hand and she froze, stilling even her breathing. Only her frantic pulse said she was still alive. "I *am* sorry if you were frightened."

There was nothing else to be said, so I unbuckled and stood, leaving her alone to get her composure. Nasil was already outside, examining the plane. It would probably need a new paint job and the landing gear was slightly damaged on one side, but it actually fared quite well.

While I loathed giving Nasil a compliment, there was really no choice. But there was nothing saying I couldn't turn it to my advantage. I lowered my brows with a studied frown, in a passable imitation of my father. "A skilled landing. I suppose I'll let you live another day."

He'd finally had enough and stood up to his full height, turning to face me with the confidence of old. "Be very careful you don't overstep yourself, Rimush. Your father didn't underestimate me, and neither should you. While I chose to serve him, I was, and *am,* every bit his equal. Who do you suppose it was he sparred with? Do you really believe he would hold back from giving his best in a battle . . . *any* battle? I wouldn't be alive today if I couldn't hold my own. You're here at *my* sufferance. If you expect to live to return to your plush life, keep your mouth *shut.*"

It was time to increase the stakes, and his nervousness. "I've seen you with a sword, Tormentor. I know your skill with all manner of weapons and potions and your magic is strong. But you should be careful as well, for my back is now fully black. I hold death in my hand—" I let the smile that bared my teeth rise into my eyes. "And I've been practicing."

Inheriting power wasn't the same as inheriting gifts and he knew it. He was likely still faster, but you can't outrun a killing touch. His eyes narrowed, but he didn't respond. He simply stared. But even the scent of burning brakes couldn't hide his anger, or his sudden fear and wariness.

Tuli found us like that, staring across the distance of half the plane, neither one giving ground nor advancing. She seemed back to her old self. She descended the stairs and stood precisely between us, turning her head from side to side. She let out a low, angry hiss and thrust her chin forward. "You both stink of challenge and we have no time for that. We have work to do. I'll go make sure the temple is safe. You two find out what happened here. If you can't work together then, for Her sake, at least stay apart!"

For *her* sake? At last we were getting somewhere. "I would like to see the temple, if I could. Father talked much about it."

Again Nasil's eyes narrowed in suspicion, but I gave nothing away except the excitement I really did feel. Tuli nodded. "Of course. You've every right to see what we work for and meet those who will serve you. You've claimed the right of succession." Now Nasil stiffened, his back going completely rigid. So, that term meant something to him too. Interesting. "Come. It's this way." She walked away and I followed, careful not to pay any attention to his reaction. After all, you don't notice those who serve. They do their job competently without your supervision or they die.

But Nasil was no ordinary servant. I'd have to watch my back from now on. It was nothing new, of course. I'd listened and tasted for his presence in every room of every home I'd lived in since I'd left Akede. What was a few more days?

TULI BECAME MORE agitated the farther we walked along the jungle path. It had been carefully cleared of undergrowth, but was hidden from above by the towering trees. Birds and insects of all descriptions swooped around us, but I could do without the biting flies. I just hoped they choked on the venom-laced blood. "Is something wrong?"

She stopped and listened for a long moment. Her tongue flicked repeatedly, tasting the air in all directions. I wasn't sure what she was searching *for,* so I remained quiet and passive to whatever might happen.

The heat was oppressive, moisture hanging in the air like steam in a sauna. Moving would at least get a breeze going. I shrugged. "What are you listening for? I hear nothing but birds."

She nodded, her teeth nibbling on her lower lip. I'd forgotten she did that and remembered how adorable I'd found it when we were children. But her words weren't childlike when she spoke. "Precisely. I don't hear anything either, and I *should.* There should be guards, many guards and the priests of the order. We're only a few steps from the temple, and it's silent. Something is horribly wrong." She broke into a sudden run and I followed, twisting and turning behind her along the rocky path.

When she stopped, I nearly ran into her, avoiding her only by sidestepping. My hands hit something solid, covered in green slime. It was a stone, cut to a perfect square and set alongside a hundred others in every direction.

We'd arrived.

Tuli didn't wait for me. She ran around the corner of the structure, calling out names. "Carlos? Jose? Where are you?" Now her voice doubled and I realized I was hearing it both outside and echoing through the stone next to me. "Syed?" She let out a loud gasp of fear and surprise and I found myself racing around the corner of the temple and into the blackened entrance before I even realized I had.

It took a moment before my eyes adjusted to the dim lighting inside the temple entrance. There were torches in sconces on the walls, but they were unlit and cool to the touch. The only light was the torch in Tuli's hand. She was fifty meters or more ahead, the only spot of light in the black that the daylight couldn't reach. "What's happened? Why did you gasp?"

"They've broken through. She's gone. Someone has stolen our queen." Her voice was flat, in the sort of shock that people get when the unimaginable has occurred.

I hadn't thought to bring a lighter with me so I walked forward with trepidation, not sure if the path to where she was standing was a straight one or if I'd fall into a black pit somewhere in the middle. But I needed to see what she was talking about. This was apparently a vital part of my father's plan for it to be so important to Tuli. I found myself wishing she wasn't involved in this, didn't actually *want* my father's goal to proceed— whatever it was. To defeat it was to defeat her, and that brought a conflict in my mind I hadn't expected.

The path was straight and sure. I stepped up behind her and tried to look around her into the breach in the far wall. But she wouldn't move, seemingly frozen by the sight before her. I finally grasped her by the shoulders and moved her bodily aside and took the torch from her hand. The flickering flame didn't reveal anything of interest to me, but it might be because I didn't know what I was looking *for.* All I could do was bluff and hope Tuli revealed more in her answer. "Are you *certain* She was here?"

Tuli shook her head and threw her hands into the air with the same frustration I could taste over the mildew, moss, and lingering sweat. I could taste other snakes too, and recently. It must be a strange sort of species that sweats. Most of us don't. "I don't know. The priests seemed so *certain.* The temple was the right size and the right location. The legends spoke of the precise layers we found here. The egg should have been in this center pyramid, the red one that was protected by her priests for millennia."

She'd taken my question at face value, and I suddenly realized just exactly what was happening down here. The torchlight revealed the deep crimson plastered over the stone next to the breach. Ochre blended with blood and then with cement. My heart started to beat so hard I could feel it my head. The tiny clues that had been gained by the blood of a dozen Wolven agents across the world for nearly a century all abruptly clicked home. Fortunately, if Tuli could smell my fear, she thought it was for another reason.

It wasn't that Father was resurrecting the Order of Marduc to be its leader. He planned on actually raising Marduc *Herself!* The great winged snake was considered to be male in Assyrian and Babylonian folklore but was, in fact, female. Only a few of the very ancient Sazi even remembered She existed, in fact. Most cultures had tales of such a creature, from dragons to quetzalcoatls and beyond. But few realized there really had been a freak of genetics in the ancient past. A Sazi, that was born of snake, fused to bird and had the strength of legions. There was no fire that breathed from her mouth, only power. Raw magical power that could freeze or burn into ash. It was said that lightning crackled around her with each wing flap and storms followed in her path. That would mean she had the equivalent power to the entire council. To the ancients, she was a goddess. And if Father had found a way to make her live again—

"Merciful Adad," I whispered, an oath I hadn't used since I was a child. I pushed the torch fully into the crack in the stone, now realizing it was just about the size and shape of an egg that could house the great and mighty Marduc. I wanted to laugh at my concern from last winter that there might be were-spiders back among us. I'd face a thousand spiders rather than one winged serpent that was born with any help from my father. Who knew what he had been putting into the process? But I now understood his desperation to have Tahira Kuric-Monier as his servant, to have a true power well that could pull on a thousand Sazi to bring her to life. He'd had an ego the size and depth of the oceans themselves, so I had no doubt he believed he could control her and make her a slave to fly before him and conquer, leaving him to rule in her wake.

I wasn't so certain.

"Yes." Tuli's voice made me flinch. "We must inform Nasil. Hurry!"

She rushed back out of the pyramid, leaving me to consider my options. I needed to get word back to Charles and Lucas. This was too important to simply stay undercover and try to undermine the process without help.

Tonight. During the hunt, I'd find a way to return to the cave and see if the magic was still strong enough to reach the young wolf. I'd marked it well so that I could both find it by scent and sight after dark.

Yes, tonight we'd begin the process of bringing down Father's plan at last. I sent out a silent mental plea, with no idea whether he could hear. *Be listening, wolf. Be waiting somewhere to speak.*

Chapter Fifteen

"—SPEAK? MR. GIODONE? Can you speak at all? We're here." I felt someone shaking me and I shot upward so fast that the shoulder belt, still strapped to the frame, slapped against my nose.

Liz winced and pulled her head out from the passenger door. A low rumble echoed around me and cool, exhaust-laden air made me sneeze four times in a row. I snorted and snuffled and tried to get my head on straight while Liz watched me with a bouncing nervousness that spoke of actual concern. Sweet kid.

I got out of the car and looked at my watch. Unfortunately, the numbers didn't really register any sort of meaning in my head. It sure would be nice if I could just pop out of these visions and be back to normal, but it wasn't that easy. I felt thick and slow, weighted down under a pile of fluff—loose and floating, but too heavy to move.

She already had the bags out, so I locked the car and started to follow her inside. She stopped and stared at me for a second, probably realizing I wasn't quite all there. "Wheel well?" Her eyes dipped to the key ring in my hand and all of a sudden, the real world came crashing back. The fuzz was gone and I was clear-headed. Thank God. "Gotcha."

I put my hand up to slow the car coming up the ramp and sprinted across to where the car was parked. Now my watch meant something when I looked. We had just over an hour left, which would work just fine. We could still grab a burger or some Chinese and get our allot-ment of meat and make it to the gates. I waited until the travelers hurrying from their cars had gone and tucked the key and chain up under the wheel well so it was sitting on the engine frame. It could still be reached, but wasn't obvious to passersby, or even a regular sneak thief.

When I reached Liz again, she smelled relieved, a little pocket of light, fresh air in the chemical-laden entry. "You look better now."

I held the door for her, which seemed to surprise her. I smiled, but dropped my chin for a little reproach. "I can *be* a gentleman, your ladyship. And yes, I'm better now."

She shook her head as we walked down the hallway toward security. "I don't know if I'll get used to the royalty thing. That's just weird."

I shrugged. "If by *royalty* you mean three hundred fiftieth in line to the throne, I suppose so. But don't be planning your coronation any time soon. Remember, no title—so probably no tickets to the ball either."

Her little pouty face had too much sunny humor un-derneath to be anything other than a joke. "Oh, sure. Ruin my fantasy."

We were at a jog now, so when I spotted a ticket kiosk, I had to do a skid that nearly sent my roll-along sailing ahead of me. "Tickets."

"Oh. Oh! Yeah, that would be good. Should I go wait in line at security?"

I grabbed her wrist in response and felt a brush of power that was pretty impressive for a new turn. "What do *you* think? No. We stick together."

The little huff of air was frustrated, but not resentful. "Okay, I deserved that. But I'm not going to run. I was just scared before."

"And now you're not?" I asked as I started to enter data into the computer. Charles had given me the paper with the confirmation number so it was pretty easy to pull up the boarding passes and hit the print button.

"No, I'm better now. I think it'll probably come back, but I'm just going with it for right now. Maybe I'm in shock."

I pulled the pages out of the printer tray and then we were off again at a race-walk clip. "Could be. Stranger things have happened."

Her voice came out a little airy from gulping for breath trying to keep up with me. "Speaking of strange things, what happened to you in the car? Where did you go?"

I let out a laugh loud enough to cause a couple of heads to turn. "You wouldn't believe me if I told you."

We reached the end of the security line, which was only three twists deep around the cordoned poles. She wouldn't let go of the bone she was chewing on. "Try me."

As I handed her the boarding pass with her name and pulled my wallet from my back pocket, I gave the short version. "I was in the head of a snake in the Honduran jungle, learning that a creature I thought was a fairy tale, or more precisely, a *Tale from the Crypt,* is actually real." I turned my head toward her as I tucked my pass and license back in my pocket and started to take off my shoes. "So, I'll be spending most of our time together on the phone, letting the right people know what they need to do to make it go bye-bye."

"Oh." She paused as my phrasing sunk home. It must have occurred to her that when a creature of legend is scared of another creature of an even weirder legend, it's a bad thing. "Oh! Yeah, okay then. Is it . . . um, *nearby*?"

"Hope not." My shoes and bag sailed through the scanner and I passed through the detector without a fuss. "They lost it. That's part of the problem."

Dammit, I'd been right earlier. A serious-looking uniformed guard walked up to us when we were putting back on our shoes and asked politely, "Could you two step over into the office for a minute?"

Liz groaned and we both looked at our watches simultaneously. Eleven o'clock. The hand search of the luggage probably wouldn't take very long. I was just hoping there wouldn't be a cavity search involved.

IF THE RUSH to the airport had been frantic and exciting, the rest of the trip to Newark was deadly dull. I had no luck contacting anyone at the clinic and Lucas's cell phone was in a perpetually busy state. Or he had it turned off. It didn't matter which. So I told everything to Sue mentally. I was interested that she hadn't any idea about the scene in the jungle, but distinctly remembered certain things about Ahmad and Tuli in the plane. She didn't know *how* she knew, but she remembered the green tank top and camo pants and the taste of honey. That was weird and I wished I could figure out what the hell was going on.

I'm sure it looked to Liz like I was out again, so when we touched down in Newark, I explained a little bit about how mating works.

"You mean if I find *the one,* the right person in the whole world for me, I'll have some sort of mental link to him forever?"

I nodded, but then winked. "Unless you're actually gay, and it's a *her* instead of a him."

She gave a little shudder, which surprised me since she said she was liberally bent. "No, that's not an issue. I'm very, *very* straight. I don't even know anyone who's gay."

That made me smile. "Actually, you do. Remember Linda and Bab . . . I mean, *Barbara* in the car? They're a couple."

Her mouth opened wide and she turned to me in the aisle of the plane where we were waiting for the flight attendant to open the door. "But she's *pregnant!*"

A couple of people stopped talking, moving from passive to active listening, while trying to appear not to. I leaned close to her ear. "Yep. With Carmine's baby. They're a threesome. Carmine and Linda. Carmine and Babs. Babs and Linda."

She blinked and shook her head and put her hands up in front of her like she could push away the image. "Whoa. Um . . . wow. I . . . that is, that *never* would have occurred to me."

"And they were sweet as pie, weren't they? Just two best friends shopping for the kid and trying to protect their man. Is that such a bad thing? I'm straight too, and don't share well. But if *they're* happy, is that a crime?"

I knew I was going to have to stop throwing all this esoteric shit at the poor kid. But she had a lot of promise. It seemed a shame to have all the independent thought beat out of her by the system before she even has the chance to think about real-life stuff.

I opened my mouth again, but she held up a hand to stop me. She just kept blinking and shaking her head in tiny little movements. "Sorry. Brain's on overload right now. Try again later."

That made me chuckle, which was just about the time the door opened with a whoosh and sunlight filled the narrow cabin.

We exited into the busy airport and started to head toward the ceiling-mounted screens to find out where Nigel might be arriving. "Charles said American flight one-twelve from New York. I'll bet *that* was a slap in his face."

She turned to look at the side of my face. I could see her brow furrow in my peripheral vision. "Whose face?"

"Lucas told me once that your grandfather's a British loyalist. Thinks King George never should have given up putting down the *colonial rebellion.* He apparently vowed never to set foot on American soil."

She got it in one. Again. "Eww . . . and he's flying in on *American* Airlines. Ouch." Then she shrugged. "Well, I'm about as American as they come, so he'll just have to deal with it. I can be polite and learn what he has to teach me, but he won't convince me that America isn't the best place on earth to live."

I just shrugged. I'd been a lot of places in the world, and there are a lot of very cool cities and countrysides. But that was for her to learn. I wasn't going to argue. We started to move toward the B-numbered gates. It was going to be a long walk to B-47, since we were starting at A-19. But there was no hurry. The screen said it was delayed and wouldn't arrive for another hour.

It was when we had just stepped onto the down escalator that I had to backpedal fast and hard, pulling her with me out of the line of other passengers. She nearly dropped her suitcase and did drop her purse, but grabbed it before it went downstairs without her. I motioned for her to follow me quietly. We went to the railing above the main terminal. "Look over there. Isn't that the same guy you saw at the hospital? Louis Perricone?"

I knew it was. He was walking with Scotty, which was a stroke of luck I couldn't believe. Unless, of course, they were here looking for me. But how would they get here before us?

She peered over the rail and looked around. Her eyes moved past the pair standing talking at least three times, with no sign of recognition. "Sorry. I don't see anyone I saw at the hospital."

"He's right there. In the center, with the blond kid in the gray suit. Next to the hotdog stand." I pointed, making sure to be very casual. Then I turned around in case they happened to look up.

She shook her head again. "Nope. Sorry. I see the teenager, but that's not the guy from the hospital."

It made me stop and think. While I hadn't actually seen Louis in the hallway, Mike and Marvin have known him for *years.* It would be tough to pull the wool over their eyes. Plus, I remembered a friendly scent, even if I couldn't place it with certainty. I ducked behind a pillar, but kept them in my sights. "Describe him. The guy you didn't like the smell of in the hospital."

"Probably forty and beefy. Very Italian face. Big nose, dark complexion and hair sticking out his nostrils. Yuk."

Yeah, that was Louis all right. Linda keeps telling him to cut the nose hairs. Even bought him one of those trimmers a few years back. But he won't. Said he likes the body God gave him and he's not going to change it and insult the Big Guy.

"Now, describe the guy and the kid."

She flicked her gaze downward and squinted a little for a closer look. "The teenager is probably sixteen, and he looks like a normal teenager, just dressed up. He's blond and slender, but he looks like he doesn't smile much. Has more frown lines than someone his age should have. Hard to judge the other guy's age, but I'd say thiry-five. Mexican, or . . . no, maybe Middle Eastern. Yeah, sort of an olivey complexion. Straight black hair and dark eyes." About halfway through, when she said *Mexican,* I had to look over the rail again. No, that sure looked like Louis to me.

"Wow. That's some talent you've got, kid."

"What is?" She peered down again, trying to figure out what *I* was seeing.

"That guy is a Sazi. He's projecting an image to make himself look like Louis. You remember how you looked away from Charles when he changed back at the clinic? You saw him as naked, right?" She nodded. "Well, the rest of us saw him in a three-piece suit. Not a bit of skin. And we all saw the *same* suit. We could testify in court or take a lie detector and pass." I motioned downward with my chin. "Same thing here. Nobody can fool you with illusion, which is an awesome thing, like seeing through a magician's trick. But your gift will keep you *alive.*"

"So is that boy seeing the same thing as you? Is he pretending to be someone the kid knows?"

She's quick on the uptake. "You've got it. But I don't think he's a predator . . . at least in the way you're thinking. But he does want to get him alone. He's going to lie to him and try to get the kid to give up an article he stole, and—"

"Oh. That's not so bad, I guess."

I finished it, because she was still being naive. "And . . . then he'll kill him. I would bet it won't be quick, either. I'm thinking this is one of the same guys who sliced the crap out of Carmine . . . my friend in the hospital."

"So we have to save the thief from the attempted murderer? That doesn't seem right."

I shrugged and started to drag her back in the other direction, toward the stairwell. "Actually, we're saving the murderer from the murderer. Sometimes the ethics are confusing in this biz. Scotty took over my place in Carmine's family. Don't underestimate him, and don't turn your back for a second. In fact—" I paused and rethought the whole thing, liking the second scenario better. "You're going to stay here and watch the bags." I fished the cell phone from my pocket and held it out to her. "You're an official lookout. I'm going down to meet with them, and try to figure out what's up. Your mission—"

"Should I choose to accept it—" She didn't reach to take the phone.

I opened her hand and put it in. "*Whether or not* you choose to accept it . . . is to use the speed dial to call Lucas and leave a message in case this goes badly. Then I expect you to go find your grandfather at his gate and tell him what happened too. After that, your life is up to you. But remember you'll need to change tonight on the moon, so if you're going to duck and run, go somewhere private. Don't get caught and wind up ratting out all the little shifter kids who'll end up like you someday. You'll condemn them to waste away in some prison compound they'll probably call a *reservation* for the rest of their lives."

The last line got through. She blinked and then nodded solemnly and scrolled down the screen until she found *Address Book.* She took a deep breath and gave a shaky smile. "Okay. All set. Go . . . do whatever it is you do."

I went and started thinking furiously as I did. I didn't have a gun, or a knife. In fact, the only thing I had was a garrote hidden in my belt. But that particular belt was up in the bags, so even that didn't help. If this guy could cast an illusion wide enough to reach me on the balcony, *and* keep his magic inside enough that I didn't see the glow, then it was going to be tricky.

Could I pull off happy and effusive? With Scotty and "Louis"? The kid wouldn't buy it for a second. He's known me for too long. He'd be suspicious as hell.

I let out a small smile as I headed toward the escalator.

And that was my *in*.

Chapter Sixteen

MY MIND WAS moving with lightning speed as I kept myself hidden behind the large woman in the flowered dress. As the escalator descended, the little Chihuahua in her arms peeked over her shoulder and let out a fierce tinny growl. But then I *looked* at him and let the tiniest bit of power slide forward. His bulging eyes went even wider and his ears flattened tight against his furry head. He ducked back into the safety of his owner's arms and began to tremble until the woman patted him in a comforting way.

They were still talking, not even looking my way. But the Sazi would smell the wolf in me pretty soon. I had to be quicker. My goal was to get the guy to do something very un-Louis-like. Scotty probably didn't hobnob with the made guys like Louis yet, but he'd been exposed enough that he'd notice something *really* unusual.

I threw open the door to Sue's mind as I touched bottom and felt her respond. **I need some bright and sunny to pull this off, sweetheart. Can you read some jokes and laugh a little to help?**

She spotted Scotty at the same time I did and I felt a moment of panic from her. He'd scared the crap out of her more than once. She didn't underestimate him a bit. **Remember. Bright and sunny. You wanted** *agent,* **you got it. The man you're seeing isn't Louis. It's illusion, and I need to expose him to Scotty.**

I felt her scrambling in her mind and could actually hear the clicking of keys as she logged in on the computer. **I've got a jokes folder here. I'll try to find some funny one.**

Until then, I'd have to make do. I raised my hand and raced toward them at a half run, hand held out in front of my body and a smile broad on my face. "Hey! Scotty! Louis! How you guys doing? Haven't seen you in *forever!*"

Airports are the place to meet up with people, so nobody even noticed another bunch of guys being surprised by an arriving passenger.

Scotty turned and his jaw dropped. The Louis-clone's eyes narrowed and I could tell he was thinking frantically, trying to figure out who I was and how he should respond. It took a couple of stammers before the kid responded. "Mr. Giodone. Um, *sir.* It's a . . . well, it's a real surprise to see you here."

He'd cut his hair short, keeping to the dress code Carmine insists on. He looked older than his fourteen . . . or, no, he must be nearly fifteen now. He'd started young, taking his first life at six. But he still smelled of fresh yellow mustard, so at least I knew it was him. I grabbed him and wrapped him in a bear hug, rasping my fist against his hair in a big brotherly noogie that flat left him speechless.

Then it was the Louis-clone's turn. He did smell like Louis, sort of dry and dusty, but so did most of the snakes I'd met. He tried to back away from me, but I wouldn't have any of it. I threw open my arms, and twitched my fingers for him to come closer. "Aw, c'mon, you old reprobate. We go through this every time. Gimme a hug."

The light came on in his eyes, figuring that if it was what we *always did,* he should do it. When he smiled and threw his arms around me with a laugh, I saw the first glimmer of suspicion in Scotty's eyes. He wasn't sure who he was suspicious *about* yet, but there was a definite chink in the armor.

Louis doesn't hug. Anyone, even girlfriends. He's that paranoid.

I backed away quick, so it didn't seem icky and clapped Scotty on the shoulder. "So, how's everything back home? Everybody good?"

He nodded, confused again. "Uh, yeah. Sure, I guess. Everybody's fine." Then he amended, probably figuring I hadn't heard. "Except, well, Carmine's a little under the weather. You might want to call and cheer him up."

A little under the weather. Now, there's an understatement. "Really?" I asked, completely innocently, all the while waiting for Sue to get me bubbly again. I'm not really good at it for very long. "Well, he's tough. He'll be better soon, I'm sure."

A moment later, I felt her in my head again. She might be late to the party, but when she came through, it was in spades. **Geez! I almost forgot! Ask Louis about Carol. They're getting married, and he's thrilled. Can't talk about anything else lately, according to Linda.**

I nodded a couple of times and then looked at the Louis-clone again. "So how's Caroline? You two still fighting? She move out yet?"

He paused for a moment, probably trying to remember if that was the right name. He decided to fake it, and that was his downfall. He shrugged. "Eh. You know. Some nights are worse than others."

Scotty's eyes narrowed and he glanced at me when the Louis-clone checked his watch. He was probably hoping to end this fast and get Scotty out the door. I nodded once, the smile off my face completely for that split second, and the deal was done.

Now the kid smiled too and I had to fight the laughter that tried to sneak out at what he said. "Gosh, Mr. Giodone. It was great to see you! We're headed out to the shuttles to get to my car. Want to come along and talk about old times?"

The Louis-clone didn't like that much. "We really don't have time, Scotty. We've got to pick up that package so I can get home."

I walked behind them and put an arm around each of their shoulders. "No time wasted. We're going in the same direction. I'm heading to the shuttles too."

Call my cell phone. Liz has it. Tell her not to follow me. I'll be back in thirty minutes, tops. If I don't show up, go to Plan B. We already discussed the details.

I didn't wait for a response. I shut down the connection with Sue and turned on my smile again. As we walked away, chatting like the old buddies we were all pretending to be, I saw Liz answer the call and nod, then put her thumb up in the air where I could see. Good girl.

* * *

I SAT NEXT to Scotty with Louis on the other side of him. My jacket was off now, both because it was too warm, and I would need it later. The shuttle was full, so looking squished together wasn't tough. About halfway to the lot, I nudged his thigh with a thumb and then made slapping motions with several fingers. He started sneezing all of a sudden and reached into his front pocket. The kid had a real handkerchief . . . embroidered. I was betting it was a gift from Linda, but maybe a girlfriend. Either way, after he blew his nose lightly and started to tuck it in his pocket with an apology, I felt a pocket knife fall onto my hand. Yeah, I figured he had more than one blade. I cautiously slid it into my back pocket, all without the Louis-clone realizing it.

When we reached the lot, Scotty called out, "J-ten, please."

It was probably the farthest lot from the building, and the farthest drop in the lot. That's what I'd do, anyway. The Louis-clone's eyes lit up, probably excited that they were going to be alone. I waited, talking fast until we were about six stops in and then said, "Shoot! That was my stop, back at A-eight. Oh, well. I'll just ride with you guys and then walk back. No big deal."

"You could get out at the next stop and not have to walk so far." The Louis-clone was sounding surly now, so Scotty had to jump in.

"No way! I'll give you a ride back, Mr. Giodone. There's no reason he can't tag along, is there, Mr. Perricone?"

Now, the Louis-clone wasn't stupid enough to *not* know what Scotty did for a living, so he probably expected a little paranoia. He changed his tune almost immediately. "Oh, you're right. Why not chat? What's a few more minutes?"

So we chatted, and chatted, and chatted some more, until the whole bus was empty and the end of the lot was near. We talked sports and weather and even, ick, men's fashion. Finally we were at the stop. We got off together and stayed together until the bus left. Scotty pulled a set of car keys from his pocket. I was a little surprised he had a license. I was betting Carmine took care of that little problem for him with a fake ID.

"Okay," the Louis-clone said, clapping his hands once and rubbing them together with a smile. "Let's just get that box and I'll be on my way." I was thinking that he was either planning to kill us both, or just take the item and go, rather than risk not getting it at all.

"It's over on the next line." He raised his hand like he was going to beep the doors, but then shrugged when there was no answering tone. Hey, wait. I'd seen that key chain before, now that I looked at it closer. It was something Carmine had given to Linda years ago. The "door opener" was actually a switchblade. It opened straight out and locked like a push knife. Linda wound up hitting the button by mistake once and sliced right through her favorite purse. She told Carmine thanks, but no thanks. No big surprise that it had found its way to the kid. Like Carmine said, he likes pointy things. In fact, his trademark as an assassin was to use a blade. As a kid, he could get close pretty easily and the little sicko likes to see the lights go out in a person's eyes.

We didn't have a signal, but like I say, he'd watched me for a long time when I was freelancing. I didn't realize it at first, but then I was sort of flattered, so I didn't care. I knew he wouldn't turn me in, because he had more strikes than I did.

I figured the only sign I needed to give him was to drop the persona, and I was right. My face went blank when the Louis-clone turned to walk toward the car and a second later, so did Scotty's. I opened the blade and then flipped the coat over the Louis-clone's head. Scotty dove low and knocked his legs out from under him. As a team, we weren't half bad. He didn't know about the head and heart thing, but when he drove his push blade upward between the guy's ribs, I slammed mine into his temple with enough force to get through the skull into the brain. It not only went to the hilt, I pushed the whole damn thing inside the hole. If Scotty wanted it back, he'd have to dig it out.

There just flat wasn't time for the guy to respond with his magic, which I considered a plus. He might have kicked our collective ass. His thrashing went suddenly still and Scotty tore off the coat down to his neck so he could watch that rare, beautiful sight. Except it wasn't Louis anymore and he smelled distinctly of snake . . . viper to be precise. The eyes with the light going out weren't green anymore, they were brown. It was the man Liz had described. The light had faded quickly with the application of the dual blades, silver or not, so Scotty didn't get to see much. My nice new jacket was soaking up the blood, and unless we dumped him over on the ground, nobody would ever know there'd been a murder here.

But Scotty's face was confused and I wasn't sure how I was going to explain that the guy we killed wasn't the guy he thought we were killing.

I could only think of one thing that he might buy. I'd

used the coat over his head so I wouldn't touch his skin directly and get sucked inside a hindsight, but maybe there could be another reason."That's why I covered his face, kid. He'd swallowed some sort of new drug so that every time he breathed, he was making everyone hallucinate. I heard you call him Mr. Perricone from up on the escalator, but I knew this wasn't him. I was just playing along with what you saw. Carmine told me about this new shit. Said he was afraid the guy was part of that gang from Jersey, wanting revenge, and it looks like he was right." He looked up at me, not really certain, so I slammed the ball out of the park. "Because, c'mon. Would the Louis you know ever miss a *poker game*? It's this weekend. I'll bet he's planning to bring a table into the hospital!"

That made him laugh and suddenly whatever I said was okay. He'd buy it. He'd buy it even more when it turned out I was right about the table in the room. He looked at me with something approaching awe as we picked the guy up and started to carry him to Scotty's car. "So this was a hitter from Jersey, looking for me? And Mr. Leone sent you to save my life? He's not mad at me?"

"Oh, no," I said honestly and with a stern face. "He's *very* mad at you. You fucked up big time, kid. You *never* take a trophy from a job without his express order. This is what happens. I was told to beat the crap out of you if I didn't think you had the proper respect. But—" I added with a generous air once we'd relieved the guy of the garrote in his pocket and had the body stashed in the trunk, "I think you just got your respect back. Near-death will do that to you. So we'll leave you with kneecaps. Carmine's willing to forgive and for-

get. Provided you give me the trophy to take to him."
He hesitated and I shrugged. "Call him if you want to
confirm it. I don't care. You have Mike's number, don't
you? He'll hand Carmine the phone. I got my orders
straight from his mouth this morning."

That was all she wrote. He knew full well I wouldn't
bluff. Not using Carmine's name. He shook his head
and opened the back door. "I'll be glad to get rid of it.
It's been nothin' but trouble."

"Why'd you take it, anyway? Planning to pawn it?"

He handed me a plain cardboard shoe box, wrapped
to look like a present. He could use lessons in gift wrapping."Nah. It's probably not worth any money. It was
gonna be a gift. For my girl."

Oh-ho! I'd forgotten he had a girlfriend. Must be
some gold jewelry. Maybe a ring. "The one from last
year? The hooker?"

He shook his head forcefully and there was a certain
amount of pride that drifted over the mustard scent.
"Yeah, but she don't do that any more. I sort of knocked
her up." I let out a noise of disapproval, because even
at his age, he should know better. But he added quickly,
"It's okay. It was on purpose. We wanna start a family.
We planned it this way. It was the only way her pimp
would dump her. She's staying with her brother here in
Jersey until she has the kid. Then we'll skip town and
move in together. Her family don't like me much, but
I'll be good to her and the kid. Mr. Leone will keep me
working and said I could have that little apartment out
by the pool."

I didn't doubt it. Family takes care of their own, even
when it's a weird situation.

"Mrs. Leone said I should get her something pretty,

to let her know I was serious. When I saw this, I decided it was perfect." He glanced at the trunk again. "But it wasn't worth it. Not by half. I'll find her something else. Maybe this guy has a few bucks in his wallet. I'll go to a real store and have them wrap it nice."

I opened the wrapping and then took off the lid. I was sort of expecting something fancy and gold, so this just sort of floored me. "A knife. You got your girl a *knife*? Not a ring or necklace?"

He turned serious as death. "Oh, Sally *loves* knives. Probably more than me. She's not a girly-girl who wears gold and silver and crap. And you have to admit, it's really pretty."

It was, in a weird sort of way. The black obsidian blade was wide and probably six inches long. It had been chipped to a razor's edge and the patterns of the chips sort of resembled scales. The handle was bone, decorated with inset turquoise and what might be rubies or garnets.

I started to reach for it to take it from the box for a better look, but changed my mind when it started to glow. Another tentative finger toward it said this wasn't an ordinary knife. I could actually watch as my aura was pulled into the black blade while I sucked in my breath. It *hurt*. That couldn't be good.

Yeah, I might use a knife to kill the guys who cut Carmine, but it wouldn't be *this* knife. I didn't want it anywhere close to me. Plus, Scotty didn't need to know I'd been given the job, and especially with a blade. "Okay, then. I'll take this back, and you head back yourself. I give my word that nobody has a contract on you, except maybe for these goons and I'll see what I can do about that. Consider it a wedding gift."

"Man," he said, walking around to open his door. "You are something else, Mr. Giodone."

Another gift. "Call me Tony."

He beamed, and stayed that way until he dropped me off at the shuttle stop at the terminal.

Chapter Seventeen

I SETTLED A paw into the cool water slowly, not making even a tiny splash. Birds of all descriptions were at the water's edge and I could see them gleam with near phosphorescence under the bright full moon.

Liz was somewhere over the ocean about now, being held in form by her grandfather. He was a right old grouch and I felt sort of sorry for her. His picture would be beside *curmudgeon* in the dictionary. Still, he had greeted Liz politely and commented that she looked very much like his late wife. His black hair had streaks of white that matched her animal form. She noticed it too and raised her brows at me in a *How weird is that?* sort of way when he wasn't looking. I thanked her for her help, not mentioning *what* help she gave in front of gramps and, on impulse, gave her a quick hug.

I got a hindsight flash that only lasted moments, but confirmed what her father had suspected. I whispered in her ear before I let her go. "You really did take down the tower. It's good you're doing this."

She smiled, shaky. It told me she remembered too, which often happens after a hindsight. "I don't want to hurt anyone. I'll get this under control. I promise." She turned to go, but then stopped. "Will I see you again?"

I winked. "You never know, kiddo. There's a whole new life out there for you. Almost anyone could show up in it."

Nigel had growled lightly and I decided to take that as a message. I raised my hand and smiled. "Sure. No problem. I'll send Lucas and Charles your regards, your Lordship."

He managed a really excellent *harrumph* but dipped his head in a brief nod after Liz preceded him into the skyway. He said more words then than he had the entire previous ten minutes. He stared after her for a long moment and I thought I might have seen a slip in his grumpy persona. Was that a twinge of affection? But then it was gone. "Thank you for delivering her safely. Having a young lady in my home will take some getting used to after so many years. But tell Charles I'll do my best."

I'd gotten a surprise after I watched the London-bound jet take off. Sue called to say she was also on board a plane, headed my way. When I asked why, she said it was a secret, and I couldn't even drag it out of her in my head.

And speaking of my head, I hadn't yet heard from Ahmad. It might be he couldn't find the cave, but I really needed to get some meat in me before anything weird happened. I didn't need to wake up in a cage somewhere because I passed out in full view of the interstate.

Another slow step into the mud. There were both ducks and geese along the shore, heads tucked under their wings for the night. I don't really like the taste of

Canada goose. Too greasy. But these were their smaller cousins—snow geese, and I was wondering if flying over that ocean on the way to their winter grounds wouldn't make them taste pretty good. A likely suspect was just on the other side of the reeds and cattails where I was chest deep in water. The cattails had exploded along ago, so with each movement I made through the tall stalks, fluffy seeds rained down on me and tried to go up my nose. I tried not to breathe, so I wouldn't sneeze.

The thick, succulent scent of bird shut down my higher brain functions and I felt my head go down, ready to pounce. With a sudden burst outward, I threw myself into the nesting birds and grabbed the wing of one goose before it could get away. It honked and squawked, but I soon silenced that. Then I was padding back to the hole under the tree root I'd found to use as a den to feast.

Sweet and warm and the feathers felt soft going down my throat.

Feathers? No, the rat had soft fur, not feathers. But it was soft and smooth as it slid down to my stomach. It wasn't enough for the night, but it was a start. The undergrowth down here was made for snakes. I was a little surprised I'd never visited before. There were a thousand places to lie in wait for small burrowing creatures, or I could hunt for a larger animal in the trees. Most cobras couldn't climb trees, but I'd always been able to.

I needed to find the cave to talk to the wolf, but eating had to come first. I wondered where Tuli had gone. She'd disappeared shortly after the incident in the shower.

She'd been talking to Nasil when I arrived back from the temple. I confirmed that the inner chamber was indeed empty and speculated that perhaps someone in their group had betrayed them, believing they could raise Marduc without their help.

They'd answered simultaneously, and anger rose from them in a cloud of choking sweetness. "Paolo."

Nasil started to storm around the camp, looking for any documents he could find that might say where they'd gone. He suggested that we go to hunt and he'd find gasoline and supplies so we could take off before morning. He just had to find out where the traitors had gone.

I'd still, as Tuli had less-than-affectionately referred to it, *stank* of challenge, as well as smoke from the brakes and from the village. While the roofs had burned and the buildings were open to the air, the plumbing still functioned. I decided to avail myself of the shower before the hunt.

I found myself enjoying the feeling of the warm water under the night sky, which was how Tuli managed to watch me for so long without my realizing it. I turned with the unscented soap my father favored still in my hair and saw her there, eyes gleaming and body naked under the moon. I let the water run until my hair was clean and then spoke. "You're welcome to join me if you'd like."

She didn't speak, just shook her head. But she didn't leave either. It was difficult not to respond to the scent and sight of her, so I didn't bother to try to hide it when my body reacted to her presence. I glanced down at the erection jutting out and gave her a small smile. "I'm afraid I'm going to have to relieve this before I change forms. You might wish to leave if you don't want to participate."

Still she didn't move. Her eyes glowed even brighter until it seemed her body would disappear inside them.

There was something extremely erotic about the thought of her watching me take pleasure, so I closed my eyes and began to stroke my length. The soap was slick in my hand and as I let out a small hiss of pleasure, she returned it, only louder. It sent my heart racing and I stroked myself with abandon, back pressed against the wall while water rained down on me. It wasn't long before a shudder overtook me and I climaxed onto the water-soaked floor. When my breathing slowed after a moment, I opened my eyes. She was gone, the towel she'd been holding discarded on the ground. But the taste of her arousal was heavy on the air, which made it all the more curious that she continued to deny her passion. Yet, it was oddly satisfying, the effect I was having on her.

And she on me.

I slithered through the leaves again, feeling each rock and twig against my belly. Another mouse fell prey to my fangs when I struck out into a hole where I'd seen movement. It was small, not at all like the rat, but added to the meat in my stomach. But now I sought larger prey, so I went on the hunt.

An odd sound found my ears so I went to investigate. It was like a strangled cough, which often means easy food. But when I tasted the air, I found Tuli's sweet honey and nuts, the exact flavor of baklava on the wind. But it was blended with panic, and that hurried my movements.

She'd found dinner—a large rodent of some sort, with russet fur and a short stubby tail. But something had gone wrong and the beast was upside down in her wide open jaw. She'd also been too anxious to feed and hadn't waited until it was dead. The prey was still alive, and was kicking frantically upward, trying to free itself from her pulling muscles. One leg was already impaled on her fang, but was continuing to kick. It was going to break off the tooth if she wasn't careful. But she couldn't even bite down again to still the frantic motions. I slithered out and her eyes saw the movement. That's when I noticed the other problem. The animal must have front teeth and it was trying to chew its way out of her from the inside. It could damage her lungs or even worse. She would eventually manage to free herself and feed, but she would be too injured tomorrow to travel.

"Remain still," I whispered and slithered up alongside her. She needed to roll over so I could bite through her skin to paralyze the rodent. But the beast was wide and fat and she couldn't turn. The only hope I had was to wrap around her and physically force her over. "Close your eyes and try to relax."

She did and the scent of both fear and relief blended on my tongue. I worked my way around her tail, then slowly began to travel upward. Around and around I coiled, letting myself enjoy the sensation of her scales on mine. There was no reason this had to be a painful process. When I reached the thinnest part of her throat, the membrane just behind her jaw, I paused. "I'm going to kill it now. Do you want it out of you after, or want to feed?"

Out. The word was clear to my ears, but I couldn't fathom how she'd said it with her mouth full. Still, if that was her choice, it was easy enough. I slowly pierced her skin with my fangs and felt a little shiver run over her as I did. I pressed forward farther and felt another pierce, followed by thick meat. It was a good meal and would probably have been the only one she'd needed tonight. But some things aren't meant to be.

I struck forward hard, felt the venom pump into the

furred body. The death was sudden, taking no more than a few seconds. Such is Sazi poison. Then I started to convulse my muscles, pushing upward from her stomach to her mouth. I felt her relax under me, so that her jaw teeth that held the animal and firmly pulled it inch by inch to her stomach would release the prey as I pushed. Since it wasn't very far down, it only took a few slow stroking motions to move the animal up out of her mouth once I'd pulled the leg loose from her fang. After it was disgorged, she could breathe properly again. Somehow her windpipe hadn't moved forward like it should so she could breathe. A series of misfortunes.

"Are you all right?" I relaxed my coils, but left myself wrapped around her until the trembling of her muscles ceased.

She moved her jaw up and down and flicked her tongue against her fang. "I will be in a moment. That wasn't the way I'd planned the meal."

I let out a hissing chuckle. "It never is. That's why they call it *hunting,* and not catching."

We remained like that for long moments, until I felt the warmth of her body start to heat mine too. I'm fully capable of sex in either form, but she'd already said no twice. I nuzzled my mouth against hers, enjoying the slick feel of her scales. "Shall I leave you to your dinner now, or are you enjoying this as much as I?"

She didn't answer with words. Instead, she just slipped her tail around mine and tightened the coil. I hadn't realized quite where my coil was, but my erection was abruptly inside her. The same muscles that pulled her dinner in worked on me and I couldn't resist the contractions that dragged me in. There were no words, just our bodies twisting and turning around each other on the soft leaves. At some unspoken signal, we shifted forms simultaneously and then my mouth was on hers and my hands were caressing her breasts while her fingers dug into my back. She moved against me hungrily and it was difficult to imagine that I'd only relieved this need an hour ago.

"I've never gotten over the desire to feel you under me." The whispered words came out of me unbidden, but they were the truth. Every other lover had been compared to Tuli, and all had been found lacking.

She bit my neck as I felt her muscles start to contract around me. Another venom-filled bite punctured my skin and then a word filled my ears. *"Ahmad."* It was a whisper and a hiss and I let her revel in her climax while I flooded her body with tickling, stinging magic and traced my tongue down her frantic pulse.

I followed her into the abyss moments later and then collapsed on top of her while she laughed lightly.

I stroked my fingers through her long hair, removing some of the leaves clinging to the strands. "There. Was that so terrible?"

She sighed. "It probably will be later. But let's not think about that now. Just hold me for a few more minutes. Then I'll need to find a new dinner." She glanced down at the rodent that had caused her so much trouble. "This one has lost its appeal."

I couldn't help but chuckle.

WOLF. CAN YOU hear me, wolf?

I shook my head and realized it was still furry. Feathers, a wing, and one leg ending with a webbed foot was all that was left of the snow goose. It was good. Much better than the other kind. I'd have to keep in mind.

Ahmad called again and I shook my head to get the stinging of his magic from my brain. Whatever he was doing was different than the visions I'd been getting. Wolf!

The name's *Tony,* Ahmad. I'd appreciate you deigning to either call me Agent or by name.

A pause. Very well. Tony. Have you been in contact with Lucas or Charles recently?

I didn't want to get into a long recitation of what had been a really weird day, so I just said, Yes.

I have information that absolutely must reach them. Will you deliver the message, or must I kill you when I return?

Oh, for God's sake. I picked up the rest of the leg and started to chew on it, pretending it was his snakey head my fangs were sinking into. Look, snake boy. I don't like you. You don't like me. But let's be civil here, huh? It's bad enough I have to go along for your little sex romps with your main squeeze—which takes on a whole new meaning in your case, but—

What did you say? I could hear the panic note in his voice.

I sighed, as much as I could and rested my muzzle on my paws. It had been a long day and it wasn't getting any better. Look. I've been inside your head since you were chained down in Boulder this morning. You can't hear me, but I can hear you. I presume you found the cave so it works both ways for the moment. Oh, and I've also been able to smell through your tongue—which is freaky weird, and get fired up enough to have to have sex every few hours. I was there for the breakout, and for the flight where you got cozy with Tuli and talked about your whole sad history. Then when you landed and found the camp and just now when you had steamy snake sex. But we're not going to discuss that. Ever. 'Kay? Just tell me what I *don't* know yet. I saw the temple and heard you thinking out loud about the legends. What else you got for me to pass on when I call?

He sounded a little shell-shocked when he replied, and I guess I would be too in his place. That will speed up this discussion, I suppose.

I would have snapped my fingers together if I had any in wolf form. Oh, by the way, anything in your legend about a weird obsidian blade? I came by one today on another case and it's definitely of Sazi origin. Or, at least, it affects us by cutting off pieces of our magic aura, which hurts like blazes. Anything you've heard about?

There was a pause long enough that I wondered if we'd been cut off, but since all I wanted to do was sleep anyway, I figured I might as well let myself drift off. He'd either wake me or he wouldn't. I already had plenty to discuss with Lucas and Charles in the morning. My eyes eased closed just as I let out a slow breath that blew bits of white fluff into the air. Hmm. Actually—

I pulled over the remaining wing and put my muzzle down into the soft feathers. Perfect. A goose down pillow. It'd feel a lot better on my skin than mud and wood when I changed back in the morning

Pain. An ache of something missing inside.

I opened my eyes and I was back inside the cave where Ahmad was. Except Ahmad wasn't there. It was empty, silent even of insects. I felt my hands being pulled to the cool stone wall. They flattened and pressed and the ache filled me again. There was no heartbeat, no fire to warm the bodies of what used to live here. I got a flash of the cave again, but filled with jungle life—bugs and bats wandering through the depths, monkeys playing in the cool shade, eating fruit and grooming.

And then the ache when it was taken.

Wol . . . Tony? Ahmad's voice shattered the image, and it fell to shards of color on the floor of my mind. I blinked my eyes again and I was back under the tree.

God! What? I sounded grumpy, even to myself. I wanted to get back to sleep. I don't know why I was dreaming about the cave, but it wasn't a bad dream, as things go. Sort of a mental Discovery Channel special, which is often what I go to sleep by anyway.

I had to leave the cave to check on some things. Are you already aware of them, or should I tell you?

The quiet night sounds of the wetlands were lulling me again, so I wanted to get this over with. **Tell me.**

Nasil found documents that indicate there's a second temple and we all agree that Paolo might have taken the egg there to hatch. But strangely, it appears to exist on the East Coast of America somewhere. I wasn't aware the Mayans extended their territory that far. I know of some burial mounds in the Midwest that could conceivably be attributed to Mayan descendants, but a temple?

Okay, he'd managed to get my attention enough that I was awake again. Geez, I can be dense sometimes. **No. Not a temple. A *casino*.**

A cas . . . Explain.

So I did. I told him about what had happened to Carmine and the new gang of . . . duh! Central-American guys. It was all clicking in my head now. I'm betting this Paolo of yours is either legit in some part of his life, or knows someone who is. They didn't *find* a temple, they're *building* one! It's called *Quetzalcoatl* and is being raised in Atlantic City. Carmine said the new gang is into drugs and didn't Nasil say something about a lab down there maybe exploding?

Even more pieces were falling into place and Ahmad picked up where I left off. The Order of Marduc likely has many tentacles. My father would have seen to that. So, at some point they must have decided to expand their drug selling into your former employer's town. They were pushed out, but didn't understand the Mafia culture there and killed someone important.

I found my head nodding, the moonlight now making my brain race even faster, instead of slowing it down. And Carmine, of course, immediately ordered a hit of someone there. But the hitter Carmine sent got greedy and took a knife that's critical to raising Marduc, which is the knife I have now.

I could tell Ahmad agreed, but there was one kink in the theory. Except nobody here knew anything about a knife. Either it's not involved or was something the priests of the order were aware of that they didn't tell anyone about . . . even Sargon.

Or, I amended, maybe they just found it. You said nobody had breached the wall to get to the egg until recently. Could it have been in with the egg? An offering of some sort that they're not quite sure what to do with? But it would still be sacred and they'd want it back.

Ahmad's voice sounded pleased, not that I really cared. So, it sounds as if our destination tomorrow needs to be that temple. I'll let Nasil know we fly to New Jersey.

Fly. New Jersey. Crap! That's right. There's one more piece to the puzzle. After you left, Angelique went nuts in the clinic when I said I was going to New Jersey. She kept repeating that she had to get there and it took Charles, Lucas, and Amber to sedate her. Amber wanted to run blood tests to find out why both she and you went berserk. She mentioned something to my wife about a virus or . . . a drug. What exactly were they making in that lab?

He paused and replied slowly, thoughtfully. I'd presumed regular street drugs, cocaine or heroin, but now . . . now I'm not certain. I'll definitely check and get samples for Amber before we leave here. He sighed and I could feel a wave of frustration, tinged with fear, as though they were my own. I'll have to confront Nasil. He is the key to most of this information. He was Father's right hand and despite what I might have told Tuli, there was little he didn't know about what Sargon did. I'll advise you of the results.

I let out a little huff that would have been a chuckle in human form and inhaled another breath of moist, musty air. I'll probably be there for it. I seem to get stuck inside you for the big four: food, water, survival, and sex. Just try to keep it to the first three for the next few days if you would.

The next noise might have been a cough, or maybe it was a mumbled swear word I couldn't make out. But the rest was clear. I'll keep that in mind. Good night, w . . . Tony. Your help has indeed been valuable.

I'd like to say he left and I was able to get back to sleep, but that wasn't to be my life. Like the telephone ringing every time you step into the shower, I heard Sue in my mind next.

Tony? Where are you?

I sighed. *Trying* to sleep under a tree. What's up?

I'm in Newark and rented a car. I was driving down the interstate and got the feeling you were nearby. Would you like to sleep in a bed tonight?

You'd think that would be an easy answer, but it wasn't. There was nothing quite like falling asleep next to my mate, regardless of my form. But tonight I was feeling the moon like few other times in my life. It was powerful, compelling and yet comforting. No. I don't think so. I've got my feather pillow and I'm comfortable. But hey, if you want to meet me at mile marker two-forty-six tomorrow morning, I could use a ride back.

I liked that it was okay with her. She didn't question or whine. She just said, Okay. Love you. See you tomorrow.

My eyes drifted closed, and I successfully ignored the buzzing of my cell phone, set on vibrate. Yeah, I could answer it in wolf form. Touch pads are just made for pointed claws. But it was already sealed in the plastic bag where I'd put my clothes after I stripped. I'd have to tear it open with teeth and claws and then all my stuff would be damp in the morning.

But the knowledge that there were still things to be done made it so my mind wouldn't follow my closed eyes down into the depths of the night. It's interesting how things replay in your mind when you're in the netherworld between light and dark.

All roads lead to New Jersey.

But what roads lead *out*?

My eyes snapped open in the darkness and I raised my head so fast I cracked it against the massive old root roof. The pain spurred my mind to full wakefulness. Where did Ricky and Stuart fit in? Yeah, they were Jersey guys, but they worked for Prezza, not the snakes. Or, was Prezza *in* with the snakes? But they weren't looking for Scotty. They were looking for *me*. How did they get to Boulder and, in fact, how did they find out about our trip to Hansen, Kansas? Not a snowball's chance in hell *that* was coincidence.

I opened the door in my mind again with a sigh, and uncurled my body out from the cozy nest under the tree. Sue?

She answered immediately. Yes?

Changed my mind. Can you come pick me up after all? I won't be sleeping, though, I'm afraid. Did you bring your laptop with you, and does it have remote access to the Wolven files?

Her voice sounded amused, excited and curious. Sure, yes, and yes. I'm on the way.

Chapter Eighteen

"AND THAT'S WHEN I discovered *this*." Another phone bill popped up on the laptop screen. Two items were highlighted in yellow. One was an incoming call from an international number. The other was an outgoing international call. But the numbers weren't the same, not even the country code.

"What am I looking at?" While she'd made a compelling case so far that a current Wolven agent was on the take, this part wasn't making sense to me.

She leaned back against the edge of the desk in the hotel room so she could look at me. I leaned back in the chair and gave her my full attention. "When Lucas asked me to pull up the phone records for each of the Wolven-issued phones, he asked me to look for any irregularities in the billing. It didn't take a rocket scientist to know it wasn't just billing issues he was looking for. We still haven't found the mole who planted all the trackers in things. It had to be someone high up in the organization. Regular agents just don't have access to the stuff that was tampered with. So, I started looking for numbers that were called often and then cross-checked the dates with weird things in the files . . . you know, people supposedly in one place but got calls in another. That sort of thing." She tapped the screen with one shiny fingernail. "Look at the *dates* of the calls and tell me what you see."

I did, and when she said it that way, I noticed something odd. "They're exactly one day apart. *Exactly.* Down to the minute."

She nodded and crossed her arms over her chest. "And so are the dozen other ones over the course of a year or so. I haven't looked any further back yet. And check this out." She turned around slightly and grabbed the mouse and moved the scroll bar down to the next pair of yellowed entries. "Every incoming call I've marked on this phone is a hang-up, like a wrong number . . . but it's the *same* number. Lucas got a plan that lists the numbers, but doesn't charge for the first ten seconds. That way, he can call and just say something like 'Report in,' and then they call him back from a secure number."

I nodded. He'd done that to me more than once.

"Of course, it could just be something simple like spam calls. We have a few of those stupid investment companies that call week after week."

She nodded and then grabbed another chair to sit down in. "I considered that. It would make sense except for those calls the day after. Every time."

She was right. I scrolled down and call after call. One spam, one outgoing the day after of varying length, but around ten minutes. "Where does the outgoing ring to?"

"Our agent Rayna in Mexico City. A landline in her apartment. It's definitely her number. I've called it to verify."

"So you're saying we've got *two* moles. Working together." I tapped my finger on the tabletop and considered what to do with the information.

She shook her head. "I thought that too, but scroll down to the bottom. This bill came in just yesterday."

I did and noticed two more highlighted calls and realized exactly what she meant. "Wait. This can't be right. You're sure it's a landline? Rayna was a prisoner in the jungle when this call was made. She wasn't anywhere near Mexico City."

The look I got said it all. I didn't even need the scents of determination and annoyance. "Precisely. Someone's trying to frame her. I got her permission to do some checking around and discovered a Mexico City bank account in her name, in a different branch as her regular accounts, with a bunch of money in it. And a bunch of activity, too. Including one rather large withdrawal . . . on the same date as the last call."

I put my hands behind my head and thought. "Wow. So this is your surprise. Quite the coup, sweetheart. Whose phone is this?"

She laughed brightly and stood up. "Oh, no. This isn't the surprise. I wouldn't have even brought it up to you if it wasn't for the fact that you'll probably have to verify to the council where Rayna was on the date of the last call. And I don't know whose number this is . . . yet. Only Lucas and Charles have the list of numbers that match the agent names." She walked across the room to the closet near the door and pulled out a large cardboard tube that you might mail documents in. "No, *this* is the surprise, and I was damned proud of myself for pulling it off."

Now she had me curious. She opened the top of the

tube and poured out the document onto the bed. I couldn't help but let out a low, delighted whistle when I opened the thick roll of stapled papers. It was a blueprint . . . of the Quetzalcoatl casino! Pages and pages of details about the construction, including the lower basement—set below sea level, with a small room blocked off with a red 'X' and surrounded by pumps to keep out the seawater. "Oh, you *have* been a busy girl! Where in the world did you dig *this* up?"

She preened brightly. She should be proud of herself. This was just short of amazing! "Well, I tried the easy routes first. I figured they would have to file the plans with the building department there. They did, but nobody can seem to find the file. Big surprise that, if there's really a plot going on. So then I called around to all the architects in the city. I found the right one, but of course they wouldn't talk to me. But I remembered Will Kerchee was in New York for a law enforcement conference this week. It's why he had to race to get back to work from the jungle. I called and told him that Lucas *really* needed those blueprints and asked if could do a little chore. I told him Lucas thought it up so he'd do it, but it was really my idea."

She was turning into quite the little spy. My smile turned to a grin as she continued. "Anyway, I had Will call the architect, speaking Spanish, and asked to have another set of the prints sent over to the site. He said he tried to sound really annoyed and told them that some idiot got the plans too close to a cutting torch or welder or something. Anyway, they burned up and they needed another set immediately. Then he changed forms and flew down to Jersey and waited outside the architect's office for the delivery boy to come out. He followed him for a few blocks until he was alone and froze him and took the prints. Did you know that Will can do magical persuasion? He made the poor delivery guy *remember* he'd delivered the package, so nobody's even going to call to check! Well, until they get a bill for them next month, and we'll be done by then."

We'll be done by then. I smiled again. Well, she'd sort of earned a piece of the action. But I'd still try to give her something to do that wouldn't put her in direct danger.

"Then Will gave them to me when my flight arrived in New York and I brought them down."

I looked up at her with a small amount of reality. "You do realize Lucas isn't going to be pleased about this, right? I don't know that he'll hurt you physically like he would one of us, but you could lose your job for overstepping your authority."

She nodded and looked contrite. "Yeah, I know. But it's looking more and more like he really *will* need them. If everything you and Ahmad found plays out, that is."

It was a lot of *ifs*, but I wasn't arguing that the plans were going to come in handy. I shook my head again. "I'm going to have to start calling you Nora if you keep this up."

She smiled. "Only if I get to call you Nick." She leaned over and gave me a quick kiss. "But I like Tony better."

The room phone rang just then and I figured it was probably Lucas. We've been playing phone tag since he left the message on my cell out by the lake. But it wasn't. "This is the front desk. There's a FedEx delivery at the front desk for Mrs. Giambrocco. I'm afraid it got put in the storeroom by mistake earlier. Shall I have a bellman bring it up now or in the morning?"

I raised my brows and covered the handset. "Are you expecting a FedEx?"

Her face brightened. "Oh! Yes. Have them bring it up." I repeated the instructions and when I hung up, she went to get her purse for a tip. "This is surprise number two. I couldn't bring it on the plane, so I had it shipped same-day air."

My little cough was automatic. For the price of same-day air, you could buy the package its own airline seat. In fact, that's *exactly* what you were doing. But the knock on the door didn't give me a chance to ask the obvious question of *what the hell did you have delivered?* The question mark in my head was even bigger when I opened the door. The package was *huge,* as tall as the doorway and probably two feet across. But the bellhop didn't appear to struggle with it, so it must not be heavy. Sue inched past me as I took the box from him and gave him a fiver.

"Put it on the couch. It'll be out of the way there." I did as instructed, but felt more cat than wolf right then, wondering what Sue was up to.

"Should I open it?" I pulled out a pocketknife and looked at her questioningly. She nodded with a sly smile on her face, so I sliced.

Oh, baby! Inside the box, wrapped in tissue and surrounded by poofy sheets of bubble wrap were two big honking swords! "Whoa, nelly. What are these for?"

She shrugged. "Snakes, mostly. You said Carmine insisted on a blade, and these belonged to Lucas and Jack, from way back when they ran Wolven together. I found them totally by accident, wrapped in an old bedsheet behind some filing cabinets when we were cleaning out the Paris office. I had them shipped to our place in Chicago, because that's where the last spider was found. I thought Nikoli might end up needing them. But we need them more right now as far as I'm concerned. Nobody even knows they're missing, so if something happens to one it's no big deal."

I picked up the smaller of the two. It had a two-foot-long double-edged Damascus blade, and from the sting I got when I ran a light finger over the patterns, I was betting there was a high silver content hammered in during the creation. The pommel guard was worn and beat all to hell, meaning it had seen a lot of action in its day. The hilt was bound with leather strips, well stained with both sweat and blood. It's hard to beat a weapon that's seen this much action. I really liked the feel of it in my hand. I couldn't help but swing it around a few times, feeling the perfect balance of it slicing the air.

The lights went out and while I was still swinging a sword, it suddenly wasn't a sword. It was a machete. Okay, I was starting to figure this out. Apparently, I was going to connect to Ahmad every time we did something at the same time. Well that was annoying.

But there was no helping it, because the room dissolved. I just had time to toss the sword aside before I collapsed to the carpeting. Then I was cutting apart another of the bags I found stashed in the corner of the metal building farthest from the camp. The room was still filled with glass vials and burners, even though most of whatever had been made here was gone. I dipped a test tube into the hideous-smelling chemical mixture and put a stopper in it, making sure I kept my glove-covered hands from touching any skin. Tony had been right. This wasn't ordinary street drugs. But what it was and what it was for would have to be decided by another.

"What are you doing in here, Ahmad?"

I didn't stop opening packages, just in case they were different substances. Each of the sample bags had a different label and I dutifully marked each tube with a marker from the table. "Exactly what it looks like, Nasil. I'm taking back samples of the lab product." I turned to look at him, my grip tightening on the hilt of the machete even though I gave no sign of alarm in my scent or on my face. "I would think you'd be just as interested in making sure the quality is kept up to par. After all, if they're lying to you about one thing, why not another?" I paused and then gave him a look that made it seem like I already knew the answer. "Exactly how many people has it been tested on?"

The split-second look of surprise was quickly washed away in his usual disdain. "Only the ones absolutely necessary."

I shook my head and turned back to my work. "I grow tired of you, Nasil. Perhaps Paolo will be more cooperative. We have the same goal after all." I paused, but didn't look his way. It was time to try a bluff, just to see what happened. "Or do we? Why Angelique? Why risk giving her the drug when it could bring down the entire council on our heads?"

It was the right thing to ask. He sighed and started pulling more sample bags from other hidden locations that I hadn't found yet. "I wasn't in favor of that experiment, but we were running out of time. We still haven't found a thunderbird, and the eve of Her birth is expected at the next moon, according to the old carvings

we found. We'd hoped that Angelique might be powerful enough to make up for the fact she doesn't have the
genes, but so far we haven't had any luck."

I feigned surprise, which wasn't difficult, since I
was getting more surprised by the minute. I threw another bone out to see how he would react. "Not *any* of
the girls from Texas? Not even the young Mayan girl?"
I knew Nasil had been in south Texas recently—calling
himself *Roberto,* and that he left abruptly after killing
a number of intentional attack victims. A group of girls
had been captured and made into birds against their
will. One was able to attach to the Texas wolf pack and
was still sane, but the others . . . yes, it was probably
best Nasil killed them. They were completely feral, and
getting so bold as to attack livestock in the area, making the human ranchers nervous. But the report also
said Roberto had been very interested in one particular
Mayan child. Charles moved her and her family to an
unknown location.

He shook his head. "Another failed plan. We lost
Ziri to the council, which was the only girl who held
true promise." Ah. Now it was *the council,* rather than
you.

Excellent.

"What are the benefits of the latest batch? As you
can guess, I haven't had new information since my
father was . . . put down." There would be no more
snide comments or arguments about who did what with
that phrasing. Another dip and then another slam of the
machete down crossway on a sample bag to split it in
two.

He nodded and marked a sample number on another
tube. "The compliance level is *much* better, equal to

the very first batch, but without the mental instability Fiona's suffering."

My charade was ruined in that moment, when I exclaimed, "Fiona?! Fiona Monier? You gave the drug to *her*?"

But I was wrong about being discovered, because Nasil shook his head and shrugged with no emotion attached to taste. "You didn't know either, hmm? Yes, but I only discovered it myself after your father died. She's been quite a challenge to keep on task lately. I'm afraid the council is going to have to have her put down soon. She's absolutely *fixated* on bringing down Lucas Santiago. The constant plots to ruin his life and have him removed from Wolven aren't going to work, but I can't seem to get her to believe that. Still, this new batch is much better, from early reports. We're distributing it to a wide area through the drug cartels as free samples to regular junkies and have found a novel way to activate the people once they've taken the required doses."

My mouth was suddenly dry and there was a buzzing in my ears. My head felt fuzzy and unfocused. But this might be the only opportunity I had to have the entire plot revealed. I forced my voice to sound stronger than I felt, but couldn't meet his eyes or he'd know the truth. "Which is?"

He let out a laugh as he pulled the gloves from his hands with a snap. "Ring tones! I proved with Fiona this year that we could use the compliance drug to make her download a ring tone that would only go off when we called. Then, when she called back our router, we would give her instructions to follow. Afterward, she didn't even remember what had happened. We don't need that same level for the general populace, of course. All we need to tell them is to obey Marduc with the same fanatical loyalty as the priests already have. Of course, Sargon's goal was to have the entire of Wolven just as devoted by use of the drug so that they would run interference against anyone who tried to stop us. We were hoping for the same thing with Angelique, but we're not certain now, since Wolven recaptured her. Still, Paolo told me that he gave her instructions right at the end that would make sure she showed up at the ceremony on time."

Merciful Adad. I couldn't tell Nasil about my conversations with Tony, but since Angelique was in the clinic when they took me . . . yes, now was the time to reveal what I knew in a way that would earn me further confidence. "Ah," I offered with sincere satisfaction. "Then I know where the new temple is!"

Nasil paused and looked at me open-mouthed and his taste held honest astonishment. "You do? Where?"

"Atlantic City, New Jersey. Charles and Lucas had to chain Angelique down to prevent her from flying there. It was when I was trying to free her that they captured me." It wasn't precisely a lie, since I could well have been doing just that when I went berserk.

He furrowed his brow and tapped a finger on the table. "Atlant . . . but the Mayans didn't travel that far north."

I smiled and it was more sinister than happy. "Why find a temple when you can *build* one? In a city of glitz and worship of almighty gold, who would notice one new temple, dedicated to the gods of decadence?"

Now he smiled too, but closer to a leer. "A *casino*. That is brilliant, which means it can't have been Paolo's idea. He's vicious and ruthless, but doesn't have the brains to plan that. No, this must have been Sargon's Plan B. He'd talked of something else in the works, but had never revealed the details. You know how he was about keeping secrets."

Oh, I did indeed. "We should make plans immediately to fly there. Where is Tuli?"

Nasil shrugged. "I haven't seen her this morning. Perhaps you should go look for her. Or—" He paused and looked at me with a significance I didn't grasp. "Maybe you should just concentrate and tell *me* where she is."

I shook my head, not understanding. "You're speaking in riddles. Just get the plane ready. I'll go find her."

He gathered up the vials and put them in a burlap bag and answered with seeming innocence. "As you wish. But my way would be faster."

I walked out into the sunlight and had to shield my eyes until my pupils could adjust to the brightness. Then the brightness wasn't the sun. It was a lamp and I was staring directly into the bulb from underneath. I rose to my elbows and heard Sue breathe a sigh of relief.

"Oh, good. You're back. Lucas called while you were . . . out."

Ah. That would explain the buzzing in Ahmad's mind and feeling fuzzy. I was trying to wake up on this side. "What did you tell him?"

"We just hung up. I pretty much told him everything that had happened so far . . . at least what you've told me. But I did say that you were probably in his head again and might have more information when you came to."

"Did you mention the swords or the prints?"

She looked at me askance. "Do I *look* like an idiot?"

"Good. Then we're going in quiet. Ahmad might make it here in time, or not. But either way the goalpost has moved a little. We're going to see what we can do to make sure a bad-ass baby snake is never born and I think I know just how to make it happen."

Chapter Nineteen

CASING A PLACE is always critical to any successful operation. The blueprints were terrific, but they're one-dimensional. I needed to see things, smell them, taste them—and the only way to do that was to actually visit the casino. It was afternoon by the time we got there, after studying the prints, reporting in on the new information, and putting on a disguise so I might actually make it back out of town alive.

The Quetzalcoatl Casino was open for business, which made it more surprising that Sue was able to get the prints. It's hard for me to walk in a casino during the moon. There are too many noises and smells that make keeping the wolf at bay really hard. So I had to really concentrate, which meant I wasn't going to be much good at keeping track of tiny details. That's what Sue was for. We decided I was the big-picture guy and she was the detail girl. There were still sections walled off with notices of *UNDER CONSTRUCTION* and *TEMPLE LOUNGE—COMING SOON!* plastered everywhere, but the main area was abuzz with happy gamblers. It was a Mayan temple theme, with stepped stone façades everywhere, but they seemed to have stolen heavily from Egypt. I was pretty sure the Mayans didn't use the ankh symbols to decorate their pyramids.

When a waitress came around offering cups of soda, Sue and I each took one. I was in disguise, naturally, wearing a blond wig and moustache, along with green contacts that very nearly matched Sue's irises. She'd lost so much weight from her illness, and carried herself so differently that she didn't need to do a thing except put on some tight, touristy clothes that would make men keep their eyes on her chest, not her face.

It was still odd to see her not minding being stared at. A part of me was a little nervous about that, but her smile was just for me, so that settled the wolf inside.

I raised the cup to my lips to take a sip but one sniff made me drop mine and slap Sue's away before she could drink. I tried to make it look like an accident, apologizing to the nice lady at the slot machine next to us when she got splattered. But as Sue and I were mopping it up, I whispered into her mind. **Don't drink or eat anything here. It's loaded with the drug.** I'd told her as much as I knew about the effects. Her eyes widened and she nodded.

"Do you think they're giving it to all the visitors?" She probably should have spoken into my mind, but we tend to first think to speak out loud unless there's a reason not to.

She'd overheard all the gory details when I was talking to Lucas earlier. He'd been extremely alarmed by more than one of my revelations from Ahmad's conversation and confirmed that the phone bills Sue had tagged were Fiona's.

There was a lot of swearing after that, and whispered

side conversations I couldn't hear. But Charles got on the phone and vowed to bring her in from the field immediately, before she could do any more damage. Then I heard Amber cautioning him that she didn't want her sister put down if there was a chance the drug could be reversed.

They started arguing again, so Lucas took back the phone. "I don't want you anywhere near this, Tony. Come back in."

"I agree with you totally." I didn't *want* me near this, either. "It's just a shame I'm the only one here." Of course, I didn't actually promise to keep out of it since, after all, I had to be here when Ahmad arrived.

Charles got back on to tell me to have Ahmad leave it alone too. They wanted to talk, as a council, about how to handle this new threat . . . from Marduc and the drugs. Of course, talking's great when you've got time. I had a feeling we didn't. Otherwise, why move the egg here in the first place, risking Nasil finding them and being annoyed enough to kill them? I was thinking they found something inside that last pyramid that changed their plans. Something that moved the date up or forced the change of location.

Sue and I found a row of slot machines that we could play and watch the whole room behind us in the mirror. Every time a staff member would walk by, we'd be chatting amiably and making all the right sounds when we'd have three bars or a wild symbol show up. "It's interesting that there isn't a Sazi in the place. I'd have thought the place would be swarming with snakes."

Sue shook her head and as soon as she replied in a whisper, hand over mouth in case the mirror was two-way, I understood the logic. "No, they couldn't do that.

Snakes make people nervous, even if they can't smell them. Nobody would stay or recommend the place. They need lots of people in here. There are a lot of junkies in the world, but not nearly as many as there are gamblers. It's better to fill it with human staff, give people the drug, and then, when they're hazy and compliant, you can spring the predators on them."

So, we needed to find what rock the snakes were hiding under. Unfortunately, it was pretty tough to see whether the prints matched the final product, because so many areas were still closed to the public. I shrugged after getting turned away from entering yet another door. "We'll just have to play it by ear later."

One of the things I noticed she was doing I had to ask her about. She kept sticking her hand in her pocket and then I'd hear a click. Then she'd do it again. I motioned to her and we turned into the hallway where the bathrooms were located so she could explain. "I have a pedometer in my pocket. It has a feature that you can hit a button like a stopwatch and flag up to ten locations on your route. Like, if you know it's five hundred steps to the corner or a thousand steps to the store, then, if you forget the pedometer in future walks, you know how far you went. I was marking how many steps it was between emergency exits . . . you know, in case the lights go out or we sneak in after hours."

That just amused me to no end. "Not many *after hours* in a casino, but an interesting idea. You never know if it's going to come up."

"I'm on my last click, though, so let's go to the front entrance." We proceeded that way, with her quietly counting under her breath. Her eyes were still on her feet when I tried to make a hasty backpedal as I saw who was coming inside. Vito Prezza, in all his glory, along with several of his goons. He didn't smell happy and I had to make a sudden stop at the big slot by the door—the one you have to use both hands to pull the lever. Sue lost me for a moment but looked around and spotted me. Fortunately, Vito *didn't* see me. He spoke with one of the security people and followed him up a flight of stairs, after moving aside a chain and sign marked *EMPLOYEES ONLY.*

"I need to get up there and find out how these guys are connected with Prezza." I whispered the words out the side of my mouth while continuing to feed dollar bills into the machine.

She thought for a moment and started looking around. She apparently spotted something. "Wait here."

She was gone for a few minutes, but I didn't dare follow her in case they came back downstairs. Of course, there might be a back staircase, but I didn't remember one on the prints. I felt a tap on my shoulder and spun to see something that made me blink. It was Sue, but she was wearing a waitress outfit that showed every curve. The little white priestess dress was a mini and had a tight waist and bodice. The hose were patterned with little roses down one leg disappearing into spike heels. I raised my brows and thought into her mind. Where did you get that?

She shrugged and smelled both embarrassed and afraid. Knocked a waitress over the head in the bathroom. Tahira taught me a nifty trick. We don't have long, though. Someone's bound to ignore the OUT OF ORDER sign I put on the door pretty soon.

Um . . . wow. And you plan to do what?

She smiled and held up the tray in her hand, filled with cups of soda. Go up the stairs, of course. You get to listen in through me. I'll probably be kicked out soon, but I can adjust my panty hose or something for a few minutes once I can hear their conversation.

This was deeper than I wanted her to get involved and I could feel my heartbeat increase. You be careful. Get out if it gets rough.

She rolled her eyes. Yes, Dad. Now open up the door so you can hear.

Then she offered the tray to me in full view of the front door security and I dutifully took a glass. She walked over to the stairs like she owned the place and opened the chain. Nobody stopped her and I let out the breath I didn't know I was holding.

This new lack of fear was scaring the shit out of me. I was going to have to talk to one of the Sazi shrinks about this. Probably John-Boy or Betty. They're both psychiatrists and have worked with Sue on and off since I met her. I think they'd be equally alarmed by this new trait. Still, I couldn't deny it could be useful.

I moved to another station to sit down and stared at the video slot blindly. I'd opened the door in my mind and pushed gently inside. I didn't want to distract her, but I did need to hear. It wasn't enough so I pushed farther. I heard her gasp and then I was in. In fact, I was in all the way. I could see the hallway where she walked and I realized my wolf hearing had augmented her ears. She could stand perfectly still and hear what was happening in various rooms.

Okay, a little farther. No. Not that room. Keep walking. I could see her shoe tips as they came into view but her eyes were straight ahead, listening and watching. A glance to her left now and . . . terrific! There was an employee lounge. That could come in handy. Not yet, though. Keep walking, keep walking, okay, now *stop*.

I got the image of her knee. She'd gone to one knee to fix her shoe or her hose or something. Apparently, she was doing it okay, because the guard who walked by just looked at her chest, let out a little happy noise and moved on.

"What the fuck do you think you're pulling here, Romero?" Yeah, that was Vito all right. "You think you can cut me out of the deal? After I pulled this many strings to get you up and running? And now I find out my messenger had his throat cut and was dumped in the ocean. What's your fucking problem?"

The reply was English, but heavily accented. "*You* are my problem, my friend. We did have a deal, but you are the one who broke it. You were to distribute our product free to all your customers and now we discover you're charging for it. And now nobody is buying it because it lacks the *kick* of your other products. We discovered your messenger dumping our drug in the ocean. We simply allowed him to follow it down. That is my *fucking problem*."

Vito didn't sound upset at the news. He sounded more amused. "Hey, if your drug is crap, it's crap. I can't help it if the public doesn't like it. But you didn't pay for the services my people and I provided, and I'm here to make sure you pay up."

"Yesssss." I heard the hiss and so did Sue. Romero was Sazi, and Vito was about to learn what it meant to cross a snake. "Yes, I believe I will pay you what you're due."

Sue winced and rose to her feet when a scuffle sounded from behind the door. Then the muffled sounds of screaming reached our ears, along with a hairspray can gone mad. Were there Sazi rattlers? Because that's sure what it sounded like. The thud of a body-sized object hit the door and made Sue jump to her feet. The tiny stream of red that started flowing under the door couldn't be good, because I was betting the snake made it hurt. While I'd like to say I was sorry, and I'd probably never find out how he knew I was still alive, Vito Prezza leaving this earth wasn't such a bad thing. Get out of there now!

Good plan. She moved quickly down the hallway, nearly tripping over her feet to get out of sight before anyone exited the office. But she was halfway down the stairs when three people walked in the building. She froze, not sure what to do.

Ahmad, Nasil, and Tuli had all changed clothes and were looking cool and professional. Ahmad flicked out his tongue as though to lick his lips and turned his head to me. I nodded and tried to reach him mentally, but he narrowed his eyes, nudged Nasil, and whispered in his ear, making the other snake notice me as well.

What the hell was he up to?

A bright flash of red light filled my vision and I suddenly couldn't move. Until, that is, the security guards grabbed both of my arms and hauled me behind a curtain next to the entrance and down a long hallway to a concrete room that smelled of death and pain. Geez, what is it with casinos and torture chambers? Another Sazi bad guy had one in Vegas and I barely managed to get Sue out alive.

Unfortunately, I couldn't stop them as they tied me down to a chair with silver chains and taped my mouth.

Sue got the same treatment, although the silver wouldn't hurt her. Had Nasil managed to give Ahmad the compliance drug? Was he finally on their side?

I could hear the four of them arguing down the hallway—Nasil, Tuli, Ahmad, and Romero. Finally, Tuli's voice cut over the others. "Enough! I will discover their secrets. I fear the rest of you would simply kill them before they can talk. The guards say they've been here for some time. I'm sure they'll be *compliant*. And if not, then I know other methods."

Great. Just freaking great.

I heard her heels coming down the hallway, and nobody was stopping her. I glanced at Sue, wondering what I was going to do if Tuli started on her first. She's my mate. I could easily kill myself on the chains trying to stop it. I'd wind up insane if I couldn't.

The door opened and I let out a low growl that wasn't stopped by the duct tape on my mouth. Tuli looked cool and deadly as she stalked toward us. She did smell of honey and nuts, but it couldn't cancel out the thick creosote and desert that branded her as a snake. "So, you're a Wolven agent. Yes?" I just glared at her. She ripped the tape off Sue's mouth and she let out a little cry of pain. I struggled against my bonds, smelling the flesh burning as the chains dug into my arms. "Then *you* will tell me. I have little patience today."

Sue's mouth contorted into a sneer. "Go to hell."

This stress wasn't doing my wolf half much good. The moon was still too close. She ripped off my tape next and sat down at the chair next to me. "I would like to be reasonable with you. If you simply tell me who you work for, I'll make it worth your while."

Would it really hurt anything to tell her? I mean, it's

not like Ahmad doesn't already know. There were no secrets left to keep once they killed us. "Sure. What the heck." Sue looked at me like I was insane. "We're Wolven agents. What are you going to do about it? You might as well kill us now, because we won't be telling you any secrets."

"Say it again." She stared hard at me and started flicking her tongue into the air.

I really didn't want to remember what that tongue was capable of, so I just looked over at Sue. "We're Wolven. Do whatever you're going to do."

The room filled with fresh air and her entire persona changed. She let out a deep sigh and whispered. "Thank Anu!" Then to my utter shock, she produced a key and started to unlock my chains.

What the hell?

"I haven't been in contact with headquarters for *years*! There are so many things that I've learned, and I have to get word to Jack, so he can destroy this temple."

To *Jack*? "Jack Simpson?" I rubbed my arms where the silver had dug in and eased the chains off my legs to pool on the floor while Tuli repeated the unlocking on Sue's chains.

She looked at me oddly. "Of *course* Jack Simpson! Head of Wolven."

"Uh . . . not so much. Jack's dead. Has been for nearly a year."

Now she sat down heavily in a chair and her hand flew to her mouth. Her voice kept whispering. "No *wonder* he stopped calling." She shook her head, gathering her wits and let out a fast breath. "Fine, then. I'll contact whoever took his place." She paused, and pointed at

Sue. "Oh. And you need to scream now." Then her voice raised. *"I said TALK!"*

Sue takes hints well. She let out a piercing scream of pain that would win her an Oscar in the horror category and followed it up with a few whimpers. I gave her an incredulous look and whispered, *"You're good, woman."*

She shrugged, but smiled. "Two years of drama in high school."

"Who's in charge now?"

I didn't think that was a secret either. "Lucas Santiago."

She frowned and shook her head. "I don't know him."

Wow. How could someone who knew Jack not know Lucas? "He's old as dirt. They founded . . . oh, wait. He went by another name back then. Enrique?"

Sue provided the answer. "Inteque."

Now her eyes lit up and the relief was back. "Inteque? Oh, that's good. That's very good. He'll know what to do. But I have to get you out of here so you can get a message to him."

Sure. I'd listen and participate in my own escape. No problem. "What's the message?"

Tuli lowered her voice even further and motioned for us to come closer. Just before I did, I let out an angry growl and a sharp swear word and kicked over a chair. She nodded approval. "You must tell him that Ahmad is following in his father's footsteps. He's not to be trusted and must be removed from the council immediately. He's been spying for years apparently and has come to claim Sargon's crown."

"Since this morning? What happened on that plane?"

She stopped and reared back like I'd lost my mind. "No, no. This has been for *years*. The trip here to New Jersey was uneventful, except for Ahmad and Nasil planning their revenge on Paolo. They've probably already killed him for removing the queen egg from the temple."

I sighed, because apparently Ahmad had been playing the part too well. I couldn't decide why I trusted Tuli. Maybe it was because there was no scent of deceit or maybe I was sympathetic because we . . . well, she and Ahmad, were lovers. Either way— "Ahmad's no spy. He went undercover down there. He thinks *you're* the spy and he knows Nasil was. He's been reporting in to the council, through me, this whole time. We know everything that went on down there—" And I do mean *everything,* but I didn't say that. "So, if you need a confidante, your best bet is the snake king. Trust me. I'm one of the new seers. I've been inside his skull and he's playing straight."

Her tongue was flicking out rapidly, tasting my every word. When I stopped, she started blinking rapidly, staring at the floor. Yeah, it was a lot to process, so I motioned to Sue to not speak when her mouth opened. But she spoke anyway. "I've known Ahmad for nearly a year now. He's a total jerk—" I looked at her askance. The goal was not to piss off the nice lady with the key. Tuli turned to her with outrage on her face. "But he's honest and I'd trust him with my life."

Tuli lost some of the anger in her scent and seemed mollified. "Well, he *can* be an ass, I suppose."

Sue smiled. "But he's *your* ass, right?"

She smiled almost shyly, but didn't respond. Instead, she threw herself at me and gave me a resounding kiss on the lips. Sue just sort of sat there looking stunned.

The door slammed open just then and there was Ahmad in the doorway, his face moving from fake furious to very real furious. He took in the loose chains and our rather compromising position in one glance and then slammed the door shut as hard as he'd opened it. "What in blazesss isss going on in here?" He lowered his voice until it was a sibilant hiss and stalked toward Tuli. He grabbed her by the arm and raised her to her feet. That's when I noticed it. I hadn't when I was in Ahmad's head because I was seeing through *his* eyes. Not mine.

"Well, I'll be damned!" I forgot to whisper, but at least I didn't yell. "You're *mated.*" Her honey-gold aura was snaking its way up his black-red, turning it nearly back to the color he was a year ago.

The announcement had a definite effect. She blushed wildly and pulled her arm from his grip. He dropped his hand, boneless, his face draining of blood until he was olive-colored chalk. My head turned toward the doorway, because I should have been listening earlier and Ahmad wouldn't have surprised us. There were distinct footsteps coming down the hall. I pointed at Tuli and made my voice a harsh whisper. "She's Wolven. Working undercover for Jack." Then my finger moved to Ahmad. "He's council, working undercover for Charles." I moved the finger between Sue and I. "We're screwed, not under any cover at all and about to get eaten for lunch. We need to get out of here."

Ahmad can move quickly when he wants to. He barricaded the door with a chair under the knob and Tuli leapt onto the table to yank off the vent cover. I offered my bent hands to step on and she used them. She bounced once while Ahmad held his weight against the door. I also noticed his magic was spreading out, making a shield of sorts that would make it more difficult to get through. Once Tuli was in the duct, she reached for Sue's hand. I lifted her up by the hips and handed her over, then stood on the table myself and jumped through the hole. Wolf aim is handy for that. Ahmad was last. He jumped from the table to the ceiling like a gazelle. I had to back up for fear of knocking heads. "The seal will last only moments. We need to move. Tuli knows the way. No more talking until we're there and crawl as silently as possible."

If I thought we were leaving the casino, I was sadly mistaken. At the first intersection, Tuli took a left. We followed and I suddenly realized we were heading *down*. "We're still going with the plan?"

Ahmad gave me an annoyed look and tried to talk into my head. Wonder of wonders! It worked!

I spoke with Charles when we reached the American border, while Nasil was refueling. When we arrived, I made the excuse of going to pick up food and visited your hotel room. I reviewed the plans and brought the swords here through the sewer grates. I found the inner temple before bringing back food. I told Nasil and Tuli about the plans in your room and that I would recognize you if I saw you. It was always my plan to save you, but I thought I was going to have to kill Tuli to do it.

Wow. He was going to kill her to save us? I guess Sue wasn't kidding about trusting him with her life. It would have killed you too, being as you're mated.

I looked behind to see his reaction and smacked

my head on a support for the trouble. His scent went from a cookie spice sort of warmth to annoyance. **I didn't know that at the time, but I've nearly died for lesser causes. Charles insists you're valuable, even though I think he's a fool. Now keep your mind on our business.**

The next downslope was steeper. It was like going down a water slide with slow people going in front of you. All you can do is grab on with fingernails and heels and pray. It felt like we went down a dozen floors, but it was probably only three. Tuli came to a particular grate and slid her fingers through the expanded metal and shoved hard. The screws weren't meant to withstand Sazi-level pressure and the grate gave way with a sharp pop. It was sudden enough that she nearly fell in, but Sue grabbed her shirt and yanked her back. She turned her head, let out a slow breath, and touched Sue's arm in thanks.

Then she lowered herself slowly into a deserted hallway. This part of the building was still under construction. Open wall studs gave way to rough drywall and then taped and sanded walls, ready for paint. Ahmad opened a doorway next to the stub-out where a water fountain would probably eventually be installed and slipped down a dark flight of stairs.

He returned moments later with the two swords. He took the larger and gave me the smaller. Sue and Tuli looked at us open-mouthed with indignation plain on their faces and in their scents.

I looked at Sue and whispered, "You ever killed anyone with a sword before? It's hard work."

Ahmad nodded. "The blade often gets stuck in the neck joints or between ribs. If you've never done it before, you could easily snap the blade or lose the weapon *and* leave the attacker alive."

Sue blanched a little and nodded, but not Tuli. She stared Ahmad down, even though I knew he wouldn't budge "Well, *I've* used one before. Where's mine?"

I shrugged. "Frankly, I prefer guns, but I'm not going weaponless. These are all we have."

Or not. Ahmad pulled a Sig nine millimeter from the back of his pants, tucked under his shirt. "It's loaded with silver. Will this do?"

I reached for the semiauto with one hand and offered Tuli the sword with the other, giving her a little bow as I did. "The blade's yours, ma'am."

Sue and I stepped back as they started swinging the swords, getting the feel of them. Tuli slammed hers into a wood stud and it went nearly clean through. But that wasn't good enough for her apparently. After she jerked it back and forth a few times to get it out of the wood, she handed the sword to Ahmad and reached for the longer one. The snake king just shrugged and let go. Now she went two-handed and swung at a different stud. This time it sliced completely through. Ahmad did the same one-handed with the shorter sword and shrugged again.

She rested it on the tip and leaned on the big thing like a cane. It came nearly to her chest. But she was happy with it.

"Now what?" I looked around, not really sure where we were in the casino, so it was hard to follow the route of the lower area I'd memorized from the blueprints. "I'd sort of planned on doing this stage with C-Four and a lot more firepower. You really think we're going to stand a chance with all the guards they'll have?"

"We have all the *firepower* we need." Ahmad swung his sword again and did a fine job looking fierce.

But I liked Tuli's response better. "I have C-Four."

All three of us turned to her and spoke in chorus. "You *do*?"

She shrugged. "I don't have *much* but I never travel without it." She dropped to her knees and rolled over onto her butt and took off her shoes. I didn't realize until that minute that they were at least one size too large. She pulled out the foam insole and underneath was a thick layer of creamy white plastic explosive.

"You're walking on it." Ahmad's voice was flat and expressionless, but the surprise of his scent gave him away.

"It's perfectly stable, and you know it. The detonator isn't anywhere close to it and nobody looks at a lady's shoes.

Sue grinned. "Oh, that's just *cute*!" I agreed. She did the same with the other shoe and then she molded them back together. It was a nice fist-sized chunk that would easily lay waste to a wall.

But it would have to be the right wall.

As she was getting back to her feet, with the help of Ahmad, and putting on her now looser shoes, Sue reached inside the tight waitress top and pulled a piece of paper from inside her bra. She also shrugged. "Another place nobody checks." Tuli grinned at her and she opened the slip to show a series of dots and letters around the outside of a square. "These are the locations of where all the gas and electric lines come in, from the blueprint. I also looked to be sure when we arrived. But I'd hate to blow them with all the people upstairs. The place would burn to the ground if we blew the line and a lot of people would die. There'd be a ton of press."

Ahmad sighed. "A great many *more* will die if Marduc is allowed to be born. Even if she never gets her wings, she would be a fearsome creature. And Anu only knows what sort of *adjustments* Father made in her creation."

Tuli was gliding her finger over the paper, memorizing the locations. "Nothing to the egg itself. But her first meal will have a number of *adjustments*. Sargon planned to feed her a concentrated mass of Sazi meat, imbued with powerful magic and any number of vitamins and steroids. It wasn't still in the meat locker at the camp, so I presume it's here."

I grimaced and asked the obvious question while Sue tried to stop looking sick. "Do I even want to know how you *imbue* meat with magic?"

Ahmad raised his brows. "You probably don't. But it's in the preparation. You have to slice the meat off while the Sazi is still alive and lock the power to the meat with ritual magic. One thing we *must* do is destroy the book my father had been using."

"So, we have three goals then. Kill the egg, destroy the book, and blow the place? Heck, that's only three goals and there are four of us. Quick, someone come up with another." I was being facetious and everybody knew it, but Ahmad answered anyway.

"Very well. Add *stay alive* to the list. At least one of us should to get word back to the council."

Well, yeah. That was a point.

Sue looked around and asked the question that I had earlier, but out loud. "Where exactly are we?"

"Basement. Southwest corner. The stairs Ahmad went down lead to the entrance to the subbasement where the temple is." Tuli answered, stepping behind a half wall of drywall, probably to see if there were any tools left lying around. She came up smiling with a pair of needle-nose pliers and a flat-nose screwdriver. Couldn't beat those for playing with explosives.

She raised her collar and removed a length of det cord. I smirked. "I can't wait to see where you have the cap hidden." It came out of her skirt pocket with a flourish. She let out a low chuckle at my look of surprise and then rolled her eyes. I was expecting something a little more . . . *novel.* "The idiot guard didn't know what it was. He gave it back to me after he searched me. It had been in my bra. I told him it was an earring."

I turned to Sue. I hated to disappoint her about participating, but there was good chance we weren't going to be good enough to get through this. "I think you know I'd like you to be the *stay alive* member of the team, right?"

She shook her head sadly and my heart sank. "Actually, I'm probably going to have to be the C-Four gal *first.* They're going to be smelling for Sazi, so I can slip through the cracks while they come racing for you guys. So long as I stay to the shadows, I can get to the gas line where I need to plant it, hide it, and get out. But I don't know how to detonate it."

I held up the gun with a smile. "You just get the charge to the spot and leave the cap where I can see it and I'll make it go boom."

It finally occurred to her and she frowned. "But that means you'll have to *see* it. You won't be able to get out."

I shrugged and reached for her hand. "Like I said, you're the *stay alive* member of the team."

Ahmad looked at Tuli with an odd expression. He tipped his head and seemed truly puzzled. "I find I would like you to also be a member of the team to stay alive. How very odd."

Tuli smiled and touched his hand and I watched the color crawl up the arm. He noticed the sensation this time and stared at his arm. "It's not odd. It's sweet. But no. I've been on this mission since I first met Colecos, who became Jack Simpson, over a thousand years ago. I have to see it through . . . no matter the price."

So, it was set. We were on a suicide mission. That's actually not a bad thing. You tend to focus better when you don't expect to come out. That's not to say you won't *try* to come back alive, but pain doesn't bother you as much. You just keep going.

Sue took off the high heels and wiggled her toes. "I can't *sneak* in heels. I'd rather be barefoot." Tuli looked at her feet for a moment and then kicked off her own shoes. She removed the gel insoles and handed them to Sue.

"I'm fine in heels. Tuck these inside the panty hose. They'll keep you from getting cuts for a little while." Good idea! I helped Sue out by cutting a hole in her hose about midcalf and sliding them down. She bounced up and down a couple of times after they were both in place and they stayed reasonably well. She might have to adjust them from time to time, but it was better than nothing. They were absolutely silent too. No squeaking or sliding noises. I'd actually have to keep that in mind. I'm not above wearing hose if I can be utterly silent.

We slipped down the staircase, weapons at the ready. I didn't like that Sue wasn't armed, but I suppose in a way she was the *most* armed. She had the C-Four in one hand and the blasting cap in the other. All she had to do was stick in the cord and slam it with a brick to make it go boom if there wasn't an option of getting out. I could yell her the instructions if it came down to it.

Tuli was leading us with the long sword. When we reached the door to the temple, we came upon the first guard. I was aiming to shoot from the next level of stairs, but Ahmad grabbed my hand and shook his head. He motioned to where Tuli was slipping down the stairs like a high-heeled ghost. The dark-red glowing guard turned just as she reached the last tread and started to pull a gun. But she was faster. She swung that sword like a tennis racket, her long black hair whipping from the wind it created. His head disconnected from his body before he even had time to get the gun from the holster and the glow disappeared. Both halves fell to the floor nearly simultaneously, well before the scent of pain and blood reached my nose.

I pursed my lips and nodded, then whispered under my breath, suitably impressed. "Go, Red Sonja."

"Who?" Ahmad's face was confused. I just shook my head. It would take too long to explain.

Tuli looked out the window of the fire door and after a long moment waved us downstairs. I let the other three go through first. I pocketed the guard's gun and the wide knife from his pants and moved his body under the stairs. It wouldn't hide the blood, but at least they wouldn't know whose blood it was immediately.

Unless they tasted it.

And I suppose they'd probably do that immediately. Like I just did. It was bitter and thick with poison. I spit it out. Oh well. We'll skip the hiding the bodies part in the future. Saves time anyway. But the fact I couldn't keep myself from tasting the blood probably meant the moon was near. And me without a single meal of meat today.

I had to hurry to catch up with them. Actually it was sort of nice that nobody waited for me. We all just sort of expected each other to do our jobs. But they'd split up by the time I reached them. Sue was hidden in the shadow of the inner temple, which soared to the ceiling of the two story subbasement and was painted bloodred. I touched the wall and then put my finger to my lips. Actually, it was painted *with* blood, which was really sick, considering the size of the place.

I eased to her side and whispered as she stared at her little map. "Know where you're going?"

She nodded and pointed to the far corner of the room, where I could see a large gas pipe joint, nearly hidden behind the machinery. The massive electric pumps holding out the sea were each the size of a jet engine, which must mean there was a *bunch* of pressure against these walls. Sue started to move, but I held her back with a hand on her shoulder, thinking out loud. "How thick do you suppose these walls are?"

She shrugged. "Why?"

"Because people above could escape a *flood*."

She stopped and stared at the walls, trying to follow my reasoning. "But would it destroy the temple?"

"Does it have to, so long as it destroys the *egg*?" Ahmad was halfway across the room, moving between pump shadows with the ease of a thief. I caught his eye and motioned him back to where I was standing with Sue. Instead of moving, he burst into my mind again with an accompanying pain that made me want to deck him.

What?

I motioned to the pumps by moving my hand around in a circle. Can a snake egg *drown?* Should we skip the gas line and collapse a seawall?

He paused and raised his brows and looked around the room. Yes. An egg can drown. Snake eggs must have oxygen to survive. We might not even need to confront anyone with that method. I've no doubt the gas lines are heavily guarded, at least this near the birth. The ones we see might even be decoys. They'd be expecting sabotage there. But if we disable the electricity and the generator and then damage the wall, that would take care of it. The electricity might not be as closely watched. They wouldn't require it for the birth.

He motioned for Tuli to join him and they had a head-to-head conversation so they could hear over the hammering noise of the pumps. I was betting if they tried, they could do the mental link, but I was also certain that Ahmad would be scared to death of it. He doesn't seem to be the sort for commitments. It was even money in my mind whether they'd wind up staying together, mates or not.

Ahmad started to examine the pump he was standing near and I did the same with mine. Sue followed along behind. "So what are we doing?" Oh, that's right. She hadn't heard the conversation with Ahmad. I wasn't sure *why* she couldn't access that part of my head simultaneously, but there you go.

"Looking for a way to shut this off." Sue tucked the C-Four in the pocket of the little skirt she was wearing and tried to find a spot for the det cord. The safest place was probably right where the paper had been. I tucked it between her tightly squeezed breasts and then winked at her. "Can't think of anywhere safer than between two such pretty cushions."

She hit at my arm, but I sidestepped just in time. Then it was back to searching for a shutoff. I heard the slowing whir of another of the machines and looked over toward Ahmad. He pointed up to where Tuli was on top of the machine. She, in turn, pointed to the top of the pump, near the front. She raised her arm and I saw a small white wire that she'd apparently cut. Okay, we could do that. Sue wasn't quite as nimble as the slithering Tuli, but we made do. I tucked the knife from the guard into her apron tie and hoisted her up as far as I could reach. She grabbed onto the edge of a short ladder and pulled herself up. They really had been working with her at Wolven, because a year ago there's no way she would have been able to do the equivalent of a pull-up, combined with a rope climb. She found the wire apparently, because a second pump did the shutdown routine.

Tuli leapt to the top of the next pump but I shook my head at Sue. Let's not push it. She agreed with a nod and dropped down the same way she got up. I caught her and we moved to the next pump. There were eight in total, but when we reached the sixth pump, we heard a voice in the now nearly silent room.

"You really didn't expect to get away with this, did you?" It wasn't Nasil, which is who I expected. It was Paolo who was standing there, surrounded by a dozen guards armed with AKs. I was betting the ammo was silver too.

Ahmad raised a single brow and stared at the group

with utter dismissal. "I don't see why not." The four of us looked around at each other and at some unspoken signal . . . scattered.

The guards immediately started spraying bullets in our direction, forcing Paolo to scream at them to stop. Of course, I was really sort of hoping they'd shoot up the rest of the working pumps and save us the effort. But no such luck.

Then it turned into a game of hide-and-seek. I leapt up and grabbed the ladder where Sue had been and waited until I saw legs come around the corner. One arm let loose and I fired two quick shots into one kneecap. He went down screaming but started healing immediately. I was forced to jump down and put a bullet in his brain and another in his heart. Ahmad would probably call me wasteful for making it a four-shot kill.

But now I had an AK, which was even better. I slid along the side of the next pump. If it hadn't been so quiet, I probably never would have heard the next guard pulling back the slide. But I did, so I spun around the corner of the machine and fired a series of shots that took out his face and most of his chest. Oops. I had it set on full auto. Another waste of bullets. I moved the selector switch to semiauto. If I could fire fast enough it would be plenty.

I heard a scream from the next machine over and felt my heart race until I realized it was a man's scream. Sue came out from behind the pump, now carrying a rifle. But how had she killed him to begin with?

I gave her a questioning look and started to contact her head, but she pointed up suddenly, took aim, and fired. Another guard fell, but she's not good with two-shot kills yet, so I helped her along with a second round to the head. But nice heart shot. Then I put another bullet in his heart just to be safe.

I heard a swish and clank from the other side of the room and looked over to see Ahmad just taking the head off yet another guard. Tuli was likewise cleaning the blood from her sword with an olive-green jacket, which I expect used to be on someone. Then a sizzle of sparks came from the room and part of the lights went out. Ahmad was rubbing singed hands, but we suddenly had an advantage.

We were down to either four or five guards, or so I thought. But with a pounding of feet on the concrete, there were suddenly another ten. This could take all night and eventually we were going to wear out. But there was already a satisfying trickle of water seeping through the walls and they were down to two pumps. I called out from behind one of the pumps. "What do you want?"

Paolo snorted, which is exactly what I expected him to do. **See if you can make it to that corner of the wall, then set the charge.** I pointed to where the water was trickling and Sue nodded. It was part of the room that was without lights, and she slipped carefully into the shadows. Of course, that meant I'd have to try to hit the blast cap with no lights. But hey, I had plenty of bullets. I only needed to have enough time to hit it with one. And that required removing the rest of the guards.

There was a wide open space right next to the glowing temple mouth—at least fifty yards. She was going to have to make a break for it. I watched her pull the wire out, tuck it into the C-Four slab, and then carefully screw on the blasting cap. Then she pulled something from her pocket and pressed it into the mass and took a deep breath.

I opened the door wide and felt myself slip into her body. She knew I was there and let go of her mind. The moon was rising now and I could feel the tug of the magic at the same time it pressed me down toward the ground. I focused on nothing but Sue's feet and getting her across the room, fast and unnoticed. "You haven't answered me, Paolo."

"There is nothing to say. I want your death, and I'll have that soon enough." He was keeping hidden just beyond the door of the temple, protecting the egg. It wasn't a very big building, but I was betting it was chock full of the toughest men he had. As it was, the new batch was moving with much more stealth. I couldn't even see shadows move. But I sure as heck could see glowing. "Not as soon as you think." I raised the rifle and squeezed the trigger twice in rapid succession. One guard down. I twisted at the waist and popped two more slugs and another thud sounded. "Oh, did I mention I have second sight? Darkness doesn't bother me much."

Paolo swore and started to close the heavy stone door to secure himself and his queen. I sailed back into Sue's body and she let me. That's when the moon came calling.

I let out a howl of pain and threw Sue into motion. She jumped out into the open area like an Olympic sprinter off the mark. It was all I could do to keep her moving side to side, ducking bullets that flew. She was almost to the wall and I'd nearly lost my battle of changing forms when a blur cut across Sue's vision. She screamed as she was dragged sideways by her hair and the ball of C-Four fell from her grasp. Thankfully, it didn't explode on impact.

Nasil had Sue's neck stretched backward by her hair, a sharp knife held to her neck. She gasped and I could feel the blade cut her skin, just enough to let a small trickle flow down her neck. "If you surrender now, wolf, I might let her live. Otherwise you can watch her bleed away onto the floor."

I let out a low growl and stepped into the open. A dozen guns raised on me and I stared them all down. He hurt my mate! That wasn't allowed. The glowing snake held up the paw holding the sharp metal. "Oh, put the guns down, fools. He's of more use alive. She is nearly born and will need a meal, since it's likely the cut power line has ruined her magical treat. And when she's done with the wolf, we will have two snakes to feed her, fat with power."

I advanced another step, lowered my front legs, and raised my hackles. I let out a howl to call the pack. It echoed and sounded like a thousand more wolves. The men with their guns didn't begin to look nervous until the magic of the pack began to fill me. The man holding my mate stared at me curiously. "How very interesting."

He loosened his grip for a split second and forgot she is pack too. Her eyes glowed green as the pack entered her, held her, and made her strong. In a sudden movement, she pulled a dark sharp thing from her skirt and reached backward. She stabbed the shiny black stone claw into the snake's back and he screamed and dropped. She rolled away after grabbing another metal claw and the white ball. The snake thrashed on the floor, spraying blood from a wound that wouldn't seal. His colored light began to fall off in chunks, cut from him like meat from a bone. Two more snakes leapt out from the shadows and began to slice at the guards pointing at me. I seemed to remember them as pack. The dark-skinned men fell bleeding and stopped glowing. But the ones that were still glowing were mine. I raced forward and slammed into the nearest glowing man and closed my jaws around his neck. He beat at me and stabbed a sharp thing in my side that made me yelp. But I wouldn't let go until he was still. He didn't taste good, though, so I moved away, looking for better food. The other wolves were with me. I could feel my pack leader leading the hunt and when I pounced on another guard my bite felt stronger, my claws raked deeper.

When the last man was down, I moved toward the snake who had hurt my mate. He was still writhing on the floor, trying to reach the claw she'd left in him to pull it out. But she'd dug it in deep, all the way to the bone handle. There was a burst of color and the stink of power in the air and the snake called his true form. But the claw wouldn't fall out. He hissed again and rolled. I could already smell decay and let out a snort of air. The snake was dying. It just didn't know it yet.

Tony! I heard my mate's voice in my head and I turned to her. **Can you change back on your own? I need you to shoot the detonator.**

I blinked, not understanding what she was saying, even though I knew I should. **Concentrate, Tony. I need you back with me.**

I shook my head and felt the pack fade from my mind.

Nikoli was pulling them back and human thoughts began to flow back into my head. Ahmad and Tuli were at the temple door, using their swords to pry open the stone door, while slamming against the stone to push it even farther open.

"I've never been able to change forms, Sue. I'm not an alpha. You'll have to shoot it." I motioned with my head to the guns on the ground. I didn't know whether she'd ever practiced for distance with a rifle, but she did pretty well on the guard on top of the pump. I turned away from Nasil. He was done for. Even now his hisses were becoming weaker, as was the glow surrounding him.

"Ahmad. Tuli. Leave him. Let's move."

Ahmad stayed where he was, throwing his shoulder against the door and bending the long sword nearly double. "I'm not going to leave without the book. I saw it in there. And we can destroy the egg, rather than simply *hope* for its death." He looked at Tuli, motioning her away. "Go. Secure the other door so nobody else can come in."

She nodded once and turned. But then, on impulse, she leaned over and kissed him on the cheek. "For luck, my prince."

It apparently wasn't enough for him. He grabbed her hair and yanked her mouth to his in a fierce kiss that left her eyes glazed and a shimmering dark glow etched across her lips like neon gloss. He released her just as abruptly and turned away to put his shoulder against the door once more. "Luck is for the weak. We are not. Go to your task."

Sue and I were halfway across the room to where I thought we would have a protected spot when the wall went when the temple door finally gave way with a harsh scraping sound.

I was catapulted inside Ahmad's head once more, causing me to skitter on the concrete floor and do a face plant that slammed my jaws together.

The inner temple was pitch black, with only the acrid smoke of the torches still thick in the air to give any indication it had ever been light. It was difficult to smell anything past the taste of venom and honey still painted across my tongue, but there was no denying anymore what the wol . . . what *Tony* had said. I could feel Tuli's heartbeat as a twin in my chest. Fast when mine raced, slow and measured when deep in thought. So, then. Mated indeed. There were worse things in life so long as one didn't become too emotionally encumbered, and an extra lifeline was of immense value.

I feared the *emotionally encumbered* part would be the difficulty.

A sound stopped me. I froze with concentration, then tightened my grip on the sword and waited for another whisper of movement. Yes, there it was, just to my left. I swung the blade abruptly toward the noise and was gratified the way the blade sunk into tissue, causing a muffled scream and the scent of blood to mingle with the smoke. The problem was I couldn't tell how large the room was. I swung a second time, but met only air before hitting the stone with a sharp ting. I pressed forward, moving deeper into the room, swinging blindly, yet hoping to push Paolo into a corner where I could end this. My carefully sliding boots hit an obstruction but the sword still swung clear. An altar then, or perhaps a staircase. My hand reached forward, trying to find the egg, or the book, all the while swinging, stabbing, and moving the blade in all directions to keep anyone from ambushing me. Another whisper of movement, but this time it was a scraping, heavy and solid.

I was thrown backward, the weight of a massive block of stone hitting my chest with the force of a body. It slid me across the floor to hit the wall, head-first. With a snarl, I was up, sword still swinging toward where the stone had come from. I realized then that I was beginning to be able to see in the dark interior. Normally, my night vision wasn't good. But now I was able to make out shapes in the black. Tuli had always been exceptional at seeing in the dark. Could this be her influence? No matter. It was useful. I could see the edges of the altar now, and raced toward it. Yes! The egg was still there, just waiting to be destroyed. And the book also lay open and waiting for the words to be read.

A fist came from seemingly nowhere, hitting my temple hard enough to snap my head sideways and erupt bright lights in my vision. A net of power was thrown over my head, impressive enough to hold me frozen in place for a long moment. Yet even though I couldn't move, I felt my arm raise, under another's control. It stopped the next blow, where had I not moved, I would have been struck again.

Got your back. It was Tony's voice, coming from inside my head.

Paolo only had so much magic, though, and it wasn't more than two strikes—both defended adequately by Tony, before I could move again. The hilt of the sword became a club while I shook my head to gain my senses. It snapped forward like a steel cudgel, hitting Paolo right in the nose. Blood erupted, tasting of fresh copper and venom.

He moved like lightning, nearly as fast as Nasil could travel. Rather than strike me, he pushed my back, hard enough that I was thrown into the wall. I nearly dropped the sword when my wrist bent backward. When I pushed off and spun—

Sue was slapping my muzzle, trying to pull me out of Ahmad's head. "Come on, Tony. I need you back here with me! I can't do this alone."

A loud, vicious combination of yell and hiss, filled with pure rage, was followed by a string of swear words. They came out from inside the inner temple. We all turned and raced back to see what had happened. Ahmad was holding the book, looking a little bruised for the process, but the temple was otherwise empty. Paolo and the egg were gone and there was no sign of where they might have gone. One of the stones was probably a secret tunnel, but it would take too long to find it. We didn't have the time.

Then we got our next annoying surprise. Nasil had also disappeared while we were all otherwise occupied. Down the same hole, or did he slither out a different way?

Still, I was betting he was mortally wounded. I had seen the knife sucking away at his power, carving it away from him like a turkey on Thanksgiving day.

A hammering sounded on the far door and it sounded a lot like a battering ram. Tuli grabbed Ahmad's arm and started to pull. "I sealed the door as best I could, but I fear we're out of time."

Ahmad tucked the book under his arm and sprinted after me. One goal out of three wasn't bad for a start.

We could still hope that blowing the wall would find Nasil, Paolo, and the egg and drown them. When we got to the other side of the room, Ahmad looked through the sight to where the C-Four had been placed. "I can't see the detonator, and we have no scopes. Someone's going to have to get closer."

He looked at Sue, which I thought was pretty chicken shit. "You're the Sazi that will heal, asshole."

"No. It's okay, Tony. I said I would." Sue took a deep breath, fully expecting she was going to die. I could feel it in her mind. But that wasn't an option.

I stepped in front of her. "Lie down on the ground."

"What?"

I repeated it. "Lie down on the ground. It's the best shooting position. I'm going to see if I can take over your head. You only have to squeeze the trigger when I tell you." She did as I asked, even as the ram hammered against the door. I dropped down the tripod on the front of the AK with a kick of a foreleg, and lay down beside her. She dropped her eye to the sight, but her eyes weren't good enough to see the C-Four, much less the detonator.

I didn't plan to use *her* eyes, though. She opened the mental door this time and I felt Ahmad hiss beside me. The book dropped from his hands and landed on my back.

"It lives." His voice sounded horrified, and his scent was filled with fear. I suddenly understood what he meant. The book had a heartbeat. A steady pulse that felt warm and solid against my back.

A heartbeat.

Torn from the body.

I looked up as Ahmad stared at the snakeskin-covered

book. "It *is* alive. It's part of the cave and needs to go back."

He picked up the short sword and raised it threateningly before kicking the book away from me to spin across the concrete. "It *needs* to be destroyed!"

I grabbed onto his pant leg with my teeth before he could go any farther. He stopped and looked down at me incredulously, in a *How dare you touch me* sort of way. I released him, but only so I could talk. "Do you want to be attached to me *forever*? Think about it. It's the *cave* where I connected to you. It was the cave where you had to go to reach me in return. I've had dreams every night about that cave, either silent and lonely or filled with wildlife. I don't know how, but the whole damned cave is alive and this book is a part of it."

He paused, blade raised to cut it in two. "Do you actually believe the cave is *sentient*? That it connected us for a specific purpose? You realize that's insanity, I presume?"

I flicked my ears forward while he got more nervous. "You betcha. As insane as a book with a heartbeat or a knife that eats magic."

Tuli touched his arm and he looked at her. "Could it do any harm to take the book back there, Ahmad? If nothing happens, *then* destroy it."

The door burst suddenly open at the other end of the room. "And . . . we're out of time." Ahmad picked the book up and Sue quickly leaned into the rifle, head lowered to the sight. Tuli kept busy firing round after round at the incoming guards, keeping them too busy to fire at Sue and me.

I didn't have time to ease into it. I flooded her brain and felt myself join with her. I'd pushed deep before, until I could slip into her skin like gloves. But never as a wolf. It was a tighter fit. I didn't realize how different my brain worked in this form. Yes, I could force it to bend, but it was painful. I took a deep breath, closed my eyes, hoping the others would keep me safe and took over Sue's body. I opened my eyes and was abruptly looking through the metal sight. The white blob in the distance wasn't really that far. I could see the cord and . . . what the heck was that thing around the cap?

I nearly laughed when the image suddenly made sense in my head. It was the quarter! The one from the firing range. The cap was right in the center of the coin, giving me a larger target to shoot at. And heck, it was only a hundred fifty yards or so. I've taken longer shots.

I took a deep breath and started to squeeze the trigger when a burst of pain made the whole gun move as Sue cried out. Crap! She was hit. Right in the shoulder.

I let my calm fill her, ride over the throbbing of her arm. **It changes nothing. Concentrate on the job. Patch up later.** She nodded and tried to center herself. Her arm was trembling now, but she only had to do it once. She breathed slow and calm and I felt her mind transcend the pain. That's what needed to happen.

Feel the arc before you fire. Know where it's going to land. I calculated it in her head this first time and adjusted the front of the barrel just a bit. "Fire in the hole," I heard my wolf mouth say. The others looked at me and dove to the side, behind one of the sturdy pumps.

She squeezed once, but I felt her arm twitch from

pain and the barrel raised. No matter. I moved her finger to squeeze again a second time with a nudge of the barrel down, before there was even time to blink. The men in the doorway looked confused all of a sudden, but when one of them looked to where the bullet had landed, he screamed for everyone to evacuate. The first bullet sunk deep into the plastic, but the second bullet, that was the ticket. Concussion turned to electricity, turned to boom!

We scrambled off the floor and followed Tuli and Ahmad to the next room. A roaring sound began to follow us.

Began to catch up.

We raced through the long, narrow hallway, back to the stairwell. I reached the stairs first and turned to see the wall of water, a dozen feet high, racing our way. "Go, go, go go!" Ahmad picked Tuli up bodily and threw her onto the second level of stairs. Sue struggled behind them, bleeding profusely and without Sazi healing to fix the damage. She was in too much pain to run. The scent cut me to the core. I stopped beside her and slammed shut the solid-steel fire door with my shoulder. It wouldn't hold for long, but it didn't need to. Ahmad was holding open the door to the basement where we'd entered, three levels up, waving us up, to hurry.

"Ever ridden a wolf?" I knew I could carry her. I carried her to bed all the time. Why not give her a ride?

She didn't argue. She just straddled my back and rested her cheek against my fur, arms around me and fingers tight in my neck ruff. She had to pick up her legs a little so they didn't drag, but damned if I wasn't able to run up the stairs as the water burst through the door, sending it spinning like shrapnel against the wall. It chased us upward with a speed and force that made me glad I had supernatural speed. I passed the others by and they didn't stop me. They could fend for themselves easier than Sue could.

But even the basement wasn't safe. Nothing was until we reached outside. I was thankful that Sue knew the way. I felt her in my mind, correcting my flight as I ran. "Four hundred eight, four hundred nine," I heard her say under her breath. "We need six hundred twenty to reach the door." She pulled on my neck like it was reins. "No, left turn here."

I looked back to find that Ahmad and Tuli had changed forms as well. Even they couldn't overcome the moon forever. But they were fast as lightning in this form, racing past me down the hallway. I put on extra speed as the roaring—held back for a moment by the second fire door—finally burst onto the level through the uncompleted walls.

Sue started screaming to get the attention of the staff as we raced up the main flight of stairs. "FLOOD! The sea's coming in!"

One guard turned to see two snakes and a wolf carrying a bleeding woman with a sword. But that didn't panic him nearly as much as the sound of roaring water under his feet. He poked his head into the stairwell and then slammed the door and locked it.

He reached onto the wall and yanked down the fire alarm. Lights began to blink and a siren screamed as people began to yell and dive for the exit.

We made it out just as the seawater reached the main level and raced for the cover of darkness on the beach where we could patch up our wounds and decide what to do next.

It was going to be awhile before the Quetzalcoatl re-opened, since the casino was now an oceanfront hotel of a whole new kind.

I hoped the snakes didn't know how to swim.

Chapter Twenty

I STOOD IN the tropical heat, sweating bullets. Ahmad looked annoyingly content under the sweltering sun. "Think we should do this together?"

He shook his head. "No. My father started this by removing the book from the resting place where it lay for millennia. Since I can't imagine that anyone other than us survived that flood, it should be safe to return it where it belongs."

He stepped inside the cave and I felt a twinge in my head. Then there was another stab. I decided to sit down so I didn't fall down. The girls were back in the car about a mile back, and I couldn't blame them. Sue was still in a cast and Tuli had seen enough of this place.

A wind passed over me, a cool breeze that eased some of the heat. Then I was in the darkness, walking down a long path. The book in my hands began to throb, a steady pulse that was increasing as I walked. It wasn't hard to find the small open spot and the hole in the wall. I had no snakeskin to cover the book as before. But better it should eventually rot anyway. It was too dangerous to exist.

Still, there was no harm in testing the wol . . . Tony's theory. It would be difficult to get used to calling him by name, but he had earned the right, as had so many of the Wolven agents before him.

I shoved the book into the hole and felt a shock that ran through my body like flame. Every hair stood on end and my heart began to pound so hard it was painful. Then there were two hearts pounding. Then three, and four.

I turned and found Tony standing there and could see myself through his eyes. I looked panicked, and well I should be. He shrugged and I could feel each of his muscles move, felt the brush of cloth against skin. Was this what had happened to him? When he said he'd *been there* during my time with Tuli? Yes, it was definitely time to end this odd union.

"It seemed a good idea to follow." And both of our mouths opened to expel the words.

I closed my eyes and shook my head, pulling with effort out of Ahmad's brain and looked up to the ceiling. "Okay, you've got your book back. Now make this end!"

It felt like strings had been cut above me. I fell to my knees and suddenly could barely breathe. Stars filled my vision, threatening to make me black out. Ahmad was on his knees, his hands around his throat, his eyes showing too much white. He pulled and clawed at his neck, trying to remove an ever-tightening binding that didn't really exist. I just tried to hold my breath and take tiny sips of air so I didn't panic. After a moment of staring at the floor with hands outstretched, trying not to puke, I looked up.

A little monkey was sitting in the doorway to the

small room. He chattered at us and then spread his lips to bare his teeth before turning and racing off.

I realized my head was silent. It was just me inside. But there was also a closed kitchen door with a light in the window in the distance. Just like there should be.

I looked over at Ahmad, who was still staring at where the monkey had been with an expression of disbelief. "You okay?"

He nodded and rubbed his throat as he got his feet under him. He seemed a little at a loss for words. Yeah, welcome to my world.

"I believe so." As we walked up the steep path, I nearly squished a scorpion. Then there was a beetle trying to crawl up my boot. A bat dive-bombed us, heading deeper into the darkness.

"So," I asked as we exited, to find a near procession of life speeding into the cave, "still want to destroy it?"

Sue and Tuli had come after all. They must have felt the choking panic we experienced. They were waiting outside along with all the other life, watching us return the cave to the owners.

The Taurus holstered on Sue's belt was just about the right height to rest her cast on. I tried to tell her that she couldn't draw it out with a broken arm. She didn't mind learning to shoot with her left for the moment, but she insisted on a cross-draw rig so it could stay on the right side of her belt. Said she carried her purse on the left.

Women.

She looked happier than I'd ever known her to be and would probably be happier still when I finally told her that Lucas had approved her to handle some limited assignments . . . with a partner.

Me.

Seems she had the sponsorship of a certain snake in front of the council.

Sue held up a cell phone and raised her brows. "Finally got hold of Carmine, Tony. He wouldn't budge. He wants what he wants."

Shit. I was afraid of that. Not only had the knife left with Nasil, but I hadn't made a "messy" kill of the type that he wanted. I'm sure he's already had Scotty describe the blade, and while the kid can confirm the kill of the guy in the airport lot, everything else that happened was pretty low-key, press-wise.

"What'd you tell him?"

She shrugged. "What else *could* I tell him? That you would keep looking for the blade and those responsible. That's what you said, right?"

Ahmad gave me a *look* that said he'd probably oppose that action. But it went higher than that. It was Charles who gave the word, not him. "Those responsible . . . remember? And I'm on leave right now. Charles's orders."

He let out a small hiss of annoyance. "For a job well done. Yessss, how *well* I remember. As though Tuli and I weren't there."

I shrugged. "Hey, I told the truth. I didn't leave out a word. And I got you to come here. Sort of worth it, wasn't it?"

"Come now, Ahmad." Tuli slipped her hand through his crooked arm and smiled, pulling an imaginary leaf from his hair. "Was that so terrible?"

He sighed in a very exaggerated fashion. Yeah, he'd probably bitch about her at the next council meeting. I doubted he could help himself. But for now, there was no denying the scent of oranges and cinnamon that blended with the honey and creosote flowers on the breeze. "It probably will be later."

It was an inside joke.

Since I'd been inside, I couldn't help but laugh.